If Only He Never

T.C. CORREY

CHAMPAGNE BOOK GROUP

If Only He Never

This is a work of fiction. The characters, incidents and dialogues in this book are of the author's imagination and are not to be construed as real. Any resemblance to actual events or persons, living or dead, is completely coincidental.

Published by Champagne Book Group
2373 NE Evergreen Avenue, Albany OR 97321 U.S.A.

~ ~ ~

First Edition 2021

pISBN: 978-1-77155-440-4

Cover Art by Sevannah Storm

www.champagnebooks.com

Version_1

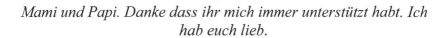

Mami und Papi. Danke dass ihr mich immer unterstützt habt. Ich hab euch lieb.

Chapter One

She wasn't a ghost. To an untrained eye, or if one's senses were hazed by what people consumed or inhaled or injected to, well, haze their senses, she could have been mistaken for one. She counted on clouded minds when she camouflaged behind corners, posts, vending machines before approaching the footpath. To her it was imperative to remain unnoticed, unidentified.

A car crawling past provided her shelter to cross the street in a flash, then scurry into a narrow alleyway where she pressed her body against the wall. The nightly chill crept under her skin, worsening her inner tremor.

She had to tell Gordon she'd failed. Failed because she was blinded. Blinded by the man holding the future of thousands if not millions of people in his hands. He could have known by now. She'd wanted to tell him, but there'd been no other option than to leave the scene, the "crime scene" as the police would soon call it. Had no other choice than to abandon him. Would he understand it was in his best interest to be in the authorities' hands? Chances were high he'd be locked up for a long time, and he wouldn't even know why.

She fished her cellphone from the pocket of her black coat— both coat and phone having been the only items she could gather in the rush. She managed to speed dial Gordon's number. He'd be so pissed off. Phone to her ear she waited for her call to be answered.

Finally, the click.

"A bit early, don't you think?"

She couldn't blame him for coming across agitated, but it still put her on alert.

"I had to compromise him." Had he heard her? She wasn't sure.

After a too-long pause, he bellowed, "How the hell did that happen?"

To muffle his roar, she held the phone against her chest. Once he'd settled she whispered, "I believe they're onto us."

"Why do you think that?"

"I'll explain it when you pick me up. I can't get to my car. Too many cops."

"Where is he?"

Contemplating her words, she decided on the truth. "The cops got him."

A heavy sigh filtered through. "You know, sweetheart, you're doing a good job. Generally. But when you screw up, you do it royally. Where are you?"

~ * ~

Five minutes earlier, less than a mile away, Curtis feared his cheekbone, firmly pinned to the cold tile floor, would crack under the increasing pressure of the boot on his face, digging painfully into his skin. He drilled his fingernails into his palm to kick-start his senses, tried to unscramble what fundamental detail he'd missed leading to this predicament, but there was nothing besides the dead woman the officer's boot forced him to stare at, her blood pooling around her head.

Curtis knew she had another wound on her back, but this wasn't about what he knew. It was about what the cop likely thought. The officer standing over him, determined to finish his job, reached for the handcuffs while clutching his gun with the other.

Curtis wanted to protest that he had the wrong man, but "humph" was all he managed to mutter. Squirming under the officer's weight was futile. Knowing it was crucial the cops didn't link him to the crime in this condo, he'd been so careful not to disturb the scene, yet the dead woman's blood smeared his face, hands, and cheek.

The officer blocked his view into the living room where he'd left Laura. She will put it straight, he told himself. Surely the commotion would lure her out. It remained quiet, but a crisp draft bounced off the floor and crawled over his skin. He couldn't remember having seen any open windows when he'd stepped into her condo. Where had the breeze come from? The officer didn't pay heed, the handcuffs now jingling in his hands. The shuffling and thudding of a second pair of shoes vibrated through the floor.

"Mendez!" a raucous disembodied voice shouted.

Definitely not Laura, but the boot's pressure eased on Curtis's cheek. *Time for a deep breath. Must keep my head straight.*

"Sutton? What are you doing here?" the boot-guy, Officer Mendez apparently, asked.

"You'd better explain what the hell *you're* doing," the voice, presumably belonging to Sutton, barked.

Curtis tried to get a glimpse of the new arrival. The gray suit told him he wasn't a beat cop. *A detective?* Still no sign from Laura. Not a peep.

"What does it look like? I'm arresting this guy," Mendez said.

"The guy got a name?"

Curtis groaned, first in relief when Mendez lifted the boot away from his cheek, then in pain as the boot's force nearly broke a rib. Curtis puffed, added assault to the list of flaws in this wrongful arrest, including not having the Miranda Rights read to him.

"Got a name?" Mendez growled.

"Curtis," he muttered.

"First? Last?" Sutton asked.

Curtis bit his tongue. He'd rather put his head under a guillotine than reveal his name. Half of the U.S. hated him more than any politician, and these two outsiders probably had no empathy for his desperate attempt to find something like a normal life, or at least a new start. New York to San Diego—one way. Chances of fewer people recognizing him here were higher, though in today's world no one went unnoticed, not with one's face plastered all over the news, internet, and TV, announcing the biggest conman of the year—Shawn Dylan Curtis.

Once these two authorities identified him, he faced certain arrest, and no judge in the world would ask if he'd committed the murder. They'd just see it as the best excuse to put him away.

"Search him for an ID, Mendez," Sutton said.

"What ID? He's not even wearing shoes. He's in a T-shirt and boxers, and I'm not digging in there. You do it."

"Just keep it coming, Mendez. You know the chief's waiting for the opportunity to strip you of your badge."

"My ID is upstairs," Curtis said before Mendez had a chance to change his mind. "Two flights. B-3. It's where I live."

"Ha! I see. Booty call gone awry, I guess," Mendez mocked.

Curtis warned himself not to get provoked.

"Anyone else here?" Sutton asked.

Unsure if Sutton had aimed the question at him, Curtis said nothing, but when Mendez denied the presence of anyone else, Curtis said, "Yes, there is." He prepared for another onslaught from the officer's boot, which thankfully didn't come.

Mendez brayed a scornful laugh. "He must be talking about the dead woman."

"Laura's in the living room," Curtis said. *I hope.*

"Who's this Laura?" Sutton asked.

"She lives here."

"Check the other rooms," Sutton ordered Mendez.

"He's not even handcuffed," Mendez protested.

"I'm sure I can handle him. Go and check the place!"

Curtis didn't dare to move or look up, but stomps confirmed Mendez had obeyed the order. *Laura will put it straight.*

"How did you end up here?" Sutton asked, his tone now companionable which confused Curtis more than calmed him.

"Laura called me and said she needed my help. I came down here and found the woman dead on the floor. Laura was in shock. I walked her to the living room then Officer Mendez arrived." Was there a point mentioning he was knocked off his feet by the officer before he had a chance to say a word? Or that the officer had arrived within minutes, by himself, which was more than strange?

"What time?" Sutton asked.

"Two."

"She called you at two in the morning? Is she a close friend?"

"No." *She could have become one, but not after this stunt.*

"You know her full name?"

"I only met her yesterday."

"You always hand out your number to women you've only just met?"

Depends on the woman. Curtis replayed yesterday's scenario through his mind.

~ * ~

He'd returned from a late-afternoon run, sweating like a pig, wanting nothing more than a nice cold shower, but there she was, lugging a suitcase behind her, losing the battle with the heavy main door, which was built to slam shut. Was she aware of the damaged bolt preventing closure, allowing every idiot to enter the building? Or the latch she could have used to keep the door open to get the suitcase through? Time for a gentleman act.

He'd asked her to step aside and hold the door while he hauled the suitcase through the entrance.

"Where're you heading?"

"B-1. Just there." He didn't need to see where her finger pointed. He'd walked past B-1 several times in the past three days. It was one of the four empty units in the condo building of twenty; a case of people not earning enough money to pay for overpriced real estate.

When Laura followed him through that door, she had managed what many women hadn't been able to accomplish in quite some time. His heartbeat sped up a notch, enough to make him check her out twice. Right away, he reprimanded himself. *You know the drama. Don't even go there.*

But something he couldn't explain drew him to her. Her hair hung loose, slightly waved, the color a mixture of dark and light brown, with a red tinge. Her smile was warm and engaging, her lips natural, her blue eyes full of life. The jeans she wore covered promising curves, and her stretched T-shirt enlivened his imagination.

She catapulted him back to his teenage years when he used to give women a score. Yes, childish, especially for a man of forty-two, but she woke his inner child. He scored her a six out of ten. A high rating. The other three points he would add once he worked out if she had some brain, intellect, and heart. But he'd never score more than a nine. Ten was too much. To him a woman needed some flaws.

He'd carried the suitcase, which weighed a ton, to the door of B-1 and checked her finger when she fed the key in to the lock. No ring or visible groove showing she'd recently divorced. Maybe she'd kicked a long-term partner to the curb? When he placed the suitcase in the hall, Laura told him to leave it there.

"Are you moving in long term?" he asked, his glance catching a sideboard with nothing on top. No photo or anything personal like a bowl or a candle or a gift a friend could have given to her.

"Yes. A new start, a new life."

That sounded familiar. Maybe it could spark a connection between them. He must have been too nosy when he tried to get a glimpse of what was further down the hall as she cleared her throat.

"I'm subleasing off a friend, for now. The furniture is his so I didn't have to sit on the floor. He said to get a feel for the place. 'If you like it, we can talk about a price'."

"I see. Is there anything else I can help you with?"

"No, but thank you so much."

He stood there for a few seconds, a rarely experienced awkwardness streaming through him. "If you need anything, just knock on my door. You'll find me in B-3. I'm Curtis." No exception made.

Even to women he introduced himself as Curtis. No reaction came from her, no wrinkle, no frown. She had no idea who he was, which meant neutral ground. An important fact before considering the not yet planned next step.

"Laura Webb," she said. "If I break my leg, I won't be able to walk upstairs. What's your number?"

~ * ~

A promising request. Best-case scenario he'd score a date. Worst case a new friend. How wrong he'd been. She'd clearly used him. Now, Curtis's neck cracked as he raised his head to look at Detective Sutton.

He guessed him around the lower end of sixty, going by his deep furrows.

"Her name is Laura Webb." He added a basic rundown of how they first met. Details weren't necessary as they wouldn't help him or her. Cops wanted facts, not how a woman caused a heartthrob.

Mendez's voice pulled him back to more important affairs. "The guy must be on drugs. There's nobody in here. Besides a locked suitcase in the bedroom, nothing indicates occupancy. Empty closets. No toiletries. Nothing."

No way. Curtis couldn't grasp why he did it—one of those out-of-body experiences—but seeing Sutton standing leisurely next to him, Curtis pushed off the floor, managed to snake past Mendez, whose hands were already moving to take him down, and lurched to the living room.

He expected to see Laura, distraught and in tears, like he'd left her, but the sliding door's white curtains twirled in the fall wind, stirring up nothing but dust particles where she sat minutes ago on the couch. In disbelief, he yanked back the curtains and stumbled ahead to the midget paved backyard, a nippy breeze kissing his cheeks. Had she seriously left him hung out to dry?

He sensed a gun pointed at him. As though coming from a far distance, he couldn't ignore Mendez ordering him to drop to the floor. Curtis did so willingly as his legs gave way beneath him. Game over.

Mendez dug a knee into his back. One handcuff already wrapped around Curtis's wrist, he was about to shackle the other.

"You're under—"

"I'll take it from here," Sutton interrupted, unruffled.

Curtis grunted as Mendez shifted on his back, barking, "What the fuck are you talking about?"

"You heard me the first time."

"This is my guy, Sutton. There's no *way*—"

"Shut up! You want to add another wrongful arrest to your list only to get it thrown out of court? Chief's just waiting for it. 'One more,' he said. 'One more and Mendez's out writing tickets for the rest of his life.' I'm taking over."

Mendez wouldn't just throw in the towel, but he pulled away, either because of Sutton's seniority or reluctance to write tickets for the rest of his life. Or was it because of additional authorities invading the crime scene?

Curtis couldn't work out who they were. Coroner's office, he assumed. The only person he wanted to see was Laura with a damn good explanation. Of course, that didn't happen.

Struck by astonishment when Sutton offered him a hand up, Curtis hesitated.

"Detective Eric Sutton. Come on. I haven't got all day."

This didn't make sense. Besides Laura's disappearance, something else didn't add up, but Curtis grabbed the hand and stood. Plagued by vertigo, he fought for footing but stiffened when Sutton gave him a onceover. Was it the moment of truth? Curtis expected his other hand to be cuffed, but Sutton conjured some keys and freed him.

"You're making a mistake," Mendez barked and stomped off.

Sutton shrugged. "Let's go to the precinct. I'll take your statement and see if you can identify Laura from a photo lineup. If not, we can get sketches done."

That's it? He'd just escaped certain arrest and now this detective wanted nothing more than a statement? Something reeked. Curtis couldn't help it but nerves kicked in, and when that happened he blabbed. "The first thing you can write in the statement is that I didn't kill this woman. I don't even know who she is… was."

"You can tell me that when I take your statement."

"Am I under arrest?" Curtis asked, rubbing his now free wrist.

"It might be advisable to find somebody who can confirm Laura's existence."

"Isn't that *your* department?"

Sutton rolled his eyes.

"Can I get changed first?" Curtis spread out his arms to show him a T-shirt and boxers and no shoes wasn't the right outfit to run around in at the end of fall.

"You may as well show me your ID when we're up there."

"So you can read me my rights while I'm getting changed?"

"Don't push your luck."

~ * ~

B-3 belonged to Wayne Cantrell. Curtis had taken up his best friend's offer to bunk there until he got his life back on track. Lavish antique furniture compensated for the lack of luxury. A blue couch, open living-dining with a marble counter created the border between dining and kitchen. It was a home for now and better than the back of his Chevvy Tahoe, in which he'd slept the past week when driving from New York to San Diego. Well, it used to be his. He'd signed ownership over to Wayne for zero dollars. Not much the lawyers and judges could do, at least for now. Would they come after a car? Nothing was impossible.

Sutton, who'd managed the winding stairs up the two floors better than Curtis expected, said, "Big difference, I assume. It must have been tough to fall as hard as you did."

Curtis snatched a breath. Every time somebody reminded him of the past, a sharp pain burned through his chest. Worse, though he hadn't given his full name to Sutton, the detective was fully aware of who he was. Could this be the reason for his reluctance to arrest him?

"I'm still falling." Curtis spoke over his shoulder and marched into the guestroom, which had a double bed with one nightstand, an antique desk, a chair, and a chest of drawers.

Sutton followed and remained in the doorway—interestingly, he didn't search the premises. "It was a ticking time bomb. You knew it. People who trusted you knew it." He paused. "You lost it all?"

"I have five hundred bucks to my name." Curtis plucked his wallet from the nightstand and faced Sutton. "I can't have a bank account. If I do every cent in there will be taken. So it's in my wallet. You want to confiscate it? Be my guest." He tossed his wallet to Sutton who caught it in a swift hand and flipped it open. He fished out Curtis's ID, checked it, shoved it back in then flung the wallet onto the bed.

"I think you'll need that money," Sutton said. "Anything that proves the call you had from this Laura?"

After taking his cellphone from the nightstand, Curtis tapped in his code and showed Sutton the call log.

"This shows it as an unknown number. You don't have her in your contacts?"

"No." Curtis scowled at Sutton. "I didn't want to push my luck." *Did I just say that?*

He pivoted, jerked down his boxers, didn't bother about Sutton's presence and showed him his naked backside while digging through the drawer. He yanked out a black T-shirt, tossed the bloody one onto the bed, tugged on the new one, then grabbed some briefs he slipped on. His gaze fell on a black button-up shirt. Unsure about the temperature outside, he thought it best to put it on too.

"People will move on, eventually," Sutton said.

But *people* hadn't moved on, and Curtis doubted they would before he saw the end of his days because they had every right not to forgive him as he barely forgave himself.

It had started off with nothing but luck some seven years ago. Back when he still had luck. He'd created a blog with stock market predictions and made money from it quicker than he could spend it. Word spread fast. Introducing a fee didn't hold people back from joining his blog, and he soon experienced what rags-to-riches meant.

With growing success, and despite increasing fees and claiming percentages of their profits, he soon had over one million people calling him the money god. Remaining with both feet on the ground, he allowed himself the luxury of a spacious apartment overlooking Central Park.

Six months ago the inevitable happened. Friends had warned him. They'd done that so many times and he'd proved them wrong so many times he started feeling too comfortable with his skills. The occasional market plunge was normal, but then, the whole thing collapsed overnight. One wrong decision broke his and thousands of other peoples' necks. It still befuddled him why it all happened or how.

The foreseeable lawsuits followed. He was under the impression he'd covered his ass with a fine print section in the policy stating they joined at their own risk and if things went wrong he wasn't to be held liable. Lawyers and financial advisers reassured Curtis it would protect him and most people wouldn't read the fine print anyway. In the end, it was worth no more than toilet paper. Mainly because Curtis owed money to every single judge making the decisions.

They wanted their money back as did all the lawyers who'd said the fine print would sustain. He had two options: cover everyone's losses or go to jail. He'd made the calculation and decided to pay the money back, which left him with nothing. He still owed… he didn't know how much. Some millions.

They processed his case at record speed because they could. Having predominantly high-profile clients, lawyers, judges, cops, doctors, scientists, and the leading pharmaceutical company in the U.S., proved to be the downside. Taking his age into account, they had given him ten years to raise the remaining money or else face prison.

In the meantime, some money was paid back to some clients by someone. Who, Curtis had no idea. So now he owed money to whoever did the good deed. Government probably. He didn't know much about court procedures, but understood many cases were settled out of court in some weird deals no one had ever heard of. Like his.

Since Curtis couldn't show his face in New York any longer after being spat at, kicked in the gut, and otherwise abused, he packed his bags and fled to his friend Wayne to whom he owed no money. Wayne had always warned him that one day the whole dream would burst like a bubble. Maybe Curtis should have listened and pulled the pin before the ship sank, as Wayne had put it with a delightful mix of metaphor. But when was it ever the right time?

Now, his mind back in B-3, he studied Sutton. Curtis had no idea who'd been paid and who hadn't. His accountant took care of those details, but to his amazement Sutton hadn't arrested him yet. Money could be the reason. Curtis behind bars meant nobody would get a dime anytime soon.

"Are you one of the people I owe or have you moved on?" he asked.

Sutton scoffed. "I don't earn enough to risk a penny on shit like that. Hard enough to survive as it is. I know a few people though. Some are within the precinct, like the chief. He made it loud and clear that he wants both. The money back and you taken down. Don't expect to be treated with kid gloves when I introduce you to him."

Curtis pulled up his jeans, buttoned and zipped them. "How big are the chances of that?" he asked, sitting on the bed to slip socks over his feet.

Sutton checked his wristwatch. "Here's the problem. Nobody will be available to do the sketches at this time of night. By the time the artist arrives, the chief will have too."

Great. "In other words, until they arrive in what four, five hours, I assume you'll put me under some kind of custody. Right?"

"I'm not too sure if custody is the right word. I'd call it protection."

Chapter Two

The coffee mug on the small rectangular table in front of him was cold by now. Curtis had asked for it when he arrived at the precinct, hoping it would keep him awake. It hadn't. After over one hour in a room no more than twenty feet square, the expected one-way mirror in the wall, cameras on each side of the ceiling, a chair bolted to the floor, a chair opposite, also bolted down, his body had forced on him what it needed. Head cushioned by arms folded on the table, he'd slept.

Now he woke with a stiff neck and muscles close to snapping when he stretched them out. He checked the time. His little nap had lasted nearly two hours. Unfortunately, no miracle had happened in the meantime. He released the brief panic rushing through him with a heavy sigh, conjuring a faint memory back to the days thirty years ago, from before his father left and never returned. "No matter what happens in life, you ride out the storm. Only wimps cry. Only wimps give in."

Curtis didn't see himself as a wimp. Yes, life hadn't been great recently, but as long as he kept his wits together, he'd be fine. He reflected on his dealings so far with Sutton, and Curtis's mental review assured him he hadn't failed to mention any crucial detail in his statement.

He'd told Sutton about Laura calling him in distress at 2 AM. The door to her condo had been ajar. He'd nudged it open. His legs nearly buckled when he spotted a woman's body splayed face down on the floor, the back of her olive dress drenched with blood, a pool of it around her head, clotted in her hair. Laura huddled on the floor next to a sideboard, clutching her arms around her knees.

"I don't know what to do," she had wept.

"I didn't know what to do either," Curtis told Sutton. "Hug her, comfort her? After I closed the door, I crouched by her and asked her what happened.

"Laura claimed she'd heard pounding on the door and a woman

screaming, 'Help me!' She said she let her in, but the woman stumbled and hit her head on the sideboard. Laura asked me if the woman was dead.

"I didn't know what to say," he explained to Sutton, "so I pulled Laura up, walked her into the living room and sat her on the couch. The sheer curtains were closed."

A crucial detail Curtis remembered he had mentioned to Sutton. Through the thin layer of curtains, he'd seen the sliding doors shut. When the officer had him pinned to the ground—the moment the draft crawled over his skin—must have been when Laura escaped through the sliding doors.

He brought his thoughts back to his statement in which he'd said, "The last place I saw Laura was on the beige leather couch. Shortly after that, Mendez pounded on the door, yelled, 'Police! Open up!' and to do that, I had to step over the dead woman's body again. Just glimpsing her profile, I knew I'd never seen her before. A second later, Mendez had me on the floor. He didn't even so much as ask a question."

At that point Curtis had broken off his recitation of events. He wasn't sure how to read Sutton's reaction. He'd said nothing. Probably didn't like his partner's failure to do what he was supposed to do, but Sutton had just jotted down notes, then left.

That had been several hours ago.

Curtis ran a hand over his face, couldn't think of any detail he'd failed to mention. Wherever Detective Sutton was right now, he probably had the luxury of sleeping in a proper bed.

Five minutes later, Sutton dragged his feet into the room, his hair ruffled, his face as creased as his suit. In one hand he clutched a tray with two coffees, a bag of donuts in the other. "You had some rest?"

"Some." Curtis realized how jaded he sounded.

His heart didn't throb anymore, just pounded at a normal rate. Reality had kicked in. He welcomed the change. He hated himself when insecurity rode him like an evil burden, forcing him to talk shit.

Sutton placed the tray on the table, passed one coffee to Curtis, and pushed the bag of donuts over. "The sketch artist will be here in ten minutes. Her name is Sally Norton. The reason I've got her is because she's fast but also accurate. It'll ensure you a quick escape. With luck before the chief arrives."

Curtis mulled over Sutton's last remark. "If I wasn't Shawn Curtis, would I be sitting here?" He held Sutton's gaze. It wasn't a stare-down, but Curtis interpreted it as testing each other's ground.

Sutton said, "You wouldn't be sitting here if it wasn't for me. If you know what I mean."

Curtis nodded. "How come you're helping me?"

"Doesn't matter what you're involved in, wherever your name turns up people want to see your head roll. I, on the other hand, am old-fashioned. I don't believe in coincidences. I think somebody is setting you up, and we can't find that person with you rotting in hell."

Curtis sipped and fought the temptation to spit the liquid back out. Regular coffee. Black. No sugar.

"How are you going to explain your supposition to your chief? From what you've been telling me, he wants nothing but to see me rot in hell," he said.

"I'll tell him what I see—a man who sank to the bottom of life but knocked back the offer of being fed by the government, being safe from people who want him dead. In ten years' time, you would have walked free, and the dust would have settled. But you chose the hard road. Chose the risk of being confronted by people who hate your guts, living a life where literally every cent you can earn will be taken from you. Anyone in their right mind would find another way. You like freedom too much."

The detective was right on the beam there. "And you suppose you're able to convince the chief of that?"

"I'll give it a shot if I have to." Sutton sat in the other bolted chair, ripped open the bag of donuts and munched away, then washed it all down with coffee. "Do you have any idea who wants to take you down?"

Curtis hiked his brows. "At least a million people."

Sutton didn't reply to that. "Who else knows you're in San Diego besides your friend…" He studied his notes. "Wayne Cantrell? What about a girlfriend? Family?"

"As you already established, I'm keeping a low profile."

"Do you believe this Laura Webb knows who you are?"

The question left Curtis thinking a little longer. "If she does, then she had a convincing way of hiding it."

Sutton jotted down more notes.

Curtis asked, "What about the dead woman in B-1. Who was she?"

"It's not like on TV where DNA tests are done within minutes. The fingerprints haven't come back with a result yet, either. Reality is they can do it in a few hours, but we're not the first in line. As for now, I'll go by your word that you've never seen her before and that there was another woman who you call Laura Webb."

Who I call Laura Webb? What was that supposed to mean? Curtis bit his tongue, heard Sutton out.

"It's undoubtedly helping you that the neighbor across the hallway has confirmed meeting a woman named Laura when she came to see the sub-let. He also confirmed a screaming woman cut short his sleep, causing havoc in the hallway by banging at B-1's door. He then called the cops."

"What about the rental agreement on B-1? Surely Laura Webb shows up there."

"Inconclusive."

"Meaning?"

"I have to make phone calls first to get the confirmation on the condo's owner. It's a bit early to do that."

It was either mendacity or the coffee causing Sutton's cheeks to blush, but unless he had a freshly brewed batch, Sutton slurped from the same lukewarm piss with which Curtis had given up on insulting his gullet.

"Anyhow," Sutton said, "these are all things helping you and me to keep the chief off your back."

"What's his name?"

"Oliver Donaghy. He's no fun."

"Noted. What happens when the sketch artist is done?"

"You can leave. Not the city, though. I want you to be reachable at all times, so keep your phone close. I'd suggest lying low."

With Wayne being his only connection in San Diego and pretty much the only friend still talking to him, but with him away doing business in L.A., Curtis couldn't quite see where to lie low.

He also realized he couldn't return to Wayne's condo. "I assume I'll have to show identification if I want to go home?"

"You said you have five hundred to your name. Book a motel somewhere. After about twenty-four hours you can return, though everybody in the building will know by then of a Shawn Curtis living there."

So much about a new start on the other side of the country. Nice, just nice.

~ * ~

One hour later, the sketch artist completed an accurate picture of Laura, just in time before the chief arrived. Sparse traffic crawled past Curtis as he stood on the street. He was stuck. A taxi would blow his budget, leaving the bus as one option. Or walking.

Knowing where to go would be a real advantage. According to the street sign he was on Broadway. A far cry from the Broadway in New York. This one was bright, meagerly lined with palm trees not providing much shade. He crossed Eighth Avenue, Seventh, Sixth, Fifth. The vicinity changed to a big open space similar to a massive roofless concert hall. A sign showed Westfield Horton Plaza.

With no option of going home for at least another day or two, which meant wearing the same clothes for just as long, he decided on a new outfit. And he needed sunglasses. The buildings' reflections on the asphalt, and the sun beaming down from the clear blue sky, nearly blinded him. On the flip side, it filled him with positivity and not the glumness he'd experienced in New York, which used to give him the feeling of the world collapsing around him, which ironically it just had.

He sauntered to the shopping mall's entrance but its doors remained shut. The sign stated 10 AM to 8 PM. His watch showed 9:42 AM. While sitting on one of the many stairs, he killed tedium by observing people passing him, but they weren't as interesting as last night.

Laura confused him. Nice woman she was. If he had to give her a score now, he would adjust the six from yesterday to a four. Leaving him in the lurch with a dead body like an idiot wiped any point for a possible brain. Her engaging smile would bring her up to a five if she wasn't so deceiving. A four at the most. Minus one point for enormously complicating his life.

Why did she run? Where did she go? She ran as soon as the cops turned up. What did that mean? Did she kill the woman? Did she mean to try to pin the murder on him?

Chapter Three

A poke on her shoulder snapped Laura out of sleep. "What's the time?" she asked, blinking.

Dark brown eyes stared down at her. Gordon grunted. "Late."

His pasted-on grimness, likely an attempt to look like a grumpy old man, failed to disguise his calm serenity. Though he wasn't yet fifty, white hair strengthened the impression of wisdom despite the beer belly classically hidden under an over-washed, moth-chewed green T-shirt hanging over a pair of faded baggy gray sweatpants.

Laura had known Gordon McNamara for many years as her mentor, professor, teacher. He'd saved her life, though she was still hesitant about appreciating and accepting the life she had now.

Last night, he had clarified that he disapproved of the proceedings by treating her like a little girl, sending her to bed, stating he wanted to sleep first to be fresh in the morning. But now, after he had had the sleep he demanded, and as soon as Laura dressed and sat at the table nearest to the kitchen sipping coffee he'd brewed, he wanted to know every detail about last night.

She glanced around the cluttered high-ceiling loft apartment with the characteristic support beams and exposed pipes. Two rectangular glass-topped tables stood in the middle of the room, each with a laptop, a printer connected to one of them, another table next to it with several external hard drives, and two screens.

Another two tables with test tubes filled with different colored chemicals, and a few smaller glass-topped tables spread throughout the room. Some empty, some with papers, some with lamps. Sparkles danced off them here and there from the sun filtering through the enormous windows offering a spectacular city view.

To the right of the entrance, Gordon hid his bedroom behind shoji blinds with chests of drawers around for added privacy. Tucked in the opposite corner sat a recliner near a small TV on a stand and the brown couch on which she had slept. It was worn, soft, but comfortable to rest on for a night. A high-rise blocked most of the impressive view from this window.

"I'm waiting," he said.

"I have no idea who she was," Laura explained after informing him about the sudden appearance knocking at her door, the screams for help. "And we'll never be able to find out."

"What makes you say that?"

"She didn't die because she was shot or hit her head."

Gordon mumbled something as though he understood. "Why did you call him and not me?"

"I panicked," she said. It was only partly true. She could have asked for Gordon's help, but she wanted to get Curtis out of there. "The cops turned up within minutes. I was hoping they'd take him in so he'd be safe for the time being because I didn't know if someone was after him or after me."

She left out how she'd reacted to him.

When Gordon had shown her Curtis's photo two weeks before, she hadn't found him particularly appealing, but when he stood in front of her, she'd readjusted her opinion. His sweaty hair had enough signs that he usually combed and gelled it into a styled mess. Facial grooves indicated he was constantly brooding. His nose wasn't knobby but not slim either. It was his blue eyes capturing her, reflecting a warm glint of hurt, carrying the unspoken message *"If I love you, I'll well and truly do everything for you for as long as you don't mess with me."*

Drawn to him by his engaging presence, and despite his sweat-stained T-shirt, she stepped close to and got a waft of his odor. It wasn't unpleasant at all. The moment he'd smiled, that's when professionalism went out the door.

"The whole thing should never have happened," she continued. "You know that. You told me he wasn't supposed to be alive, told me he reappeared from like, what, the dead? But the way it seems, other people know he's around. Or how do you explain the woman? Unless, and that really bugs me, they found *me*." She played with the mug, reality sinking in. "I don't want to get dragged back into this whole mess."

He nodded but didn't seem willing to accept the latest development. "You could have remained at the scene, kept an eye on him."

This was the statement she'd feared. "I couldn't."

Gordon's glare went under her skin.

Though he didn't ask why she'd been unable to stay, she explained, "*He* turned up."

"Who?"

"Eric Sutton."

Gordon's eyes flared. "Why is *he* here?"

She studied the coffee mug.

"Did you know?"

She shrugged, remembering the day when she'd spotted Sutton a few years ago in the deli where she was shopping. Her heart had dropped; a second later it *whumped*. He hadn't seen her sneak out. After that, she'd come to this very place and cried. She wanted to see Sutton again but didn't until the day she drove past a crime scene which appeared to be a hit-and-run. She added one and one together and stalked him sometimes when he left the precinct.

"Out of all the cops," Gordon said, shaking his head, "it had to be him. We're pretty screwed, and to make it worse your plan to keep Curtis safe didn't work out."

"What do you mean?"

He pointed at the computer screen he had played with moments ago. "Unless the cops decided to take him shopping, Curtis is out."

"Out?" Laura pushed off the chair, paced up and down, scenarios of defeat manifesting in her mind. "I have to get to him before he gets killed."

"I don't think it's a good idea to show your face."

"I'll make sure Sutton won't see me," she said promptly to kill the urgency she'd heard in Gordon's voice.

"He's here for you, don't you think?"

"I doubt it," she said but wondered why Sutton crossed her way now.

Chapter Four

Cars and people, the pulse of the city, pushed through the streets. While waiting for the shopping mall to open, Curtis sat on the stairs and contacted his friend Wayne Cantrell to inform him about last night.

"I can't leave you alone for two seconds," Wayne said and suggested getting a key from the condo which would give access to another apartment in the city.

Who knew to whom that apartment belonged? Wayne was, as far as Curtis knew, a trusted realtor, doing business with who-knew-who, having access to who-knew-whose-house. Sleeping in a condo of who-knew-who-it-belonged-to wasn't to Curtis's liking.

With his phone pressed between his chin and shoulder, he rolled up his shirt sleeves and said, "Your condo is a no-go zone for at least another twenty-four hours. I'd bank on forty-eight. I'll try to get my Tahoe later today. I slept in it for a week. Another night won't kill me."

"You're a suspect in a murder, so what do you think they'll do with your Tahoe?"

"I'm a person of interest."

"Same thing in your case. Forget the Tahoe. What about Laura? Aren't you trying to find her?"

Curtis lowered his head as a security guard walked past. "Why don't you send me to Mars and ask me to find a needle?"

"Wisely spoken. Glad you learned how to chill."

Curtis snorted. Chilled didn't resemble his feeling one bit. On the outside maybe, but on the inside a volcano was searing. "The cops have nothing against me to justify an arrest, but Sutton warned me about Chief Oliver Donaghy."

"You don't want to get in his way, mate. He'll lynch you to death."

"You know him?"

"And his reputation to act before asking questions."

Curtis swallowed hard. "Very comforting. When are you back?"

"Tomorrow around noon. That's if I can wrap up the deal by then."

Wayne had a knack for selling himself better than the house he was trying to sell, but more importantly, he was due back tomorrow.

"Big realty deal?" Curtis asked, his attention shifting to the entrance slowly crowding with people.

"Beverly Hills."

"Celebrity?"

"Can't tell you." Of course he couldn't.

"Good luck." Curtis chuckled to mask his relief, pocketed the phone, and observed the people streaming into the shopping mall—mainly women.

Caucasian, Hispanic, Asian, some hard to guess, some tall, some wide, some as wide as tall. Mixed in-between were children and men. Some ran as though it was a life or death matter to find whatever they needed.

He loosened his shirt collar as he strolled to the door but didn't enter. He hadn't been in any shopping mall for at least six months. One person recognizing his face could turn this venture into a trip from hell.

A woman his age scrambled past him, flashing him a smile as though she was saying, "Don't worry, you'll be fine."

He checked the people in front, behind, to his sides, then hurried inside to blend in with the growing crowd. The directory was one way to find any men's clothing stores, but with increasing confidence that nobody had identified him, he rode one floor up, another up, then one down. He had plenty of time to kill. And too much time to think.

A Levi's store caught his eye, which created a battle between budget and quality; the latter he liked on his skin, but the budget didn't allow. At the shop he checked once more behind. Nobody followed him. A young blonde strode up to him and asked if he needed help.

"No, thanks."

The jeans he wore should remain presentable until his return to the condo, but he needed at least two more T-shirts, maybe three, and new underwear, which he planned to buy somewhere else. And socks. Once he got those essentials, he'd purchase soap and shampoo and hope to find a public shower somewhere. By then, perhaps, the tangled mess in his stomach would untwine and he could eat something.

For now, he concentrated on a pile of T-shirts on special. One for thirty dollars, two for fifty. The young blonde remained nearby, keeping a close eye on his moves. Maybe the past six months had left him appearing desperate. Or she'd seen his face somewhere on the news, internet, TV, tabloids. Or it was a matter of paranoia?

"How much for three?" he asked her.

"Let me check." The girl went to the checkout to discuss the request with another girl, also blonde, also young. After a short conversation, she joined him again. "Seventy-five for the three."

Times are tough. Curtis skimmed through the pile, chose a black one and a blue.

The girl said, "Y'know, they're a small cut, particularly around the sleeves." She closed in on him. "Between you and me, I think the reason they're cheaper is that something went wrong in the factory. People like buying smaller cuts, not bigger. Y'know, they think they're getting too fat." She stepped back, studying him. "Not saying this applies to you, but I suggest taking them in large instead of medium."

Curtis rewarded her honesty with a warm smile, unfolded the blue shirt, and held it against his torso.

"You can try it on."

"I think it'll be fine." He didn't want to pull a new shirt over his dirty body.

While the girl dug through the pile and fished out a black in a bigger size, Curtis sensed eyes on him. Nobody in the shop. But across in a shoe store, a jeans-clad woman swiftly turned aside, then entered. As he shifted his attention back to the girl, he caught motion in the corner of his eye. There she was again—a woman in jeans, long hair. *Laura!* She weaved through the shoppers, increasing her speed.

Curtis tossed the shirt in his hand onto the pile, saying, "I'll be back shortly."

He moved fast. So did Laura, racing in a zig-zag, shoving people out of her way. Curtis followed, faster, darting into the spaces she left as she pushed others aside, leaving them perplexed. A free standing A-frame sign went flying when she knocked it over. It didn't stop Curtis. He jumped over it, closing in on her.

Less than ten yards separated them. He could easily catch her, but unexpectedly she spun around, ran up to him, flung her arms around him, and locked her lips on his. He was too stunned to protest, enjoyed this sudden change of attitude, which stopped as quickly as it started. Her session of passionate kissing was nothing more than to shut him up and distract the puzzled security guard who was closing in.

She parted her lips, waved at the guard, as if to say, "All good," clenched her hand around Curtis's, then dragged him to the corner near the restrooms.

Forced against the wall, he allowed her to pat him down, from his chest to his pants, but as her hands came dangerously close to his privates, he had to bite his tongue to distract his body from reacting in a way he didn't want to show off publicly.

He shoved her from him, gently but assertively. "What's going—" Silenced by her fingers on his lips, he let his eyes do the talking, making it clear he didn't approve of her actions.

"Trust me," she whispered into his ear and nodded back to the way they'd come.

He looked past her shoulder and spotted the security guard assessing the situation. For now, Curtis let his guard down. It was a challenge to trust a woman who dumped a dead body on him only hours ago, but he wanted to give her a chance. Doubt flooded him when she fished his cellphone from his jeans back pocket and started dismantling it by stripping out the battery first, then the SIM, shoving all the bits and pieces down her jeans pocket.

"You need to work on your security measures if you want to remain undiscovered," Laura whispered.

He got it at once. He'd long been aware that phones could be tracked, conversations listened to, text messages read, money transactions followed, every download stored and so on. Big Brother watching. The worst were apps.

People downloaded them, agreeing to have their information shared without knowing who they shared with. Few people read the fine print regarding privacy the legal departments had ensured would be upheld if it came to the crunch. Except in his case, of course.

He assumed his phone had revealed his location to her and explained her excuse to ask for his phone number in the first place. As soon as this idea itched his brain, another conclusion came to his mind. Sutton hadn't taken the phone off him as evidence. *Odd.*

She motioned for him to follow, which he did, outside to the street where she discarded the phone's body in a trash can. She stopped at a gray Rover parked some fifty yards away, opened the passenger door and gestured him inside. He complied. She slid into the driver's seat, started the engine, then hit the accelerator.

"Are you going to—"

"Not yet," she said.

Studying the scenery he swallowed his frustration. Being told by a woman what to do didn't go down well with him. A dead woman being dumped on him didn't either. Since his last experience with a woman, the entire gender displeased him.

The reason for that was a woman he once wished would stick around for a long time, hadn't. But she appeared again one year later with a little girl in her arms. The woman named Sarah identified the girl as his daughter. Judging her a decent woman, he believed it. Most stupid mistake.

She demanded money. Fine by him, but her terms were tricky. Instead of paying child support spread over the next eighteen years, she wanted a lump sum. If he paid, nobody would doubt his status. If he did not, she threatened to feed the tabloids with stuff like him doing drugs, dealing drugs, sexual misconduct, and warned of spreading the rumor he was gay.

He had no problem with the latter accusation—not that he was. But the other accusations, especially the harassment part didn't sit right with him because it wasn't him. It actually went against every belief he had. The slander would have resulted in a loss of clients who believed he was an ordinary nice guy, which he considered true.

Because his business flourished back then, and nothing indicated it would change anytime soon, he paid her a lump sum big enough to feed more than one village in Somalia. But Sarah appeared again nearly three months ago, demanding more money.

At that stage, he had no money to give to her and didn't need another debt, so he demanded a DNA test. Why she agreed to it, he still couldn't work out, but after a lengthy delay, the results contradicting her actions had come in two weeks ago.

He kicked himself in the gut, hit the grog so hard he couldn't think straight for three days. Of course he would never see Sarah or the money again. Or the child—whoever she was. His trust in women had hit rock bottom. Now being kidnapped by another he didn't really know, who dumped a body on him only hours after she'd given him a leg-weakening smile didn't help to change his mind.

Laura stopped the Rover at a beach. He wasn't familiar enough with San Diego yet to know which one. Some people strolled along the shoreline, others were swimming, and some were playing fetch with their dogs.

"Are you going to fill me in now?" he barked.

She unbuckled, pulled the key from the ignition, then shoved it in a small brown leather bag, which she tossed to the back of the car. A clear sign she wanted to keep him from getting away. Then she flicked the button, and all the locks snapped shut. Next, she activated the child lock switch. So much for thoughts of running.

"You have no idea how important you are," she said.

Curtis froze for a brief second, the words evoking a memory from many years ago, told by someone he'd loved. "You sure I'm the right guy?"

Her straight posture reflected reassurance. "Shawn Dylan Curtis.

Born March…" She rattled down every detail of his identity, his parents' names, even his blood type. "I'm positive you are the right guy."

"Do you know every woman I've slept with too?"

"That wouldn't help in this case."

"Glad my dick's still my business, but stop wasting my time. I have more urgent matters to deal with, like the dead woman in the condo. So get to the point."

She inhaled deeply as if preparing for a lengthy conversation, unless she had to digest his rant. "You know animal testing was banned six years ago?"

"What's that got to do with everything?" he growled, remembering the ban had been big news back then because for many years pharmaceutical companies relied on animals to ensure the development of cures for all the diseases plaguing the world's population. At least that was the fallacy people were supposed to believe.

"Pharmaceuticals have been searching for alternatives to beat the major diseases causing deaths, foremost cancer. They continued—"

"Don't give me that bull. The pharmaceutical companies aren't interested in providing cures for anything. There's too much money involved in keeping people sick, so they're only releasing cures in drips and drabs to keep the people in hope. Furthermore, every proven natural cure for cancer has been taken off the street, destroyed, swept under the rug, or held up in unnecessarily prolonged processes so the money keeps rolling. Tax-money by the way. Big Brother will make sure of that."

Laura had beautiful eyes, especially when they flared in annoyance, but there was no way he'd let her steer him away from his belief about politicians, governments, and all those thieves he called Big Brother, no matter how much she stared him down. Tempted to add more fuel to the fire, he said, "I'm sure you know about all that, so *please* continue."

"I'm so glad I'm dealing with a highly educated man."

Her sarcasm irritated him. "I'm all ears. I suppose you intend to further my education?"

"Maybe we should stop your education right here. I don't think you're interested in finding out why you're so important."

Wow, she wasn't only good at arguing. She was clearly confident in how to shut him up. "Okay." He would have rather said he was sorry, and always talked garbage when nervous, but she had a long way to go before he'd give her so much insight into him.

It took a few seconds before she continued, her eyes still spitting fire, "The pharmaceutical companies believed they had—"

He rapped out, "Which ones?"

"I'll get to that if you ever let me explain."

"Fine."

"They believed they had the solution at hand to stop any mutation leading to cancer. After the ban, tests continued behind closed doors on different breeds of animals. They infected them with several types of cancer then gave them the blood carrying the vaccine they thought held the key to preventing cancer. Every single animal survived, rats, rabbits, monkeys, etcetera, and ongoing tests implied a sure success. It was a breakthrough.

"However, to make sure it worked on humans, more tests were needed. That's when Operation Rabbit came to life. Short O.R. The vaccine was still in its experimental stage and could only be applied by blood transfusion. It wasn't—"

Curtis interrupted, again. "Cancer vaccines became available a decade ago."

"For some types of cancer, yes."

"So you're talking about what, the *ultimate* vaccine?"

"Ultimately," she drawled the repetition, "yes."

Where was this heading? "Go on."

"Every two seconds there are people in need of blood transfusion, so it wasn't hard to find subjects. Six years ago one hundred people were subjected to the tests."

"Only one hundred?"

"Had the tests been legit, the number would have been higher." She pursed her lips as if she cautioned herself against revealing too much. "To guarantee the best outcome and to eliminate age-related complications, they used people from as young as ten up to eighty-six, each from a different origin."

Curtis rubbed his head, wondering if she was still talking about humans or some objects.

She continued, "All of them needed blood transfusion. All of them couldn't have cancer, so…"

His stomach lurched. "But they infected the animals with cancer. Why wouldn't it work on humans who already had cancer?"

"Because the vaccine *prevents* cancer. It doesn't cure it. So if it was used on someone who already had cancer, it wouldn't have helped them."

"Like a flu shot doesn't make your flu go away?"

"In some ways, that's right."

"You're saying, they infected humans with cancer and the vaccine would get rid of it."

"That's right."

"One hundred test subjects? One hundred people?"

Laura nodded.

Curtis worked through her words once more. "Hang on. It wouldn't have been easy to find many agreeing to the tests. I mean somebody in need of a blood transfusion but having no cancer wouldn't just say, 'hey, yes, infect me with that stuff.' There was no guarantee it would work, no long-term research, side effects, and so on. At least not according to what you've told me so far. Why would anyone agree to it?"

Laura didn't reply.

"Laura?"

"They didn't."

Curtis knitted his brows. "Wow," he whispered.

"Like you said, nobody would agree to it unless they had a death wish. So they simply carried it out."

"And the government was aware of it."

"Some government, yes."

"You're telling me there are now one hundred people cancer free or immune." It wasn't a question, more his hope to hear a yes.

She stared out the windshield. "The first people died within a week. Some lasted a month, one four months."

His turn for irony. "One? I'm sure he, she, it, or whatever *one* is to you, was overly impressed with that."

"There's no need to be snarky."

"What do you expect? First, you disappear, leaving me with a dead woman I've never even met. Needless to say the cops would love to hear my explanation, which I can't give, unless you give me one. Now you're telling me about some experiments I'm certain I shouldn't even know of. How about you tell me what happened next, so I can finally head home and have a shower? Oh, hang on. That ain't possible because the cops are there, thanks to you."

She opened her mouth, must have had second thoughts about her comment, then said, "Interest in the whole experiment diminished quickly after all participants died. As far as I know they destroyed the evidence linking to the tests."

"Participants," he muttered, shook his head then shifted his glare through the windshield, spotting a boy throwing a ball and a Labrador chasing and retrieving it to claim the reward: a pat on its furry back and the common words, "Good boy."

Curtis said, "Why don't you just get to the point and tell me what I have to do with this?"

Another pause, then Laura said, "They all died."

"You already said—"

"Except one."

He tilted his head. Her deep gaze left no question.

Six years ago, she'd said.

Six years ago, the experiment had been brought to life.

Six years ago, he had the motorcycle accident. Steering clear of a car cutting him off, he was too late to avoid a collision with an oncoming vehicle, the impact catapulting him into the back of the truck carrying one-inch steel poles, two of them piercing him like a meat on a stick. To his luck, he hadn't sustained life-threatening injuries to internal organs but nearly died of blood loss. And been given a transfusion.

Sweat broke out, trickled down his spine.

"Let me out." As soon as the locks clicked, he thrust the door open, stepped out, filled his lungs with fresh air, all the while shaking his head, trying to deny what he couldn't.

The ocean roared, the waves' bubbling whitewash reflecting his turmoil. He sat in the sand next to a park bench and ran a hand over his face while he tried to make the knowledge sink in, to process it all the way to the hindmost corner of his brain. He didn't get far, didn't know what to make of it.

He heard the crunch of shoes on the sand. He sensed Laura next to him but kept his gaze on the Labrador chasing the ball, retrieving it, chasing it. Lucky for the dog it wasn't used as a guinea pig.

"Why now?" he asked. "Why not one year ago, two, three, four?"

"According to the information we had, you died during the experiment but came miraculously back to life when..."

"When I took the DNA test."

"Correct."

"You said they destroyed all the evidence of the tests. How did you find me here? I was still in New York when I received the DNA result."

"It's not that easily explained, but changing your phone didn't change the reality that the person you contacted the most was your friend Wayne Cantrell. We knew you were coming to San Diego."

Curtis wrote a mental note to warn Wayne about getting a new phone and number. "Then what? Did you follow me all the way from New York?"

"I doubt you'll believe me, but it was a coincidence that you chose San Diego. I was already here."

She was right. He didn't believe her. "Who are you? Government, FBI, CIA, ordered to take me in so I can be used again as a guinea pig?"

"I'm here to make sure you don't end up dead."

He furrowed his brows. "I was under the impression my blood could help people."

"It's time you met my friend, Professor Gordon McNamara."

Chapter Five

Detective Eric Sutton sat at his desk, a third coffee in front of him. On his mind, the man who must have swallowed a broken mirror: Shawn Dylan Curtis.

Sutton wasted a few seconds mulling over his boss's lecture for letting Curtis walk.

"What the heck were you thinking?" Chief Oliver Donaghy had spat at him. "You know he belongs in jail. Do I have to send you back to the academy?"

Sutton had taken the wind out of the chief's sails by mentioning it benefited the department's reputation, which was Donaghy's sore spot. After Sutton promised to keep him up-to-date with future developments, Donaghy let him off the hook.

For now.

Foot stomps creating a perceptible tremor drew nearer. Sutton prepared for another onslaught by Donaghy, but before he had time to tilt his head, a hand slammed a piece of paper onto his desk.

"Surprise." Officer Peter Mendez, probably still gnawing on his defeat over missing out on arresting Curtis, glared at Sutton with eyes bloodshot from lack of sleep.

Sutton picked up the paper, read it. "This can't be."

"It makes no sense to me either," Mendez replied, stepping around like a nervous chicken, "but the results can't be wrong."

"How come we got them so quickly? It usually takes much longer for a DNA test to come through."

"Maybe they caught up on the backlog. Why do I care? Explain to me how the dead woman in the condo can be Laura Webb?"

A miracle? A mistake? Curtis lied about her name? The woman lied about her name?

Sutton said, "Do me a favor. Don't let anyone see this result until we know for sure. It can never *ever* hit the chief's desk. At least not yet."

"How am I supposed to do that?"

"You'll find a way. I'll go find Curtis. He has some explaining to do."

Chapter Six

Accompanied by Laura, Curtis entered the loft on the twenty-first floor. The view was priceless, the room spacious, and the sun beaming through the colossal windows brightened the interior cluttered with computers and tables full of vials containing some colorful liquids. A million-dollar loft converted into a laboratory.

"DNA must be worth a lot of money," Curtis said.

"The government pays for it without knowing they're paying for it," a man's voice replied.

Curtis blinked. *I wouldn't mind knowing that loophole.*

Laura said, "This is the professor I told you about."

A man with curly gray-white hair, medium length, tucked behind his ears appeared from behind a wall. He wore glasses not thick enough to complete the nutty-professor look and baggy jeans with a green T-shirt riddled with holes. "You must be Shawn Curtis. Pleasure to meet you."

Curtis shook his hand, the man's flaccid grip triggering a picture of the man's persona in his head. Lack of confidence, guilt, anxiety. "Professor," he said.

"Oh, don't call me Professor. I'm Gordon McNamara. Gordon's fine. What do you prefer?"

"In the good days, I preferred Shawn. Now I prefer Curtis, and over a million people out there call me Asshole. Your pick."

His joke fell flat. Instead, Gordon's thick brow puckered. "I'll explain my theory to that part later," he said. "But right now, if you don't mind…" He turned toward Laura. "Is it okay with you if I do some tests to make sure he is who we hope he is?"

Curtis squared his shoulders in annoyance at Gordon's addressing Laura and not him.

"He's all yours."

What? Am I made of glass? Curtis thought, but said, "What type of tests are we talking about?"

"Just some blood," she said.

"I don't think so. No needles. I got poked and prodded enough in my life."

"You won't feel it," Gordon said. "Trust me."

Trust him? Who could Curtis trust after being betrayed by a woman he barely knew? A woman who just left him with a man holding a needle in his hands while she cowardly disappeared through a door? Curtis had no idea where the door led to, but hopefully there was an escape if things turned sour.

~ * ~

Laura visited the bathroom to freshen up, tried to look her best, given the circumstances. The brief moment, when Curtis was distracted getting comfortable on a chair Gordon had asked him to sit on, Gordon had fed her some news she hadn't prepared for yet.

"It's done," he'd said.

"So quickly? Doesn't that cause suspicion?"

"It'll keep them busy."

"I'll need a new one."

"I'll get that done within the next few hours. Trust me."

Trusting Gordon was no problem. Earning Curtis's trust was a different matter. Once he figured out what Gordon had done, Curtis could run. Very fast.

She promised herself to keep it all professional until things were over and he was hopefully still alive and not killed by people he wouldn't expect were after him. That was something she'd left for Gordon to explain because it meant Curtis could once more get the idea of running.

Feeding him with as little information as possible was the best bet to keep him hanging around. It ensured his safety until Gordon decided what to do with him.

At the sink, she turned on the tap, cupped her hands, and splashed water on her face. She toweled it dry, then studied her image.

"You're dead… again. Better come up with a new name," she whispered, running a hand through her hair.

She stiffened at the sound of thunderous thuds outside the bathroom. Then another. Glass shattered. A horrified shout froze her. Her heart pounded. She grabbed at the knob but the door swung open, sending her crashing against the wall.

~ * ~

On his knees, Curtis slithered inside the room, slammed the door shut, and yanked Laura to the floor.

"Hush," he hissed, searching for an escape in this, what he now recognized as a bathroom. Walls, walls, more walls. *Damn*. He tilted his head back, exhaled. Air vents. Too small to get through.

"What's going on?" she asked.

"You tell me. If this isn't somebody from the government pissed off that you're using their million dollar loft without paying rent, then you'd better tell me who the sniper is on the high-rise, sending bullets through Gordon's head while he's taking my blood."

Laura flung her hands to her face, strangling on sobs.

Curtis clutched her arms. "I need you to pull yourself together. We have to get out of here. I expect people who shouldn't be here to come through the door. We're trapped. Is there a way out?"

She shook her head. "Only the front door."

He filled his lungs and pushed out the air, more to suppress the sudden pain than the panic streaming through him.

"You're bleeding," she said.

He jerked away from her touch on his shoulder. "Just a flesh wound." *I think.*

"We have to stop the bleeding."

"We don't have time. Those chemicals on the table—how flammable are they?"

"Do you intend to set the place on fire?"

"It'll distract the sniper."

"There's irreplaceable data on the computers."

"The sniper took care of that."

Her face changed from pink to white. She stretched herself out to the cabinet under the sink, opened it and searched around until she revealed a box. He saw bandages and all sorts of medical supplies.

"It's crucial for you to stay alive," she said, wrapping a bandage tight around his shoulder. Once done, she shoved as much as possible of the box's contents into her pockets.

"Anything flammable in the box?" he asked.

She revealed a gas lighter.

"That'll do." He opened the door to a slit. There were no more shots or commotion within the loft, which meant no one besides Gordon's dead body. For now.

He gauged the distance between the door and the test tubes on the tables. Twenty-five, maybe thirty feet. He closed the door again, spotted a small round glass jar containing face cream sitting on the sink. He wrapped his hand around it.

"There's another in the cabinet," Laura said. She opened it and came out with the jar.

Now he held two in his hands. He also found a shampoo bottle.

And a soap bar. He smiled at her.

"I'm left-handed." Why he said it he didn't really know. Maybe because he needed an excuse in case he missed the target. "Wish me luck."

He struggled up, opened the door a little more. He held the shampoo bottle in his hand. He aimed. Threw. Missed. Well, he didn't hit what he wanted to. A computer screen toppled over and shattered on the floor. The response came within seconds. Curtis never heard the shot, but the TV sizzled smoke.

He forced the door shut and lowered himself. "The cops will be here soon. I have no desire in seeing them so quickly again since Gordon told me you're dead."

"I can exp—"

"Not now!" Rage flared in him.

She continuously lied. Worse, he felt defeated. Fighting a sniper with shampoo bottles and cosmetics jars—who was he kidding? And throwing with his right meant he had to open the door wider, which meant the sniper could make out their position, which so far he didn't seem to know.

Curtis grasped the jars, both at once and jerked open the door. He aimed, cast. A hit. One tube tumbled and smashed, spilling the liquids over the floor. He grabbed the soap bar then threw it too. One more hit.

To his credit, the sniper did his job, showing impressive shooting skills by smashing all the bottles at once. Their contents now oozing over the table, trickling over the rim, formed a puddle on the tiled floor. Fortunately, there were no carpets hindering the liquids from pooling to a lake.

Curtis fired up the lighter, but Laura pressed her hand on his. "Do you think that's a good idea?"

He flipped back the lid to kill the flame. "What else do you want me to do? Wait till the cops get here?"

"What if the entire building goes up in flames?" Her voice quavered with a hint of panic.

"As far as I can tell, the doors and walls are fireproofed. My only worry is the next floor up. But do you see another option?"

Her shrug was his go-ahead.

He fired up the lighter again, slid it toward the puddle oozing their direction. He had a millisecond of hope it would work, a millisecond of certainty it wouldn't. Then the flame hit the chemicals. A nanosecond sparked more doubt. At the full second, a blazing gust engulfed the room, not loud but hot. Curtis watched it growing as the flames fed off each other, spreading across the ceiling, turning blue and green.

"Holy shit." He slammed the door shut then dragged Laura down, covering her with his body. An ear-battering explosion rattled the walls, followed by another detonation. "What the hell was in those tubes?"

"I don't know. But I guess it's helping us."

"Cover your face with your shirt." He jerked the door open. Flames in all shades blinded him. Whatever types of fumes were hanging in the air, the last thing he wanted was getting trapped in his own escape route. "Ready?"

"No." She reached for a dark-blue towel, soaked it under the tap, and threw it over her head. "Now we are, once you stick your head under here."

He flung up the towel to cover both of them, held her close as he urged her on. The sprinklers kicked in too late for his liking. As the alarms went off, screams filtered through the air vents. The flames fed by the oxygen poured through the shattered windows. As long as the sniper steered away from shooting blindly, he had no target.

At the door, Curtis stopped. "We have to be quick. Opening this door could suck the flames our way." He didn't wait for her reaction. "Ready?" he asked, going for the knob.

Laura nodded.

He yanked the door open then shoved her through. He slipped through after her, shut the door and raced for the staircase, forcing her ahead as they were joined by half a dozen people from the floor above.

"Are you guys okay?" one middle-aged man yelled.

"Yes. Anyone else up there?" Curtis asked.

"Not in this part of the building."

Good. He didn't want to be accountable for killing innocent people only to save his own ass.

A woman behind him asked, "What's going on? All I heard was a big boom."

"No idea." This was good. Nobody would track the fire back to him or Laura. "Try to shove past everyone else," he whispered to her. "We need to blend with the crowd."

On the way down, he picked up a sunhat somebody must have lost and pressed it on her head. Now that he'd set an entire high-rise into a panic, he wasn't sure anymore if the fire had been such a good idea. But what other option had there been? Hope swelled up deep within him as he envisioned the fire gutting only the loft. He didn't want to have caused another 9/11 event.

Fifteenth floor. A sign on the stairway door. *Emergency*

assembly place… Blah blah. Stop and wait for instructions. No one did. People streamed out from their homes and joined the rush to safety. More people scrambled into the stairway, running, screaming. Some less able to rush moved slowly, easy to overtake, working in Curtis's favor, offering better camouflage among the ones in panic.

Tenth floor.

Fifth floor.

Third floor.

Laura's steps slowed.

"Come on. Two more," he encouraged her.

First floor.

"Stop."

She did.

Authorities stood ahead. He laced his arm around her, lowered the hat on her head. Clasping her body closer, he hunched to hide his face under the hat's wide brim. Like crammed sheep being pushed through a corral, he allowed the crowd to force them through the door. Everyone steered to the left. So did Curtis and Laura. Rescue people asked one by one about their wellbeing.

"All good." He glanced from under the shade of the hat.

People everywhere. Security, emergency, ambulance, fire department, cops, onlookers. He aimed for the latter. Seconds later, he and Laura blended in like chameleons. With more people streaming to the scene, he directed her the opposite way until the crowd thinned out.

Over his shoulder, he looked up to the building. Plumes of smoke tinged with fire belched from the shattered window but didn't pose a threat to the floor above or the adjacent dwelling. Thank God for that.

They crossed the street. "Keep going," he said when she slowed again.

A bit over a mile from the scene, he spotted an alleyway and pulled her in. They both slid down along the wall behind a dumpster. Laura gasped in exhaustion. He gasped in pain.

"You need treatment," she said.

"Oh, yeah, like where? The hospital?" He meant it to come across harsh. This woman had disappointed him more than any other before, and it pissed him off. "Let's go."

As he struggled to his feet, he noticed she was shaking, fighting to gather composure.

He knelt beside her, rubbing her arm. "Hey, chances of getting trapped are fewer if we keep on moving."

"Oh, yeah? Move where?" Her voice carried as much mockery

as his had before.

Good. This meant she wouldn't break down in tears when he gave her an earful. Just not yet.

"We can't get to my car," she added, her voice unsteady.

"We'll find a way. Right now we have to hide somewhere until we know what to do. You have friends, family, anybody nearby?"

She wiped the tears from her face. "I hardly know anyone."

"At least we have that in common." He expected a smile but heard more sobs.

"This wasn't meant to happen."

"Life doesn't always go the way we plan it. But if we don't go soon, I won't be going anywhere." Wooziness overwhelmed him; a clear sign his body fought the sudden trauma of whatever had happened to his shoulder. When he'd slid into the bathroom, the pain was a throb. Now, it nearly knocked him off his feet.

He held onto the wall as he forced himself upright again.

"Are you going to be okay?" Laura asked.

He didn't know. "We should try getting a taxi and finding a motel somewhere," he said, but she stopped him from walking on and adjusted the towel over his shoulder.

"That way it somewhat looks as if you'd been at the beach."

"Wearing jeans?"

She shrugged. "Why not?"

Chapter Seven

Clifton Wright stared at the computer, watching a small red dot on the screen, moving straight forward, then sideways, then forward again.

"Who have you got on the vision?"

Clifton startled. He hadn't heard Leon Powell, Chief of Operation, leader, controller, the man keeping an eye on everything, sneak up on him.

In a split-second click with his finger, Clifton changed one number on the setting to adjust the reading. "I don't know what or who it is yet."

Powell leaned in from behind Clifton's shoulder and studied the screen so close Clifton wrinkled his nose as Powell's stench of days old sweat wafted to him. He shifted to the side and sucked in a quick breath.

"Where's the signal from?" Powell asked.

"Asni."

"Where's that?"

"Morocco."

A long silence.

"Are you bullshitting me?"

Clifton smiled back at Powell. "That's what I'm getting." He pointed at the red dot flashing on a green grid, coordinates next to it. He shifted his index finger over to the location. "Asni," he repeated. "I don't know how it's possible. Foremost, we don't have anyone there, but according to the reading, somebody is."

"Isn't there a name connected to the location?"

He shook his head.

Powell pushed Clifton's chair so vigorously his belly crushed against the table. "You know that's impossible. Something's linked up the wrong way. Find the fault."

Watching Powell march off, Clifton relaxed, tugging on his hair.

He wanted to see what everyone was up to, but the curls obstructed his vision. He snapped the elastic band from his wrist, tamed his hair while his glance brushed over the eleven other people sitting at their computers. He shifted his glasses back up the bridge of his nose and concentrated for a moment on Martin Green, two desks up on the other side of the sterile room.

When Clifton first met Green, he'd judged the guy as being roughly ten years older than him, early forties, and thought of him as stiff as an ironing board. Green, with short light brown hair, was always perfectly groomed and neat, like his outfit. Shirt ironed. Slacks pressed. He'd laughed when he learned Green's secret. The guy folded his clothes neatly and laid them under the mattress. He claimed to have once read it in a book.

Green must have understood Clifton's silent message. He gestured with his head and left. Clifton swept his gaze over the gloomy laboratory once more. It didn't resemble what he believed he'd signed up for six years ago. The aged tables—some steel, some wooden—had marks or scratches, names or words cut into the surface. Most chairs squeaked when swiveled.

Comfort wasn't important. The money went into high-tech. Technology not invented yet—not for the usual consumer. It would take ten or so years before the nation learned that what they believed was a revolutionary discovery in the science world was actually outdated. Money kept the wheel going, but then it started drying up for reasons Clifton didn't know. Nobody here knew.

Instead of a high-profile pharmaceutical lab, he'd ended up in what may as well be a prison. There were doctors, computer techs, nurses, all sorts of people. No plumbers or mechanics. Not needed.

Some stated they didn't know how they'd ended up here. Others, like him, had signed to work on a top-secret experiment. The latter a definite because there had to be a reason why they were kept in this godforsaken shithole.

Days went by, months, years. People disappeared, wanted to disappear, had no strength after it became clear there was never a way out. Of the original thirty-four people, twenty-two remained. So far. But today something had changed.

He knew where he'd find Green. In the heart of the operation: the server room. As head operator of the technical team, Clifton had every right to be in there, but Green did not. Nevertheless, there he was. He must be smarter than he purported to be because he'd somehow created a keycard giving him access to anywhere, at any time, except the way out. Nobody could get out, and it was Green's job to prevent people from going nuts in this shithole.

Clifton entered the room, his T-shirt instantly clinging to his body like a second skin as though he'd transitioned to the Bahamas. The cooling system was failing, as always. It wouldn't be long before he needed to try to fix the problem for the trillionth time, though he'd never found any air vents in walls nor spotted evidence of them in the ceiling. This place held a lot of secrets—still no escape.

Green stood in front of the big server racks, which combined to forty-foot lengths, ten feet deep, and roughly six high. The dark walls, some flaking paint, revealed plain concrete. The ceilings were too high therefore provided little hope of an escape route in that direction even if there were air vents up there.

"What have you got?" he asked Clifton.

"It's time to get out."

Green snorted. "Are you having one of your crises again?"

"Desires. Somebody has miraculously reappeared from the dead."

"Who?"

"Rabbit 76."

"A Rabbit reappeared?" Green straightened. "Got a name?"

"You know they destroyed the list. All I have is Rabbit 76 and his location."

"Where is he?"

"San Diego."

Green chewed his bottom lip. "Does Powell know?"

Clifton shook his head. "I redirected the signal to Asni."

"But he knows we have a Rabbit."

"He knows we have a signal."

Green chewed his bottom lip once more, a habit annoying Clifton who preferred to act before someone else did. Green, being a thinker, pondered before asking, "Could it be a hoax?"

Clifton shook his head.

"A glitch?" Green asked.

"Excluded."

Again, Green bit his lip. "But somebody outside knows about him?"

"Maybe somebody kept his promise."

Green did his thinking game again. "How do you want to play it?"

Excitement streamed through Clifton. "I'll bribe Powell. We'll get out, catch Rabbit 76, and instead of delivering, we'll sell him out."

"To whom?"

"Whoever offers the most. We need money to start again, don't we? He'll be worth a few mill." Clifton couldn't help it; he had to smile, already imagining what that new life could be like. He observed Green's ever-changing face, sunny days altering to cloudy in seconds.

His face darkened, thunder on the horizon. "Do you even know where we are?"

Clifton shrugged.

"Do it again. Right there. That shrug. What if we're in Alaska or China?"

"We'll worry about that once we're out."

Green's face remained dark. This guy was so difficult to convince.

"What's your problem?" Clifton asked.

As Green lifted his arm in reminder, a pang stabbed Clifton, reminiscent of the pain when the implant was catapulted into his body part.

"They'll always know where we are," Green said. "Besides that, you know we can't get out."

"Cody got out."

"And where is he now?"

Dead. "Do you want to die in this shithole or try to have a life? Rabbit 76 is right there, and we are the only ones who know. Let's use this to our advantage."

Chapter Eight

After waving down a taxi and asking the driver if he knew a budget motel out of the city, Curtis now stood with Laura in a street as dingy as the motel in front of them. He studied the white panel with red letters. P's Motel. Whoever or whatever P referred to, he didn't want to know.

Down the street were a handful of shops, a restaurant, and several residential houses. Some had potted roses and other dried up plants. Driveways held neglected vehicles ranging from pickup trucks to sedans.

He paid the driver from a wallet running dry as if it had a hole in it, added up how much money he had left. Hopefully, Laura had more cash on her.

"Let's go," he said to her, leading the way to the shabby weathered lobby door.

A tiny bell attached to a string sent a chime tinkling through the office. Behind the counter sat a guy at the higher end of fifty, watching TV or security cameras. Curtis ran a fleeting look over the ceiling. No cameras. They'd exceed this place's budget.

The rest of the lobby didn't interest him. He already painted a picture of the room's interior, including the smell. Mr. P, so Curtis presumed, had greasy salt-and-pepper hair, a week-old beard, and an odor which, if inhaled for too long, could ruin anyone's olfaction.

Curtis drew Laura along, marched up to the counter and waited for the man to pay attention to him rather than staring at the TV, but he never did, only said, "Seventy-five a night. No discount unless you stay over three."

Robbery. But Curtis wasn't in the frame of mind to pick an argument. He plucked his wallet from the back of his jeans, fished out a fifty, a twenty and a ten, and placed the notes on the counter.

Now the guy rose from the chair and grunted as if digesting bad food. "I need ID."

Curtis ran through options. Laura's ID was useless. If she wasn't wanted, she was dead. His ID was worth nothing either. He was wanted for killing a woman who wasn't even dead. But Mr. P would have heard every lie under the sun why somebody avoided the formality of showing an ID.

Curtis added another ten to the pile.

Mr. P pointed at the towel hanging over Curtis's shoulder. Curtis was aware of the blood seeping through. He'd seen it in the rearview mirror while sitting in the taxi.

"You injured?"

"I had a run in with a surfboard down the beach. It looks worse than it is."

Mr. P shifted his gawk to Laura, then back to Curtis, flipped the ten off the stack and tapped on the twenty. At least it wasn't the fifty. He added a twenty on top of the other.

"I know nothing." Mr. P unhooked a key from the back wall. "Number 8. Last room to the left. If you lose the key, it's fifty."

Curtis grabbed the key. "Won't happen."

A touch on his back impeded his turn. Laura took the hat from her head, covering up something with it, presumably more blood on his back.

"Thank you very much," she said, and he followed her forceful push through the door. As they stepped outside, she said, "Do you think he'll call the cops?"

"Too risky. Guys like him have drugs sitting behind their counter."

She rushed ahead. Curtis, in no rush, studied the surroundings. Like most motels, each room boasted a parking space out front. Room 1 didn't exist. Room 4 and 5 had a small passage in between, which struck him as odd, but he couldn't see where it led to. A graffiti-painted wall at the end of the driveway drew his attention, separating this building from whatever was on the other side of that wall. As expected, room 8 was to the left. He expected to see room 9 on the opposite side of the driveway, but the number on the door read 15. It was a weird set up.

"You'll bleed to death by the time you get here," Laura said, standing outside room 8.

"I like to know where I am, just in case we need a quick escape." Curtis fed the key into the slot and swung the door open.

How low can life go? There was a bed in the middle, a brown loveseat at the end of the room, an old-fashioned TV, an imaginary kitchen made of a scratched up wooden table with coffee and tea packets in a small woven basket. A coffee maker sat on top of shelving between two wardrobes where shoes or a suitcase would usually go. The carpet was stained, and the room reeked like Mr. P.

"Perfect," Curtis muttered.

Ignoring her, he proceeded to the bathroom, ripped the towel from over his shoulder, and threw it into the sink, its unidentifiable color the same as the moldy shower and the walls. He left the door open while he took a leak, then washed his hands using a double load of soap. The reflection in the mirror told him he looked like shit. No other verdict.

With his foot, he slammed the door shut and slid to the floor, covering his head with his hands. A knock disturbed him.

"I have to treat your shoulder."

"I'm still alive after two hours, so I don't think I'll drop dead in the next few minutes," he said, unable to keep his voice from trembling.

"Let me know when you need me."

He didn't reply, suppressing the groans to ease the tremendous throb swishing through every nerve from his shoulder to his fingers. Compared to the pain of being pierced by the poles six years ago when he had his motorcycle accident, this was far worse.

An EMT had taught Curtis to take deep inhalations to lower pain. Today, the lessons helped considerably to disguise his real state, and the entire time he'd sat in the taxi, he'd stared out the window to avoid the driver's quick, curious looks. But if he didn't get painkillers soon, his screams would bust Laura's eardrums.

It wasn't only the physical pain torturing him. In six months, everything had turned upside down—so to speak. Down the drain was more accurate. Turned to shit even better. What else could it be after a woman swindled a lot of money, claiming he was the father of a cute little girl while he wasn't?

His business had evaporated and the court trial fast-tracked so he could get stripped of every penny he had. People wished him dead but not before they had their money back, which some wouldn't, not for a long time or maybe never. Now the woman at his side maintained his DNA or blood or whatever could save millions of people's lives. Could it really? If so, why was he clutching his bleeding shoulder? If only he never had taken that test.

He couldn't prevent it and even if he tried, a whimper forced its way out. Curtis wasn't Superman or a hero of any kind. An ordinary guy, that was how he described himself. Facing fears was one of his goals. He'd jumped out of planes, off cliffs, swum with sharks, did all sorts of things. Being shot at or getting killed wasn't on his bucket list.

Right now he wished for a hug. Anyone would have been good

for it, even a dog or a cat or a teddy bear, just not the woman knocking at the door once more.

"Are you okay?"

"I'm fine." He brushed a tear away, scrambled to his feet, pasted on a corny grin, then opened the door. To remind her that this was all her fault, he wiped the grin and presented her with a cold shoulder.

"Stop!" she cried the moment he made to peel off the bandage she had put on him earlier.

"Why?"

"Undoing the pressure bandage could leave you in a pool of blood."

"If any major artery was damaged, I would have stood in a pool of blood at the loft. I don't need to be a doctor to know I would be dead. Plus, I can move my arm and fingers. Obviously, I was lucky, which actually amazes me." She didn't need to know that when he wiggled his fingers, a thousand needles went shooting through his arm.

She slouched against the doorjamb. "I saw a pharmacy across the road. I'll get a few things, including painkillers."

"You can't use your bank cards or your phone, or anything to pay besides cash," he said. *Since you're dead and you still haven't explained that part.*

"I have about two-thirty on me."

Times were getting tougher quicker than he expected. Lucky he hadn't wasted the money on the T-shirts.

Laura said. "Do me a favor and lie on the bed. I don't want to return and pick you off the floor."

Curtis lifted up a folded towel beside the sink. "Get some towels as well. God knows if they ever washed this thing." He studied Laura, who appeared rattled by his surly tone, but he'd lost trust in her because of her lies, and now he had to trust her with his life. "Whatever you have in mind when you come back, don't kill me because if you do, I'll haunt you for the rest of your life."

Chapter Nine

Curtis's anger cut right into Laura. He would spit fire and venom once she told him everything.

At the pharmacy across the road, she purchased saline solution, hydrogen peroxide, antiseptic, gauze, tweezers, and bandages, painkillers as strong as she could get over the counter, adding whatever else she thought might be useful. A doctorate in science didn't mean she was a physician.

Two shops farther down the street she discovered T-shirts. She wasn't sure what size he was, guessed him around six feet, athletic. Better too big than too small so she got some in large. One shirt was blue, the other black. For herself she bought a different shirt, expecting the one she wore to end up bloodied. Their prices fit the tight budget, as did the towels she found. She'd purchase food after his treatment, but she bought some bottles of water.

When she returned to the motel, she found him lying on his side on the bed, shoes and socks on the floor, but jeans still on. Three small empty bottles of Jim Beam, which he must have taken from the minibar, were lined up on the nightstand. She couldn't decide if this was a good idea, bearing in mind he would add painkillers to the mix, but he knew his body better than she ever would.

"I'm back," she said. In reply he grunted. "Would you like another drink before I start?" She said it politely, with a touch of rancor.

"Nothing decent left, and I'm not into the sweet stuff."

Didn't think you were. After placing the bag on the chair, she cleaned the table with disinfectant wipes, spread her purchases over it.

Hygiene so important in this procedure, she washed her hands before slipping on the gloves she bought, then went back to where he lay. "Can you make it to the bathroom?"

"I'm not dead yet."

"I want you to sit for a minute before standing up. Lower your feet to the floor. Take it slow. I'll remove the bandage in the bathroom and after that you may step into the shower. I'll clean the wound as much as possible and get into the tricky bits after." She noticed his disturbed glower as he sat up. Her words hadn't really reflected what she meant. "That is… I…"

"Don't bother. We're far from 'tricky bits' the way things stand."

She watched him sway, grab hold of the table to stabilize. She could have helped him but two reasons kept her from it: There was no way he would accept her help, and she didn't want to miss out on the chance to watch him land on his stubborn ass. He wouldn't do her the favor, unless his body knocked him right off his feet.

Laura followed him to the bathroom, muttered a near silent "lazy" as she flipped down the toilet lid, and asked him to sit on it, but it left her hardly any room to move, and she had to weave past him to get the painkillers she'd forgotten on the table.

Back in the bathroom, while filling a glass with water, she said, "It might be better if you straddle the seat."

He peeled three pills from the packet, snatched the glass out of her hand then swallowed them. "Can't think of anything better than straddling the toilet. Saves me from looking at you."

She swallowed. *You'll soon lose your spite.* "You need to know I'm not a doctor as such."

"Oh, really? Who would have guessed?"

She glared at him, at his sarcasm. "Why don't you do it yourself?"

"I would if I could, but it's a bit hard to treat my shoulder with one hand, especially the back part." He flung his legs around, resting his arms on the cistern.

"It's a bit hard to do a good job while you're carrying on like a child." To her surprise, he didn't respond. Maybe he got the hint.

With care she unwound the bandage. The bleeding had mostly clotted, but to know for sure, she had to remove the shirt. With scissors she started cutting it.

"It's the only shirt I have," he said.

"I bought you new ones."

No reply.

Thank me later if I haven't kicked your balls beforehand.

She peeled off the shirt, making sure she left no material in the wounds. Now getting a fuller picture of the damage, she shuddered, momentarily dizzy and nauseated at seeing glass shards pierced deep into the flesh near his shoulder blade.

"How bad?" he asked.

"You really can't remember what happened?"

"How could I? There was glass flying. Gordon… I don't want to remember that bit."

"You have cuts all over and a bullet grazed you. You weren't near the window, were you?"

"Gordon knocked me onto a glass table. Or what was left of him."

She swallowed. "It's best you have the shower now."

"Are you getting naked too?"

"No. And I'd appreciate if you kept your underwear on."

"I had no intention of taking them off." Using the toilet cistern as support, he heaved himself up, slipped off his jeans.

She squeezed past him, unhooked the hand-held showerhead. It would help her clean his wound. Taking off her jeans, too, was an option. She wouldn't be able to keep them dry, but she had no desire to show off any of her body parts. Though, she swept her gaze over his body when he stepped inside the stall. Toned, brawny, athletic, sturdy, a balanced mix—likable. She turned on the shower.

"Holy shit, are you trying to freeze me?" he yelped.

What's the use of a hot body when you shriek like a girl? "Hot water will not help with the bleeding."

"I thought you weren't a doctor."

"Don't you know that hot water speeds bleeding?" She ignored the fiery scowl he shot at her, washed the bullet wound on his shoulder, but then he hit her with the question she'd known had to come.

"Tell me, how can you be dead while you're alive? Gordon didn't have the chance to explain it to me because somebody blew his head off. That's the next bit you can explain. When you're done with that, you may as well tell me who the dead woman was in your condo."

She swallowed once more. So far she hadn't found the time to process Gordon's death. It had to wait because Curtis showed no sign of grief or sympathy unless he overshadowed it with rage.

"Gordon tampered with the DNA result of the woman killed in my condo. It was meant to keep the authorities guessing for a while. In the meantime, we were hoping to find out who she really was."

"And in doing so risked saddling me with a prison sentence. The cops want to know why the hell I've given them the name of the woman who was dead in the condo. Why would you do that in the first place? Essentially, it would lead back to you."

"*Essentially…*," she repeated with acid in her tone, "the plan was to change my identity, but that didn't happen because they killed

Gordon. So yeah, it backfired. Nevertheless, it guaranteed your safety while you were in the hands of the authorities."

"Safe from whom?"

"Turn around."

As he did so, he asked once more, "Safe from whom?"

"I don't know for sure yet."

"Obviously, it's somebody who wants me dead, and I have the feeling you know who it is."

She was fairly certain who it was, but before she divulged the information it was probably nothing other than money deciding his future, she first needed reassurance her assumption was right.

She shut off the water and faced him. "Right now, I need you to dry off and sit on the toilet."

"Right now, I want you to tell me how Gordon could change the DNA reading of the woman in your condo. Who are you people? Spies? Some weird agents?"

"You're not in the right headspace. Sit down!"

"Pass me a towel and turn around. And don't tell me when I'm in the right headspace."

She turned, her gaze following the path of his wet underwear flying, landing in the sink. Interesting. Even more interesting when he straddled the toilet seat with nothing but the towel wrapped around his hips. She accomplished treating the minor cuts on his shoulder with ease and, listening to only a few groans from him, fished out the small shards with tweezers. It was a different story when she started on the deep gashes near his shoulder blade. Every time she came as far as touching it, he jerked away.

"I'm really sorry," she said. "I can only imagine how—"

"Keep going."

"I'm worried that if I pull the shard out, you'll end up—"

"Keep going."

She tried removing another shard, but he jerked away once more, rattling the cistern with his arms.

"I doubt we're going to have much success. Without morphine there's..." Her next word jammed in her throat as he clenched her by her arm, hauled her closer, kissed her, quick, sharp, still intimately, and let go of her.

"I don't consider it ladylike when a woman kisses a man first." He shot up, stomped off and lay, belly down onto the bed.

Laura stood there stupefied. *What on earth was that?*

"Are you getting this job done or do I really have to do it myself?" he called out. "And don't pump me full of morphine."

She gathered the utensils from the bathroom and went to the bed, happy to take on the fight. He should know she couldn't simply go to the pharmacy and ask for morphine.

"We have to lower your pain level as much as we can," she said.

"I want to keep my head straight."

"You won't be able to keep your head straight the way things are heading."

"Don't forget I survived what others didn't."

"You are a smartass."

"With a cute ass."

The towel had slipped high enough to reveal parts of his butt, and he squeezed his cheeks as though he was trying to bring his point across.

I know exactly how to shut you up. She reached for a syringe, undid the cap, then whacked the needle deep into his flesh. It forced a pathetic shriek out of him.

"What the hell was that?"

"Tetanus. Never argue with a woman armed with needles."

Moments later she sat next to him on a chair, dragged the table with the utensils closer and continued using the tweezers. As soon as she touched his shoulder, he said, "Tell me about you." His voice had now morphed to calmness.

Did I tame the tiger?

"I was born in Philadelphia, lived there most of my life. Already as a child, I was drawn to science, and as I grew up I dedicated my life to find a cure for—"

"Tell me about you, not your work," he mumbled from underneath the pillow he clutched with one hand, while his left arm dangled over the side of the bed.

How he managed to deal with the pain while she was poking around his wounds she didn't know, but she noticed his deep, controlled inhalations.

"I love animals," she said. "I always had a pet. Rabbits, guinea pigs, fish, cats, dogs, but I don't have time for them anymore. I like sports, but never have time for that either. I love going to the movies, but never have time. I love reading, but…" She shrugged.

"What do you do when you do have time?"

"Sleep." As he started sweating conspicuously, accompanied by groans and the occasional profanity, she said, "Tell me about your life."

He murmured something. She understood. It wasn't a good call to make him talk while he went through torment.

She rushed into speech. "I've never been overseas, but it's

always been my dream. France, England, Italy, Germany, Switzerland, Spain. All of Europe. The world. South America, Australia. I've never even crossed a border."

"Mexico is not far from here," he mumbled.

She giggled. "Yeah. Why not? But first I'll need a passport."

"No. First you need to be alive again."

Chapter Ten

Detective Eric Sutton seized the opportunity of a deserted squad room to sum up the little information he had. The man in the loft wasn't killed by the fire but a bullet to the head, likely fired by a sniper in the opposite high-rise. The windows exploded inward and not outward, therefore heat didn't cause them to burst. The lack of finding brass in the loft supported the hypothesis. Who the man was that got roasted in the loft Sutton didn't know…yet. It would take days to identify the body.

Why the loft went up in flames he didn't know either, though arson remained the main possibility, which didn't make sense because how did the person shot in the loft set the place on fire? This meant other people had been in the loft. There was the faint possibility that the chemicals caused the fire.

As if there weren't enough hiccups, the reality they couldn't notify the loft owner didn't help as the name he had at hand didn't exist. According to neighbors, they rarely observed people living in the loft besides a cleaner coming in every so often. However, the witnesses stated there had been more activity in the past two weeks.

A man was going in and out sometimes, his description matching a nutty-professor look which, going by the remains of the body, could jibe with the dead man in the loft. Now and then a woman was seen. This woman matched Curtis's description of Laura and not the dead woman in B-1.

Curtis must have found the mysterious woman he claimed was Laura Webb as CCTV showed them leaving the high-rise together. It didn't take much to add one and one together, him being once more in the building where somebody was killed. Even lotto numbers didn't come by coincidence. Buying the right ticket was pure luck. Being twice at a crime scene in less than twenty-four hours had nothing to do with luck, and when Sutton's gut gave him clenching pangs, he had to eliminate coincidence.

His gut gave him more pangs when he studied the CCTV footage closer. For one second, Curtis glanced at the CCTV from under the sunhat as though he was checking if eyes were on him. That was what Sutton believed at first. He zoomed in on the face and tried to read his expression again. He revised his conclusion. It was more like the message, "I need help."

But Sutton gasped when he zoomed in on the woman held by Curtis before being swallowed by the crowd streaming out of the building.

Better watch out, Curtis.

Sutton closed the screen of the footage and changed it to the DNA reading of the dead woman in B-1. They were wrong. Somebody had fed the system with off-beam results. Who and why and…how was it possible?

Sutton contacted his old friend Theodore, who worked in the lab, but when he said the dead woman's DNA hadn't been tested yet, it confirmed something was foul. Less than five minutes later, Theodore called Sutton back, reporting he received the results of her fingerprints and that he could only think of a computer glitch because the woman he identified as Olivia Fitzgerald died six years ago at the age of thirty-three.

"How did she die?"

"I don't think it matters because I personally ran the test once more and this time it came back with a different name. Sophia Langdon. Also dead. Also six years. I don't know what the heck we're dealing with here, Eric. It'll take at least another day to get her DNA results, but I'm not confident we can trust whatever is coming back."

"How is it possible?"

"Man, in all the twenty-six years, seven months, and twelve days since I've been doing this job, I never came across anything like this. So, thank you for giving me something new. But I don't thank you for the headache this will cause."

Sutton had already popped two Advil to settle his headache. "Can you do me a favor?"

"Haven't I just done one too many? I should be at home, drinking a beer."

Sutton chuckled. "Could you keep all this undisclosed until further notice?"

There was a lengthy pause.

"For how long?"

"For as long as it takes until we know who we're dealing with."

"You mean what we're dealing with. If she's some alien, I can keep it undisclosed for a few days. But if it's a computer glitch, I'll have to report it."

"I doubt it's a computer glitch, and she's certainly no alien. I assume the result was planted to mislead us. I bet the DNA will come back with yet another name of another dead woman."

"I'll see what I can do."

"Keep me updated." Sutton disconnected the call, typed the two women's names in the computer sitting in front of him, but the results were inconclusive.

Olivia Fitzgerald committed suicide. Her body was never found after she allegedly jumped from a bridge. Sophia Langdon went missing. The only fact possibly connecting the cases was the incidents happened six years ago, two days apart.

He checked the time, gathered his paperwork and decided to read into the cases at home over a pizza and a beer.

Chapter Eleven

When Laura visited the pharmacy earlier, it would have raised too many eyebrows had she asked for everything she needed. Therefore, she had done the best to keep Curtis comfortable during the horror treatment he endured with bravery. Now that night had set in, and he was exhausted, and the pharmacy was closed, and the streets were deserted, and the guy at the office had called it a day, she continued carrying out her plan.

She changed into the gray T-shirt she'd bought earlier, took the white one she'd worn and cut holes into it. It was without question a different approach for a burglar to wear a white mask with blood spots, but she didn't want to ruin Curtis's new black shirt.

On her first visit to the pharmacy, she'd studied the vicinity and after leaving the dwelling, she'd checked the parking lot behind the building and found the backdoor she stood in front of now. The CCTV didn't bother her. Everything she needed would be in closed-up cabinets in the pharmacy's backroom.

Getting in wasn't the problem. Gordon had not only been a good mentor in science, he had also shown her many ways of entering buildings with little force, so she easily picked the backdoor. It didn't trigger an alarm, unless there was a silent one, but she'd be gone long before the cops arrived.

After ten minutes manipulating some locks of cabinets to get what she was after, she'd gathered what she needed. She didn't hear any cops, doubted she would, also doubted the break-in was ever discovered until the pharmacy took out an inventory.

Back in Room 8, she broke through the skin of Curtis's hand and inserted a cannula. She would have rather done it on his arm but didn't want to disturb him by rotating his body. Keeping his fluids up was a crucial part for him to survive, so she connected a drip, added antibiotic to the cocktail and a small dose of morphine. Curtis wouldn't know. He was in a delirium of exhaustion and his body fighting trauma, but to her relief he showed no sign of shock.

Despite the reality that a gunshot wound should be kept open so it could heal from the inside out to prevent an infection, she wanted to stitch it up because her poking around had left the wound seeping, so did the big cut near his shoulder blade. She contemplated the use of surgical glue, steered away from the idea since the wounds were located on body parts under constant stress and pull. So she cleaned the wounds once more and bandaged them up.

She observed his body closer than he would ever know, down to the towel. Who wouldn't be tempted to peek? A smile tugged at her lips. She went for the blanket and covered him up, made herself as comfortable as possible next to him and hoped to find sleep.

Chapter Twelve

Rasp, tap. Rasp, tap. Curtis cracked his eyes open. A strobe of light filtered through the window as if exploring the room's contents. It took him a moment to sort out his memory. The dead woman. Gordon. The explosion. The motel.

Curtis was still in the motel, though it was dark now. He touched his shoulder, hammering as though a baseball bat had bashed it.

Rasp, tap.

He pricked his ears. The sound came from the outside, close to the entry door, then the bathroom window, back to the door. Another shaft of light flashed through the room. Pulse pounding in his neck, he turned his head to the side. Laura was sleeping next to him. Dressed. He poked her.

"Laura." She purred like a cat. His next nudge was harder. "Laura." To stop her possible scream, he pressed his hand to her mouth. "Somebody's outside."

Her eyes wide open, she nodded.

Curtis pulled the IV needle out of his hand, marveling at its unexpected presence, tiptoed to the chair where he spotted his jeans. Next to them was his underwear—dried. The benefit of a woman's company.

Amused by her likely unintentional but attentive action—he hated the pants zip rubbing on his holy highness—he peeled off the towel from his waist, wiggled the underwear over his hips, followed by his jeans. A black T-shirt lay folded on the chair. Quality: two shirts for twenty dollars. Laura well and truly showed qualities he hadn't expected though valued since money was running thin.

He snaked his injured arm through the sleeve before he slipped the rest over his head and body. Getting the shoes on was much easier.

She mouthed, "Which way?"

The entry door wasn't a good idea. The bathroom had a small

window. He studied a door he didn't know where it led to, pressed his ears against it, listening to any noise. Nothing. His heart jumped. *Rasp, tap.* This came again from outside Room 8.

Laura crouched as though she got spooked. Curtis mimed to her he wanted to get through the door. She duckwalked to him, rose, fished a gift card out of her jeans pocket. The main door to the room had a deadbolt, therefore the card wouldn't work. But the lock to the connector door seemed to have a spring latch. She slid the card vertically between the frame and the doorjamb and in less than two seconds Curtis heard the click.

Impressive. He opened the door by an inch, listened, peeked inside the room. Nobody there. He motioned for her to follow and repeated the scenario at the next door. No noise, no snoring. Same game. Card, *click*. Now they stood in what had to be room 6.

Curiosity taking over, he inched to the window and glanced through the curtains. He couldn't draw a clear picture of the features, but the muscled guy outside was of dark origin. He stood tall, an easy six-four. Curtis had no intention of getting into a direct combat at three in the morning, not in his physical state, but the guy outside didn't come to share a pizza.

At the next door, Curtis listened and cursed silently. Snoring.

She whispered, "I know there's a passage between room 5 and 4. If we get through the next door, we can get out the back."

He remembered having seen a passage when they'd walked to room 8. She used another card as the previous one was bent. *Click*. He peeked into the room. Some obese guy slept on the bed. His snore could be of benefit, warning Curtis if he woke. He looked ahead. Nothing but wall. No door to escape through. Damn. He turned to Laura.

"We have to go out through the front and slip into the passage." He read panic on her face. "We can make it," he said, encouraging himself as much as her.

Her reluctant nod showed bravery.

"Ready?"

This nod came instantly. Tiptoeing, he crept through the room toward the entrance. She followed, the tremble from her hand on his back forcing his pulse to speed up. Curtis inhaled deeply to block the nervousness he felt streaming from her.

The obese guy's snore was regular. Curtis listened to it with the utmost attention, prepared for any disruption of his grating sound.

Through the curtain, he peeked to his left, expecting to see the black guy. No silhouette or shade. Not good. The option he wished for he doubted the most. The guy left after an unaccomplished mission. The chance he waited around the corner was much greater.

Curtis's next concern was Laura. She could run straight into the guy's arms. This wasn't the time to rely on hope, especially since the guy's posture reminded Curtis of a mini godzilla. Going first was the best bet. With the greatest care, he clicked the door open and waited for a few seconds. No rasp, no tap, just continuous snoring.

Inch by inch he opened the door wider and stuck his head around the corner. No sign of Rasp Tap. Curtis slipped through, Laura behind him. He steered to the right toward the passage, hustled into it and checked behind. So far, so good. At the end of the passage, he stopped. Left, right, straight? She tapped him on the shoulder and pointed to the left.

By now, Curtis doubted Rasp Tap chose to attack from ahead. If anything, he came from behind. Curtis gestured for her to proceed to the left, checked his back and waited until she disappeared around the bend. He checked once more behind.

A shriek. Laura!

He ran to the left, stopped as her legs folded like a flower stem clipped by a hoe. Motionlessly, she remained on the ground. Tall and strong, Rasp Tap stood above her. Curtis had to reassess his earlier estimation. The guy was at least six-six, three-hundred-something pounds.

I'm fucked.

What would Dmitri do? Before everything went pear shape in Curtis's life, Dmitri used to be his trainer of four years, four times a week, two hours a day. In the good days, Curtis had enough time and money to follow his passion: martial arts, aikido, karate, jeet kune do, and a combination of them all, which Dmitri called dmi kune do.

He had lit up his Russian passport when he became a US citizen, and the last time Curtis spoke to him, contemplated renaming himself to David. His features were similar to Rasp Tap. However, this guy surely had been in direct combat in real life before. An advantage Curtis didn't have. His experience was limited to the inside of the spacious apartment he once owned, and he'd never hit anyone other than Dmitri. And he'd never knocked out Dmitri, no matter how hard he'd tried.

What would Dmitri tell him to do? Wait for the attacker. Moves would be slow, the size working as a hindrance. Duck, go for the groin, make him stoop, and in his winding, whack him with an uppercut, then kick the back of his head, wallop your knee against his forehead or better even the nose, followed by a thrust into his knee, making sure the cap shattered and the leg kinked in an unnatural way. The opponent would fall, no other way. Seize him in a rear neck choke. Finish him off by breaking his neck. Curtis wiped the last bit.

One thing Dmitri always said about tall, strong guys, "Never ever get hit or you'll be wiped off your feet before you can think about your next move.

Curtis had experienced that once. He was too sluggish blocking Dmitri. Colliding with his head against Dmitri's elbow resembled smashing against a concrete wall. Not that Curtis remembered much of it besides the tremendous headache he had for days.

Rasp Tap hadn't moved yet. Curtis waited him out. A game of patience. First point for Curtis. The guy charged. Straight for the head. Curtis ducked, went for the groin, made him stoop. In his winding, he whacked him with an uppercut, kicked the back of his head, walloped the knee against his head and followed up with a thrust against the guy's knee. *Crack.* The guy came down like an uprooted tree.

Curtis arm-locked him and choked him out, and breathed for the first time since he ducked. By the time the guy would come to, his head would feel as if it went through a washing machine in spinning mode, and he would have an imperative limp.

Curtis groaned. The benefit of adrenalin before it streamed out of the body. His shoulder pumped after that little session. No time to cry. He rushed to Laura, checked her consciousness. Nothing. He fed his hand under her head, elevated it slightly as he clapped her cheek—not the one that started bruising.

"Come on, wake up." A few more claps before she reacted, her eyes circling.

"What happened?"

"Rasp Tap hit you on the head."

She rubbed her cheek. "He could have just slapped me." Her brow creased. "Are you calling him Rasp Tap?"

"Knocking you out was the whole point of it," he said and smiled. "And yeah. Come on. We gotta go. I don't know how long he'll be in a dreamworld."

"Did you do that?" Laura asked as he helped her to her feet. She pointed at the guy.

He reddened with a nod. "I was lucky," he said. *And faster.* But right now he had enough of all the bullshit. "Let's get out of here."

Chapter Thirteen

Clifton Wright focused on the signal on the screen. Still there. He craned his neck, checked the room. Green wasn't sitting at his table or had his rest on one of the thirty small bunks. Fifteen on one side, fifteen on the other. Green usually claimed the same one as his—the last one at the top. No one had ever fought it. Rest was taken in rotation, no matter what genres, all in one room though there were no women left.

They were the first ones to break under the pressure once it became clear this hellhole was the future with no way out. Some killed themselves, others got sick, others died of complications after being assaulted. Some men got so desperate they raped men. Clifton was lucky, kept Green close at all times. The peacemaker. The guy who straightened out trouble.

Powell had, as the only one, a separate room, his eyes everywhere at all times. If he rested, which he didn't do often, he put Green in charge. Green was good at playing both sides which would work in Clifton's favor.

Unconcerned, Powell sat at his desk. He didn't know that what Clifton concentrated on would determine if there was a need to get out of here. The red light kept blinking. So was the blue. If everything went according to plan, all Powell could see was the blue light. He would concentrate on it.

Clifton contemplated which outcome he anticipated more. If the red light faded, he had no pull to get out of this shithole. But if it remained and the blue light faded, he and Green had to get out of here real fast and seize the opportunity. One thing was sure. One light would stop blinking soon.

Chapter Fourteen

His hand clenched around Laura's, Curtis zigzagged past parked cars, bushes, dumpster, rushed down the gloomy residential street, then another, then through a narrow dark alleyway out the other end, farther down a street, through another alley, then he stopped so abruptly, Laura collided with him.

"How did he find us?" he said.

"What did Gordon do?"

"What do you mean?"

"How far ahead did he get to examine you before he was shot?" She grabbed him by his right arm and ran her index over his inner forearm. "Dammit."

"What?"

"He implanted a tracker."

"Meaning?"

"It sends out a signal of your location."

Curtis yanked back his arm and glided his finger over the part where hers had stopped moments before. Heat started smoldering in him when he felt a small object, like a tiny tube no more than one inch long.

Before Gordon had tried to pull some blood, he'd belted Curtis's arm down on an armrest. "So you won't hit me in the head," he'd said. "It'll hurt a little," and before Curtis could ask "What?" Gordon had operated a gun-like device, implanting something into his forearm. The pain was sharp but short, and Gordon said Laura would explain what this was all about. If only she ever would.

He challenged Laura with a deep glower. "What the fuck's going on?"

"Like I said, it sends out a signal."

"To whom?"

"I honestly don't know. It makes no sense why Gordon implanted the device."

Her next words jammed his upcoming rant.

"But I know this much. If the device is tampered with as in if you try to remove it, it'll implode and inject poison into your blood. You'll be dead in seconds, minutes at the most."

Curtis spread his feet wider apart, tilted slightly back to feel the ground from toes to heels. The fury boiling in him was about to burst out, but a tremor filtered from his ears to his brain. An engine? A car? It faded out. He disregarded it, his anger switching to awareness.

"Did you just say this thing could kill me?" He studied Laura and followed her gaze steering away from him, ending at his boots. "Laura?"

She nodded.

"I thought I was supposed to help people?"

"There's more to it."

"Be more specific?"

"Your blood and potential would have been worth a lot four, five years ago if anyone had known you were alive. But things have changed, and now you're worth five-billion dollars. Dead."

Curtis swallowed. It didn't take a mastermind to grasp people wanted him dead, but for this amount of money, every single person would want to kill him.

"I promise I'll explain everything once we know we're safe," she said. "Right now we have to stop the signal."

When is she ever going to spill the beans? "How do you plan on finding a way to do that?"

Laura pointed at a bracelet she wore—silver with a dash of copper. "I also have a device in me."

"How come you have one?"

"We don't have time for details, but Gordon invented the bracelet. It scrambles the tube's signal, including the one from a person wearing the same implant. Up to twenty yards."

Mistrust grew. "We were never more than twenty yards apart since we left the loft."

"Yes, we were. I left you at the motel when I went to the pharmacy. In that time he must have located you."

Curtis mulled over the information because it didn't explain how the sniper was aware of his presence in the loft. Not only that… "This means more people know I'm in San Diego."

"That's why we have to stop the signal as soon as possible. I can only hope Gordon had more bracelets in the loft."

"Well, we can't go there, and they would have melted."

"They're heat-resistant, waterproof, and I know Gordon wore a bracelet."

"Why did he wear one?"

"He didn't have a device in him but wore one as a precaution in case anyone from Operation Rabbit would suddenly be in front of him."

Operation Rabbit. It sounded like one of the Grimm fairytales. Give it a cute name but watch out, you'll get mauled by the wolf. Curtis suppressed his frustration, speculated where Gordon's body could be. The morgue? That posed a problem. The suggestion to break in came to mind.

Laura had proven skills of picking locks at the motel but checking her friend's scorched wrist to see if he had the bracelet on it surely wasn't the way go to. But then, any jewelry he wore would have been removed and sealed in a bag made available to the next of kin—if there were any—once they released the body.

Another option was that he burned to near ash. Then the bracelet slipped off his wrist, and as they removed his remains, the bracelet ended up on the loft floor, either seized by the authorities or still there, undiscovered. There were too many possibilities where this bracelet could be and too many ways to be arrested when attempting to get it.

Curtis shook his head. "Why would Gordon implant a device into my arm intending to jam the signal?"

"I'm sure he had his reasons, but he had no time to explain it. For now, we have no other option than sticking together."

An outlook he wasn't sure whether to appreciate or deem as one of the worst options at hand. Something much worse started to develop. A perception, a feeling. When Laura's eyes grew bigger, her cheeks tensing, her lips tightening, he sensed something bad stood behind him.

~ * ~

Laura stumbled over her own feet when Curtis shoved her to the side. She managed to catch her fall with her hands and raise her head, unsure what to think of him stretching out his body as though he tried to match the size of the guy in front of him, which he never would.

It had strangled her vocal cords when Rasp Tap appeared out of nowhere. Somehow he'd shaken off his injuries, located them, and he appeared taller than before. Laura hadn't seen the previous fight, didn't know if Curtis had enough skills to take this godzilla down a second time.

She readied to run when the guy propelled his fist toward Curtis, but he ducked under the swinging arm. One nil Curtis.

She kneaded her hands, hoping, praying this would somehow have a good outcome.

Your turn, Shawn. Take him down. She widened her eyes. Curtis did anything but that. He just stood there, legs slightly apart, his body wide open. Did he have a death wish?

Rasp Tap attempted another blow. Curtis dived under the arm once more, this time though he bounced up swiftly and whacked his elbow into the guy's kidney. It didn't impress the guy one bit, shook it off as if a mosquito had stung him.

She started to understand Curtis's game. Rasp Tap's size hindered his moves, but his apparent strengths would make up for it. It wasn't that Curtis didn't appear strong, but his thighs barely matched the size of Rasp Tap's arms. And these arms had a longer reach. Laura couldn't find anything within close vicinity to help extend Curtis's arms or something she could use to step in on the fight, besides naked blacktop and walls.

She studied Rasp Tap once more. His injured knee handicapped him. He was trying to keep his distance, only approaching Curtis to land a strike.

So far, Curtis was quick enough and bowed away. At one time he swung a kick aimed at the guy's injured knee. But Rasp Tap wasn't stupid after all and retreated in time. The two men resembled lions trying to find each other's weak spot, luring for the one mistake. Unfortunately, it was Curtis making the mistake.

Rasp Tap aimed for another clout. Curtis mustn't have realized it was a bluff, so he'd dodged away, only to run his head straight into the guy's other first. Curtis flew back landing on his coccyx, annoyance on his face as much as a laceration. Rasp Tap seized the moment of Curtis's weakness, followed up with a boot.

He rolled away, scrabbled monkey-like on his hands and feet over the blacktop, trying to retreat from his predator, who clung to him like a shadow. As he surged to his feet, he pivoted and collected the next blow on his back, knocking him forward but not off his feet. He skipped away, puffed once twice. Rasp Tap didn't follow.

Curtis's demeanor altered to a grimness she'd never seen on him before, then he smiled like a little child kicking the ball to victory. He started hopping around, putting on a Mohamed Ali show.

"Are you going to tell me who you are before I take you down?" Curtis snarled.

He had better know what he was doing because the show didn't impress Rasp Tap.

Left, right, right, left—Curtis darted behind the guy who wasn't able to spin in time when Curtis struck him in the knee pit. The blow threw Rasp Tap off balance but not enough to be of Curtis's advantage.

He continued his dance, seeming to gain confidence with every kick he landed: one on the thigh, another on the back, one on the hip. Rasp Tap's anger built, but every swing ended in hitting dead air.

He roared. Even more so when Curtis teased, "Come get me. Hit me." To Laura's disbelief, he remained motionless for a few seconds, pointing at his face. "Right here, buddy. Hit me again." He bobbed and weaved, shadow boxing in reverse, one step at the time, and beckoned for Rasp Tap to follow.

The guy did, his fists balled, his face like steel. The faster Curtis stepped back, the faster Rasp Tap came at him. Or tried to, with a limp. A hobble maybe, a hopple more accurate. He closed in on Curtis, only because he slowed, then stopped.

Laura's heart dropped. Rasp Tap focused on Curtis like a bulldozer ready to squash a mouse. Curtis didn't seem fazed by it. He ran straight at the guy. They were no more than twenty feet apart. Fifteen, ten. Rasp Tap roared, hands balled, ready for anything.

She wasn't sure if she should laugh or cry when Curtis took two, three short steps, jumped up, one leg horizontally straightened, the other angled, like Bruce Lee in an amateur style. His boot, sole first, hit the guy in the face. *Wham!* Rasp Tap flew backward, landing hard, arms and legs sprawling. His head thudded on the blacktop, blood streaming from his nose. He was out for sure.

The success was short-lived. She'd seen a slight fault in Curtis's glamorous kick. The moment he had jumped, it was written on his face—the surprise, the shock, the realization. He'd slipped on loose gravel, enough to throw him off balance. He didn't land the way he should have: on his feet enabling him to roll to the side.

Instead, he came down like a sack of potatoes, crashing on his back, smashing his head on the concrete. No movement. Two guys, foot to foot, supine, blacked out.

Laura wasted some seconds to see if Rasp Tap showed any sign of motion. Once in the clear, she leaped to Curtis.

"Shawn?" she whispered, kneeling. "Shawn?"

Maybe she should say Curtis. He'd made clear he didn't like the name Shawn any longer. She preferred Shawn, but it didn't matter what name she used, he didn't move. Besides him breathing, he showed no sign of life.

"Oh my god, Shawn, please. React." A groan raised every hair on her body. The only problem was it didn't come from Curtis.

It was Rasp Tap, struggling to lift an arm. No way. She marched to him and kicked her foot in his face. Something cracked, but she didn't give a shit what it was. The guy didn't move. Good.

Back with Curtis, she ran a hand over his face. "Shawn, please.

Wake up. React. Anything. Blink if you can hear me."

~ * ~

"Shawn? Can you hear me?"

The voice was faint. A woman. Curtis squinted.

"Thank god you're alive. Do you remember your name?"

Idiot, you said my name. Shawn. Shawn what? Curtis. That's it. There was something in the middle, though.

"Shawn, talk to me, please."

Can somebody shut this woman up? I gotta think. Dyl. Dylan.

"Shawn Dylan Curtis," he whispered, felt a kiss on his forehand, a hand caressing his hurting cheek.

"I'm so glad you're back," the woman said.

Would be good if I knew who you are. He opened his eyes. Blue eyes, fair hair with a reddish tinge. *Laura.* He groaned. Coughed. *Did a truck run over me?*

"What happened?" He listened to the story about Rasp Tap he apparently flattened with a Bruce Lee kick, only that it went wrong when it came to the landing.

Curtis tried to sit up, but once his head left the horizontal position, his world blurred and swayed. He lay back down and flung an arm over his head.

"Just give me a moment," he said, slightly disgruntled.

He had one big memory issue. He remembered her name, but she didn't fit into his life. To put this puzzle together, he needed a few minutes, mainly because he didn't want to make a fool out of himself and ask her for details. A pang jolting through his shoulder stopped his attempt to turn to his side. Wiggling back, he caught a glimpse of the bracelet she wore. Scrambling signal. Experiment. Billions of dollars. The picture manifested bit by bit. The dead woman in her condo. Gordon. Glass.

"I hate to interrupt your little snooze," she said, "but the guy just moved."

With a stretch of his neck, Curtis assessed the situation. The guy whimpered like a baby. His kick wouldn't have caused this much injury, not that Curtis remembered where he hit the guy or that he'd hit him.

Curtis squirmed end to end as he rolled in slow motion from back to front. Hands on the ground he struggled to his knees, remaining like that for a moment to find orientation; the pounding in his head was unbearable.

Refusing Laura's help, he scrambled to his feet and stumbled to the guy on the ground. Rasp Tap was one big mess, barely conscious, his jaw out of whack.

"I kicked him in the head when he came to," she said. "I had to stop him somehow."

Even though he understood her fear-driven action, she'd created a snag. "Now he can't talk." Ignoring her blush, he riffled through the guy's pants and found the car keys which he held up like a trophy. "We're mobile now. Keep an eye out for a Ford. Maybe a truck. A guy like him doesn't drive around in a sedan. Old model by the looks of it. New cars don't have that type of key any longer."

Smart keys had taken over the world on the latest model cars. Voice recognition the newest invention, even thumbprints—anything to keep thieves away. Hybrid and electro cars had become the norm. Some loved them, the greenies particularly, some hated them.

Curtis didn't like them because too much technology meant too many possible failures. He preferred being in charge of a car instead of relying on a computer, especially in avoiding an accident, since latest onboard-computers forced a car to a halt before the crash.

Was that what the car industry wanted? Didn't they need the smashed up cars, so people had to buy new ones? Another of Big Brother's shady inconsistency. At least his brain was gradually overcoming the blow from moments ago, though his head hurt.

Laura had taken the keys. He watched her disappear around the corner. Seconds later a flash sparked in the darkness, followed by an engine revving up. A Ford Raptor nosed around the same corner and came to a halt next to him.

Told you so.

She jumped out of the car. As they lugged Rasp Tap in the back seat, Curtis discovered the source for the rasp. One of the guy's shoes had a loose sole. Surely his profession earned him enough for a good pair of shoes. Killing people was generally lavishly rewarded. First-time killer?

Curtis closed the door. "Let's go."

She pressed the car key in his hands, unsnapped the bracelet from her wrist, adjusted it, and fixed it around his. It was too late to protest; she turned on her heels and ran away, calling out, "I'll find you."

Chapter Fifteen

Detective Eric Sutton woke with a start when the vibration of his cellphone sent his nightstand into a quake. He slid the device to his hand, checked the number, which he didn't know. He answered, he listened, his jaw dropped.

"I delivered a tall, dark guy to the UCSD hospital. Since he refused admittance, I made sure he couldn't go anywhere, and I'm certain somebody is taking care of him as we speak. I don't know his name, but I know this much: he'll be able to tell you that I didn't kill the woman in B-1. And if I judged you correctly, you'll do anything to find the real killer. So do your job. I'll call you back in four hours."

"Curtis, don't hang up."

"So you can trace me? Save yourself the hassle. I'm outside the hospital, and I'm leaving now."

"I can only help you if you let me. What happened in the loft?" Crackling was all Sutton heard. "For fuck's sake, Curtis. How am I supposed to help you if you don't talk?"

"There was a sniper. I'm not sure if it's the same man I delivered to the hospital."

"Are you okay?"

"I'll survive."

"Why were you in the loft?"

"I'm not answering this question until I know what's going on."

A wall was easier cracked than Curtis. "Who was the man in the loft?"

Silence.

"Curtis. It'll give me a head start if I knew who he was."

"Gordon McNamara. He was a professor... science I believe."

"How did you get involved with a scientist?"

"I'm not answering this question until I know what's going on."

Sutton exhaled sharply. "You're in a lot more danger than you think."

"Oh, yeah? I've survived a blast, a bullet, and a godzilla. I'm not too worried about what's coming next."

"What about Laura?"

"What about her?"

"According to CCTV, you're walking the streets with her."

No reply.

"Is she still with you?"

No reply.

"Is she alive?"

No reply. Instead, Curtis said, "I gotta go. Four hours." He clicked out.

Sutton tossed the phone onto the blanket, disgruntled, disappointed, and worried. "Is a tiny yes too much to ask for?"

~ * ~

Forty-three minutes later, Sutton stood in the UCSD hospital, showered, unshaven, and he had confirmed that they found a big, dark guy outside of the emergency, choked out. According to the tall and bony specialist, who Sutton got to know as Doctor Michael Valensky and became a friend, the guy Curtis had delivered suffered maxillofacial traumas.

"Can you be more specific?"

"Broken nose, shattered jaw. A scan will reveal the rest. And in layman's term, his knee is a big mess."

"Can he talk?" In return, Sutton received a glower portraying, 'Are you for real?'

"Not in a very long time," Valensky finally said, his hands playing around in his gown's pocket.

"He can write though, can't he? Can I question him, try getting his name at least?"

"If you're able to get him to reveal his identity that'd be great. So far he's been refusing to let us take any blood, fingerprints, anything. All he allowed us was to insert an IV."

"What caused the injuries?"

"I'd say he either fell from somewhere high, flat on his face, which I doubt because his skin shows no abrasion, plus he'd have some other broken bones or bruises than just the ones on his head. My next guess is a good strong kick or two. No fist causes fractures like this. Not on a guy his size. And the knee... I'd say another strong kick."

"I need to talk with him," Sutton persisted.

"Go ahead. To be honest, I'm not sure if he understands a word we say. Since we took him in, he's been staring holes into the ceiling.

But while you're at it, find out who's going to foot the bill, unless you want to bear it."

"I'm a cop, not the pope."

"Dr. Valensky!" A young nurse in a green gown ran up, presented her back to Sutton as she whispered something into Valensky's ear.

"I'll be there in a second," he said to her. "Don't go anywhere. It's your guy," he said to Sutton and disappeared through the blue door.

Waiting wasn't Sutton's forte, especially when something apparently urgent had just happened. He shifted up to the blue door, the temptation to follow Valensky enticing, the knowledge of trouble brewing keeping him at bay. He pondered about Curtis and his uncertainty if the man here at the hospital was the loft's sniper.

Fifteen minutes it took before Valensky returned, slightly pale.

"It's going to be interesting to see what the medical examiner will put down for cause of death," he said.

"What are you talking about? He was alive a minute ago."

"Was. He was dead before we could even think of reviving him. The way it seems, he savaged his underarm with the IV needle. He didn't hit an artery or anything that could have caused his death, so I arranged a test on the surrounding tissue."

Sutton shook his head, deflated by this blow. "Handling a victim's body without—"

"Did you want to wait three weeks before forensics gives you the result or do you want to know *now* what's going on?"

The door swung open, a man appeared, handing a paper to Valensky and disappeared. Valensky read it and said, "The first results show traces of Digoxin and Batrachotoxin."

"Poison?"

Valensky nodded.

"How did it get there?"

"Question is how did the cylinder containing the poison get into his arm? And what else was in the cylinder?"

"What cylinder?"

Valensky directed him from the corridor into a small room. "The main reason I rushed the results is that whatever he had in his arm dissolved so quickly, I was lucky to retrieve some of it and run tests before it was all gone."

"What do you mean, all gone?"

"It liquefies, evaporates, disappears, melts, I don't know. It leaves no traces." Valensky whispered, "I've only ever seen it once before, and that person worked for NOKS."

"NOKS is in New Jersey."

"Maybe the guy wanted to get a tan in California."

"How many years back?"

"Less than six."

Sutton ran an eye over Valensky. "Do you remember his name?"

"He could never be identified."

Sutton studied his friend closely. "Tell me, Michael, is there a way to change fingerprints? Or someone's DNA?"

"Fingerprints can be altered, but the epidermis grows back after thirty days. DNA is trickier. Give me more detail about what you're after."

"People being dead but returning alive."

Valensky shook his head. "Impossible."

Sutton informed him about Sophia Langdon and Olivia Fitzgerald. "The first DNA result came back with Laura Webb. I'd say somebody tampered with the system because the dead woman in the condo looks nothing like Laura Webb, or Olivia Fitzgerald, or Sophia Langdon."

"Sounds like somebody found a convincing way to cover the tracks."

"I believe that somebody is NOKS."

Valensky scoffed insultingly. "I know you have it in for NOKS. I also know you want to be a step ahead of everyone else to take them down, but remember NOKS is one of the biggest pharmaceutical companies in the States, backed by the government."

"I've waited six and a half years for this opportunity." Being reminded of his daughter's death, Emily, Sutton's heart tightened.

NOKS had claimed they couldn't retrieve her out of the lab they had conducted tests in with highly flammable chemicals. According to them, it came to an explosion which left no remains for forensics of her body and the ones of another eight victims. NOKS claimed it was due to the extreme heat and the combination of chemicals involved. Sutton had lost his big love. She was only twenty-nine. The daughter he never had time for.

Time was the factor causing the divorce from her mother, Christine. She'd claimed he didn't spend enough time with the family, was too obsessed with chasing the bad guys. Emily was thirteen then, which meant she could still be shaped and accept opinions from her parents rather than being influenced by people who wanted her to do what they thought was best for her. Luckily, Emily built her own opinion.

Despite the divorce, he and Christine remained good friends, and Emily had decided to step into her mother's shoes and study science.

Much better than chasing the bad guys.

Christine had also worked for NOKS and started telling him about NOKS carrying out unethical animal testing behind closed doors. This was before the ban. Eight years ago, when he went to see Emily, Christine complained about a bad headache. Next, she collapsed and died instantly. Brain aneurysm doctors said caused her death. Back then, Sutton couldn't do more than believe it, but after Emily died while working for NOKS, he started doubting the company.

Backing his suspicion was Dr. Michael Valensky. One of the first people Sutton had met when he relocated from Trenton to San Diego, the same as Valensky, with the difference that he was from Princeton. Since they didn't know anyone at this end of the country, they became friends.

But as much as a good friend he was, it didn't mean Sutton shared everything with him, like the main reason he chose San Diego. Never would he forget the night when he left work. An elderly man walked up to him, pressed a piece of paper in his hand, and strode away. The words on the paper said 'She's in San Diego'. Sutton wasn't sure who 'she' referred to, but only a father could have that feeling no one else could describe.

"Thank you, Michael. Let me know his ID once you're done with the tests." Sutton left puzzled about the developments. Only one person had the answers. He had to find Curtis.

Chapter Sixteen

Clifton Wright held his breath. He checked the screen once more. The blue signal was gone. Kind of. It blinked: ERASED. It would do so for ten minutes, then vanish forever. Minutes before he expected it to happen, a signal came to life after years of hibernation—not the red light Clifton had kept an eye on and had hidden from Powell. This signal was also red, but bigger, fatter, alarming. Clifton rerouted it the moment it appeared so Powell wouldn't discover it. It didn't eliminate the problem.

A door slammed shut. Clifton lifted his head, held his breath.

Leon Powell stormed up to him, nearly hyperventilating in a panic. "Tell me this is some god damn computer glitch."

Clifton shook his head. "I doubt it."

"What happened to him?"

"According to the last readings, he was poisoned."

"By what?"

"The tube."

Powell crossed his arms. "Somebody fiddled with it."

"I doubt anyone on the outside knows about the tube, besides the ones who should. I think he did it himself."

"What makes you say that?"

Clifton gathered all his bravery, readied for Powell to have one of his fits. The master of skills was dead. No way would he accept that.

"I backtracked to previous recordings that came in when I had my break. Nearly two hours ago, his vitals showed signs of stress. Even a simple nightmare while sleeping could have caused those." Clifton left out the detail that those vitals needed reporting because they displayed obvious signs that TOX-1 was blacked out, but he wanted to find out first why the person in charge kept quiet about it.

He continued, "One hour later, more stress readings came in. Some of them showed he lost consciousness several times before he…"

Clifton hiked his shoulders.

"Why didn't I get the readings?"

He shrugged once more.

"And where is he?"

"I still haven't been able to find the glitch why we can't get a proper location." Biggest lie. Clifton created the glitch, guessing TOX-1 had located the red light, and therefore Rabbit 76. For as long as Powell didn't know about it, Rabbit 76 was safe.

"Let's hope the tube disintegrated before it was discovered." Until now, Powell had kept his serenity, but his next words brought the entire laboratory to a quake. "How on earth is it possible that we lose the best man? Our entire mission is on the verge of being discovered because TOX-1 is in the hands of fucking whoever!" Every clutter, breath, tap, stopped in the room. All eyes were on Powell, his face as red as if dunked in paint. "And you, Wright." He leaned in closer to him. "You seriously think I believe that two hours before all this, his vitals didn't need reporting? Whose shift was it?"

Clifton cleared his throat. "Sanders."

"Sir!"

The moment Clifton put a face to the voice, his muscles tensed.

The man spoke again. "Sir, I have reason to believe that Clifton Wright and Martin Green are plot—"

Clifton thrust his chair back. It crashed into Powell, knocking him over. Swiftly, Clifton launched from the seat, flung out a hand to help Powell back to his feet.

"I'm terribly sorry, sir. I thought you'd moved from behind me." When Powell ironed his pants with his hands, Clifton shot a murderous stare at Sanders, making a throat-cutting gesture.

"In my office. Both of you!" Powell shouted, his jugular vein about to explode.

At first, Clifton followed him but shortened his stride to let Sanders feed in behind the boss. Clifton wanted the backstabber in front of him, move in on him and whisper in his ears, "You'd better watch out what you say. You're not the first one to disappear if you know what I mean."

Benjamin Sanders was a chicken. Tall, bony body, thin fair hair, thick, black-framed glasses. Ass-kisser when it came to Powell, and a bad spy. Clifton had noticed Sander's inept presence several times; Sanders seemed to pass them by a happenstance when Green and Clifton discussed recent developments.

While Green shrugged it off and suggested not worrying about the ass-kisser, Clifton remained on alert. Although a little wind and a little jangle would scare Sanders, Clifton was more worried about how much he knew.

Right now he wished for Martin Green to appear. He could deal with any type of problem with ease, rattle down some bullshit story convincing enough to mute the other party involved. But there was no sign of Green.

Once in the office, Powell hadn't walked behind his desk as usual. He remained in front of it, in front of Sanders and Clifton, his posture straight.

Powell rubbed his chin. "Why has TOX-1 been compromised?"

Clifton shrugged. "I don't know."

"Who is your source outside?"

He stiffened. "Is this a trick question?"

"Maybe I have to make myself clearer. Have you been in contact with Gordon McNamara?"

Goosebumps crawled over Clifton's back right up to his scalp. Powell had been on his ass. For how long? What else did he know? Did he know Gordon had promised to get them out once a Rabbit was discovered? Any Rabbit, because there had to be some out there.

It had taken six years to find one. Six agonizing years to receive a sign from Gordon. It happened to be Rabbit 76. Since Powell knew about Gordon, the chance existed Powell knew about Rabbit 76 whereabouts. Did he also know about the new signal Clifton had killed the moment it appeared on the screen? That would screw up the entire plan.

"I don't know where Gordon is," Clifton managed to say.

"I can tell you where Gordon is. He's dead."

He struggled to find his breath.

Powell said, "TOX-1 killed him. I have no idea why. Maybe TOX-1 went rogue. I don't know what the fuck is happening out there because nobody is telling me anything, but Gordon is dead." He steered his stare to Sanders. "Sanders? Finish what you were going to say before."

"I believe Green and Wright are plotting against us. I'm sure they're keeping the location of a Rabbit disclosed by tampering with the system. I also believe in—"

"God!"

The door flung open, Green in the frame, gun straight out. He fired, point blank in the back of Sander's head. He collapsed like a rigid thin log, the bullet drilling into its final destination: the wall, now splattered with blood and whatever brain-mass the bullet had carried with it. Ten inches from Powell's head.

"It's a simple deal, Powell. You show us the way out; we'll bring The Rabbit to you," Green barked.

Powell's laugh carried sarcasm. "You're out of your mind."

Clifton shot a look at Green, cringed when his colleague aimed the gun lower. "Don't!" An ear-battering bang deafened him.

He covered his ears, the jarring whistle hurting his brain. Green, amused by it all, the gun still in his hands right next to Clifton's head, smiled. Clifton couldn't hear Powell scream but his mouth wide open communicated his pain. He clutched his thigh. Green said something. Clifton didn't know what he said but the whistle eased to a shallow humming.

"Idiot," Clifton murmured.

"Who's the idiot here?" Green said. "You stood in my firing line. I would have killed the guy otherwise."

Clifton wasn't sure if it had ever been a good idea to team up with Green. His finger sat too loose on the trigger.

"You may have done exactly that," Clifton said, Powell's scream now reached his sensitive ears.

Green said, "He'll be fine. Flesh wound. Won't kill him. Hurts for a while. Depending on how much of a wimp he is, a little longer."

Powell bent like a bow, both hands on his thigh. "You won't get out of here."

"You sure of that?" Green mocked. "By the way, I suggest wrapping a belt above the wound. I don't want you to bleed to death. I'm sure you're keen to walk out of here alive."

Powell unfed the belt from his pants and wrapped it tight above the wound with a loud whimper. "There's no way out. Only through the hatch, and I can't open it."

Clifton and Green exchanged puzzled looks. The hatch. Whoever got too close to the wheel got grilled like a steak. Only one ever tried. Since then, everyone avoided it as if it were the devil himself. Trapped.

"You're trying to convince me that in all the years you were never out?" Green asked.

Powell nodded.

If this was true, then he was as much a victim as they were. Clifton didn't understand what would drive a man to give up his life, knowing he would rot in hell.

"Why did you sign up?" Clifton asked.

Powell breathed heavily. Despite Green's prediction, his pain must be getting worse. "It was either here or prison."

"What did you do?" Clifton said.

"Fraud."

Green said, "You were responsible for the money going missing from NOKS?"

Powell nodded.

"Man, oh man," Clifton said, remembering the headlines when the IRS investigated NOKS over money that never made it into the accounts. "Maybe I underestimated you, but somebody has to be able to open that damn hatch. What happened to the bodies of the people who died in here? How is the food delivered?"

Powell said nothing.

Clifton stepped up to him, close enough to get a whiff of his bad breath. "There has to be an easier way out than the hatch," he said. "We were all brought here by a bus, were driven through some countryside. Next thing I remember was this shithole."

"Can I sit down?" Powell asked. Green pointed the gun at the chair beside the desk, and Powell sat down heavily. "You never drove through the country. You were drugged, were connected to a machine, your memory tampered with. Transferred from Trenton to this shithole."

"With no way out."

Powell didn't answer.

"Where is this shithole?"

Powell shrugged.

Clifton faced Green. "We're doomed."

Green lifted his gun. "If he can't get us out of here, he may as well be dead."

"No! Stop!" Powel flung out his hands as though he was hoping he could stop a bullet. "Let's strike a deal."

Chapter Seventeen

Curtis made his way back to the city. To leave no trails he concentrated on his weighing-a-ton feet. Sleep would have provided more luxury than the T-shirts he hadn't bought at Levi's. His shoulder hammered as if an army of tiny elephants were trapped inside. Oncoming fever warned him his body fought bacteria growing at rapid rate, but he'd rather drop dead than go to a hospital. His grumbling stomach reminded him he hadn't eaten in hours. A decent meal could help him recuperate, as would sleep.

He scanned the immediate area, in the hope to spot some place where he could grab a bite, at the same time contemplating whether to go to Wayne's condo to see if his friend had returned early, or back to Gordon's loft. Laura could be somewhere near there.

Standing next to a patio café, open for the keen and hungry and early risers, Curtis observed a businessman flop a copy of the *San Diego Tribune*, open to the crosswords, onto the table, turn and busy himself digging into a bag that hung on the back of his chair.

In one swift move, Curtis snitched the paper off the table and hurried around a corner of a building. He thumbed through the pages back to front, expecting to find an item about the loft but found nothing until he reached the front page. A shudder traveled through him as he looked at himself.

The photo was the same one most major dailies had run, above the caption "Conman of the year." This time it displayed a big fat "WANTED", like a nineteenth-century sheriff's office poster, listing his crime, name, and his desperado status in sparse terms.

Shawn Dylan Curtis. Wanted by police for escaping custody. Anyone with information about his whereabouts, call this number immediately. Considered dangerous. Do not try to apprehend.

The heat streaming through him wasn't merely fever. His desire for food now killed, the call he'd planned to make later bumped right to the top of his agenda. Where could he find a public phone? He remembered having seen one in the shopping mall where Laura had stalked him, but it was far from ten o'clock.

A young man walked his way, behind him an elderly woman. They both sauntered at the same pace, though appeared independent of each other. Curtis tossed a coin in his mind. The elderly woman might be understanding, but chances were high she'd read the paper. The young man could tell him to fuck off.

Curtis held his head low as he passed a twenty-dollar bill toward the young man, hoping he'd made the right decision.

"Hey." The young man had a 49ers cap slipped sideways on his head, which Curtis liked. "Is there a chance I could use your phone for a few minutes?"

"Just like that?" the young man asked.

"Mine died, and I have to make an urgent call."

The young man snatched the twenty out of Curtis's hand. "Make it quick," he said, handing over the phone.

He could have kept the phone and the twenty and raced away. For a change something worked in Curtis's favor.

The phone rang twice before a voice said, "Detective Sutton."

"Do you seriously think you can intimidate me by putting my face and headlines on the same page?" Curtis gnashed his teeth.

"We can sort this out in peace."

"Peace?" Curtis scoffed. "I'm not the one who started this war."

"Neither did I. There's no search warrant out for you. I don't know who's playing the media, but somebody wants all eyes on you. We have to find out who that somebody is."

"There's a phone number."

"The number is a dead end. But the next logical move somebody will make when seeing you is calling us."

"And who would benefit from playing the media?"

"I'm doing my best to find out." Like a flip of a switch, Sutton's tone altered from agitated to inquisitive. "How well do you know Laura Webb?"

"Really well. I met her briefly two days ago so what do you want to know? Her favorite movie, food, her history or her flaws? You might strike luck and I know the answer." Sutton may as well know how stupid that question was.

"No reason to get snarky. Do you trust her?"

"I don't know yet."

"Then don't. I know you've been in contact with her, so if you know where she is or you intend to stay with her, be careful."

Curtis tightened his fingers over the rim of the phone as an ambulance with wailing sirens drove past. "What are you talking about?"

"I don't know what game she's playing, but staying away from her is your best bet."

"Why don't you tell me what I need to know about her?"

"I will, once I'm one hundred percent certain."

"Certain about what?"

A groan came from the speaker. "She looks so much like..." Sutton's sigh sounded as if he was about to unload a heavy bag he'd carried for a long time. "Like someone I knew years ago."

The detective *knew* Laura? How? Why? If what he said was true, then why had Laura lied? What was she hiding? But worse than her hiding something, if it was true, then Sutton had good reason to hang around closer than Curtis wished.

He said, "I need to know more."

"I can't give you more. Not before I know for sure."

"What about the guy I took to the hospital?"

"He's dead. Killed by poison in a tube in his arm. Listen, Curtis, I don't..."

The sudden roaring in his ears washed out whatever else Sutton added. *The guy was killed by poison in a tube in his arm. The same type of tube as the one sitting deep in my arm?*

"Curtis? You still there?"

"Sorry, yes."

"Olivia Fitzgerald. Sophia Langdon. Do you know these women?"

"Am I accused of killing them too?"

"No. Somebody is trying really hard to cover the identity of the woman in B-1 as well as the one of the man you delivered to UCSD's Emergency."

"Don't you have his name yet?"

"Take your pick. Samuel Dunbar or Christian Fisher."

"He didn't necessarily look like a Christian Fisher. Why two names?"

"We keep receiving different results. They're all incorrect. All I know is these people are dead or went missing six years ago."

Was it the making of the device? Was there more in this tube than just a death sentence? Curtis wasn't sure. He checked if the young man was in a rush for getting the cellphone back, but he only watched the passing traffic.

"What about his truck?" Curtis asked. "I left it at the hospital so you could pin down who he is. Didn't you run his license plate?"

"It leads nowhere."

"You got his body, his truck, but you can't tell me who he was?"

"Listen, I've been keeping my reports short, but if I don't deliver soon, Chief Donaghy will be up my ass. Once he gets wind that the dead woman's identity came back as Laura Webb and that you were responsible for, let's say the *condition* of the man ending up at the UCSD, hell will break loose. We have to meet up, so we can work through this together."

Sutton's calm voice failed to settle Curtis's nerves. "Yesterday you had no problem letting me go and now you want to take me back in?"

"I had no idea what we're involved in."

That makes two of us. "Explain one thing to me, Sutton. By law I'm innocent until proven guilty. Right?"

"Yes."

"So tell me, why am I chasing proof that I'm innocent?"

"No charges have been laid over the woman's death in B-1. And I'm closing my eyes and ears at the moment about the dead guy. Explain to me why you're chasing proof of your innocence."

"Because we both know if I'm arrested for whatever reason, I'll never walk free again." Sutton didn't reply. Probably didn't know what to say. "I'll contact you later."

Curtis disconnected and deleted the number from the log. Though rattled by the news about Rasp Tap's death caused by the toxins in the device in his arm, the information about Laura bothered Curtis more.

Once more he glanced over his shoulder to see if the phone's owner showed signs of impatience, but since he was busy studying a young chick's short skirt—probably imagining the hidden parts underneath—Curtis made one more quick call before giving back the cellphone to its owner, saying, "Thank you very much."

"Quickest twenty I've ever made. If you don't mind me giving you some advice, I hope one of your calls was for an ambulance. I was actually hoping the one driving past was for you. You don't look too well."

"Thanks to you, I might see tomorrow." They exchanged a friendly smile, and Curtis pointed at his 49er cap. "How much for that?"

The young man ripped it off his head, beat it a few of times on his cargo pants while running a hand through his thick sun-bleached hair.

"It's yours. I have more of them. And the way you look, you better hide before you get arrested."

Curtis replied to this unaccustomed friendliness with a spurious smile. Did it mean the kid recognized him or did he simply look like shit? Hopefully, the latter.

They walked in opposite directions. Despite Sutton's bad news, the last boosted his spirit. Wayne Cantrell would arrive in San Diego in less than an hour from now.

Chapter Eighteen

Leaving Curtis behind hadn't been Laura's plan but the only option. He was worth nothing dead, and for as long as he had no bracelet, chances of him dying were high. She hoped the bracelet she'd sacrificed scrambled his signal as it had with hers, but it still puzzled her why Gordon implanted the device into Curtis's arm in the first place. Had Gordon had different motives? Who received Curtis's readings? If only the computers in the loft wouldn't have gone up in smoke, she could have searched them for clues.

How many people had been killed by the tube's fatal ingredients she didn't know, but the woman at her condo didn't die because she hit her head on the sideboard or because someone shot her in the back.

Several ideas started spinning in Laura's head. Maybe the bracelet didn't scramble the signal any longer, which meant it wouldn't scramble Curtis's signal either, which meant he was in danger. Or she'd been followed. Either way, she was a target. She had to find a new bracelet. Gordon's loft was her only option to find one.

After catching a cab, she stopped the driver one block short of her destination and grumbled a silent *fuck* when handing the quickly-diminishing money to the driver. Keeping her head low, she risked a fleeting look to the high-rise, to the window where only yesterday smoke billowed out, but authorities and plainclothes investigators conferring the high-rise's main entrance quickly drew her attention.

Also working against her was the subtle sheen starting to filter through the buildings, illuminating the streets, exposing her more. Every authority could possibly identify her and that provoked additional danger. It didn't matter for the people able to locate her on the tracker; they could find her day or night, in fog or rain.

A clatter captured her attention. A man shuffled a cart loaded with sunglasses and T-shirts and placed it neatly next to another. Upon closer inspection, she discovered sundries like nappies, toothpaste, and something that gave her an idea.

Twenty minutes later, at the beach in a public restroom, she wanted to lock herself in, but to do so she needed a key. With no chair in sight she could jam under the door-handle, she had to chance it.

Bloodshot eyes in a pale and tired face reflecting in the mirror unsettled her. She riffled through the paper bag she'd put next to the sink and pulled out scissors. Once more she looked in the mirror and ran her fingers through her hair. Tucking a hank in between her index and middle finger, she started cutting. One inch, then two, then three.

Confidence growing with every cut, she chopped away until the tendril leveled with her chin, clamped a big junk in her fist and performed a courageous big cut. She continued all around until she had a layered bob. It wasn't professional but good enough to help change her appearance.

Before gathering the trimmings, she fished out a box with dark brown hair dye, but giggles warning her of unwelcomed company, she shoved everything into the bag and locked herself into one of the stalls. She didn't need a mirror to complete the next step.

Two girls, so it sounded, entered the restroom. Busy applying the dye, Laura listened to their gossip, one girl in particular overly daunted by a guy she met while surfing, but the girl's friend pointed out the obvious, "He's got his brain between his legs."

Amused by the girls' conversation, Laura snickered a few times silently. Minutes later, the door snap shut, and the girls' voices fade out. Aware the restroom was going to get busier, Laura transferred to one of the three shower cabins, sat on the bench while waiting for the half hour to pass before being able to wash out the dye.

Thirty minutes could feel like an eternity in a place like this. The eternity filled her with guilt for leaving Curtis behind, but before she could go out and find him, she had to make sure she wouldn't end up dead.

Chapter Nineteen

Curtis paced up and down the bustling street before he discovered the Lincoln Navigator in the traffic, standing out like a queen ant amongst their workers: white, modern, polished, brand new—his friend's pride.

Wayne must have seen Curtis and, terrible driver as he was, killed speed without warning. The driver behind in a blue Toyota honked as the green light switched to yellow. Wayne's Lincoln and the Toyota would have gone through had the Lincoln maintained normal speed, but it sat waiting for Curtis. The Toyota driver lifted his fist, shouting, screaming, and Curtis prepared for a possible road rage, but the Toyota driver remained seated, his face glowing as red as did the changed lights.

Curtis limped off the sidewalk, yanked the door open. Sinking into the leather luxury was like leaning back into a first class jet. Spacious interior, massive center console with store compartments and armrests on both sides were the first things he noticed. And the big screen in the middle. He turned his head to check on the grumpy driver behind, but the Lincoln's backseats astounded him even more. One could have a party back there.

"You drive worse than a grandmother," he said, to pull his brain back to the affairs.

"I was looking for parking," Wayne said grudgingly.

Curtis pulled down the sun visor to once more check the Toyota driver's moves, but he'd lowered in the seat, maybe deflated by being outnumbered as two men occupied the Lincoln. It didn't stop him from inching the Toyota's nose closer and closer to the Lincoln's trunk.

"What the fuck is that wanker doing?" Wayne yelped.

"You pissed him off. I suggest…" A force pushed Curtis into the seat. Wayne punched the gas, ran the red light.

"That's how you deal with idiots like that," he called out, carrying a grin from ear to ear, showing off his perfectly white teeth. He was forty-five, and he looked it too. It was hard to find an Aussie bloke looking younger than their age, Wayne always said. Courtesy of the sun.

Beer was his favorite after work, or a good Scotch, and the lack of exercise started bulging under his perfectly ironed mauve shirt. The black tie was knotted to, of course, perfection and his sandy brown hair showed off the latest pompadour, pedantically gelled in place with great pomposity. The only part he hadn't planned on was his receding hairline, which he said sucked.

For the first time since Curtis sat in the car, Wayne actually looked at him. "I was worried about you, mate. Gee, man. You look like shit. What happened?"

Wayne. There was no in-between. People either loved or hated him.

Curtis gave him a quick rundown of the past days while Wayne steered the car through the city and stopped in a parking lot. Unfamiliar with the location Curtis spotted an inlet where a river connected with the ocean, docked yachts to his left.

"You're saying you're worth five billion dollars?" Wayne said, killing the engine.

"No. I'm worth five billion dead. That's as far as she got to explain stuff to me."

"Considering how much time you've spent together, there's not much she revealed." He reached past Curtis, ransacked the glove box and exposed a black pouch big enough to hold a book. He fumbled in it, fished something out, turned it in a flash of motion.

Curtis's heartbeat stalled at the sickening sensation of a gun muzzle pressed up under his chin.

"No one out there is your friend," Wayne said, raucously. "Not for five billion dollars. It doesn't matter where you go, who you meet. Everyone wants a share, wants a reward. Everyone you think is your friend might be your biggest enemy. Let this be today's lesson."

Curtis didn't dare swallow, or speak, when Wayne poked the gun deeper into his chin's flesh. His brain crammed with ideas. He didn't know which one to hold on to. Did Wayne just turn to a money-hungry prick? Anything was possible with him.

After agonizingly seconds, his friend released the pressure, leveled the gun, and forced the grip into Curtis's hands. "You'll need it. Don't hit me."

He fought off the cocktail of relief and fury. "You fucking damn fucking prick," he roared, started a backhander at Wayne, but a pang in his shoulder stopped him. He groaned.

Wayne snickered next to him. "It's called karma."

"Asshole."

"Yep, I've heard that before. You didn't tell me you were injured, besides that new addition to your face. That black guy must have had a hell of a wham. Does it hurt?"

"As if you cared." It did hurt. Not the laceration but the cheekbone protested under every word he spoke.

Wayne said, "Lighten up, buddy. I just wanted to make sure you know what you're dealing with. What would I do with a share of that money, ay? I'd suddenly have friends I never had before and don't want in the first place. My ex would be knocking at my door. Next my kids. You know I'd rather let them do the hard yards, even though I don't know what yards they're doing. But it's not all about computers and technology. You still need your brain and guts and muscles to survive in this world."

"Besides that you can't control your kids' yards since they're on the other side of the world," Curtis said, ignoring his friend's scowl.

"Why hasn't Hollywood come up with my story, yet, ay? Aussie meets Yank. He follows her to the States, gets married, bangs her up a couple of times. He takes her with the kids Down Under, and she doesn't know better than being banged up by my rich prick friend. Aussie returns to States with no wife and kids, while she remains Down Under. It's what people call economic growth with an international transaction."

Curtis had to work through this flood of information only to realize there was nothing new in it. Same old, I'm-such-a-poor-guy story. Worse. Fourteen years on and Wayne still said banged up instead of knocked up.

Wayne said, "But somebody had to shake your naivety out of your brain because I don't think I understand the whole severity of it yet. I mean, who is this Laura Webb? You're telling me you met this woman in my apartment building's lobby. Next thing she calls you, tells you she has a dead woman in her condo. Then Laura's gone, and the cops suspect you killed the woman. Then she stalks you and tells you they used you in an experiment and that you're worth five billion dollars."

"Was worth."

"Come on, mate. Don't give me that crap. Gold doesn't suddenly lose its value. Has it at any stage entered your mind that somebody is taking the mickey out of you?"

"The what?" Over the years Curtis familiarized to some strange phrases Wayne had brought over from Down Under, but he still came up with idioms he'd never heard of before.

"Playing you, mucking around with you," Wayne said. "You have over one million people hating your guts. Most of them want their money back, which is probably the only reason why you're still alive. It's all about the dollar, but they still want to see you bleed. So, some of your ex-customers are giving you a hard time, made up the story about your DNA and all that crap, feed shit into your brain about your..."

"Okay, okay. I get it." Curtis shook his head. "That doesn't explain the dead woman or why Gordon's head was blown to pieces. And what about the device in my arm?"

"I admit Gordon's story is a bit sick, but the device is nothing but bull."

"I can feel it." Curtis let Wayne examine his forearm with his finger.

"And she told you it'll implode if you fiddle with it, and the bracelet, which comes across as though you are a poofter, is scrambling the signal so you can't be traced?"

Curtis refrained from asking about the poofter comment; he had an idea. "Apparently the device is filled with poison. The guy from last night was killed by it." He studied the console to escape his friend's deep scrutiny.

"I've known you for about fourteen years, and I never thought somebody was able to load you up with so much crap."

Curtis wasn't sure if the word *crap* triggered it, but his stomach churned. Just in time he opened the door and retched.

"Oh man, don't lay a pizza into my baby." Wayne moaned.

Curtis didn't reply. To keep his head from spinning, he rested it on the headrest, THEN ran the back his hand over his mouth.

"Fine then." Wayne started the Lincoln.

"Where're you heading?" Curtis asked.

"A friend. She can check that thing in your arm and your health before you cark it."

Chapter Twenty

Armed with a new hairstyle and new-grown confidence, Laura stood in front of the door to Gordon's loft, barricaded by yellow DO-NOT-CROSS tapes. It didn't mean they stopped anyone willing to take on a possible charge by trespassing a crime scene. Her only problem was to remain undetected if somebody appeared.

She snaked her hand through to the door handle and turned the knob. To her surprise, as much as relief, it was unlocked. Hesitant to proceed, aware authorities could occupy the loft, she chanced luck, bumped the door strong enough to swing it open. If anyone was in there, she'd have enough time to escape. There was no one. She unclipped the top crime tape, weaved her feet and body over the bottom tape, then tucked the top tape back onto the doorframe before she closed the door behind her.

A quick scan of the loft showed it had undergone a major makeover. Soot smudged the once white walls. Glass shards glittered on the floor. Dry blood adhered to the chair where Curtis must have been sitting. A lot more puddled on the floor below had caked. That raised a concern. If any of it was his, which it likely was, it would lead back to him.

She hurried toward Gordon's sleeping area on the right side corner of the loft, now mostly visible through the burned shoji blinds.

Three aluminum chests of drawers lined up next to each other claimed her focus. One he must have used as a nightstand as a lamp perched on top next to a clock. Nothing of interest was in the first two drawers, but she struck luck when she slid the third open. Three bracelets sat in a small black box as if waiting for her to pick them up. To the authorities, they would have been meaningless, but to her they meant staying alive a little longer.

With one clipped around her wrist, she heaved a deep, relieved sigh and shoved the other two into her jeans pocket before combing through all the drawers. Nothing of use turned up.

He was a thorough man, kept a record of every development of his work. She'd seen the external hard drive on the floor near the shattered screens when she entered the loft. It was now one deformed black glob of plastic. Near the hard drive, she spotted memory sticks scattered around. Each item had a number tag adjacent.

She assumed they'd been filed as evidence but not yet bagged. They could contain key information why Gordon had been killed, like why he implanted the device into Curtis, but before she could retrieve them, a male voice startled her.

"Is anyone in here?"

She hunched behind the chests of drawers then peeked through a gap between the two chests. The uniformed officer was dark-skinned, boxer nosed, wide-cheeked, and his belly bulged over the too-tight belt of his black pants. Though he held his hand on the holster, insecurity streamed from him as his eyes fluttered from side-to-side. He progressed deeper into the loft which Laura deemed her only chance.

With the door wide open, the crime tape undone, she'd outrun the officer without a puff. It was then when the officer occupied himself with checking the bathroom that Laura ran, her feet hardly causing a tremble. Like a gazelle dancing through the desert, she slipped through the door. In her imagination the escape already a success. Unexpectedly, a hand clutched her arm, the force of reversed momentum propelling her straight into the arms of a man.

"Where do you think you're going?"

The shock froze her, worse was his voice. It shook her up to the core of her body, flooding memories to her brain she wasn't sure if they belonged to her life. Gordon had warned her about the possible consequences and complications if the past challenged her. She closed her eyes, wishing this moment away, the moment she had longed for but had feared even more.

She stiffened in the man's grip, at the sound of footfalls approaching fast.

"I've got it under control," the man said, his hand still clutching her arm. "Check if anything is missing."

"Okay, sir."

Footfalls faded out.

"Fine," the man said. "Easiest way is you tell me your name and why you were in there. Then we discuss the options. My name is Detective Eric Sutton."

Her heart pulsated in her neck. *Don't look at him.*

"Easiest way is you simply let me go," she said.

"Sorry, but that's a no go."

His hand now under her chin, she resisted his force to lift her head, her legs nearly folding beneath her as the urge to hug him enveloped her.

Not now, she reprimanded herself and remembered a well-known saying: Offence is the best defense. His holster's undone safety snap gave her an idea. Her stealthy act so easy to pursue, she promised herself if the chance arose to scold him about this slackness. She jerked his weapon out, but didn't point it at him, watched not only surprise dawn on his face, also recognition.

"You have to let me go or innocent people will die." She stepped away, drew closer to the emergency exit.

"You're really good at it, Laura," he hissed through his teeth, "but I'll never forget who you are and what you've done. I hated you for six-and-a-half years and you can never change your appearance enough to remain unrecognized."

"If you kill me, you'll never know the truth."

"The truth? She's dead. You killed her. You knew what experiment she was involved in. You knew the dangers. You could have made sure she wouldn't be part of it. NOKS's reports stated you led those people into a death trap, but it was still treated as an accident. And you disappeared the same day as the accident happened. Isn't that enough to show your guilt?"

"It's far more complicated than you think."

"There's nothing complicated about it. You couldn't stand the fact Emily was successful while you struggled to make a name for yourself. You were always one step behind her. You wouldn't be the first best friend eliminating the reason for coming second."

His words twisted her stomach. "I know it won't make sense when I tell you she died because it was the only way for her to—"

Her muscles constricted at the sound of a ding. Sutton's turn to the arriving elevator gave her opportunity to act. She darted through the emergency door to the stairwell, cursing to have divulged too much. Now he would be out there hunting her for the wrong reasons.

As she reached floor 19, she wiped the gun to destroy her fingerprints and dropped it. Chances were high he followed her by foot. If he opted for the elevator, he'd be on the first floor long before her, but her goal was floor 12. There was a door connecting this high-rise with the neighboring building, leading to a spa, a gym, a pool, and ten floors down, shops she could use to hide out.

Chapter Twenty-One

Wayne waited outside the treatment room while his friend, Katherine, examined Curtis. She was a veterinarian, experienced enough to treat an alien. Curtis qualified close enough for it, though he would never have admitted he needed medical help.

Seeing him had sent a shockwave through Wayne, who was able to read the physical and emotional pain his friend tried to hide by clenching his teeth after every word he spoke. Wayne had no intention of watching him suffer any longer—Curtis was a good guy.

He treated everyone equal, gave everyone the same chance, but people had broken him like a horse by its rider. The past six years hadn't given him an easy ride. The motorcycle accident had put a full stop to his active life, but he didn't give up, practiced any kind of self-defense sport on top of swimming, running, and bench pressing to regain health—his way of proving he couldn't be broken.

But he nearly snapped in half when three years later life claimed the woman he loved the most from him. When Wayne had word that Curtis was held in custody after hitting drugs and abusing an officer, Wayne had taken the first flight to New York, bailed him out and lived with him for a few months, helped him to concentrate on his prone-to-fail business. At that time, Curtis needed to find belief and not reality since it had kicked him more than enough. When he got his life back together it all turned upside down.

First Sarah, the woman he saw as a chance to find love again but stripped him of his money after the fraudulent news about the daughter who was supposedly his. After that the business crashed. The DNA test wiped him entirely off his feet. And now? Wayne didn't know what to make of it, and Curtis surely didn't know either. Blood transfusion, tests, his blood worth billions… or death.

Katherine came out of the treatment room, her brown hair knotted up, her hands dug in the jeans back pocket, the blue gown over a blue shirt swung back.

"How's he doing?" Wayne asked.

"He's in real bad shape. More than he's letting on. He's got a concussion. I drugged him up, but please be aware he could fall unconscious at any time. The full severity of concussions can happen hours even days later. I wished he'd agree to go to a hospital, but I'm hitting a wall there. You didn't tell me he was shot at."

"You kiddin'?"

"Unfortunately not. He suffered scratches and cuts from glass, some deep. And he's got a bullet-graze on the verge of an infection, so is a deep cut near his shoulder blade. That's why he has a fever. If his temperature rises, call me. If any pus shows on his wounds, call me. If he falls unconscious, call an ambulance. He won't be able to debate then. He needs sleep, but check on him at least every hour to make sure he's responsive. I've given him some drugs to calm him. He's stressed, even though he's trying to hide it. Don't use anything but the medication I gave him as some can cause complications with his concussion. He needs to keep his fluids up. No coffee, no alcohol. Garlic is helpful, onion, ginger, all things that help to fight the infection. He'll be crying for a steak. He told me he hasn't eaten for a while. Give him chicken soup first. If he keeps that down for four hours, he can have his steak."

Wayne wasn't prepared for such a lengthy list. "Maybe I should try becoming his mother. What else?"

"Don't be surprised if he suddenly suffers a mental breakdown. He'll need a good old hug."

"Isn't that your department?"

"I only hug animals." Her nose crinkled as she smiled.

"You know I'd love to be your dog." He moaned as she ran a hand over his bottom.

"You know we tried that, sweetie, and all we achieved was doggie style."

"It was good, though."

"Not denying that. But on a serious note, he needs a good friend now."

"What about the device in his arm? Is it real?"

"As real as me."

Chapter Twenty-Two

Four hours after seeing Katherine, Curtis and Wayne sat at the shoreline of a secluded beach. No people, no dogs, nothing but beach. The sun's reflection glittered on the water, the cliffs behind them beaming in an orange-red. Peaceful.

Curtis sipped from a whiskey bottle wrapped in a towel. The Jameson had caused an argument when he proposed his wish to drown his sorrows after he woke in a bed he didn't know how he ended up in it.

"You're pumped up with drugs, mate," Wayne had protested. "If you want to kill yourself, do it without me,"

"Wasn't it you who told me once: when shit hits, kill it with booze?"

"Fuck you."

"Glad that's sorted."

In the end, Wayne had bought the whiskey, admitting he could do with a drink himself. It was his way of showing that his own wisdom had beaten him.

As Curtis observed the ocean—the calmest he'd ever seen it in contrast to his inner self—the vet's result spooked through his mind. Katherine had examined every angle of the device in his arm, X-rayed it, ultra-sounded it, scanned it, ran pictures through a database. She had nothing more to say than: "I've never seen anything like this before, but playing around with it may not be a good idea in case it does what you were told it does. All I can say for sure is it's a capsule concealing liquid." The little hope he had that somebody was playing games went up in smoke.

"I'm screwed," he said. "I could drop dead any second. Who knows what this shit thing in my arm is capable of?"

"Do you think the bullet was meant to kill you or Gordon?" Wayne asked.

Curtis reflected back to the moment when Gordon shot the

device into his arm and released the belt he'd used to restrict any disagreement. Gordon had gotten the needle ready to draw blood but didn't get to proceed as his head blew to shreds.

Curtis's reaction trying to push Gordon back had come instinctively, but dead meat could weigh a ton, especially when it came down without warning. As Gordon sagged, the chair flipped, and they both crashed onto the glass table. Now, Curtis realized the bullet grazing his shoulder must have been the one that killed Gordon.

"Hard to tell," Curtis said.

"Where's this Laura now?"

"No idea. Don't really want to know either. She gives me the shits."

Wayne ripped the whiskey out of Curtis's hand and took a good pull. "Last time I heard you say *'she gives me the shits'* you were in love."

Curtis scoffed. "First of all, I only met her two days ago, and I'm too old for the falling-in-love-head-over-heel stuff. And you couldn't be more wrong."

"I know it's not the right time to bring it up, but I was right the last time."

The talent Wayne had of bringing up a story at the most inappropriate moment was incredible. Did he do it intentionally or was it simply his clumsiness? Curtis brought it down to Wayne. Successful, caring, but he spoke before the consequences of his words crossed his mind. Or when he was about to say something hurtful, he would feed a tiny excuse before he dropped the bomb. Like moments ago.

He knew it wasn't the right time to stir up old wounds, though he still had to add that he was right the last time. Which he was, essentially.

The woman Wayne was talking about was Jessica. Was. Curtis would still be with her if life hadn't decided differently. When he first met Jessica, he didn't necessarily like her but something drew him to her. In other words, she knew how to press his buttons.

They fought their way together as they couldn't be with or without each other. In the end they both stopped fighting, which freed the path for love.

Three years of happiness, goals, dreams, until some drunken idiot decided to smash into her car, which flipped off the bridge. She was dead before her car hit the water. The only consolation Curtis had—the reckless driver veered after impact straight into a truck and got squashed to death.

It all happened when his business started to fly high, and as much as he tried to make it fail after Jessica's death, it took off even more. Thanks to Wayne. Forever grateful for his friend's selfless help, Curtis managed to deal with his grief.

Not quite two years after Jessica's death, a glimmer of love came his way when he met Sarah. If only he'd known she'd rob him of the last penny he had. Since then, women meant nothing to him. Until Laura. She was a different kettle of fish, knew how to press his buttons—the same way Jessica had. The way she…

A nudge on his shoulder snapped Curtis out of his thoughts. He'd totally forgotten about Wayne sitting next to him, still being a pain in the butt.

"You're pondering about Laura, aren't you?"

"I'm wondering how I'm supposed to get out of this mess." Curtis had no intention of sharing his opinion about her yet. Not before he worked her out himself. Not before he knew her secrets because according to Sutton, she was hiding something.

"The only person able to help you out of this is Laura," Wayne said. "It might be a good idea if I check her out. You know, she seems to screw you around a bit."

"She's not your type," Curtis said quicker than he could think.

"Not that way, dumb fuck. I want to find out who she is. Her history, if she is who she purports to be."

"How do you want to do that?"

"I have my ways, or how do you think I find out my clients' history? I'm a realtor. I know who is getting married, divorced, who killed a wife or a husband. I want to know who I'm dealing with before I meet them. So while I'm digging, I want you to find Laura and be the nice guy you usually are."

"Not interested."

"Yes, you are. She's either your only way out or the closest way to death. That's if you haven't killed yourself beforehand with whiskey."

It happened as though someone had unclogged a tab. They just came out, unstoppable. Curtis didn't try to fight the tears, had no shame to let them flow in front of Wayne, and Wayne, for a change, had the right words.

"I'll help you through this, mate. Don't worry." The brotherly hug sealed his commitment.

Chapter Twenty-Three

A rasp annoyed Curtis's ears. After sleeping in so many beds in the past few days, he started losing track and had to find orientation as he opened his eyes. The mix of whiskey and medication had left him lacking memory.

The rasp was different from the one he remembered from early yesterday coming from the man who stalked him and Laura at the motel. This one sounded more like a chainsaw.

He guessed the rasp's source, reached for a pillow, and flung it hard. A clonk, a groan, a bang, a thud. He switched on the light and cracked up laughing. Tangled between the chair and the bed end hung Wayne like a monkey. He gaped around. One hand on the bed, he used other to free his foot from the chair.

"Glad you haven't lost your humor," he said with a smile. "You 'lright?"

Curtis nodded despite his hammering head. "Why don't you go to bed?"

"You're in it. I can't stand it when people fart while sleeping."

Both chuckled, and Wayne disappeared through the door to the living room. Now that quietness had settled in, Curtis snuggled up, longing for sleep. Wishful thinking. Laura spooked around his head and with it Sutton's comment, "She looks awfully similar to someone I knew years ago."

Curtis crawled out of the bed. While he slipped on the T-shirt he'd taken from the chair off which he'd knocked Wayne, he familiarized himself with the new area. The generous bedroom, all furniture in white, had a built-in closet with three sliding doors and nightstands to each side of the bed. An entire home office could have easily fit in the room, but only a tiny coffee table stood near the wall next to the door leading to the bathroom which he used before he entered the living room.

In the left corner sat a white small table on which Wayne had scattered some paperwork. The big window front to its right had no balcony, and centered in front was a black dining table with four chairs. There were no paintings on the wall, no decoration, no personal touch. And nothing hinted it belonged to Wayne. He liked solid wooden furniture. This had to be the apartment he mentioned yesterday.

Curtis had Wayne's head in his view. His friend rested in the beige three-seat couch and he hadn't started chopping down trees again.

"You should be in bed, recovering," Wayne said without parting his attention from the laptop he had in front of him.

"The only thing I need is a conclusion."

"Don't forget you're suffering a concussion, so your conclusions might be a little blurred, but since you had an over ten hour beauty sleep and I only had an hour nap because I was too busy making sure you don't cark it, I suggest we swap. Bed for the laptop." Wayne tilted his head back, his eyes reflecting a begging puppy.

"Deal," Curtis said.

Wayne got up. "I hope you didn't shit in it."

It didn't need a reply.

He added, "I suggest you eat something. I cooked up some chicken soup. It's in the fridge. Microwave's in the kitchen."

"I hope you didn't spit in it."

Wayne giggled before he shut the bedroom door.

Curtis waited until the lights dimmed, sat where Wayne had been moment ago, pulled the laptop closer and typed her name into the search bar: Laura Webb. The result revealed a heap of women, mostly linked to all types of social media. Not one of them resembled Laura. Curtis entered Philadelphia next to her name, remembering she'd mentioned it was her birthplace. Match. In some ways.

He read into Laura Webb, eighty-seven-years old, claimed a hero four years ago because she'd rescued the neighbor's cat from the burning house. The article remembered her; she died a few months ago. More Laura Webb's from Philadelphia showed up on the screen, but not the one he wanted to see. He deleted Philadelphia from the search bar, added scientist to it. About to click through the pages, a different name caught his eye: NOKS, named after the founder Henry Knox.

Rumor had it the company should have been named KNOX, but due to a legal dispute with a company already named the same, they founded NOKS Organic Toxin. Short NOKS O.T. though the Organic Toxin seemed more like a fallacy.

NOKS was of other interest. It used to be one of his main clients. Not NOKS itself, but Henry's son Sebastian Knox, who'd taken over the reins since his father's retirement. Curtis read deeper into the story and stored the result deep in his mind. Laura had some explaining to do.

He also remembered that Sutton mentioned two women and so far nothing he said came by accident. Olivia Fitzgerald and Sophia Langdon.

The search delivered several results. Olivia Fitzgerald was thirty-three when she supposedly jumped off the pedestrian bridge in Elizabeth Park in Trenton—on a rainy day, the river roaring—leaving a note in her car that life wasn't good enough.

Several reasons concluded suicide: the note, her one shoe found at the bridge, and the jacket she allegedly wore the day she was last seen. But no one had seen her jump. Her parents were convinced their daughter was murdered but lack of evidence, and no body, caused the case to go cold.

Curtis read into Sophia Langdon. She disappeared two days after Olivia, though nothing connected the two women, not even their jobs. Olivia was a computer tech in Philadelphia, Sophia a nurse in Edison and aged forty-one.

The next names he typed were Samuel Dunbar and Christian Fisher. The result on Fisher came back similar to Sophia Langdon's. He went missing two weeks after Sophia, aged twenty-seven, and had studied medicine in Princeton.

The search on Samuel Dunbar, however, returned a result that made Curtis frown. He died in an explosion while working for NOKS, but because of the extreme heat caused by the fire, no body could be retrieved. *Interesting.*

Though nothing appeared to link them all together, one thing was certain: six years ago appeared frequently. Six years ago he had his accident and nearly died. Six years ago he was used for the experiment Laura mentioned. Six years ago Olivia, Sophia, Christian, and Samuel died or disappeared. Too much of a coincidence?

Curtis needed fuel. Time for chicken soup.

Many times Wayne had proven himself as being the worst cook in the world. Every steak resembled an old boot. But the first spoon of chicken soup Curtis slurped from surprised him. *No way.* He slid from the barstool at the kitchen counter and checked the trash and found scrapes from chicken and vegetables in it.

He chuckled, continued eating the soup, enjoying every bit of it so much that he filled the bowl a second time, heated it up in the microwave and would have gone for a third, but he didn't like sleeping on a full stomach since it gave him nightmares. He already had enough of them.

Chapter Twenty-Four

One hour before he had to be officially at work, Sutton sat at his desk, skimming through files about Laura Webb. Deep inside it gnawed at him that she tricked him and stripped him of his gun, though it reflected her deceiving persona. Luckily he'd decided to follow her down the stairwell and found the gun on floor 19. God knows what would have happened had it fallen into the hands of a child.

Why was Laura alive? Her files stated she disappeared six years ago just hours after the explosion in which Emily died. Laura's belongings were at her desk: her jacket, handbag, wallet, phone, though no sign of her.

The last place she went to, according to the videos installed all over NOKS's premises was the storage room where drums of chemicals were held.

One question arose back then. What was she doing there?

Nobody had knowledge of how she gained access because the area was off limits for unauthorized staff and could only be accessed with a code and a key. But she simply opened the door. This led to the conclusion the door was tampered with, either with paper or something strong enough to prevent the door from locking. Therefore somebody knew she was going there. Every employee who went in before her came out again. Just not Laura. There was always the option of CCTV manipulation.

However, Gordon McNamara disappeared the same day as her, or actually one day after. His movements were normal the day she vanished and nothing indicated he was near the storage room. The following day, he simply didn't show up at work.

Two people from NOKS had vanished and the cases turned cold. Some believed they couldn't handle the loss of their eight colleagues dying in the explosion and chose to go underground. Still, it sounded fishy.

Years ago, facial recognition came into place to eliminate identity fraud, but it appeared Gordon and Laura had found a way to cheat the system, with the risk that one day their scam could flop. Both were listed missing in New Jersey at the same time, both had lived a life in San Diego under their names, but with different SSN, birthdates, birth certificates, and driver licenses.

For as long as their faces weren't checked, or their fingerprints, nothing would raise suspicion. There were two of the same, with different lives, like another John Smith story.

Gordon's scant history didn't give Sutton much to go on. It showed Gordon had a law degree but never practiced. He'd listed himself as a car salesman, but mentioned no dealership. And nothing linked him to being a scientist.

In Laura's new life she'd been working as a waitress and room attendant. It contradicted her previous career path, and Sutton found it difficult picturing her cleaning toilets. He brought back the feeling he had when she was, literally, in his arms. That she wasn't the success-driven, money-hungry chick he'd dealt with in the past. Instead, it woke a familiar feeling he couldn't explain.

He lifted his head. Mendez strode into the squad room, dragged his chair from his desk over to him, and straddled it, resting his arms on the backrest.

"You're early," Sutton said.

"Baby's been crying all night. I needed peace. Anything new?"

Besides the fact you are never early. "Nothing that will crack the case. What about you?"

"Labs and techs are working frantically to find the hiccup in the system and hope they'll be able to come up with the identity of the woman in B-1 within the next few days."

Sutton leaned back and folded his hands behind his head. "What was your first impression of Curtis when you got to B-1?" He studied his partner's reaction closely.

Sutton had offered to assess officers to see if they were ready to take on the next step, in other words, step into his shoes. When Mendez was assigned to him, he had a good feeling about him, but then he started to ignore simple rules, became a hot-head, and something Sutton couldn't explain yet happened the night when the incident at B-1 was called in.

"He was nervous," Mendez said.

"Did you know who he was when he opened the door?"

"No."

"What's your gut telling you?"

"I think he killed her."

He said it so quickly Sutton wondered about it. "When did he mention Laura the first time to you?"

"Not before you turned up."

Sutton wrote a mental note of the statement.

Chapter Twenty-Five

When Wayne woke in the morning, he found Curtis on the couch, sound asleep. His breathing was steady, a few groans, a few twitches, no snoring. To avoid waking him up, Wayne returned to the bedroom, gathered some clothes he'd take to the condo, where he hoped the cops had packed up their investigation.

Stuck in the usual early morning crawl, he noticed the increased presence of black and whites circling the streets.

He parked the Lincoln in his allocated lot in the underground parking, spotted Curtis's Tahoe in the visitor spot with a note jammed under the wipers. He ripped it out, read it. *This not permanent parking.* The handwriting was poor, and obviously the friendly writer needed some spelling lessons. Plus, how long determined permanent? Could be a visitor for a day, two, seven.

Wayne crunched up the note, shoved it down his jeans pocket, fished out his cellphone to insert the battery and SIM. Curtis had warned him over and over about Big Brother watching and listening, and with those two parts not in the phone, a location couldn't be traced, calls not listened to.

"Wayne Cantrell?"

The voice came from behind. He turned and saw a tall man in a suit, the demeanor of an authority written on his face. His age was hard to guess. Sixty give or take three years. His profession, however, easier observed. Private eye or cop.

"How can I help you?"

"Detective Eric Sutton."

Wayne shook his hand, firm enough to communicate he didn't enjoy being bullshitted. He shoved his cellphone back into his pocket. No point deactivating anything. A cop will always find you unless you're hiding.

"Do you mind answering a few questions?" Sutton asked.

"Depends on the questions."

"Shawn Curtis?"

"What about him?"

"Have you seen him recently?"

"It depends on what you classify as recently. I just got back from L.A."

"He moved into your condo?"

"He moved in while I was away." Wayne loved to play this game.

Quick, short answers left no doubt for the detective to question his integrity. When Sutton stepped closer, invading his personal space, Wayne didn't budge. Curtis had told him about Sutton and that was all Wayne needed to know.

"Have you spoken to him?" Sutton asked.

"The other day. Are you going to tell me what this is about?"

"Did he mention any trouble?"

"What trouble?"

Sutton eyed him. "You're best friends, and he's living in your condo. I'm sure he told you something."

"The only trouble I know of is that about one million people hate him and that he owes money to a bunch of crooks."

"Glad you mentioned that. Do you know if he has any specific enemies?"

"It depends on what you classify as specific. Why?"

"Because I think his company didn't go down by accident."

This speculation came as no surprise. Wayne had discussed the option with Curtis many times, but he'd vehemently denied the supposition, foremost because he didn't see the point in why high profile customers would want to destroy themselves. Eventually, Wayne flushed the idea too.

Sutton said, "You need to know, Mr. Cantrell, I'm not here to take Curtis in or take him down. I'm trying to get him out of the mess he's in. To do that, I need your help."

"And why do you want to help him?"

"Personal reason."

Wayne deliberated what this personal reason could be. Money? "Last time I spoke to him, he told me my condo was a no-go zone because of a woman killed in B-1. He also told me he wouldn't be here because the cops suspect he has something to do with it. All I know is he's out to prove them wrong. So are you wrong?"

"You can help prove us wrong."

Wayne's annoyance grew like yeast. Did this moron seriously

think he would rat on his friend? "Look. I don't know where he is, so I don't know how I can help."

"I can tell you how you can help. When he contacts you, you make sure I'll be able to meet up with him."

"So you can rock up with a team and arrest him?"

Sutton scratched his head, his puzzlement on his face.

Wayne understood. *Yanks don't know how to speak English, let alone Aussie.* "Rock up means turn up," he said, craning his neck. He would have liked to look down on Sutton.

"Essentially," Sutton said, "I need him to help me find the woman who got him into this mess—" The detective paused so abruptly, Wayne had the impression he'd just said too much. "What I'm discussing with you will never hit the record. To me, he's worth far more out here than behind bars."

"What's he worth to you?"

"Not a cent."

If it wasn't money, what else could it be? "What about the woman? Laura Webb."

"She's the wrong woman to play games with. In fact, she'll play him till nothing's left of him."

"And who is she exactly?"

"I can't give you details in case I'm wrong."

Wayne scoffed about the typical cop-blurb. "Curtis can take care of himself, and he'd kill no one."

"The way things stand, Curtis is involved in the deaths of two people in less than twenty-four hours."

Scare tactic. Wayne didn't buy it, kept his poker face as if dealing with a salesman trying to trade him a VW for a Porsche. Time to get rid of him.

"Since he's not worth a cent to you but a whole lot to me, I might go and see if I can find him. Regardless of that, I want to check if everything is still at its place in my condo. I believe your colleagues entered it without a warrant. Needless to say what it means for the SDPD if I find out that's the case. What about you give me your card, and I'll contact you if I hear from Curtis?"

Chapter Twenty-Six

At one stage during the morning, Curtis shifted from the couch to the bed. It hadn't helped improve his condition. He woke washed out, his shoulder hammering, his head pounding.

Wayne stuck his head through the door as if he'd waited behind it eavesdropping for a noise. "You okay?"

"Where have you been?"

A bundled pair of jeans and cargo pants and several shirts landed next to Curtis.

Wayne said, "I thought I'd get you some shirts instead of tees. Easier to handle while your arm is all screwed up."

"Thanks, buddy." From the staggering selection of three button-up shirts, Curtis chose a black one, but Wayne remained there as if he had something important to say. "What else?"

"I got your laptop."

Which couldn't have been the reason why Wayne still made a face as if the words were about to explode in him. "Spit it out before you choke on it."

"What do you know about Eric Sutton?"

"The detective?"

"That's the one," Wayne said, joining him.

"As far as I know he's handling the case. *My* case if you want to call it that." He propped himself up, swung his legs over the side of the bed, dressed in the shirt and cargo pants his friend had brought from the condo. "Why?"

"He stalked me in the parking lot said something that made me think. He has a personal interest in you. Any idea what that is?"

"I've never met the guy before all this, so how personal can it be?"

"The other thing he said was he doesn't believe your company came down by accident."

"Hmm, I know you said it before, but I still can't see the sense in it."

"He also said he wanted to find you so you can lead him to the woman involved."

"Laura?"

"No, Jennifer Lawrence. Anyhow, I've been checking out Sutton, thought I'd find what he could be after. Does he know about the experiment six years ago and that thing in your arm?"

Curtis shook his head. "As far as I know, it was a top secret experiment, and I haven't told him anything about it."

"I got some details about him. He used to be a detective in New Jersey, transferred on his request to the West Coast after his daughter's death. He started off in L.A. but relocated to San Diego."

"On request?"

"I couldn't find that out."

"Family?"

"He lost his wife. He blamed her employer for her death because of her exposure to hazardous chemicals. Six years ago his daughter died too. She worked for the same company."

"What was her name?"

"Emily."

Curtis studied the printout of the photo Wayne passed to him. She was slightly plump, her hair lamely styled, the old-fashioned blouse resting crookedly on her torso. Even though he liked a natural appearance, some women were too inconspicuous or lacked confidence, though the latter could be boosted.

Her pleasant face promised potential. Too late now. "How did she die?"

"Her remains were never found after an experiment went wrong. The company claimed it was due to the combination of heat and chemicals."

"Come with me." Curtis went to the living room and fired up the laptop. "What company are we talking about?"

"You already know it's NOKS, don't you?"

Curtis smirked.

"Why are you always a step ahead of me?" Wayne said, discouraged.

"Because I don't just have a pretty face."

"You're flattering yourself."

"Who else does?" With the laptop now ready, Curtis typed in the name Samuel Dunbar, pointed the finger at the article which reported his tragic death while working for NOKS, killed in the same fire as Emily

Sutton.

Wayne slouched, his cheeks sagging. "You already knew everything I just told you?"

"I didn't know about Sutton's past. What were you able to find out about Laura?"

"Why do I have the feeling you already know that too?"

Curtis shot him a wide grin. "I didn't come across anything about Laura Webb. But when I stumbled over NOKS, I discovered an article referring to a Laura W. She worked for NOKS. She was involved in the experiment in which Dunbar and Emily died. The same day, Laura mysteriously disappeared. And here is the interesting part. One day after her disappearance, Gordon McNamara disappeared too. Interestingly, I couldn't find any photos of Laura, but I have the feeling Laura W. is Laura Webb, and that would explain Sutton's personal interest. Does this match your result?"

If it were possible, Wayne's chin would have hit the ground. Then he rolled his lips like a cheeky boy up to mischief. "Why don't you use your charm and shag Laura? That would speed up things enormously."

"Very funny. I don't know where she is, anyway."

"She'll find you someday soon. Until then there's somebody else who can help."

"Who?"

"The surgeon who operated on you."

"How's he supposed to help?"

"Maybe he knew the blood he gave you was more than just blood."

True. "Good luck with finding him. As far as I know, he quit and was never seen again after he released me from treatment."

"Looking back now, it was a bit of a strange procedure. I mean, I didn't know where you were for weeks. Maybe there was already something going on then. That's why I thought I'd see if I could find him. He's on his way."

Goosebumps swarmed Curtis. "Phil Merkow is on his way?"

"Dr. Phil Merkow, yes."

"That's impossible."

"Well, I spoke to a Dr. Phil Merkow who knows exactly who you are."

"How did you find him?"

"There must be a reason he shows up in the White Pages. Usually, when you reach voicemail, it says, 'Please leave a message, yadda-yadda-yadda,' but his said, 'If your name is Shawn Dylan Curtis, please leave your number, and I'll call you back. If not, hang up.'"

Curtis had to chew through it all. "Did you just say he mentioned my name?"

"Yeah, mate. Okay, I lied about who I was but we'll meet him at three."

A blast of adrenaline whooshed through Curtis. Wayne could be right. The surgeon well and truly could have known something.

Chapter Twenty-Seven

The phone's beep shook him. It hadn't rung in many weeks, many months. It was just as long since he had spoken to HIM and much longer since he had seen HIM. He only ever spoke to HIM over the phone. And the phone only rang when HE had bad news. That was why he hesitated.

He reflected on the past six years when it all started. When the lucrative idea was proposed so the business would flourish again after the bitter losses—which were peanuts since it was a billion-dollar business anyhow—due to the government cuts. That day HE lost his name and was only called HE or HIM, sometimes HIM HIM to avoid confusion because HE didn't deserve a name. Because HE was a delusional, derogatory, smarmy miscreant with no respect for life in any type or form.

The idea of using humans sounded logical, though he should never have said it out loud that he'd condemned the game HE'd planned. And he should never have embezzled part of the money meant to bolster the shady tests.

One morning he went to work and HE said they had an important meeting and the private jet was ready. His worries being late for dinner was set at naught when reassured by HIM he'd be back long before then. He never enjoyed another of his wife's delicious meatloaves, instead survived on shabby canteen food, which later changed to nothing but boxes of microwavable crap with the occasional change to… He left this thought for later.

He never saw HIM again. Only heard from HIM over the phone and the promise to hang in there a few days longer before things returned to normal.

This was six years ago, give or take. Whenever he asked why they were still here, he got excuses in return. Sometimes mice and rabbits were delivered together with gruesome instructions for tests that needed to be carried out.

Once, there was a monkey. The animal didn't last long. It snapped itself with wires cutting its own head off. The delivery of animals stopped after a while because instead of using them for tests, they were eaten, and so were the people who died within these walls. How else were they supposed to survive on a minimal budget dramatically shortened over the years?

One day, it all changed. When they left the fumigation cell, they found stacks of computers waiting for them in the lab. The immediate realization that there had to be a way out of this filthy shithole since someone had a way in to deliver equipment caused turmoil. The obsession to find freedom created the near impossible challenge to keep everyone at bay and accept it wouldn't get any better than simply being alive. Thankfully, the idea of finding freedom died with another two people killed in the uproar, which meant more food.

A few years back, one man managed to escape. He'd realized too late that this man was missing while everyone hunkered in the fumigation cell, its door sealed for one hour. The man, Cody, must have hidden in the lab and when somebody entered, Cody slipped through. He didn't get far, though.

His signal died on the monitor. TOX-1 had taken care of him like he had of others. People who'd worked for HIM. People who'd been sworn to silence but were silenced anyway. TOX-1 had no feelings or remorse.

Unquestionably furious about the loss of TOX-1, HE was definitely blowing a gasket over the latest developments.

The buzzing phone drew him back to the present. He couldn't refrain from answering the summons. He had no excuse like getting a coffee or not hearing the call, though he kept the phone hidden in the desk drawer. No one was aware it existed. It took only incoming calls from only one person, which meant it couldn't have helped anyone anyhow.

The buzzing continued. He could say he was using the toilet but what impression would that leave? The phone only rang once in a blue moon but right that moment he was following nature's call? Not that reputation mattered, but who'd throw fuel into a fire when it delayed freedom… or death?

He could let it ring a few more times, let HIM sweat. But then the caller would hang up. That couldn't happen.

He opened the drawer, lifted the phone from its cradle and pressed the button. "Yes?"

"What the fuck took you so long?"

"We're battling technical issues."

"Technical issues my ass. Explain to me why I have the reading of two men walking the streets?"

So HE knew. "We had a complete blackout. Two men got out."

"Got out." A derisive laugh came through the line. "Who?"

It confused him because if HE was aware of the two men being out, HE should know who they were. "Aren't you getting the reading?"

"I do get the reading, but I want you to confirm the names."

"Clifton Wright and Martin Green."

The silence streamed a sizzle through the line.

To cut the silence, he said, "I could do with some medical supplies."

"Why's that?"

"Because I've been shot."

"By Green?"

"Yes. And he shot Sanders. He's dead."

More silence.

He added, "I put him in the cool room for now."

"I'll send you medical supplies once we've done the quarantine procedure."

"But... we only recently had—"

"You've been shot. You might get an infection. We can't take the chance of you spreading bacteria and god knows what. And I need you alive."

Since when do you care if I'm alive, or anyone else in this shithole? Something fishy is going on.

"Okay. When do you want to proceed?"

"Right now."

Right now? This was odd. HE always gave at least a twenty-four-hour notice. "It'll take some time to round them all up. Some of them have their rest."

"One hour enough?"

"Two would be better."

"Ninety minutes, no longer. I'll call you back with instructions."

"Okay." He put the phone back on the cradle, closed the drawer and sat there, contemplating if he should round them all up.

Circumstances given it could go either way—death or formal procedure. Unless he took the same road as Green and Clifton. Out. He'd actually been out in the early hours today, drugged up Clifton and Green enough so they wouldn't remember a thing. HE could follow the signal, not only of Green and Clifton, also of the car he'd used—the car he should have gotten rid of years ago but kept for, well, situations like

Green and Clifton. But there was no other way.

He'd always known how to get out but decided against it because he had nothing out there besides a nagging wife and two daughters. He'd failed them so many times he was convinced they were happy he was gone. Here, he had a name, had a reputation, was the boss, ran the show. Out there he was no one, had nothing. Struggle at best. Plus, *out* meant death anyway, as Green and Clifton would soon learn. Not having TOX-1 to do the jobs didn't mean that HE didn't have other ways to get rid of unwanted pests even if HE had to get his own hands dirty.

So he returned after he 'dropped off' Green and Clifton. Maybe the two men could complete their tasks before HE got to them.

His eyes on the switchboard, he weighed up once more which way to go. Everyone would know what to do if he pressed the orange button. Proceed to the decontamination cell, endure the hour of fumigation, shower with the chemicals provided, take up normal procedure.

Day in, day out, with no way out, no way to change things. He could change things, add a little drama to it since everything was already so ridiculously lost. Even if it was the last thing he'd do—which he knew it was.

He pulled the keyboard closer and started typing, a tear running down his cheek when he wrote his wife's name and his two lovely daughters. And the name of the one man who held it all in his hands.

Chapter Twenty-Eight

The lively airport streamed out energy waking in Curtis the memory of excitement as much as the fear of coming down quicker than anticipated. Flying. It was less than a week since a plane had disappeared, reason unknown, exact location unknown, no wreckage to be found. Undoubtedly, events like this clung to the minds of some travelers about to board a plane.

People stretched their necks at the departure board. Some gathered in a crowd, some in tears, kissing or hugging a loved one they wouldn't see for a while. Some thrilled to go on a trip they'd worked their butt off for.

A group of men, five in all, wearing suits and carrying briefcases, hustled past him and Wayne. None showed emotion, and none of them was the doctor.

Curtis turned his head and caught his friend in the act of eying up two gorgeous stewardesses. "Explain to me why we're in departures and not arrivals," he asked, nearly missing Wayne's stealthy hand dive into the pocket of his loose-fitting cargo pants and, some delayed seconds later, emerge holding his cellphone as if it had been the sole purpose of poking his hand in there.

"Did you just pinch your dick?" Curtis said, not knowing if he should be disgusted or ashamed.

Wayne wiggled as if he had to shake things back into place. "Man, if I don't get laid soon, I'll rape a pillow."

Curtis snorted. "Been that long?"

"Way too long."

"Katherine not good enough?"

"Don't even go there."

A gaunt man caught Curtis's attention. He'd styled his mousy hair to a tousled mess and left it longer than it suited his age, which Curtis guessed was early fifty. He wore jeans and a black leather jacket over a black T-shirt. The whole outfit resembled a stay-at-home-dad-pretend-biker.

Curtis kept an eye on him mainly because he seemed nervous and hid behind sunglasses while pacing next to the magazine store, his head held high as though he was scanning the crowd. It was the aquiline nose and thin lips Curtis remembered as the last features before he had to undergo a long and complicated operation to get the poles out of his body. And it was the first face smiling at him when he came to. 'I'm glad to see you back,' the doctor, Phil Merkow, had said.

Curtis nudged Wayne and whispered, "Two o'clock. The man with the sunglasses."

He craned his neck toward the direction. "Hmm, a bit skinny for a doctor. And for somebody who doesn't want to raise suspicion, he's doing a damn good job wearing sunnies in an airport lobby."

Curtis lowered his cap and shoved his sunglasses up the bridge of his nose. Wayne clapped him on the shoulder. "You're a different case. You're a wanted man. Want to talk to him alone?"

"You can get me out if shit hits the fan." Curtis trudged ahead, Wayne behind him.

A few feet in, Merkow twisted his head left, right, behind before turning toward Curtis.

His face starting to ease, he stretched out his hand. "I'm glad to see you, Mr. Curtis."

Curtis shook his hand and introduced Wayne.

Once more Merkow's head twisted left, right, behind. "I'm not sure if it's a good idea to meet here, but then the more people the better."

"We can go somewhere else," Wayne said.

"Not enough time. I'm on the next plane out."

"Busy surgery schedule?" Curtis said.

"Busy hiding schedule," Merkow replied.

They chose a coffee bar hectic enough for them to remain unnoticed and sat at a small square table in the corner. Merkow faced the wall, while Curtis and Wayne kept an eye on the people hustling past. They ordered coffees. Curtis a Cappuccino, Wayne the same. Merkow a black.

I hope that won't give you a heart attack, Curtis thought, as the doctor resembled a Coffee Shakerato, still covering his eyes with sunglasses as if fearing the wall would smile back. Curtis freed his face from his sunglasses but hadn't stripped the baseball cap from his head.

He and the others hardly exchanged words until the coffees were served, and Merkow managed to sprinkle the saucer with sugar. With his tongue, he wet his finger, played it over the saucer's rim, then sucked his finger like a child. It must have given him an energy boost as he didn't wind down after that.

"I've waited a long time for this moment. All the years I wanted to contact you, tell you what was done to you. At first I couldn't, and when I could, I thought you wouldn't believe me anyway. I knew if you figured out something was wrong you'd come looking for me. To be honest, I feared this day. It's already a miracle you didn't die the day of the operation, but reflecting back, maybe I should have let you die."

Curtis swallowed. "So why did you let me live?"

Merkow leaned in closer. "I need you to know I have less than an hour to tell you as much as I can so you don't end up dead. The more questions you have, the less time I have to talk. What I need to know first is how much you know."

Curtis kept his report brief, told him about Laura and the test she'd mentioned.

Merkow sipped his coffee before he spoke again. "Are you talking about Laura Webb?"

After exchanging a quick look with Wayne, Curtis confirmed with a nod.

Merkow said, "The woman you call Laura Webb doesn't know everything either, but I'll get to that later. I know this much—you are in grave danger. And I didn't save your life six years ago to watch you get killed now." Merkow wiped his face with a napkin, crunched it to a ball and kept it in his fist. "Before I explain how you fit in, Mr. Curtis, I need to clarify a few things so you understand the basics. I assume you've heard of NOKS and Sebastian Knox?"

Curtis nodded again, and from corner of his eye observed Wayne going for his shirt pocket, tugging out a notepad and pen, jotting down notes. They'd agreed on an old-fashioned style. No cellphones.

Merkow continued, "You see, there are many underground experiments, especially since the ban on animal testing, but Knox went further. Why waste time and money in finding avenues other than animals? Why not go straight to the intended recipients: humans? And here's the catch.

"As you may know, the FDA used to approve meds before they could be sold. The decision to ban animal testing came with consequences not only for the FDA, also for the entire pharmaceutical empire. Companies had millions cut from their budgets because no more feeding animals, breeding them, or testing meant money saved. The government went beyond that.

"The FDA was renamed to FQA, Food Quality Administration, and a new company was created: PRDA, Pharmaceutical Research and

Development Administration. You might want to write this down, Mr. Cantrell."

Merkow took an audible breath. "The people behind the PRDA remained mostly the same crew who ran the FDA, and they had to come up with an idea to cover the losses the fund-cut caused. To speed things up, NOKS and the PRDA struck a deal. Whenever the PRDA came across a potentially successful drug, they claimed it a failure and passed it on to NOKS. NOKS then altered the drug, returned the new version back to the PRDA, and they okayed it. The PRDA and NOKS shared the profits from selling those drugs. This was step one.

"Step two. After passing the drug, NOKS didn't sell the drug approved by the PRDA. Without the knowledge of the PRDA, NOKS produced placebos, an innocent pill or liquid containing nothing but, for example, lemon, and sold it as the drug passed by the PRDA. This could have been painkillers regularly sold over the counter. It didn't harm anyone.

"To ensure the scam remained undiscovered, they included placebos with regular drugs under recognized labels. So let's say you bought a packet of twenty painkillers, at least five of them were fake. It was cheap and profitable. After a while, the drug under whatever name got replaced by the actual drug and the fake one taken off the market and sent to third-world countries."

"I thought it was regulated so all this couldn't happen any longer!" Wayne exclaimed.

"It always depends on who sits at the other end," Merkow said, his voice convincing enough to keep Wayne from interrupting. "As you can imagine, it's not something everybody within these companies knew, only the, the…"

"Big bosses," Curtis provided.

"Yes, the big bosses. Whenever somebody got too close to the truth, that person went missing or was found dead. Whenever somebody got too loud, that person went missing or was found dead. Whoever found a cure for specific diseases went missing or was found dead.

"Natural sources to heal disease were and still are destroyed. The government doesn't want people to heal themselves with alternative medicine, because there's no money in it. But the main thing is, why do people actually get sick, and why was there such an enormous hike in cancer cases in the past two decades?

"The government is covering their actual game, blaming cigarettes as the biggest causes of cancer. It's an easy way to whack a good tax on tobacco so the people can pay their own medical bills because the tobacco industry can't cover the costs associated with smoking any longer. You get the drift. We all believe if we want to stay healthy, we'd be better off growing everything ourselves, but I'm not going into detail here. If we start thinking too much about what we're eating, we'll starve to death. Even the rain coming down isn't much healthier and neither is the air we're breathing. However, no one should ever hear the government is spraying the atmosphere with toxins to use every single living creature as guinea pigs."

"Why would they do that?" Wayne asked.

"To keep the money coming," Curtis said and wished Laura was sitting there as his theory was confirmed. "What I don't quite understand is, it's nothing new. These conspiracies are spread all over the internet, media, blogs."

Merkow said, "They are the little fish. The ones who jumped on the boat to keep the conspiracy alive. Like the ones about the man on the moon or 9/11. There'll always be people saying, 'Hang on, wasn't there something wrong?' For as long as there's no proof, it's hot air. But the ones with solid proof—they are the ones silenced."

He slurped more coffee. "You see, the government needs the sick people. Sickness means more funds for the pharma industry. To cover the costs, the government increases taxes. At the same time they… let's say, create more diseases. People get sick, let's find a cure, and so on.

"But it bit the government in the butt. It ended up costing more because they didn't expect such a spike in cancer cases, Alzheimer, and many other crippling diseases. At the same time it's a balancing act; how much is made available to heal people? In other words, everything spiraled out of control.

"To cut the story short, when the government pushed for answers on how to deal with the problem, NOKS and the PRDA worked together to develop a vaccine to primarily kill cancer once and for all. This should have put the government back into the good books since the people are lacking trust, already disgruntled about the past few presidents failing them.

"But Sebastian Knox isn't a sharing guy, and as far as I know, there was a dispute between Knox and the former FDA commissioner, which I believe was over NOKS's scandalous reputation for altering drugs behind the PRDA's back."

Curtis lifted his hand. "I might be slow in understanding the whole game, but how do I fit in?" In return, he received a how-dare-you-interrupt-me glower, accompanied by Merkow's disdainful sigh.

"You'll understand how it connects once I'm finished." He played his finger over the saucer once more and sucked the sugar from his fingertips. "Days before you had your accident six years ago, I was at a conference and was pulled aside by Sebastian Knox. Him coming to me with a spurious request; you don't think twice. He told me he was trying to find participants for a test involving people at risk of hypovolemic shock. The substance…"

"What's hypo… whatever you just said?" Wayne asked.

"It's a life-threatening condition when the body loses more than twenty percent of its blood. The substance Knox wanted me to use was supposed to lower the risk of cardiac arrest and organ failure—common causes of death in relation to blood loss. Since the world in general never has enough blood, the substance was also supposed to increase the ability of the body to produce more blood when needed… In layman's term, let's call the substance a vitamin boost because as it later turned out it was a swindle. That's where you come in, Mr. Curtis."

After a few long seconds, he continued, "I don't know how many specialists were involved, but I signed the confidentiality agreement simply because I believed the whole experiment could benefit not only the patients, but also doctors.

"When you were admitted to the hospital with two steel poles sticking out of you, I contacted Knox and told him I had the perfect patient. You were fit, healthy, and you needed several pints of blood and were at a high risk of organ failure. He then encouraged me to use the drug on you, but my initial euphoria about the experiment had diminished, and I had pangs of conscience. Something in the back of my head told me it was a scam, but Knox made sure I would proceed, promised me what I wanted to hear—the fame to follow. Yes, I was an asshole and naïve, and I had no time for second thoughts because you were about to die on me.

"The following day, after I used the… let's say 'altered' blood on you, I was attacked on the way home, hauled into a black car. In there was Knox and another guy. Knox told me I needed to understand that participating in this top-secret experiment came with a price, and he made pretty clear that I had no choice other than to continue what he called Operation Rabbit. Most people involved called it O.R."

"You never considered the authorities?" Curtis asked.

"And tell them what? That you were injected with a vitamin boost?"

"When did you know for sure it wasn't vitamins?"

"The moment I was hauled into the car. I don't know why Knox trusted me to return to my practice. Maybe because I had a reputable name. I continued my normal business and behind closed doors, I worked for him, mainly because I was scared, but I also wanted to find out what he was up to and what O.R. was about. I discovered the true reason for the tests and how people were involuntarily used as guinea pigs in cancer tests. I was disgusted but too deeply involved and knew I'd end up dead if I spoke up."

Merkow snatched a breath. "The whole excitement about the cancer vaccine was short-lived because the participants dropped like flies. Except you. Already in the early stages, your blood readings showed signs the vaccine would work, and since I had control of your readings, I faked your death."

Curtis lifted his finger as though he was sitting at school asking the teacher for permission to speak. "How did you fake my death?"

"A falsified death certificate was enough to convince Knox you'd died of complications in relation to your injuries and not the vaccine's side effects. In my favor was our agreement to eliminate all evidence that the test was ever carried out. And I made damn sure I did."

"How exactly did you do that?" Merkow conveyed he was asking too many questions. Curtis changed tack. "Why did you fake my death?"

"I knew your life would be over if Knox ever discovered the potential of your blood and DNA. So, I had you transferred to a different place. I'm sure you remember."

Curtis did. It was the second time he'd come to. Instead of the ICU, he woke in an unfamiliar room in a sanatorium surrounded by beautiful green meadows, his only attendants two nurses and Merkow. Curtis had argued the move but couldn't fight it either. No one was allowed to visit him. With no phones or computers accessible to him, he couldn't contact anyone.

Over one month later, Merkow had driven him home, though he'd taken so many detours Curtis could never find the sanatorium again. Also fruitless were his efforts to find Merkow at the hospital. According to the staff, Dr. Phil Merkow had resigned and was never seen again.

"I've always wondered about your special treatment, the isolation, and your disappearance," Curtis said.

"It was the only way. I left the city, changed my name, which I, for my own protection, keep undisclosed. But I've always made sure a phone number remained in the directory, which I changed regularly. I knew one day you'd contact me." Merkow paused a beat. "How did they find you?"

"I carried out a DNA test."

"And your blood reading triggered an alarm in the system only linked to Knox."

"Only Knox?" Curtis asked.

"I'm not sure, but I'd say so. My biggest mistake was not telling you about the tests, the potential your blood has, but I don't think any of us would be sitting here right now if I said something."

Curtis silently agreed to that. "Am I the only one?"

"As far as I know you're the only one surviving the tests."

Curtis welcomed the seconds of silence to let the new information sink in. So far it all made sense, but plenty of questions remained. "What's your theory on why Knox wants me dead?"

Merkow eyed his empty coffee mug.

Wayne stood, glancing at Curtis. "You want another one too?"

Curtis shook his head. He wanted Merkow's answer.

Merkow continued once Wayne had trotted off. "One person surviving the test isn't enough to call the experiment a success. The tests failed. End of story. However, if the government hears about you, hears there's actually one participant who has fought the cancer cells introduced into his body, Knox or any other company doing cancer research will be out of luck receiving the big bonus for creating a vaccine. And Knox can't afford that nor can anyone else."

"Five billion," Curtis mumbled.

"Spread over three years."

Curtis sat back in the chair, realizing it wasn't him at all they were after. Not as a person, or his blood or DNA. It was driven by money.

Before he could single out a question of the hundreds swarming his head, Merkow continued, "Unfortunately, there's another problem for you. If you were found by any of these companies, your life is over. If you're not dead, you'll become a guinea pig. You need to weigh your moves very carefully. And I know what I'd do."

"What's that?"

"Disappear."

"I only just left New York."

"You haven't established a new life yet and won't be able to. There's one other thing. It doesn't mean because you've survived the past six years that it's not all coming down on you. There's no long-term study on the vaccine. It only takes one DNA to not repair itself and you're dead before you know what struck you."

Curtis rubbed his scalp, but it didn't release the tension. He flinched when someone nudged him on his shoulder.

"You all right?" It was Wayne.

"Yeah."

Wayne sat down, slid the coffee across the table to Merkow. "How does Laura Webb fit into all of this?" he asked.

"If Laura is who I think she is, then her name isn't Laura Webb.

Well, in some way it is. To fast-track finding qualified people to work for O.R., they were chosen, like I was. No questions asked. They promised others good money and all that bull. There were some lonely wolves who didn't need convincing. Others had no choice, like Emily Sutton."

Curtis lifted a brow. "Detective Eric Sutton's daughter?"

Merkow nodded.

"Were you there when she died?"

Merkow skipped answering this question and said, "Gordon McNamara, Emily Sutton, and Laura Webb were a talented team. But Laura was always in Emily's shadow and the once great team with Emily, Laura, and Gordon started to falter because Laura's interests were different from Emily's. Laura wanted to be the famous scientist, while Emily and Gordon wanted to help prevent and cure diseases. Where do you go when you want to reach the top? You go to the top. Laura started playing Knox and plotted against Emily and got rid of her."

"The explosion," Curtis said.

"The explosion that never took place. Emily was snatched off the street, put under drugs and brainwashed, made to believe she was sitting on a bus driving to a facility called Operation Rabbit."

Curtis lifted his finger to stop the doctor. "Did you just say the explosion never took place?" The interruption garnered him a didn't-you-know-that glower.

"To keep the families and friends from looking for the disappeared, they received statements that their husband, wife, daughter, son, whoever, were victims of a test gone wrong."

"Some went missing, some supposedly committed suicide," Curtis said.

"I see you've done some research."

"I stumbled over some names," Curtis said, but something, he couldn't explain what, held him back from mentioning Sophia, Olivia, Dunbar, and Fisher. "Does Operation Rabbit still exist?"

"As far as I know everything was destroyed. Knowing Knox, I doubt anyone involved is still alive, besides Laura by the sounds of it."

"Where is this facility?" Curtis asked.

"I don't know."

"What do you mean you don't know? Weren't you in contact with the people from O.R.?"

"I was never in the facility. Most facts I figured out after I turned my back on everything. You need to understand the original plan was to transfer, sorry to use this word, the guinea pigs used for the tests to the O.R. lab. But they all died, except you. And nobody knew that, besides me."

Curtis exhaled heavily, the gravity of the situation slowly sinking in and with it, the pressure in his head intensified. Nausea bubbled in his stomach.

Merkow said, "You can't trust anyone who knows about O.R. The person in front of you may not be the one you think it is. However, I'm going to take a big jump here because we're running out of time and my story is primarily based on an assumption.

"Emily was a much bigger asset than Laura. Gordon knew that. But Knox was more interested in Laura's skills. Primarily, in making him happy. You get the drift. As you already know, the explosion Emily supposedly died in was nothing but a farce. But the same day the explosion supposedly happened, Laura disappeared and the next day, Gordon. My assumption is Gordon was sick of Laura's game, so he eliminated her and gave Emily her identity."

Curtis let that sink in for a while. "Can't be. She doesn't look like Emily."

"My mistake. The woman you're looking at is Laura, but the brain is Emily's. This gave Gordon the ultimate advantage. He had a woman able to play both sides."

Saliva crawled up in Curtis. *Did I get kissed by an alien?* "I either need fresh air or a drink."

Wayne shambled to the bar and shortly after balanced three glasses in his hands. The three men swapped coffee for whiskey. Curtis would have liked downing it in a single gulp and was glad Wayne took over to lead the conversation.

"If I understand it correctly, Gordon transferred Laura's face onto Emily, and they both got away?"

"No, he swapped brains. As I said, it's an assumption but the only explanation I have. If it was Laura, Mr. Curtis wouldn't be sitting here. He'd be in Sebastian Knox's hands. The differences between Laura and Emily went as far as to live and let die. Laura wanted to get rid of Emily, so she made sure she ended up in O.R. Laura didn't care what it took to achieve fame."

"You're saying Gordon got Emily out of O.R. and swapped her brain with Laura's," Curtis said.

After a why-is-that-so-hard-to-grasp roll of his eyes, Merkow nodded.

"Just like that?" Wayne said. "Just like changing a hard drive?"

Merkow rolled his eyes once more, obviously unwilling to spill the beans.

"So, where is the real Laura?" Wayne asked.

"Dead, I assume."

"Let's say you're right, then why hasn't Emily revealed herself to her father?" Wayne was on fire.

"What's she supposed to tell him? Oh, hi Dad. Thanks for the funeral and sorry for all the grief you've had over the years. And by the way, I changed my appearance."

Acid accumulating, Curtis's stomach churned harder. "I have to excuse myself."

He had no time to hear the answer when Wayne asked Merkow about his informant. Bumped a few times as he weaved through the crowd, Curtis pushed the door to the men's room open and stumbled to the nearest stall. The reek hitting him did the rest to send his stomach into turmoil. Whiskey, coffee, scrambled eggs, and burned toast Wayne served him earlier—it all ended in the bowl. His brain was as messy as what was in front of him.

He wiped his face with yards of toilet paper, again and again and flushed it all down. He needed answers like, how to get rid of that thing in his arm? Which he had no chance to mention. And the dead woman from B-1.

He got up, swayed, sat back down.

"Why me?" he mumbled. The bang of a slammed door got his attention.

"Curtis?" It was Wayne.

"Yeah?"

"He's left."

Curtis shot up, now as bright as day and yanked the door opened. "What do you mean he's left?"

"He said he had to catch his flight. He ran out. I couldn't hold him back."

"Fuck, no! Where to?"

"The last announcement I heard was the final call for a flight to Dallas."

"Let's go." Curtis ran ahead, checked in his jog long enough to read the board and discovered the flight to Dallas was leaving at Gate 7.

Hope vanished when he drew in on the gate. From the distance, he could see none of the few faces in the small remaining line up of people at check in was Merkow. Curtis darted straight to the counter, the lady behind it welcoming him with a disapproving glare.

"Sir, please line up."

"There's a man who can save my life."

"Sir, please. If you don't line up and if you don't calm down, I must call security."

"I have to get in there!" he shouted, but restraining hands on his arms forced him back from the counter.

Wayne said, "Calm down, mate. She won't let you in. To be honest, I doubt he's on this plane. It was nothing but a distraction so he could get away."

Was there an earthquake or why did the ground suddenly sway? Curtis clutched onto Wayne as his legs turned to water. "I don't feel too well."

Chapter Twenty-Nine

"Why didn't we grab him then?" Clifton groaned, now sitting in a black Range Rover Green had stolen. The owner had left the vehicle unlocked in the gas station when he went to pay for his fuel. So many people do that.

Green had parked the car down the street from where they'd later watched two men enter an apartment building, one supported by the other. When a woman entered the building, Green and Clifton decided she wasn't of interest. More people of no interest went in and out.

After an hour or so, the man who'd supported the other man earlier left the building, returning forty minutes later while the sun was still warming the air. Two more hours passed and night had set in. The streets were deserted.

Clifton groaned once more. "We should have grabbed him when we had the chance."

"He's not alone," Green said.

"He just was."

"I'm waiting for somebody to turn up. We need her since she's been able to hide her location for six years. We better have the same advantage before we sell him. Otherwise, Powell will make sure we're dead before we even start. For now, we wait."

"For how long?"

Green pointed at the building's door. A woman walked out. Another woman slipped through before the door shut tight. "Not much longer."

Chapter Thirty

Curtis flung the blanket back. Not good either. He dragged it up over his body again. His head hammered, his shoulder throbbed.

"How are you feeling?"

He opened his eyes to a slit. Wayne's head hung over his, a grin on his face. Curtis vaguely remembered that Wayne had helped him to the car and somehow managed to lug him to the apartment.

"I owe you, man. I've made a complete idiot out of myself," Curtis said.

"Oh, I think you had everyone's empathy when your legs buckled."

"I hope you have a truckload of painkillers."

"Katherine already loaded you up with a truckload. I can't give you any more for at least four hours. You'll have to ride it out."

His words reminded Curtis of his father's, but he wasn't sure if he wanted to ride this one out. "I can't remember Katherine being here. How long was I out?"

"It's ten at night. Katherine isn't too happy with the healing process, and your concussion isn't helping. You should be in a hospital, get proper treatment. I told her it was the last place you could go. She wanted to put you on a drip. I told her you'd just rip it out anyhow."

"You know me well."

"Yeah, well, gotta say we took advantage of you being out like a light, and she hooked you up to an I.V. You didn't know that, did you?" Wayne flashed his teeth but dropped his grin. "No kidding, mate. She said it's very important for you to rest. And no bloody alcohol. I know you're stressing out, I would be too, and I'd drink a whole bloody bottle of Bundy Rum to wash out my brain, but in your case, it'll bloody kill you."

Curtis said nothing though felt, oddly enough, flattered by his friend's concern.

"Please don't screw this up for me and do as you're told. Last thing I need is to upset Katherine because I want to shag her again one day," Wayne added.

Curtis laughed out loud, tried to prop up but slumped back down. "I have to get out of here."

"Sorry, mate. I'm the boss here now. Rest, and I'll get you some chicken soup."

"What happened to the steak?"

"Postponed." Wayne turned to leave, 'stopped, turned back, wearing a facetious grin. "You got undies on?"

Curtis lifted the blanket and checked. "Looks like it."

Wayne walked to the dresser, revealed a blue T-shirt and flung it onto the bed. "Good idea to dress appropriately."

"Appropriately for what?"

"You have a visitor."

"Who?"

"Run your fingers through your hair. Sort it out."

"Who?"

"Me."

Curtis's breath hitched. The woman standing in the door had a resemblance to someone he wanted to know more about, but she'd provoked him in so many ways he wasn't sure if he'd rather kill her. Her hair was now darker, shorter. It suited her.

He struggled up in bed, leaned against the back wall, reached for the T-shirt but putting it on was an impossible mission.

"Do you want help?" she asked.

He hurled it to the side, pulled up the blanket and ran an eye over her. Obviously, she'd managed to get a bracelet since she wore 'one around her wrist. "How did you find me?"

"I think she followed me back from the condo where I've got a few things while you were out," Wayne threw in from behind her.

Her head turned back to him.

"I'll get some soup," he said and left.

She faced Curtis again. He noticed her eyes had lost the shine which, not so long ago, warmed his heart.

"I couldn't tell you the truth," she said.

For however long she'd been here, she must have had a conversation with Wayne, and the idiot probably presented everything on a plate about the meeting with Merkow.

"I'm used to your lying to me, but lying to your father is atrocious," Curtis said, unable to hide his mockery.

"He would never understand."

"So you'd rather be killed than tell him who you are?"

She blinked and tightened her lips as though fighting back tears. "It's easier for him to remember his daughter as the woman he knew than looking at a face of a woman he never liked."

Merkow's assumption seemed correct. Laura was Emily or the other way around.

Nevertheless, Curtis was too pissed off about her lies to care about her tears. "How did it all come about with you and Laura? I mean, the actual Laura. Where is she? Who are you, really?"

Her chest deflated. "Laura and I were friends at school. Dad didn't like her, said she was too sure of herself and only out for her own benefits, used me because I made sure she would pass exams. Maybe it was true, but I looked up to her. She was what I wasn't—pretty. Having her as a friend was a privilege.

"When we both started working for NOKS, she found other ways to succeed. Nice body and a pretty face can achieve a lot." She hesitated, blushing as if the comment had embarrassed her since she now had the pretty face and good body. "I heard rumors about Operation Rabbit, a facility planned to run tests I couldn't agree with. Too late I learned to never get loud about what you do support and what you don't. I was taken off the street and woke up somewhere in a laboratory. No sign of Laura, no sign of Gordon. It was like a prison. No communication with the outside world. Nothing. We all had the device implanted so we couldn't go anywhere without them knowing where we were. A precaution in case we found a way out. One day a guy tried to escape through the hatch. He got roasted the moment he touched it. The reek from burnt meat hung in the room for days." She lowered her head, hiding her emotions. It didn't help.

Curtis saw a tear or two falling. "How long were you there?"

"A few months."

"How did you get out?"

She composed herself and lifted her head again, though she avoided eye contact. "They ordered us into a lab to undergo a procedure designed to eliminate bacteria and viruses infesting the facility. My next solid memory is a house. I couldn't leave. The doors and windows were bolted shut." She sighed. "When I checked the mirror, my reflection was Laura."

Curtis straightened up in bed. "You didn't know about the brain transfer?"

She shook her head, her eyes watering. "The only other person in the house was Gordon. He helped me get used to the changes, refusing to give me answers to all the questions I had. At some point I gave up asking. One day he said it was time to start a new life. The next place I remember was the beach where I took you to a few days ago."

This changed the perspective. She wasn't an alien. Instead, she was guinea pig like he. But it opened a zillion questions in Curtis. "How long ago was that?"

"Roughly six years ago. The first time I was at that beach was close to one year later."

"Six years ago you were taken in Trenton. Months later you ended up on the other side of the country. Even worse, you were someone else. You agree it sounds a little…" She could put the rest together. "You never asked Gordon for details?"

"Gordon's lips remained sealed, no matter what I asked. The loft was at first my home, and Gordon continued experimenting with whatever it was he did. I lost interest in science as though I had fallen through a crack. I had to find out who I was, what life was about, so I started working at different jobs, trying to make ends meet."

"Gordon was your friend, right?"

Her nod made no sense to him. After everything Gordon had done to her, how could she call him a friend? Maybe the brain transplant fried a few brain cells. "What did he say was the reason for the change of your… I don't know what to call it."

"He said it was the only way for me to have a life."

Very vague, but he left it at that. "What happened to Laura?"

She inched behind a chair.

He had enough. "Tell me!"

"It was out of my control."

Her tears and his senses told him the truth would be more than disturbing. He lowered his voice. "If we can't trust each other, then how are we going to get out of all this?" No reaction from her. "You need to tell me!"

With her palms, she wiped the tears from her face. "I don't know if it's true or if Gordon wanted to shut me up, but he told me he dumped her body in a drum of lye."

Why the hell did I have to ask? Curtis shook his head in disbelief, his hands forming tight fists, cramping up. If he'd known all this the day he met Gordon, he would have… He didn't know what he would have done, but he wished he had known what Gordon was capable of.

Laura sobbed out, "I couldn't tell you. All I wanted was to make sure you could help save people's lives."

"This has gone way beyond helping people. You ever thought about how to get out of all of this?"

She must have realized for the first time trouble brewed, even for her. Her lips quivered as she said, "This isn't about me."

"Isn't it? How can this not be about you? I wouldn't be in this situation if it wasn't for you in the first place."

She didn't react. Didn't say a word.

He had to gather his thoughts anyhow, which wasn't easy since his head started spinning. Information overload and shocking news: a poison mix for his concussion. But there were still too many loose ends. "Where are the people from O.R. now?"

"Gordon told me he lost contact and presumed them dead."

Or Gordon told her he'd lost contact so she wouldn't go looking for the people trapped in O.R. Somehow his actions became shadier, and Laura had just lost another point for cruelty. Leaving people behind without caring for their fate. But her stupidity angered Curtis more.

He wiggled himself straighter in the bed, would have liked to get up but knew his legs would resemble jelly. "How could Gordon know about me if he hadn't had contact with either O.R. or Knox?"

Her face whitened, her expression remaining blank. How could she be so naïve? "You never asked him, did you?"

"He told me the less I knew the better."

"So if he'd told you to jump off a bridge, you would have jumped?"

"You have no idea what I've been through."

Curtis couldn't read her, couldn't tell if she remained persistent because she was telling him the truth or if it was her way to hide it. "When did you find out about me?"

"About two weeks ago. He asked for my help because you'd been discovered."

It still didn't answer where Gordon had got the information from, but Curtis concluded he must have taken the truth with him. "Who are Olivia Fitzgerald, Sophia Langdon, Christian Fisher, and Samuel Dunbar?"

His abrupt question sparked a reaction. Her eyes darkened. "How do you know about them?"

"It happens their names come up as an identity for the woman in B-1 and the black guy I took to the hospital, who is dead, killed by the poison in his tube."

"They are people from O.R."

"Were," he corrected. "They're dead. Or missing."

Her eyes widened. Once more Curtis couldn't read her expression. Genuine surprise or she had no idea what he was talking about.

"They were alive when I was taken from O.R.," she said, inching back.

"So there's a chance they're still alive."

"I don't know."

Challenged by her reluctance to share her secrets, Curtis tried a different approach. "Is Knox behind it all or somebody else within NOKS?"

"I'm honestly not sure."

"What about the woman in B-1?"

Laura studied the floor. "I don't know who she was, but her true identity will never be found."

He hurled the blanket back, swung his legs to the side, challenged them to keep him straight as he stood, his care-factor as low as zero that he only wore boxers. "Why?"

She hung her head as she said, "Because whoever has an implanted device and dies disappears not only in real life... also in the system."

"What system?"

"To make sure there's never a link found to O.R., a virus gets planted into the government's system."

"A virus?"

"Computer virus. Not a human virus. If the guy you took to the hospital was working for NOKS or O.R., or for whatever reason had a device, then his files were corrupted the moment his blood readings hit the system."

"Can you for once be black and white and not talk in riddles?"

"Let's assume you die tomorrow; the device in your arm will be activated. It'll change your blood readings, including hair, teeth, DNA, everything. Even though we know you as Shawn Dylan Curtis, the system will spit out a different name. Any name. Your identity will vanish as if you never existed. Or to be clearer, every search will produce a different name, just not Shawn Dylan Curtis because the name Shawn Dylan Curtis doesn't exist. At least not as you. There might be another Shawn Dylan Curtis out there like there is an abundance of John Smiths. None of them will be you because the device evaporates and the causes for the discrepancy will never the found."

He studied the wall. It helped to unclog his fogged head and focus as otherwise he would wring her neck. Her confession explained why no identification was found on the dead woman in B-1 and Rasp Tap, but something didn't add up.

"Can't be," he said. "They could check my fingerprints."

She shook her head.

"My SSN? License."

"Invalid. You don't exist in the legal world. All they can go by is that you existed as Mr. Unknown using the name Shawn Dylan Curtis."

"Newspapers. I'm in them everywhere, especially in the past year, let alone yesterday with a big 'Wanted' sign over my head."

"It doesn't identify you as Shawn Dylan Curtis. Not in an official way."

"Medical records?"

"The bug is programmed to eliminate any medical record, birth certificate, bank account, etc. Anything that could identify you as Shawn Dylan Curtis."

"Facial recognition?"

She shook her head.

"So when I die, I'll be on the record as a regular John Doe, birth unknown, parents unknown, history unknown. I don't exist."

She nodded. "The result will come back with someone else, but it'll never match you."

"You should leave."

Her eyes grew big, her jaw jammed, but he didn't care if he'd hurt her, and he cared even less when she said, "I can't help you get out of this mess if we don't stick together."

"Sticking to you is the last thing on my mind." He wanted his words to wound her, wanted her gone before she witnessed his true vulnerability.

She turned to leave.

"Laura?"

She stopped.

"Did you kill the woman in B-1?"

"No!"

He kept his eyes on her as she left, uncertain what to believe. When he was sure she'd gone, he slid back into the bed, onto his back, then his side, his head running through the second cycle of spin mode, his stomach… *Bucket. Bucket.*

"Hey, Laura? Do you want…" Wayne called out, seconds later standing in the door. "…some soup?"

"Bucket, get me…" Too late. Curtis hung his head over the side of the bed then emptied the little his gut could spit out.

"Gee, you really are allergic to this woman." Wayne snorted, left, before returning with a wet towel he hauled at Curtis and a bucket Wayne had filled with water to clean the mess off the tile floor with a rag. "Glad you've got nothing in your tummy as otherwise I'd be spewing too."

"That's the whole problem. I need food and not some soup. Don't know what Katherine's pumped me full of, but it's not agreeing with me."

"She said it may turn your gut inside out."

Curtis rolled onto his back, wiped his mouth with the towel, grabbed the T-shirt, and tried to cover his body once more with it. Why bother?

"Is Laura coming back?" Wayne asked.

"Nope."

Wayne poked his head up.

Eyes on him, Curtis said, "I didn't want to throw up in front of her."

"You're such a gentleman."

"It's better she left."

"You are the biggest idiot in the world."

"My life was normal before she turned up. And I don't need to be helped by an alien."

"Ah, yeah? The alien still gave you a boner when you first met her."

"You're a real charmer."

"She's out there all alone, fighting against god knows who. She was good enough for you to let her help and now you let her take care of things herself?"

"Why don't you go after her then?"

Wayne slouched. "Not sure if she can be trusted."

"She's lied more than once."

"Didn't you lie to over one million people, purporting you had god knows what skills predicting the stock market while it was nothing but luck?"

"Do you doubt my skills?"

Wayne rolled his eyes. "Well done, mate. Let's get you something to eat."

"Steak?" Curtis puckered his brows to a puppy look.

"As long as you don't plaster my floor with it."

"I'll cook."

"I don't think so."

"I want a steak, not a shoe sole."

"I'll do the veggies."

Curtis grinned about this victory.

Chapter Thirty-One

Laura regretted leaving Curtis behind—again. When Wayne informed her about the meeting with Merkow, she couldn't see the benefit of him coming to the scene. Considering his familiarity with O.R. raised one question. How did he know so much?

After she'd retrieved the bracelets earlier, she'd chanced luck, hoping Curtis would go back to Wayne's condo. But it was Wayne who did. She'd seen photos of him when Gordon first introduced her to the case. The rest was easy. When Wayne jumped back into his Lincoln, she caught a cab and followed him. The mission paid off. Partly.

She found Curtis. That was the only positive. She had not so much as dime left now. She'd failed to convince him of the danger he was in and that he needed help. She also observed he was on the verge of collapsing, not only because of his injuries, and there was nothing she could do to help.

Now, defeated, she waited for the elevator, which had a long way to come from the third floor to the nineteenth. The doors squeaked open. The cabin was empty, as expected. Normal people were snuggled up.

Tired enough to fall asleep while standing against the cabin wall while the elevator descended, she remained on alert, fearing she'd been discovered during the time when she had no bracelet, which she'd given to Curtis. The bracelet seemed to protect him since nobody had tried to kill him. Wearing the bracelet she found in Gordon's loft filled her with confidence, but the confrontation with Sutton perturbed her. How was she ever going to tell him the truth?

The ding threw her back to reality. She readied herself to step out, expecting the elevator to have reached ground floor, but as the doors opened a man appeared. She didn't check the face, only the jeans and the white shirt, then steered her attention to the elevator panel. Floor fourteen. This thing was slow. She let the man in, which he did. The doors shut.

"Life's full of surprises."

Laura shuddered, recognizing the voice. She couldn't run, wasn't sure if it was necessary to run, wasn't sure if she was happy to hear the voice.

"Martin. You're alive?" She studied him. He'd aged, was pale. The cost of years of darkness?

He must have recently escaped that damn forsaken prison created by men who didn't give a shit about people. A cold aura surrounded him, which supported her assumption freedom had come to him recently. But the reason he was there worried her far more.

Green hit the stop button before the elevator started to decline. "I only have about thirty seconds to fill you in. Once we leave here, you must follow your instincts."

Chapter Thirty-Two

The sparsely equipped kitchen was open to the living room, but the neighboring high-rise blocked what could have been a spectacular view. The floor-to-ceiling window had one colossal black rectangular terracotta pot planted with some kind of fern. As much as Curtis liked nature, he didn't have a green thumb but had enough of an eye for detail to question if the design flattered the apartment. The pot was too high, too wide, and sat there like one oversized piece of junk.

According to Wayne, the apartment belonged to one of his client's client other client and was an investment, hardly used because the owner from Australia came to visit only once or twice a year. In the vacant times, he could access it and had agreed to renovate it preparatory to selling it for his client's client other client for top dollar. The concern Curtis raised that it may have been compromised since Laura now knew about it was set at naught.

"She's only interested in your dick," Wayne said, slid out two plates from the cabinet and placed them on the counter.

Curtis checked the frying pan in which he was sizzling one steak, looked over to his friend, who drained the vegetables he'd steamed.

"Steak done?" Wayne asked.

"Yup." Curtis got shoved out of the way and confusedly watched Wayne fishing the steak from the frying pan, flipping it onto one plate, cutting it in half, spearing one half with a fork and sliding it on the other plate. "Where's the rest of it?"

Wayne smirked. "I never said you were going the get the whole steak. Small meals at a time because I don't want to clean up your puke again."

Curtis blew him a raspberry, went for his plate, prepared to sit down.

"Veggies, mate. Or I'll eat your half of the steak too," Wayne said.

Curtis held the plate toward Wayne, who filled it with broccoli, carrots, pumpkin, and mashed potato.

"Any sauce?" Curtis asked.

"I'm out of sauce. Now eat and keep it where it belongs."

Dry streak, dry vegetables. The soup sounded much better.

When Wayne accompanied Curtis at the small white table, he stuck his teeth not into his dinner, but straight into one topic—Laura. "Gee, man. She's hot. Not hot-hot like some, you know, big boobs, hot ass. She's got something."

"Don't be blinded. She's as shady as a chameleon; alien fits even better."

"It doesn't make her an alien because she's got somebody else's face. It's still her as a person."

"Her brain in Laura's body. Does it even make her a person? I mean, who is she as a person?"

For once Wayne was speechless. Yes, it could happen. Curtis continued before being bombarded with questions he didn't want to answer, "Did Merkow reveal where he had all the information from?"

"Have a guess."

"He didn't tell." Curtis chewed on his steak as much as the events, but again Wayne didn't know better than being a pain.

"You haven't told me yet what she wanted."

In a few brief words Curtis clarified his existence would be wiped by the cylinder when he died, which explained how Olivia and the others fitted in. "I also assume Gordon was playing both sides and Laura's either dumb or playing dumb." He rubbed his forehead. "You want to hear something confusing? She didn't know about the brain transplant. Gordon just carried it out. And she had no idea how she got to San Diego."

Wayne scratched his head. "You know, her being in San Diego and her dad being here gives me the impression it's no coincidence they're both in this city. At least he must have had an idea. Why else did Sutton leave New Jersey?"

"Unless she was following his steps."

"You just said she didn't know how she ended up here."

Right. "I'm getting the feeling O.R. is or was somewhere here in San Diego."

"You kicked out the only person who knows."

"She doesn't know."

"Or she knows but doesn't share. You keep saying she's a liar. Why don't you turn the game around? Let her lead you. If you keep pushing her away, you'll never get to the bottom of it."

Curtis shoved the plate with the remaining few bites of the steak and pumpkin away and crossed his arms.

"I see," Wayne mumbled. "Wanna talk about it?"

"Not really."

Wayne gobbled down the last piece of meat, stabbed the leftover pumpkin and steak off Curtis's plate then swallowed it. He cleared the table, sat again, shifting from one position to another.

Curtis suspected he was trying to decide if leaning on the table or a stilted relaxed manner was more appropriate for what he wanted to say. And Curtis knew his friend had things to say.

At length, hands folded on the table, his tone as subtle as he could manage, Wayne finally said, "You can't carry the guilt with you for the rest of your life. It won't bring her back."

Did he leave the fork purposely on the table? Curtis grabbed it. Kneading it, he awakened the day he wanted to keep buried. The day Jessica was killed.

He had swapped cars with her because she needed a bigger one for the day. She had a Toyota Yaris, and he drove a Toyota SUV. Later that day, she'd called him with a cry for help, asking if he could come to her shop with her car, take his car and pick up a painting at a gallery, then bring it to hers. She couldn't go because she had to prepare other paintings for the customer and only had an hour to get it all done.

Any other day, he would have dumped everything and rescued her, but he was in the process of an important meeting with a pivotal client he couldn't risk of slipping away. She understood his dilemma. He understood her frustration.

In the following hour, he sealed the biggest deal he had with an investor and couldn't wait to share the news with Jessica. He hoped there was still enough time to do what she'd asked, which would have made it the perfect day. But her phone remained unanswered. He drove to her gallery to find the doors shut. Assuming her busy, he returned home but kept on calling her.

Two hours later, the cops showed up at Curtis's door, in tow her father bringing the bad news. In his grief, he lamented failing to do as she asked, and her father, hearing that, snapped. Curtis will never forget his words, 'You're responsible for my daughter's death.'

After that, Curtis called off the deal with the investor, told him doing business with him would always remind him of his girlfriend's death. It was the most honest statement he ever made to a stranger.

He played the fork through his fingers. "It's difficult to shake off the guilt or the idea that I should have been in that car and that she'd still be alive if I hadn't been such a selfish prick." He withstood the temptation to drive the fork into the wooden table. He dropped it instead. His chest compressed, wringing a sigh out of him. "I'm going to lie down. I'll do the dishes later." He thrust the chair back, stood, and started for the bedroom.

"Brother?"

Curtis stopped. The only time his friend called him 'brother' was when he had something significant to say.

"After all that's been going on, I think your whole life has been a lie, has been staged, controlled, monitored, call it what you think fits."

A raw egg in the face would have felt better than Wayne's words. "I'll see you in the morning."

~ * ~

It was over an hour since Curtis escaped to the bedroom. At least his stomach had ceased rebelling. The aches in his shoulder and head were now a manageable pulsing after he popped more pills Katherine had left for him.

But a new ache tormented him. His heart. Wounds, which should have remained in a closed box hoarded nowhere else but his heart, were now excavated. Nobody, unless they'd experienced the same pain, knew what it was like to be robbed of the chance to say one last goodbye to a loved one. No more last kiss, no more "I love you", no more "take care", no more crossing off the adventures from the bucket list drawn together. Everything—just wiped, leaving nothing but emptiness and the unheard words, "I wish you were here."

Everyone handled losses like this differently. For Curtis, drugs had provided a world of forgetting. The ultimate glob in his history: knocking out an officer when stopped for a DUI test while he was drugged up from top to toe. Luckily, Wayne had come to his aid before Curtis had to spend years behind bars. A situation when true friendship was determined. As much as a pain in the ass he could be, Wayne became a brother.

Curtis never touched drugs again, even stopped smoking but wouldn't spurn a good drink.

Just as he wanted to grant his body the sleep it so desperately demanded, knocks at the door annoyed him. For as long as he remained quiet, chances existed that Wayne would give up. Not Wayne. Whatever applied to other people didn't apply to him. Curtis swung the blanket over his head before he sensed Wayne's presence in the room.

"You know, mate, it wasn't smart to kick her out."

"Wake me when you find her," Curtis mumbled from underneath the blanket. Only a few hours ago, he silently crucified Laura for leaving people behind without caring about their fate. Now he'd left her fighting the battle by herself. *I'm a hypocrite.*

Wayne was still there. Speechless for a change.

Curtis peeked up from beneath the blanket. "Sorry, mate. I know you're trying to help, but I honestly don't know which way to turn. Right now, I'm happy if I can keep the steak where it belongs. But I wouldn't know where I'd be without your help."

"Aww, you make me cry, mate. But somebody has to keep your ass out of trouble and who's better than me? By the way, you'd better get in touch with your accountant. I forgot to tell you I had three missed calls on my phone."

"Today?"

"While I was in L.A. No message attached to it. It slipped my mind. Sorry."

The door snapped into the lock. Maybe it was time to contact the accountant to see if anything had happened at his end. Something Curtis had avoided because it would come with bad news. You owe money here and more money there. Lawyers after it like starving lions. The inevitable question, 'What do you want to do? You'll never be able to earn enough money in ten years to pay them all. And you know what that means.'

Curtis was no idiot. He worked it out. He had nine years, eight months and thirteen days left to find the money, twelve days as of a few minutes ago or end up in prison. He could have gone straight for the prison option, like Sutton said, be fed by the government. But like Sutton had also said, Curtis liked freedom too much. Plus, he wanted to give himself the chance to achieve the impossible.

If he miraculously managed to pay most of the money back, the judges could take into account his goodwill, extend the deadline and add another ten years to gather the rest of the money. With sixty-two, he voluntarily deemed prison a good option. However, the deal had a downside.

Every new one-hundred grand claimed in debt since his penalty added another year to his sentence. Since there were still people out there who hadn't made any claims—and if they imprisoned him at fifty-two— he may never walk out, and at sixty-two it was a slam dunk. Something Wayne didn't know, which was good, as otherwise he would suggest robbing a bank.

Why wasn't there a way to flick off thoughts? Laura spooked around again. Wayne was right; Curtis should have kept her there.

He crawled out of bed, dressed in jeans, a black shirt, and a sweater. He ran a hand through his hair, preparing for the confrontation with Wayne in the living room.

"Where are you going?" Wayne asked, sunken in the love seat, laptop on his legs, his eyes focused on the screen.

"I need fresh air."

"Take a gun."

"I've got my charm."

"Grab my phone at least. You're a wanted man. People might snatch you off the street."

"It's two in the morning."

"That's what I mean."

"I'll be fine." Curtis remained there a few seconds, torn between worlds of right and wrong and messing things up more. "Thank you for everything you've done for me. I understand if…"

"Mate!" Wayne shoved the laptop onto the coffee table and rose, his face creasing in a way Curtis hadn't seen often. "Wind back fourteen years, mate. It's me who has to thank you. I can see you're falling apart, and I don't like that. I miss your sarcasm, and I saw a glimpse of it after Laura left. You need that chick, and you need to open up, mate. She's a victim as much as you are. Get that in your head. Now piss off. If you're not back in half, I'll come looking for you."

Chapter Thirty-Three

Curtis had a long wait for the elevator to come all the way up from the ground floor to the nineteenth. Plenty of time to ponder Wayne's words, about how right he was, about Laura, about where she could be. She had no car, not enough money for a plane ticket or a bus to go far. There were many places where she could be if she stuck close. There was a hotel right across the road and a motel one block down, which could have been her choice if her finances weren't drained.

The ding announced the ancient contraption's arrival. The door squeaked open, but Curtis hesitated as a man inside leaned against the stainless steel wall. He wore jeans and a white shirt, which didn't suit his pale and freshly shaven skin. His light-brown hair shimmered green in the elevator light. Curtis guessed his age the same as his.

The man nodded as if to say, "I don't like elevators either." No hello or any other acknowledgment. He kept his arms crossed over his buff, tall body, and he streamed out confidence, which Curtis didn't like to encounter at this time of night. Or morning.

As he stepped inside, he noticed ground floor button was already lit, which struck him as strange since the elevator had come up.

With his back pressed against the stainless steel wall, opposite the white-shirt guy, he innocently read the few flyers sticky taped to the wall but just as innocently stayed on alert.

The doors squeaked closed, and the elevator started its decline.

"Should you be going out?" the man asked.

Curtis chewed through the comment not making any sense to him, then studied the man. No sign of threat on his face. "Excuse me?"

"There must be an urgent reason for you to go out because, sorry to say this, you don't look overly well."

"I've had better days." Curtis kept occupied reading the flyers, leaving a corner of his eye on the man.

"You mind me asking why you're going out?" the man asked.

Weird. There were several ways to play this. Polite: Going to catch up with some friends. Impolite: None of your business. Curtis chose the in-between way.

"Cabin fever." He wasn't sure if he should face the guy or keep his eyes on the flyer. He decided for the flyer.

"I see. Is it not the case that you're trying to catch up with Laura?"

Don't react. "Don't know a Laura."

The elevator joggled to a stop. Curtis's heartbeat sped up. As he faced the guy, it galloped.

The guy pointed a gun at him. "You want the easy way or the hard way?"

If there had been the slightest energy in Curtis, he would have decided for direct combat, but lifting an arm was like lifting a bag of cement. Plus, it was never a good idea to go for combat in a small, enclosed room, especially when you're at the other end of the gun barrel. "Who are you?"

"Martin Green. What's your name?"

Did he seriously ask that?

Green must have noticed Curtis's befuddlement. "All we know you under is Rabbit 76."

Tsk-tsk. Rabbit. "Samuel Macintosh." Good name. That would sell.

"I guess Laura will be able to confirm it."

"You know where she is?"

"Downstairs, in a car, waiting with my partner."

Curtis's muscles stiffened. No point lying about the name. Laura would have told him. "Shawn Curtis. People call me Curtis."

"Good. When we get downstairs, I want you to walk ahead, outside to a black Rover. I want you to get in the backseat." Green pressed the button, and the elevator continued its descent from floor thirteen.

"Where are you taking me?"

"I want you to follow my orders at all times. Clifton can be a hothead."

"Clifton who?"

"Wright."

Curtis made a mental note of the name. "When was the last time you saw Laura? Besides today."

"It's been a while."

Green didn't reveal much. Curtis decided to be just as secretive.

"I assume you know about O.R." Green asked.

Curtis nodded.

"Clifton and I got out a few days ago. While Clifton may have other things in mind, my interest is in taking down Powell and whoever else is involved."

"Powell?"

"Leon Powell. Chief Execution Officer."

"What about Knox?"

"Ha! You know the game. The little ones bleed, so the big ones can proceed. There's no way we'll be able to take him down. But there are another nineteen people rotting in a facility with no way out."

A charge traveled through Curtis. There were people alive. "Why didn't you get them out?"

"This probably won't make much sense, but I don't know how we got out, nor do I know where the others are."

Like Merkow had explained—brainwashed.

Though the gun was still pointed at him, Curtis didn't feel threatened by it. "How well do you know Laura?"

"You need to watch her. She'll wrap you up and present you to Knox like a Christmas present. You heard about Emily?"

He didn't know what to say, so he said nothing.

"She was Laura's best friend, but she got rid of her, transferred her to O.R. Same with me. The day before they took me to O.R., I proposed to Laura. She even said yes."

Wow! "How do you know it was her decision you ended up at O.R.?"

"Because she was the one deciding who from within NOKS had to go. Laura was eating grass from two sides of the fence and decided Knox had the juicer field. But like I said, watch Clifton. And don't trust Laura. If you stick with me, you might live."

I don't stick to anyone.

At the ground floor, Curtis spotted the black Range Rover, the silhouettes of two people sitting in the front. Laura, he guessed, and Clifton Wright. Twelve short steps separated Curtis from the laser-activated glass door. Like a shadow, Green hung behind as Curtis approached it.

"Get in the back," Green said.

Closing in on the Rover, Curtis kept his focus on Laura. Her window was up, but she stared right at him. Her features were tense and, as he was two steps away, she shook her head. A tiny shake. Almost imperceptible in the darkness.

He guessed Green still behind him, presumably holding a gun. Clifton's hands were on the steering wheel. As their eyes met, Curtis wasn't sure if he read slight haughtiness. Did Clifton see Laura's shake of her head?

His window crawled down, halfway. "Get in."

Curtis caught a glimpse of Laura once more, now clearly visible. She shook her head again, ever so slightly. Something solid poked him in the back. The gun.

Curtis spun around so Green had no chance to mull over pulling the trigger, which he probably never did in the first place, which was the reason his grip on the gun was slack, which enabled Curtis to clutch both hands around it and rip it out of Green's hands. Green stood there as if he'd been stripped naked.

With no next move planned, Curtis pointed the gun at Green to win some time.

The engine behind him revved up, the tires whirling up dust and smoke, the stench of burned rubber stinging Curtis's nose. Before he could react, the Rover careened around the bend.

"What the fuck were you thinking?" Green snapped.

"Shut the fuck up." Curtis whacked the gun on his head. Hard enough to knock him out, not hard enough to cause damage. Hopefully. As Green folded, Curtis caught his fall and laid him on the ground. He had no intention of hurting him. All he needed was time.

"Oy! Ay! I saw that."

From thirty feet away, a solid dark-skinned man marched closer, his hand going for his pocket. Gun? Phone? For a few seconds, Curtis contemplated if it was worthwhile explaining his situation. Better not take the chances since he had Green's gun in his hand. He could have dropped it, but it had his fingerprints on it. He ran. Despite his heavy legs, they carried him.

"Police! Police! Somebody call the cops!" The voice faded out as Curtis crossed the street to follow the Rover's path and stopped in an alleyway to catch his breath. What a mess! But Laura's warning was clear. If this idiot hadn't witnessed the knock out, he could have Green in hand. Now he had nothing. No Laura, no Green, no Clifton.

Little point checking on Green's movements, but he wanted to warn Wayne. Green must have been on his way up there, scheming on a kidnap or even a killing, and Curtis's simple desire for fresh air had ruined that.

The streets were deserted besides some stray cars. One taxi rested on a curb, lights on.

Curtis approached it, knocked at the window which lowered straight away. The driver eyed him. "Need a ride?"

"I was wondering if there's the chance to use your phone. My missus is going to kill me if I don't call her and let her know I'm running late 'cause my car's playing up."

"Car, ay?"

Stupid excuse. Curtis reached for his back pocket—an international gesture for getting money out—but the guy waved him off and handed him his cellphone.

"Make it quick."

Seconds later, Curtis made the call to Wayne but got no reply. He tried once more. It went straight to message. Curtis passed the cellphone to the taxi driver, thanked him and started back the way he came. Wayne always had the cellphone with him, on him, slept with it next to his pillow. Even took it with him when he did his... you know.

Curtis had told him to remove the battery whenever they were together as otherwise it could be traced, but it would fall on deaf ears. The moment Curtis left the apartment, Wayne would have switched it on to be available for any unplanned incidents. Like now. It unsettled Curtis that Wayne didn't pick up.

When Curtis was back on the street of the apartment building, Green wasn't in front of it any longer. Neither was the guy who called for the cops. Green could be at the apartment to follow up with the initial plan, with the difference to take Wayne instead. Wayne could defend himself to a certain degree and Green no longer had a gun, but compared to Wayne, Green was tall and muscular.

At war with his gut feeling telling him not to go up there, Curtis's conscience demanded he couldn't leave Wayne in the lurch. Conscience won, supported by the advantage of having the gun Green no longer had.

Curtis entered the building and headed straight for the elevator which parked on the ground floor. This left him with mixed feelings. Green either went up to the nineteenth floor, grabbed Wayne, and came down with him, or Green never went up. Chances somebody used the elevator to leave the building at this time of the morning were slim.

The ride up was slow, giving his body time enough to torture him with hot and cold sweats, his mind conjuring pictures of Wayne puffing out his last breath as he bled to death. Curtis checked the gun in his hand. A Beretta 9mm. Not that he knew much about guns.

He collided with the doors as they sluggishly opened. Gun in his hand, he unlocked the apartment door, swung it open, trudged through the hallway, calling out for Wayne. If Green was there, he may as well surprise him. There was no Green. Not in the living room, kitchen, bedroom, bathroom. And no Wayne. One discrepancy startled Curtis: Wayne's cellphone sat on the coffee table. No sign of any scuffle or anything that suggested a fight, but the phone was there, and it was switched on. Wayne hadn't left the apartment of his own free will. That much was sure.

With a deep sigh, Curtis relaxed his cramping chest. It would only be a matter of time and the phone would ring, a voice demanding the obvious: You for Wayne.

Realizing he was outnumbered, Curtis bunched his shoulders. He snatched the phone to his hand and checked for a clue or a message. The last incoming call, besides the two from himself, came from Harry, one of Wayne's clients. The previous call from another client. The last outgoing call went to Katherine, at the time which he guessed was after the meeting with Merkow.

He sank into the loveseat. He needed help, and only one person could provide it.

Chapter Thirty-Four

Forty minutes had passed since Curtis made the call and received the expected gruff answer from the man whom he'd dragged out of sleep. "This better be important," he'd growled.

"Two lives at stake important enough?"

"As long as it's not yours, I'm all ears."

Charmer.

Sutton directed him to meet up at Embarcadero Marina Park South, which Curtis found with the help of the GPS in Wayne's Lincoln he used with utmost reluctance. He deactivated it as soon as he knew the directions, fully aware Wayne's phone in his pocket gave away his location. He carried it in the hope Green or Clifton would call. Or Wayne.

Curtis sat in the car waiting. Though the sun hadn't broken through the night yet, he could envision the spectacular views of the San Diego Bay, Coronado shimmering on the other side of the rippling water. Trees with ghostly pale bark lined the park, and expensive yachts laid at anchor in the harbor.

Laura came to his mind, a constant brooding about possibilities of finding her torturing his imagination. Was she with Wayne? She could be tied up inside one of these million-dollar yachts and Wayne thrown off the Coronado Bridge. Fish food. Curtis's throat tightened. He'd let Laura down, failed Wayne, failed himself. Giving up wasn't in his cards, but *hell!* Where should Curtis start looking?

He focused on the parking lot as lights hinted at an incoming car. A black Dodge Charger crawled along. As it closed in, a hand waved at him, and Sutton stuck his head through the tinted window.

Curtis left the Lincoln and slid into the Charger's seat, but Sutton didn't drive off. He killed the engine.

"You alone?" Curtis asked.

"When I agree to something I tend to keep my word."

"I'll hold you to that."

"Fill me in."

Straight to the point. He kept his rundown of events equally straight.

Sutton said, "You sure it's Martin Green who has Wayne?"

"If not him then Clifton Wright. But I assume he's busy keeping Laura chained."

Sutton sucked in his lips, bit on them, pursed them out like a child trying to get air into a balloon, not knowing it needed to give the lungs a little workout to succeed.

Then he straightened his shoulders as if he'd come to a conclusion. "Before we do anything, I want you to hand me Green's gun."

"I might need it."

"I don't think I need to explain what happens should you kill somebody with it."

Curtis puffed a sigh, ripped it from his waistband and handed it reluctantly over but to his uneasiness, Sutton kept the Beretta in his hand.

"How did you meet?" Sutton asked.

"Who?"

"Wayne."

Curtis prepared to get lynched about every detail of his life. "I was driving home one early morning when I saw him losing his footing while trying to find his way on the pavement to wherever. At one stage he hugged a pole. He never got to make the next step. He landed flat-faced on the road. I picked him up, saw his wedding band on his finger. He kept saying the name Debbie, called her all type of names. I concluded it must be a bad I-hate-my-wife case, so I took him home and after he sobered up, he told me he'd taken her and their two kids to Australia, where she got knocked up by some rich dude, who was supposed to be his best friend. It was his first night back in New York when I helped him out. We became good friends. That was about fourteen years ago. Five years later, he went to San Diego because it reminded him of home. He never went back to Australia, never saw his kids again."

Sutton cleared his throat. "I think something in your life previously to what's going on now must be the cause for all this. Tell me about your childhood. Your parents."

In vain Curtis studied Sutton's face to see where this was heading. "Shouldn't we be more worried about Laura and Wayne?"

"You are the reason they are in this situation, aren't you?"

Touché. "My parents are dead." Curtis remembered how every few months they were packing bags, no reason ever given to him. He didn't know much about his father, Charles. Charlie, they called him. According to his mother, Iris, he'd worked as an engineer. He was hardly around and when he was, he made his presence clear.

Curtis recalled he always had to wear a watch. His parents had insisted he never take it off. He hated that thing. The solid band cut in his flesh and the oversized watch was stiff and never accurate.

One day he took it off. Less than one hour later, his father interrupted his adventure and beat the living daylights out of him. After retrieving the watch from the bush where Curtis had hidden it, his father jammed it around his wrist and said, "Next time you take it off, you won't be able to walk."

At home, his father sealed the buckle on the watch strap. Every so often, as Curtis grew, his father enlarged the band. Curtis never quite understood the story behind it and never understood why they were constantly on the move, the packing always done in a rush.

Shortly after he'd turned twelve-years old it changed. His father came home. Curtis had never seen him flustered before. He snapped off the watch and said to take care of Mom. His mother gathered all their belongings in a hurry and they moved to New York, where he had a settled life for the first time. Curtis never saw his father again.

"Three years later my mother died of, what I was told, a heart attack. I wasn't eighteen then, and the last thing I needed was to end up in foster care. I was used to packing bags, so I grabbed what I could and ran. Jobbed around to make a living."

Sutton rested his chin on his hand, groaned a few times in his deep deliberation, lifted his head and tensed his shoulders. "Was your name always Shawn Dylan Curtis?"

Sutton's deep glower jammed Curtis's nod.

"You see," Sutton continued, "I checked your history or Shawn Dylan Curtis's history. What you're telling me doesn't quite match. According to what I've found so far, Shawn Dylan Curtis had a normal life. Was born in Brooklyn to Charles Dylan Curtis and Iris Elizabeth Curtis, formerly Sullivan. Went to several schools in Brooklyn, caused no major dramas, and was apparently rather shy. He vanished after graduation from the system and resurfaced at twenty-one, which is the only part matching your story. Any explanation?"

"Can't be. I wasn't born in Brooklyn, and I certainly wasn't shy."

"Who are you really?" It was Sutton's deadeye stare that nearly propelled Curtis to boiling point. But it was Sutton boiling over. His face reddening, he growled like a grizzly bear tearing down a tree. "Who are you?"

Curtis's breath hitched as the cold muzzle of the gun hit his chin. A scream tried to escape. He gulped it down and cursed the tinted windows when he wasted a brief second to see if anyone was walking past. Wasted a second thinking to fight him off. Dmitri taught him to stay calm in situations like this. Ha! What a joke when it happened in reality. He wanted to swallow, but his mouth was like a desert.

"Shawn Dylan Curtis, born in Michigan," he managed to croak. "My father was Charles Dylan Curtis, who disappeared when I was twelve. I never saw him again. My mother, Iris Elizabeth Curtis, formerly Sullivan, died twenty-seven years ago. I didn't set a foot in New York before I was twelve, and I never graduated because I never went to any school. My mother was my teacher, which probably wasn't bad after all because she taught me enough to see when somebody is bullshitting me." He held Sutton's stare as the gun's pressure eased.

"I assume you don't have anything to prove your point? A birth certificate would be helpful."

"Social workers were already at the doorstep when I climbed through the window, so paperwork was the least of my worries. And as you already figured out, I didn't worry about any of it before I was twenty-one. I do admit now and then I did take advantage of having three names that could be either used as first or last, so you might find stuff under Dylan Shawn Curtis or Curtis Shawn Dylan or Dylan Curtis Shawn, but if you were a good detective, you would have checked the yearbook, because I won't be in there."

Sutton flipped the glove box open, chucked the gun inside as if it had finished its duty, reached behind to a duffel bag. Seconds after rummaging around, he withdrew a big book. His fingers flicked open a page marked with a Post-it. He pointed to a photo.

A quiver ran down Curtis's back as he looked at a young man wearing a black gown and a cap he never wore, but the face was too familiar. He ignored Sutton's glower. "I was never there."

"I contacted a few people who are in this school annual. They said they'd never heard of you. I compared this book with theirs through video calls. All of them were identical to this one, but not one person has heard of Shawn Dylan Curtis. I contacted the schools your history claims you went to. Interestingly, the system showed a Shawn Dylan Curtis. I tried to track down teachers, principals, but I didn't find many who are still alive, and I haven't had a chance yet to call the ones who can give me answers. Somehow, I already know what they're going to tell me anyhow. But the way it seems, somebody has given you a life you never had. I want to know why." He snapped the book close and tossed it to the backseat. "The DNA test. I looked into it a little. Why did you pay

Sarah such an enormous amount?"

He looked into it a little? Obviously, Sutton hadn't held back in turning his entire finances upside down. Curtis swallowed his anger down. "I had no reason to believe I wasn't the father. It's why I didn't hesitate to pay her the lump sum she demanded."

"You paid her first and carried out the DNA test later?" Sutton asked, evincing doubt.

"She approached me again about six months later, only days after my business went downhill. This time I got suspicious and wanted to make sure I was the father."

"The test came back negative. What else was involved in the test?"

Curtis studied Sutton's deep creases. When he'd first met him, he had the impression of Sutton being a switched on guy. Honest. Not stupid. It dawned on Curtis. "You don't know why this is all happening, do you?"

"I know there's much more involved than what I could figure out so far."

"Much more," Curtis said. Sutton had been around all this time and didn't really know why. 'Personal reasons,' he'd told Wayne.

Curtis filled the holes and told him about the tests that were done on him, conducted by Phil Merkow, who was hauled from the street by Knox. He brushed over Laura's involvement, left out who she really was or what happened to the real Laura. The truth held the risk of giving Sutton a mental breakdown.

"Somehow in all this mess," Curtis said, "Knox or somebody within NOKS wants me dead because… I'm not sure. It's got something to do with a five-billion-dollar deal the government pays to the company for a cancer vaccine."

"I had no idea how big this is."

Curtis seized the moment to steer Sutton's attention away. "When you stalked Wayne in the parking lot, you told him you were after me for personal reasons. What are they? The most genuine cop wouldn't go as far as you do to help a guy he doesn't know."

There was a silence.

"Sutton?"

"I keep receiving messages. I can't find the source."

"Get to the point."

"They state it is my responsibility to keep you safe."

"Safe from whom?"

"What do you think I've been trying to find out? But after everything you just told me, it must be someone who knows about you."

"Did it take some unknown felon sending you text messages to convince you of my innocence?"

Sutton said nothing.

"Why should you be responsible?" Curtis asked.

"I don't read anything into that part."

"When did you get the first text?"

"A few days before you came to San Diego."

"How does that make sense?"

"You tell me. The next message came shortly before I reached B-1. It didn't mention the shooting or the place, but I had the feeling it had something to do with the call from dispatch about B-1. Next I know, you mentioned Laura Webb, and I knew I was there for a reason."

As Sutton said it, Curtis realized he checkmated himself.

Sutton said, "Tell me about Laura."

Curtis bit his bottom lip. The question alone purported that Sutton had a suspicion.

"I don't know more than you do." He tried to plant on a neutral face.

A whoosh flashed past his cheek. Something robbed him of air before his brain translated it to Sutton's hand clutched around his throat, dangerously tight. Curtis wanted to fight the hand, had to fight it, tried to fight it. Grabbed Sutton's wrist.

"If you don't let go of my hand," Sutton warned, "I'll make sure you never lift an arm again."

Curtis clawed the seat instead. *Air. I need air.*

Sutton snarled, "You have a bunch of crooks after you, and I don't know if I'm willing to help you out the next time. We can end it right here, and I can sleep again. So don't play me for a sucker. Who is she?"

Curtis shook his head. Not a good idea. Sutton's fingers tightened. Panic strangled Curtis as much as the lack of air. He searched Sutton's eyes for a slight sign of mercy. There was none. Blank, dead brown eyes. He didn't want to betray Laura, but he couldn't swallow, couldn't breathe. Flashes behind his eyelids warned him of the first wave of fainting. He managed a nod. Sutton let go.

Curtis dragged in air, tears close to winning. *No way.* Like a fish on land he snapped for oxygen, coughed a few times more than needed to gain composure. Sutton had scared him right down to the core of his being. Just as Curtis found the next breath, Sutton's hand flung once more up to his throat.

Before his grip tightened, Curtis wheezed, "Emily."

Sutton hit the dashboard hard with his hand. "I knew it. I fucking knew it!" Just a spurt of anger. Suddenly composed he said, "I saw her yesterday. At first, I thought it was Laura, but there was something off. I don't know what it was, but you know when it's your own flesh and blood."

The difference though that, theoretically, she wasn't Sutton's flesh and blood, but Curtis didn't want to complicate things. He remained deep in the seat, had no intention of straightening himself. A subdued low profile could keep Sutton from another attack.

"Where... did you... see her?" Curtis said, his voice rasping.

"At Gordon's loft or whoever it belongs to. I caught her out. I don't know if or what she took from there."

The bracelet, Curtis concluded. The uneasiness streaming from Sutton infected Curtis. The disappointment for Sutton had to be demoralizing, foremost the question of why she'd never contacted him. It could only be explained by her shame and fear he might reject her.

Curtis said, "She was at the apartment last night."

"How could you let her go?"

How could I not?

Was there a point in explaining he'd been furious with her for holding back the truth that his existence would be wiped from the system the moment he died? Or that she was responsible for the real Laura's death, even though she couldn't have prevented it?

"We didn't agree on proceedings." His voice now guttural, Curtis hoped it wasn't permanently damaged. "I told her it was atrocious to keep her identity from you."

That would shut him up. It did, and Sutton relaxed his shoulders.

Curtis put his next words carefully together, unsure if they would infuriate him again. "There's a good chance Green and Wright have Laura."

"*Emily.* I... Stay here." Reality must have sunk in on Sutton. He heaved himself out of the car, strode away, but not far enough for Curtis to escape, which he didn't want to anyway.

He looked the other way, giving the detective the privacy he needed. As Curtis waited, a couple of tears pressed out of his eyes. With the back of his hand, he brushed them off and propped himself up, but not enough to be at eye level when the cop joined again, which he did, minutes later. The car door swung open, Sutton sat back in, no redness in his eyes. Tough guy.

His voice was softer, though. "How's your throat?"

"I'll live."

"Sorry."

"I'd probably boil over too." Better to make friends with him again.

"I want you to go home, get some rest. I'll be in touch with you."

"What about Laura and Wayne?"

"All you need to do right now is stay alive. As for Wayne, there's the possibility he came looking for you, left his phone at the apartment. He might be there right now."

"If not Green and Clifton."

"I doubt they'll return because they doubt you'll return."

Strange theory.

"But I want you to look over your shoulder at all times."

Somehow these words sounded familiar.

Chapter Thirty-Five

Curtis sat in the Lincoln, watching Sutton's Dodge disappear. There was a fresh fall nip in the air, the first light of day glittering on the water. He started the car and drove, not knowing what prompted him to remain close to the ocean instead of searching for Wayne or Laura.

When Curtis spotted a familiar beach, he parked five slots from the one Laura had used a few days ago. He killed the engine. Engulfed by an urge for freedom, he stripped off his boots and shoved his socks into them before leaving them in the car and striding the few yards to dig his feet into the sand. He enjoyed the way it filtered between his toes.

The clean, crisp air he inhaled deeper than he had in many days, the realization within him that without Laura he'd be dead. Sutton didn't give a damn about him, would have gone for the kill and dumped him somewhere, or used the gun and pinned the blame on Green, if it wasn't for Laura.

The ocean in his vision, Curtis trudged through the sand, every step waking in him gratitude that he was still alive. He stopped one time, rolled his jeans up to his calves, and kept walking to let the water enliven him more. In any other situation, he would have taken a dip and ridden a wave, but this wasn't the right time.

As he waded through the water, his gaze occasionally swept the beach in the unlikely hope of spotting Laura.

His mind drifted to his parents. For as long as he could remember they were always on the move, always chose small towns to live in. How could his photo be in a yearbook?

The watch he had to wear. Now he understood, or thought he did, its purpose. His parents kept track of where he was and where he was going. Like that damn thing in his arm. But why? Was it their overprotective nature to keep him safe? Safe from what? He remembered his mom pulled his blood on every first day of the month. He'd dreaded that day. He hadn't mentioned it to Sutton because it didn't seem important, but once his father had disappeared, the ritual of drawing blood had stopped too.

His mother always said it was for his own good. For Curtis, his own good came with pain and sometimes he wondered if his parents had to test their blood, too, for their own good. He asked his mom once, but her answer gave no conclusion.

"We only want to make sure you're healthy." When he asked about the watch she'd said, "We only want to make sure you're always on time."

His father drummed into him what being on time meant. Though he had only rare occasions to explore the neighborhood, Curtis had taken advantage to the fullest whenever he had permission to go out and play. Soon he was familiar with every dog barking behind a fence, every rock, every tree, every squirrel in them. Sometimes on his adventures, he crossed paths with other like-minded kids, who weren't easy to find because they were usually at school or busy killing virtual enemies on their computer games. Curtis loved nature, grew up with it, and the only computer in his home was solely for his father's use.

His mother was more relaxed about how long she allowed him to do his explorations. Most times he could go for one hour, sometimes two, even three when his mother rewarded him for being a good boy. But when his father was around, as rare as once every six to eight weeks for a few days at a time, the limit was strictly one hour.

One day Curtis got sidetracked watching a deer and was ten minutes late at home. The belt his father used left a scar on Curtis's back. Luckily, his mother had stepped in to stop his ferocity. "He doesn't understand how important he is," she'd said.

He still didn't understand. Not then. Not when Laura had taken him to this beach and said, "You have no idea how important you are."

With the sun still rising, the glitter of shallow water was broken by a shadow thrown by a woman dressed in jeans and a black T-shirt, huddling at the shore. Her dark hair had a shimmer of red. A healthy new cut. Short on the neck, longer on the side. A stray ringlet fluttered into her face. She tamed it by keeping a finger on the tendril as if trying to glue it down. As she lowered her hand, it broke free again. Untamed, the lock danced around her face once more.

She turned her head, an annoyed move, and stared right at him. If she was surprised, then she hid it persuasively. The strand of hair now restrained by the ocean wind, her body bobbed up once, twice, as though she battled the decision if whether getting up or remaining seated was the better option.

He lengthened his stride, sat next to her and observed the calm ocean, inhaling the salty freshness to suck in his relief.

"How did you find me?" she asked.

"I played a hunch."

She didn't reply, swung her arms around him, and cried. Cradling her back, he swayed her body. It comforted him, no matter how much she trembled. Did she understand he needed just as much sympathy? That he wasn't the hero so many women sought in a man? He hadn't been too scared when the rasp-tap guy challenged him, at least not to death. And Green hadn't scared him either. But death knocked at his door, showed him what it meant to be scared. Terrified even.

Being killed by a bullet you couldn't hear coming sounded pleasant compared to facing the man who wanted to kill you with his bare hands. Curtis didn't think Sutton would have gone all the way, but he'd held his grip for one, two seconds too long, catapulting the full extent of mortality into Curtis's brain. That fear sat deep in his bones and he would have liked to release it with either tears or a scream.

Before he had the chance to allow his hurt to escape, Laura freed herself, looked to the left, right, behind. Then at him. He had no idea what he read in her eyes, but they didn't reflect what he expected to see: the devastation of having faced a near-death experience. More like she was still expecting that kind of ordeal at any moment.

"Were you followed?" she asked as she wiped the tears from her face.

"I've been here for a while, still alive." Studied by her with puzzlement, he asked, "Did you expect me to be dead?"

Once more she craned her neck, checked left, right, behind. Whoever she expected wouldn't appear from the ocean. "We have to go. You can't leave my side at any time."

She spoke in riddles again. "What's changed?"

"Martin Green is the one we can trust."

"I wouldn't be so sure since you dumped him after he proposed."

She opened her mouth, closed it. She tried again, and this time something came out. "It was Laura, not me."

He would have liked to know her intended comment. "Tell me about the two men."

"When Clifton smells money, he'll do anything to get it."

"Green's helping him."

"Green's keeping an eye on him, making sure no one gets hurt who shouldn't."

Curtis wasn't too sure if he should believe that. "And how did you get away?"

"I might be a woman but am not totally defenseless."

It was then that he noticed some scratches and bruises on her arm. Her jeans were torn near her hip and thigh, dark marks marbling the material. She hadn't been in a scuffle, but it looked like she'd jumped out of a moving car. "Are you in pain?"

"Nowhere as much as you are."

If only she knew in how much pain he really was. "Where's he now?"

"Don't know. With Green I guess."

"We have to find them. They have Wayne."

"What?"

He told her about Wayne's disappearance, that Curtis had no other option than to contact Sutton. The detail why his gullet still hurt every time he swallowed, Curtis left out. When she drilled her stare into him, the same way her father had earlier but with blue eyes, he bit his tongue.

"You didn't *tell* him, did you?" she whispered.

It was one of those moments when you force your body to disguise any sign of betrayal. You don't want to breathe, tense a muscle or twitch a brow. But it's exactly that stillness that gives you away. That moment when you exhale and your body sags.

Wham.

He'd expected a blow to land on his face but she'd shot up like a torpedo and kicked him hard in his side, bellowing, "How *could* you?"

Ouch. He hoisted himself up, taking a moment to find his voice. "How could I not? I had his…" He couldn't tell her Sutton's hand had been around Curtis's throat. It would be such a petty excuse, and she most certainly wouldn't believe him if he told her about her father's dark side.

He lowered his head. "I had no option." His words didn't reduce her ferocity.

"It wasn't up to you to tell him. It wasn't up to you to tell me he knows, either."

"Fine then. Let's deal with this by lying to each other like you've lied to me since the day we first met. If you want to go through life like this, then so be it, but don't drag me into your lying bullshit, playing games with my life. If you had the slightest humanity in you, you'd tell me from A to Z what's going on. I understand why they're after me. I understand why they're after you. But tell me who the fuck *they* are."

Her chest grew bigger and bigger, then deflated. "When Gordon told me about your existence, it was our plan to… present you to the PRDA as the living example that cancer could be prevented. We were sure we could convince you that it was the best way to proceed in this matter. The plan was to expose Knox's controversial methods, including the existence of Operation Rabbit and the underground experiments. But we got no farther than discussing how to expose anything because there wasn't enough time. You didn't exist before a few weeks ago. I mean, you did but not… you know what I mean.

"Until last night, I thought no one from O.R. was alive. The main problem we were facing was, either way, if you were in the hands of Knox or the PRDA or any pharmaceutical company, you would end up a guinea pig. That's something I wanted to avoid the day Gordon told me about you."

Curtis searched her face for a hint that the same emotion growing in him blossomed in her, but her scowl suggested differently.

"How did you find out about me?" he asked.

"I told you. From Gordon."

"Did you know about me before Gordon told you?"

"No. I mean, obviously, I knew about Operation Rabbit. I knew about the tests, but I didn't know a man had survived."

"Gordon told you."

She nodded.

"And who told Gordon?"

She shrugged.

"Gordon didn't tell you by any chance why he implanted the device in my arm, did he?"

She shook her head.

"He didn't tell you by any chance why the fuck Green and Clifton knew my whereabouts?"

"I'm starting to believe the bracelet I gave you isn't scrambling your signal."

"No shit." He had to pump his fists so as not to hit the roof. "I think Gordon linked my signal to Green and Clifton so they can deliver me to O.R., if not kill me. And if you didn't play along nicely, Gordon would have sold you off too."

She didn't argue back. Something had changed and whatever Green or Clifton told her scared her enough to change tack.

Voices reached his ears. Behind them, he spotted a group of eight, nine people with five dogs were coming their way.

"Let's get away from here."

Chapter Thirty-Six

Back at the car, Curtis slipped the socks and shoes over his feet and offered to buy Laura new clothes to replace her ripped jeans.

Since no shops were open, he suggested breakfast first. Deep inside, guilt brooded for disobeying Sutton's order to return to Wayne's apartment. However, neither Green nor Clifton had demanded anything, therefore it was possible Sutton was right about Wayne being safe.

Curtis and Laura sat opposite each other in a high-backed booth at a cold silver table the farthest from the street. She ordered pancakes. He ordered a hearty breakfast of bacon, eggs, and toast. He was hungry enough to eat two meals but wasn't sure if his stomach could handle it, although since the steak last night the rumbles had stopped. Painkillers would have been a good addition to the menu to stop his shoulder from aching and his head pricking like needles.

Wayne's phone in his pocket interrupted their silence. Swiftly, he fished it out, his feelings going through a whirlwind when he identified Sutton as the caller.

Curtis asked Laura, "Do I tell him you're with me?"

She shook her head.

He answered the call. "Any news?"

"Do you have news?"

"Not yet. But I'll get a new phone. I don't want to risk being traced."

"Not possible. I had it blocked for the time being so you're not being caught."

"What do you mean?"

"Thank me later, but I know people who know how to do that stuff. But you didn't follow my order. Now guess who contacted me in panic, reporting his phone and car stolen?"

"Wayne?"

"Maybe in the future, you'll take me at my word. He went

looking for you and in all his panic, he forgot his phone. You, in your panic, took his phone and his car and… you can fill in the rest."

It wasn't an earthquake, but Curtis felt as though the mountain falling from his back could have caused one. "Is he okay?"

"Yes. I'm keeping him off the street for the time being. Location undisclosed. Even to you. Any sign of her?"

"No." Forced to lie for the woman who seemed a pro at it, Curtis feared his quick reply had given the truth away. "You'll be the first to know when I find her."

After a short hesitation, Sutton said, "Where are you?"

"You know where I am."

"I know where the Lincoln is. Don't use it. And I don't want to know where you are. Too much is at stake. In five minutes my friend has to open the signal to Wayne's phone again. Everybody will know then where you are, and you don't want that."

Why on earth couldn't Sutton spit out the rest? "Why?"

"Check the latest newspaper. You need to understand this is not my doing or from our side. But you better disappear. The quicker the better."

Curtis had totally forgotten about the 'WANTED' notice in the paper from the other day. Instinctively, he lowered his head. "You ever found out who put the notice in the paper?"

"This is much worse. Go and hide."

Curtis swept the coffee shop with a quick look to see if anyone had recognized him. The older couple he'd seen when entering was still sitting in the same booth, munching their breakfast, sipping their coffee. Nobody else was in here, besides the waitress busying herself with cleaning countertops. She showed no sign of recognition, no interest in his or Laura's business.

Sutton said, "Make a note of this number."

Curtis listened and scribbled down the number.

"Get a burner. Send me a text with your new number. Do not call me. I'll call you. As soon as we hang up, destroy Wayne's. He told me he backed up his numbers and information so you don't have to worry about the phone or SIM or anything else. You got that?"

"Yes."

"Take care. Talk soon."

Cutis dismantled the cellphone, shoved the SIM and battery into his pocket and said to Laura, "We have to go." He shoveled more bacon and egg, chewed it up in seconds and washed it down with coffee. Who knew when there was a next time to eat something so palatable?

"What's happening?" she asked.

"Don't know yet." Back in the street, he chucked the phone's insides down a drain and flung the cover over a fence. The SIM, he broke in half and tossed one half into the bush, another into a trash can.

Next, they searched for a shop selling sunglasses and ball caps, which they found around the corner. They were the first customers. Two streets over, he waited outside another, pretending to study a flyer he'd plucked off a free newsstand, while Laura replaced her ripped jeans. She wasn't one of those women who took hours to please her desires. Jeans, one black T-shirt, and one blue blouse, along with, she said, underwear. She also picked out hoodies for them both. The nights were becoming fresh. Money, however, was running thin.

"What about the car?" she asked when she rejoined him.

"Can't use it."

"Are you going to tell me what's going on?"

"I need the internet or some way to watch the latest news. Then we'll know what's going on."

Laura stopped him when they hurried past a bar, the TV blaring through the windows and open doors.

Curtis focused on the TV. A dark-haired woman wearing a red blouse sat behind the desk, obviously talking to Chief Oliver Donaghy over the open phone as his picture flashed on the side of the screen.

"Do we know for sure the name Seb relates to Sebastian Knox?" the woman asked.

"I can't answer that question."

"What about Rabbit 76? Do we know who would qualify for the criteria? I mean, there are a lot of forty-two-year-old Caucasian men living in San Diego. Is there any way to determine who the email in the newspaper refers to? Who this 'Rabbit 76' is?"

"Like I said, I can't answer these questions. The SDPD is working closely with the FBI to find Rabbit 76."

Curtis stared at Laura. "We need a newspaper."

Which they found sticking out of a nearby trashcan. The headline alone gave Curtis the shivers.

Who is Rabbit 76?

She started reading, but he ripped the paper from her hand.

"Sorry." He skipped through all the *blah-blah*, his eyes straight onto the part referring to an email.

This is a message to the public, and to my beloved Eleanor, Tracey, and Alicia.

To Rabbit 76: I know you are alive. So am I, though I'll soon be dead, along with 19 other innocent souls, by the time this message reaches you. In the beginning, we were 34 but some died of stress, others were beaten as life in captivity led to rape, assault, and insanity.

We were taken 6 years ago. Some of us were involved in illegal tests on humans used for the purpose of finding cures and preventions for several diseases plaguing the world. Others were brought here to help, often involuntarily. None of us was meant to walk free again. Even if we did escape this place, we would never survive. HE would make sure of that.

I don't know where we are and only by luck did I find a way to reach the world.

I hope this will reach you, Rabbit 76.

I don't know your real name as all data has been destroyed to keep evidence of the tests under wraps. It's also believed you had died like another 98 people who were subjected to the tests. I don't know if you're aware of your potential, but I know you're alive. You're 42 years of age, Caucasian, and male. To my knowledge, you are in San Diego. You are the only survivor of tests on the cancer vaccine.

You cannot trust anyone. The purpose of the vaccine wasn't only to prevent cancer. Its purpose was to give the developer power to sell you out for, as you can imagine, a significant amount of money.

Your capture will lead to your death. Your death will lead to the loss of the biggest hope the humans ever had. The world needs you in the right hands, people who will use your potential to the fullest without sacrificing you. I believe in the good in people, despite us being victimized by who I call the biggest delusional, derogatory, smarmy miscreant with no respect for life in any type or form. How do you like this, Seb?

I added a list of the 34 people who were involved in what was called Operation Rabbit. I write in past tense as the remaining 19 are about to die.

Let me introduce myself. My name is Leon Powell, former Chief Execution Officer from NOKS O.T.

I'll always love you Eleanor, Tracey, and Alicia.

Below, Curtis read a small print line from the editor: *The list of names has been forwarded to the authorities and will remain undisclosed until further notice.*

Curtis trembled. He passed the paper to Laura, distanced himself to digest this revelation. Did Knox go as far as creating the email to catch him? A possible notion, but Curtis disregarded it. The email clearly stated NOKS's involvement with O.R. And the name Seb unmistakably referred to Sebastian Knox.

An idea crept up. Curtis could leave, give up selfish needs, avoid getting kicked in the gut by a status-chasing society. Maybe that's what his dad had done. Escape it all, sleep under the stars, not worry about anything. Not a good idea. The entire world was looking for him. In a matter of time Rabbit 76 would be linked to him. Merkow could leak and so could Sutton. Laura could sell him out. And there were Clifton and Green. Curtis would never be able to leave the country, jump on a boat, ship, plane. He could drive until he'd run out of gas, run like Thelma and Louise.

He toyed with the ideas before rejecting them. Something might come up. He could negotiate. Something he was good at. But who could he trust to negotiate with?

Laura joined him. "What do you want to do?"

He sighed. "Die."

"Is there a chance we can get hold of Wayne?"

"He's under protection because your dad believes there might be people out there who want him dead or use him to get to me. I need a phone to keep in touch with your dad."

Burner phones were a dime a dozen. She purchased it in a drugstore, leaving Curtis with one-hundred-and-twenty-three dollars in his pocket. He activated the phone and sent Sutton the text with the number. Seconds later he called.

Sutton said, "I assume you heard the news?"

"And read it."

"I'll keep this very brief. I'm sure you understand this is a game changer, and it's not in your favor. This will be our last conversation. As of five minutes ago the FBI has taken over. The only way for me to keep you safe is by cutting the cord."

"I understand. Any idea of where the email was sent from?"

"No lead yet, but it was his wife who received it, and she forwarded it to the media before talking to the authorities. In some ways it's good because you should have every cop out there on your side. They all want you alive."

Unless they want to make money out of me. "Where's Knox?"

"I presume he's hiding, though nothing yet confirms that Seb refers to Sebastian Knox."

Curtis laughed. "Who else could it be?"

"Don't get carried away yet. I'll contact you once I have more details. Until then I want you to disappear."

"Starting to run low on resources to do that, but I'll find a way." Before he could add a comment, Laura snatched the phone from his hands.

"Dad, it's me. I'm sorry for what I've done, and I'll explain it all to you, but right now we need a car so we can leave the city. And we need money." She pressed the phone back to Curtis's ear, who heard nothing but a man breathing and what sounded like sniffling.

"It's me back on the phone," Curtis said.

"I'm not sure whether to give her an earful or tell her how much I missed her."

Curtis heard him blowing his nose.

Sutton then said, "Can you give me a rough location where you are, so I can get a car delivered?"

"Ocean Beach."

"Make your way to Newport Avenue. Opposite the Ocean Beach Hotel is a parking lot. I'll let you know the model of the car once I've got one delivered. Stay low." He hung up.

"Ocean Beach Hotel?"

"We can get there along the beach. In case somebody recognizes you, you can drown that person."

He liked her sardonic humor.

~ * ~

The clear skies, no cloud, just blue, enveloped Curtis in indescribable comfort. Once more he slipped the boots and socks from his feet, wanted to feel the sand, the life it streamed through him. Laura did the same.

Carrying his footwear, Laura doing the same, he strolled with her along the beach as if the threats had stopped. Nobody expected a wanted man to promenade alongside the ocean in the company of a woman. To steer clear of surprises, he kept his baseball cap low, avoiding eye contact with anyone crossing their path.

To know any day, any minute, any second could be his last forced him to reflect on his life. What he still wanted to do. What he wouldn't be able to do. What he didn't want to miss out on. He stopped his stride, waited until she stopped too.

"What is it?" she asked.

He pulled her closer by her hands. "I'm a little rusty at these things, and I've never been good at it, but I want you to know I appreciate what you're doing for me, though you really piss me off sometimes." He flashed a grin. "I haven't been a gentleman myself, and I apologize for it. In all honesty, I can't think of anyone better at my side than you. If... If we get out of this alive, I wouldn't mind... you know... getting to know you better. You as Laura or who you were as Emily."

Her face was as blank as an unpainted canvas.

He scratched the back of his head. "I just wanted to get that off my chest in case there's no tomorrow, or if... Anyhow, I—" His buzzing phone put a halt to his next words. Typical father, making his disapproval clear without being at the scene.

Curtis answered.

"How far away are you?" Sutton asked.

"How far are we?" Curtis asked Laura.

"About ten."

"Ten minutes," he said to Sutton.

"Last lot, second to the right. Key is under the left front door in a magnetic holder. There's a bag under the passenger seat. And Curtis?"

"Yeah."

"If you let anything happen to Emily, I'll personally kill you." Sutton hung up.

Curtis smiled at Laura. "We should go," he said, but she wrapped her arms around his neck, pressed a kiss so intimate on his lips his jeans grew uncomfortably tight.

The hunger for more engulfing him, he answered her kiss with growing passion, fighting the yearning to lower her onto the sand and explore her body in front of everyone walking at the beach. It was nice to have a racing heart not caused by panic, but instead of answering his fervor, she gently pushed him away.

"We should go," she said.

He grinned. The first challenge was right ahead but he'd learned from his relationship with Jessica it was best to not deny equality to a woman.

~ * ~

As they approached the parking lot, Curtis focused on the last lot, second car to the right. There it was. Black, dark tinted windows. Sutton's Dodge Charger. Curtis hesitated in approaching it, expecting to find Sutton inside. He didn't.

Curtis slid into the driver's seat, while Laura tossed the newspaper onto the dashboard before she wiggled into the seat. Shortly after, she revealed a duffel bag from under it, searched through it, and fished out an envelope. She thumbed through its contents.

"Three grand," she said.

"Wow! Is he planning for a long haul?"

Her hand disappeared back into the duffel. This time she came up with a plastic pouch containing bandages and medication.

"He's good," he said, then snapped the packet from her hands to click out two pills before swallowing them dry. Not his favorite method, but he needed to settle the pain.

"There's a gun too."

"I'm starting to like your dad."

"I think you liked him before all this."

"Not too sure if it works both ways." He flicked her a mischievous smile, the fear he now had of her father still scratching at his dignity.

"I'm sure you'd be behind bars if it wasn't both ways," she said. From the envelope where the money was, she withdrew a note, read it, then passed it to him.

> *I deactivated any device enabling the car to be traced, and no one knows about the Dodge. Take care, both of you. Emily, I'm trying to understand what you've done. I'm sure one day I will. I can't wait to hold you in my arms. Eric*

"I'll make sure he'll be able to hug you," Curtis said.

"You see, the difference between you hugging me and him hugging me is he'll always miss Emily. I still have my thoughts, my memory, just not my body. I'll always look like a stranger to him. That's why I never got in touch with him." Her voice carried remorse as much as a firmness that she wasn't sure if she ever wanted to change that belief. "Let's go."

Chapter Thirty-Seven

As soon as Sutton entered the precinct, Mendez approached him, clenched him by his arm and forced him along, all the way to the parking lot.

Sutton hand-ironed his jacket after Mendez eased his grip. "What's going on?"

"The chief doesn't know it yet or anyone else."

"Spit it out."

"I went to B-1, thought maybe we overlooked something. Forensics did a sloppy job and, well, you and I did too. I found a cellphone under the cabinet where the woman hit her head. It belonged to a Felicity Pike. I have had little time to check her details, but she's from Manhattan."

"Was. What connects Laura with Felicity?"

"I have no idea. Where have you been anyway?"

Sutton didn't know how to reply, didn't like lying since he judged Mendez as being honest, generally. He deemed it wiser to remain silent.

"You know where Curtis is, don't you? Probably know where Laura is too," Mendez said.

"I don't know where either of them is." It wasn't a lie.

Mendez lowered his head. "Probably better if I don't know."

A siren's howl echoed through the parking lot. Sutton didn't need to check who it was. Donaghy always made a big deal of his arrival.

"Let's get back to work." Sutton pushed Mendez on to avoid confrontation with the chief. He wasn't in the mood to talk to him.

"Sutton!"

And Donaghy wasn't in a good mood either.

"You want me to wait?" Mendez asked.

"No. But you can come to my funeral."

"I'll bring flowers." Mendez smirked and left.

"Sutton!"

"Yes, Chief. I'm right here." Sutton tried to face his boss, but he stomped right past him.

"In my office," Donaghy ordered.

Sounds like fun. Sutton trudged a few feet behind Donaghy, hesitated before entering the office, waited until the chief had made himself comfortable, which he normally would behind his cluttered desk. But after he shut the blinds, he posed in front of it, his arms crossed.

As soon as Sutton closed the door, Donaghy stepped uncomfortably close, his breath carrying either beer or wine. Sutton inched back, the wall hindering him from escaping further.

The chief's fist bunched Sutton's collar, nearly cutting off his airway. "If I, at any stage, find out that you're hiding Curtis's whereabouts, you won't see tomorrow."

"I suggest you let go or I'll make sure you're up for assault," Sutton growled through his teeth.

"Oh yeah, try to prove it."

"I can easily bruise myself and everyone out there will see it."

"I can easily spare you the hassle and shoot you in the head and claim it was self-defense. It's your fault I have everybody climbing up my ass. Curtis was right under your nose but you let the sucker go." Donaghy let go of his clench. "Clean up the mess. Find him, or I'll make sure some accident happens."

Sutton stared coldly. Too proud to cough to clear his throat, he spoke through tormented vocal cords. "I'll make sure I chase down everybody responsible for this mess. Including you." The temptation to throw the badge at him came close, but he wanted to remain within the precinct. It guaranteed him a close eye on the developments.

As he reached for the door handle, he hesitated, and this time managed to face Donaghy. "Why are you more interested in finding Curtis than Rabbit 76?"

"Get out!"

Mendez was outside the door as Sutton left the chief's office. With no intention of exposing to Donaghy that he'd hurt him physically not mentally, Sutton strode to the coffee room before he allowed his body the coughing fit it forced on him.

"What the heck was that all about?" Mendez asked.

"He thinks I'm hiding Curtis."

"Are you?"

"Do I look like someone with a death wish?"

But Sutton didn't like the state of affairs. Donaghy's actions revealed he had to have a suspicion about Curtis and Rabbit 76.

Chapter Thirty-Eight

Fearing roadblocks more likely in the city, Laura directed the quickest way out. Once they hit the city's outskirts and she left him to decide how to continue the trip, Curtis weighed the options. Long or short, country roads or the highway. The highway meant more cops, and if not cops, more drivers and passengers capable of recognizing him. Country roads meant more time in transit, which meant longer exposure.

"How much longer is longer?" he asked.

"Hard to tell since we don't have a destination."

"Countryside," he said.

She navigated him through El Cajon, then Lakeside. A street sign announced Wildcat Canyon Road, but there were no wildcats and no visible canyon. When they reached a town called Ramona, he clenched his hands around the steering wheel. Despite the tinted windows, paranoia constantly with him, he kept the sunglasses and ball cap on.

Once past the town, the landscape changed to golden, fading into a dry brown. It must have been a long time since the grounds had been fed by enough rain to sprout grass. Trees shrank to bushes, shallow hills bracketed the road for at least ten or more miles. A sign ahead required decisions.

"If we go straight, we might end up in the desert, which I don't think is a good idea. We should get up the mountains. Better chances to hide there," she said.

He left Highway 78, steered onto Highway 79, then took a right when he read a sign for Palomar Mountain. "Have you been up there?"

She shook her head.

The road narrowed, the sides now more rocks and gravel, here and there the chance to stop, which Curtis did to suck in the breathtaking views.

He gasped, awed by a lake shimmering in the distance, which

Laura identified as Lake Hemshaw. "I had no idea it was so beautiful around here. You've been here?"

"I saw the sign."

He promised himself to pay more attention to the signage instead of being blindly driven by the desire to be away from the turmoil that gripped San Diego.

Once more the scenery changed, the road now lined with dominant pine trees, high and proud, countless years old, having withstood all kinds of weather and events during their lives. Then Laura got lost.

"How can you get lost when we don't even know where we're going?" Curtis snapped.

"I realized I've been up here before. This road leads to the Palomar Observatory. It's a dead end. We took the wrong turn somewhere."

"We?" He U-turned and headed back down the winding road. "Is there any cellphone reception out here?"

She checked the phone. "I have one bar kicking in and out. Why?"

"In case we run out of gas."

"We're not that far from civilization."

"It might be far enough if you keep directing us the wrong way."

"How can it be the wrong way when we don't know where we're going?"

"Before, you said you've never been up here and now you say the road is leading to a dead end." Luckily, the gun was still in the duffel shoved under her seat. Too complicated to retrieve it and shoot him right there and now. "I need a break, and we have to make plans," he said to take the wind out of his own sails.

He pulled to a stop at a graveled pit with a track leading into the woods, allowing him to park the Dodge far enough into the trees to remain unseen. In one simultaneous move, he ran a hand over his face, ripped the cap from his head with the other, and ruffled up his hair. No relief.

Annoyed, he pushed the door open, left the car and paced around. No relief. But before Laura could join him, he sat on a rock, and asked her for some painkillers. After she gave him the packet— surprisingly, she didn't throw it at him—he swallowed two pills down, as dry as he did earlier. Proof they were running around like headless chicken. Not once did they stop to buy water or food.

He puffed out air. "I like your idea about hiding in the hills. I admit I'm worried sick about Green and Clifton, and I don't understand why they haven't turned up again."

"I think they're licking their wounds. One has a headache; the other is trying to figure out if he can ever produce children."

He chuckled. It gave some answers as to what she did to Clifton. "I also admit I'm over hiding. Running from problems isn't solving the problem." He didn't get any further. As unlikely as it was, his phone buzzed.

"It's a strange way of cutting cords," he said to Sutton on the other end.

"I need to talk with Emily."

Curtis gave her the phone. He didn't hear Sutton's comments but cocked his head and pricked his ears when she said, "Felicity Pike? Who is she?"

After a few seconds, Curtis said, "Can I talk to him?"

Laura handed him the phone.

"It's me. Can you check if there's anything about Gregory Whitehurst in Manhattan?"

"Give me a moment."

A few seconds passed with tapping, accompanied by Sutton's unidentifiable mumbles. "Gregory Whitehurst. Hmm, he was found shot dead in his office in Manhattan four days ago. Authorities believe it was a burglary since his place was ransacked. Fill me in."

Curtis's eyes hazed. He cleared a throat plagued by a golf-ball-size lump of grief. "Gregory was my accountant. Felicity his long-term girlfriend. I've never met her, but he spoke a lot about her."

"Explain to me how she ended up dead in Laura's condo?"

"I have absolutely no idea. I'll put Laura back on." He handed the phone to her. "I'll go for a walk." Hardly able to will his legs to keep him going, he stumbled deeper into the forest.

What did Gregory have to do with all this? Curtis had gotten to know him as a humorous but switched on guy, also professional. It was only a few months after Curtis started his business that Gregory had approached him at a party, told him he was an accountant. At that point Curtis didn't dream he'd ever need an accountant, but he kept Gregory's number and contacted him when the business flourished.

They became good friends, despite not sharing many interests. Friday afternoon beer buddies, and Gregory let loose about the grief Felicity caused him sometimes, jealous of every woman crossing his path. He never revealed her face, never showed a photo, so Curtis would never have recognized her in the street. Essentially, it was a good thing. Until now the dead woman in B-1 had been a stranger to him.

Nothing made sense right now.

Gregory must have stumbled onto something unless he'd been put under pressure like: Tell me where Curtis is or you'll be dead.

Why hadn't Felicity just made a call, warned him, told him Gregory had been killed? Curtis had every type of social media killed, including his email address. Before he left New York, there was a trail of different cellphone numbers ranging from defunct to destroyed to burner phones. And Wayne... Only last night had he mentioned the missed calls he had from Gregory. It must have been Felicity on the other end, which confirmed she didn't have Curtis's phone number before Laura took his cellphone from him in the shopping mall.

Therefore, if Felicity knew he was here, she must have flown to San Diego. Would she still be alive if Wayne had answered those calls? Curtis promised himself to never tell Wayne.

Why did Felicity knock on Laura's door? Even though her goal was to reach B-3, she was already shot, must have gone for the first door possible to find help. B-1.

How did she enter the apartment building without the use of any doorbells, waste seconds before dying? The lock was broken. The door closed but didn't lock. She got in, banged at B-1's door, died either because she hit her head on the sideboard or because she was shot. It sounded so farfetched Curtis had to scoff. It also sounded so plausible despite the holes in his theory.

Who shot her? Whoever it was had been disrupted because Laura made the call for help, unfortunately not to the cops. He remembered nobody stopped him when he ran down the stairs to come to her aid. Nobody ran away either. The first person at the scene was Officer Peter Mendez, followed by Detective Eric Sutton. Unless, and that was the theory Curtis feared the most: Laura shot her.

He returned to the car where Laura waited.

"Are you okay?" she asked.

He didn't know what to say since two people were dead because of him. He took the phone from the passenger seat, the call he made answered in seconds. "Sutton. I need a favor. I believe Felicity either knew Gregory's killer or overheard the conversation in which he was killed. She flew to San Diego to warn me about something, but she was followed or somebody at the Manhattan end tipped off whomever at this end. She was shot before she got to B-3, tried to find shelter in B-1 unaware Laura was there or who she was."

"A far-fetched coincidence."

"I agree. However, can you get onto someone from the lab and find out how far they are with examining her body?"

"Are you after something specific?"

"I want to know where the bullet in her back ended up. Also, do you trust Mendez?"

"As much as he can be trusted. He's a cop."

"So are you."

"Ha. Ha."

"Call me back once you know more." Curtis hung up, Laura's stare on him.

"What are you after?"

"Not sure yet," he replied but hoped something specific would come back from his request. The wait was silent. Five minutes, eight minutes, twenty-three minutes. The phone buzzed.

Curtis answered, "Shoot."

Sutton said, "They have a hiccup. They can't find the bullet."

"That's because there is none. It wasn't a bullet that killed her. It was a capsule. The gun-like device Gordon used on me would have enough velocity for the capsule to perforate soft tissue even from a few yards away. The impact would have shattered the capsule when entering her body, trickling poison straight into her while the capsule dissolved. That's why her identity came back scrambled, giving the first result which Gordon tampered with, using the name Laura Webb." Once more he ignored Laura, who stepped closer. "Which got me in the shits."

"That's good thinking. I'll follow up on that, but what has Mendez to do with it?"

The sudden headache hitting Curtis created an avalanche of realizations. Had he been played all along? "Nothing. Forget I said it."

He hung up, bent inside the car where he yanked out the gun from the duffel. The gun was Green's. Sutton must have checked if it was a throw down. Curtis rammed it down his waistband as he trudged off. He wanted Laura to follow with no invitation. She would. She was a woman. Bingo. Within less than twenty seconds she called out his name. He waited until she caught up.

"What's going on?" Her face was blank, lost. She would be more lost once he shared his thoughts.

"You knew it, didn't you?" he barked. "All this time you kept it to yourself that Felicity was killed by the device."

"I didn't know who she was."

"That still doesn't explain why you kept it from me, from your father, why she died."

She said nothing.

Fine by him. "Where was Gordon the night Felicity was killed?"

"Home, I guess."

"You guess," he scoffed. "She died because of the device. Hours later, Gordon implanted the same shit into me. Who else has the equipment? It can't be Green or Clifton. So who?" *Besides you.*

"I honestly don't know."

"What about Knox?"

"Possibly."

He studied her face, searched for anything giving away deceit, but there was none. Nothing. For the first time he read true honesty. But he had to blame her for something because too much wasn't right.

"You know what I can't get my head around?" He pulled the gun from his waistband. "How come you and your father ended up here in San Diego? Don't tell me it was a coincidence because it can't be." Gun chest high, he pointed it at her, captured by hope as much as sorrow when her eyes grew big. "You set me up, both of you!" he yelled, his voice cracking under the pressure.

"For fuck's sake, Shawn, he's doing everything to help you, help me, out of this mess."

"Then why was he one inch from killing me?"

She backtracked, shock and disbelief at once in her face. Her eyes narrowed. "Obviously, he didn't kill you, and I don't think he would touch anyone unless he needed to."

"He demanded I tell him who you are," he spat. At least he got that off his chest. It felt good. "Would you have run from the scene in your condo if he hadn't turned up?"

"I needed you in safe hands. The cops provided that, and it gave me time to contact Gordon. The woman in my condo wasn't planned."

It flustered him that she avoided answering his question. "What was your plan? Become friends with me, take me to bed, seduce me, drug me so you could take as much of my blood as you want? Become Gordon's guinea pig? Your guinea pig?"

She rolled her eyes. "You don't seem to understand that Gordon and I wanted to help."

Wanted to help. It sounded more vague than a glass of water. "I doubt Gordon wanted to help. Felicity is dead. Gregory is dead, and I'm only alive because I was lucky. Can't you see that?"

"The only thing I see is a man suffering a bad concussion and losing perspective."

A wind gust whirled up dry leaves, the rustling snapping him out of his outburst. His arm gave in, the gun now pointing to the ground, but he held on to it when she tried to wrest it from his hand. She'd played him, betrayed him in every direction.

Or had she?

She didn't say a word, only passed the phone to him when it

buzzed. It was Sutton.

"According to the lab, it's ruled out the head injuries killed her. So they focused on the wound on her back. They confirmed the entry wound showed signs of an object traveling through several organs including the liver, and then stopped with no evidence what it actually was, which could corroborate your suspicion. Good work."

"All we have to find now is the shooter."

"Which won't be easy."

"What about Knox?"

"I doubt he'd want to get his fingers dirty. Anyway, leave that part to me. Why did you ask about Mendez?"

"Because he was very quickly at the scene."

"He's a good guy, but he's given me a reason to keep a closer eye on him since he claims to have found Felicity's phone in Laura's condo. Keep that to yourself. Okay?"

Very interesting. "Keep me posted." Curtis disconnected, a thought manifesting in his already blurred mind. He inched up to Laura while putting his words together. "You knew your father was in San Diego, didn't you? You knew if anything bad happened in your life he'd come. Right?"

No reaction from her. Fine then. He would find a way to shake the truth out of her. Somehow. She'd make a mistake or he could trick her into one.

He carried on, "When Felicity, at that stage a woman unknown to you, turned up at your door, you sent Sutton a text stating my innocence before or shortly after you contacted me. Right? That way you made sure I would end up in his hands and no one else's. Right?"

Still no reaction. Time for the strike. "Only the shooter and you knew about the woman in B-1, and I doubt the shooter sent Sutton a message. And… you were the only one who knew you were going to contact me."

No reaction. Again.

"I'm not stupid, Laura. Let's go back to the car." Frustrated and expecting her to follow, he walked ahead, but he couldn't hear rustling behind or arguing. He stopped, turned. She posed there like a statue, hands on her hips. Her eyes spat fire.

"Who do you think you are?" she yelled. "You just walked all over me, deciding something that's not true. Yes, I might have lied to you in the past, and I'm sorry about that, but don't accuse me of something I haven't done. Got it?"

His first impulse was to act in response to her outburst, but her snit, reminding him of a small child trying to prove a point, forced him to backtrack and bite back his laugh. He had to say it. "Has anyone ever told you how adorable you are when you're angry?"

"Has anyone ever told you that you can be a jerk?" She left him standing there, which was fine by him. At least she didn't say he was a jerk. Slight difference in her slander.

When he returned to the Dodge, Laura leaned against a tree. He noticed her shudder.

I'm not only a jerk, I'm a dickhead. He closed in on her, though not enough to invade her private space.

"I'm sorry." He wished she'd say something. "I'll be more—"

"What if all of this brings *her* back?"

He had to chew through her remark first to understand that maybe some of her actions were out of her control. Like his actions before, driven by an overload of stress, not to mention the concussion and the drugs doing his head in.

He laced his arms around her and whispered, "It's a face, Laura. It's not who you are." He was confident his words would calm her, but this woman knew how to bring him to the end of his tether.

"You know, a few days ago you wouldn't have looked at me if I still had Emily's face or body." She freed herself from his arms. "And there's no point denying that."

No point in proving her wrong either. Or was there?

Chapter Thirty-Nine

During the silent drive, Curtis added puzzles together, only to conclude he was stuck. Laura thumbed through the newspaper, the puff of air annoying his cheek every time she flicked a page. Worse, she held the paper high, a boxed in ad on the front page drawing his attention like a magnet. Inevitably, he had to read it.

He checked the traffic behind—no car there—lifted his foot from the accelerator and slowed the car to a crawl. It was just a small ad, located right beneath the article about Powell's email.

Sometimes in life, things don't appear the way they are.

The wording woke a memory in Curtis's mind, but he couldn't put a finger on it. There was a phone number. Nothing else. The car's clock read 3:48 PM. Before dinner, after lunch, the dead time in-between. Perfect. He ripped the paper from her.

"Hey," she protested.

He flipped it back to the front page, flung it onto her lap, and pointed at the article. "Call this number."

"What for?"

"Just call it." The burner phone was way behind modern otherwise he could have synchronized the device to the car's media, but he'd chosen this old style because the less modern technology meant fewer chances of being traced. Seconds later, he held the phone in his hand, his impatience gnawing as no one answered, ring tone after ring tone.

Finally, there was a click, followed by a timid female voice. "Yes?"

"I'm very sorry to disturb you, ma'am. I'm replying to your ad in the paper."

"I don't know of any ad."

A gruff voice echoed in from the distance. "Who is it?"

It suddenly sounded as if she were miles away. Maybe she held her hand on the speaker, but he heard her murmuring, "A man. Says he's…"

"Who is this?"

Curtis connected the cantankerous voice to an older man. "I'm replying to your ad in the paper."

"What's your father's name?"

Taken aback Curtis said, "Charles."

"Wait." An unbearable pause. Then a muffled, "Why don't you go feed the chicken?"

The woman with the timid voice came through loud and clear. "Why don't you simply tell me that you want to be alone? It's the seventh call today, and you're acting all suspicious about it. Whose phone is…?"

Her voice trailed off. More silent seconds. The man apparently waiting for the woman, his wife presumably, to be out of earshot. Then he said, "Is your line secure?"

Curtis guessed this man was no novice when it came to Big Brother listening. "It's a burner."

"Good. How did you get this number?"

Strange question. "It was in the *San Diego Tribune*."

"Where were you born?"

Curtis startled at the man's immediacy. "I was born in Allen."

"Last place you saw your father?"

Who is this guy? "London, Kentucky."

"How many years ago?"

"Thirty."

"Your first kiss?"

How could this man possibly know something so personal? "Jocelyn was her name. I was thirteen. Are you going to—"

"You were a bit of a late starter in that regard." The man chuckled. "I'm beyond relieved to hear your voice, Shawn. Glad they haven't caught you yet. And make damn sure they don't."

"What am I missing here? How do you know me? Who are you?"

"I thought you already figured that out since you called me."

"I haven't been able to connect you to my life, but what you wrote sounds familiar."

"Are you driving?"

"Yes."

"Pull over. I don't want you to cause an accident."

The voice was urgent enough for Curtis to pull over. He

switched the phone to speaker, wanted Laura to hear the conversation. "Okay."

"What do you know about your parents?"

In vain, he tried to connect any dots. "My father was an engineer, my—"

"Charlie was a very smart man and was anything but an engineer. He was a professor, scientist, physician. At the same time, he was a pro in IT and worked for companies you don't know exist. He was like a sponge, learning about anything was his life. Bugs, viruses, as much the human ones as computer bugs, and I don't know how many other things. He was successful and witty and purported. An engineer to cover up what he really was. To be honest, I don't even know what he really was, who he was, who he worked for. FBI, CIA, some dubious organization. I honestly don't know.

"However, what I'm telling you next is not something you want to hear, but it's been long overdue for you to know the truth." An audible sigh came through the speaker. "I'm sorry to tell you that you're not *who* you think you are or *what* you think you are. Your father isn't your father; your mother isn't your mother. In fact you don't have parents."

The pause fried Curtis's patience. "What are you talking about?"

"It was always in your father's interest to remain undiscovered, and family didn't fit into his life. But you can't control love. Iris... her desire to have a baby nearly brought their marriage to a breakdown, but he couldn't give her what she wanted because he was shooting blanks. The two had a bond not many couples have, at least not nowadays. He did anything he could for her, especially since his spurious profession required him to be away often."

"You knew him personally?"

"Sometimes in life, things don't appear the way they are."

Hearing the words from this voice unraveled the deepest memories. A man with black hair, black beard, long enough to knot it up. He was only present when his father was. Curtis remembered him as a teacher in ways his parents weren't. Enjoyed it when he took him fishing, hunting. He always told him things weren't the way they were but added something to the phrase.

Curtis said, "And sometimes it's wiser to accept things how they are rather than trying to change them. You are Uncle Buck."

"I don't know if you ever knew my real name. Arthur Buckley. You always called me Uncle Buck, though you probably are aware I'm not your uncle."

Curtis ran a hand over his face and cast a brief look at Laura to see if she'd discerned his goosebumps. She smiled back.

Buckley continued, "I honestly wished the circumstances were different. Are you ready for the truth?"

"Shoot."

"This may not be easy to take, and I'm keeping this as short as possible because there's no point in sweet-talking anything. You were created. You were an experiment. Developed to withstand diseases, especially the ones related to DNA mutation like cancer. There were others, let's call them embryos Charlie could have chosen, but he destroyed the others and picked you. Either purposely or not, he never told me. I never asked. I then implanted the fertilized embryo into Iris's uterus and less than nine months later you were born. Iris was your surrogate mother. Charlie's sperm was never used."

Curtis wasn't sure if he should vomit or be relieved about finally closing in on the events that turned his life upside down. "Who is my father?"

"No one. Artificial sperm was created a long time ago, though were rarely used for the purpose of IVF etc. Anyhow, are you prepared for more news or do you need a break and want to call me back later?"

How much worse could it get? "Tell me."

"One problem is you are theoretically stolen property. You actually belong to the government because you were created in their facility. If the government wants to use your hair, there's nothing you can do. If they want to use your eyes, there's nothing you can do. If they want to chop off your balls, there's nothing you can do. You don't have rights. You are government property, and they want you back. Besides the fact some people want you dead to hide your existence."

The mix of fury and disappointment nearly prompted Curtis to jump out of the car. He would have gladly accepted being hit by oncoming traffic, if only there was any.

"I'll call you back." He pushed the door open, his legs buckling beneath him as he struggled out of the seat, buried his head in his arms, but he was too devastated to weep. Laura's touch on his shoulders gave him no comfort. Unintentionally, he shoved her aside as he scrambled to his feet.

"I'm fucking nobody!" He kicked up dust, sending a stone flying over the road. Kicked up another and hit a tree. His next kick nearly dislocated his kneecap. "Fucking assholes! Fucking shit! Fuck this shit!" He collapsed to his knees and tears won him over. "I'm done."

"You are not."

Right now, he would have liked to tell her to piss off. A bottle of whatever strong enough to blur his mind from this nightmare was what he needed.

"Didn't you hear what he said?" he growled. "I don't exist. I'm not even human. Made, created. Some species. Hah, and here is the real irony. I once said to Wayne *you* were an alien. Look at me! Who is the fucking alien?" He shot up, stomped off.

A few yards, then a couple more, until he realized he'd said something horrible. He stopped, looked back. She stood there, proud, tall, straight shoulders.

"How do you think I've felt for the past few years, huh? Do you think it was easy to look in the mirror and see somebody who's not me? That face I actually always admired and now hate because it's not mine? Call me an alien all you want, but at least I learned to live with it. So fuck you, man. You either get your shit together or jump off the cliff."

I'm starting to like you more every second. "I'm sorry," he whispered. "I'm sorry," he said louder.

"Sorry me later and get back on that phone and call him again so we can work on this."

Back in the car, he redialed the number. "Me again."

"That was quicker than I thought," Buckley said.

"I guess that makes me half human."

"There's no doubt about you being human. And what I told you about the government may never happen. I don't know if Knox will be smart enough to play that card, but you need to be aware of it and lawyer up should you ever get caught."

"You already mentioned Knox. Who else knows about it?"

"Besides Charlie, I assume Hank Hiddleston."

"Who's he?"

"He was once the Commissioner of the PRDA, or actually the FDA before it became the PRDA. All I know is there were differences between the two and Hiddleston quit before the transfer from the FDA to the PRDA. As far as I know he's since enjoying retirement. Knox, Hiddleston, and Charlie created you, but Charlie told me Hiddleston never wanted to proceed with giving you a life, especially since DNA editing was illegal back then and still is, including artificially creating human life out of stem cells. The latter isn't actually illegal, but a human was never supposed to grow into an adult and walk the world. Apparently, Hiddleston was a bit of a chicken and wanted to pull out and destroy the entire experiment, but your father had stolen you before it happened. Knox always blamed Hiddleston for it, never suspected Charlie behind it. At least not for a while."

"What are you suggesting we do?"

"Running is probably the best bet. I don't know if Charlie would have a better idea."

Curtis scoffed. "He hasn't been around in thirty years and back then he packed his bags and left. I doubt he has any interest in helping. I don't even know if he's still alive."

"He is."

A spasm charged through Curtis. "Do you know where to find him?"

"No. But I know he's alive."

Curtis wasn't sure if he wanted that. Love or hate? What do you choose? "The system doesn't tell me anything about him besides lies about some family in Brooklyn, that my mom was a nurse. Apparently, I graduated, which I never did."

"He covered your every step for as long as he could."

Wayne's words came to Curtis's mind: "I think your whole life has been a lie, has been staged, controlled, monitored, call it what you think fits." Maybe there was some truth to it.

Curtis said, "What do you mean, he covered my every step? Did he put the photo in the yearbook? How did he get my photo?"

"How hard is it to get a photo? How hard is it to make it look as if you were at the graduation? You know enough about computers."

He did. "And before it came to printing the book he added the photo."

"Correct."

"Why did he leave?"

"It was the only way to keep you safe. Wherever he was, Knox or Hiddleston suspected you were too."

This didn't mean Curtis forgave him. His devastated mother tried to stay strong and support them both. He started working before he reached the teens to help financially. "His name isn't taking me anywhere."

"You won't find him under Charles Dylan Curtis. He only used that name in… let's call it real life. All his other activities were under different names, which he changed all the time. Knox only knew him under a different name."

"Which was?"

"Frank Gillespie. No need to look him up. He made sure no traces are found, other than his supposed death when he disappeared out of your life."

Curtis wasn't surprised. "Does he ever contact you?"

"Sometimes."

"How often?"

"Every few weeks, months. Sometimes it takes four, sometimes six."

"When was the last time you heard from him?"

"Two days ago."

The comment, worse than a slap in the face, just sat there for a few dead seconds. A knife in the heart, that's what it felt like to Curtis. The words from Buckley washed over him, all the excuses why his father had to leave, why they couldn't be seen together. All the la-de-dah was nothing but thirty years too late, and since the words didn't come from his father, they meant nothing to him. Curtis observed Laura. Seemingly consumed by Buckley's words, she wiped a tear or two from her face and turned her head away.

"Curtis?"

Now he paid attention. "Yes."

"Does the name Share-On ring a bell?"

How could it not? Share-On used to be Curtis's main investor besides Knox. He risked a surreptitious glance at Laura. She was once more fully engaged in what Buckley had to say, but Curtis couldn't send her away—it would only lead to suspicion. He decided to play the game, despite the conversation leading into a direction he didn't want to disclose.

"Yes," he said.

"It had taken a while before you understood the pattern, but eventually you did. The rest was a walk in the park."

Curtis had to mull over that. "You're saying the success of my company was the making of my father?"

"The majority was your making."

"How does that make sense? How did he know I was getting into shares?"

"He didn't. He made you do it by sending flyers to your home about the share market. Pop-ups on your computer screen, which you eventually blocked. But the seed was planted. It's funny how the brain works. When you constantly see something you start checking it out. He knew you were an opportunist. Curious. You would see the potential."

"You gain, you share." Curtis remembered the flyer in his mail, which he ended up framing and pinning to the wall.

He also remembered the flyers about the stock market and the annoying pop-ups on his computer. When he discovered the company Share-On, he had the idea to buy some of their shares.

It was the start of an incredible journey until… "Why did he crash it?"

"He didn't. It was nothing but bad luck."

"I don't believe that. It came crashing down too quickly. The final straw was Share-On making a move it never made before. Or actually, it didn't make a move at all."

"If he did take it down, then he did it for a reason."

"Wouldn't mind knowing that reason," Curtis mumbled, realizing Buckley had heard when he said, "He wouldn't have done it to hurt you."

Curtis bit back the comment that he'd been hurt by his father more than he wished for. Starting with that he wasn't his father after all. "Do you know anything about Doctor Phil Merkow?" He wanted to mention Laura but refrained.

"No one I've heard of."

"What about the accident I had six years ago. When I nearly died."

"Charlie told me about the accident. He was worried sick. So was I."

Curtis frowned. "You know nothing about a test involving blood transfusion containing a substance which acts as a cancer vaccine?"

Buckley's voice sounded like a cat treading on a branch about to snap when he said, "Oh my god, why didn't I add it all up? You are Rabbit 76."

Curtis was genuinely confused. "I thought it's the reason you put the ad in the paper."

"Charlie saw the 'Wanted poster' in the paper, and so did I. It was time you knew the truth. I had no idea then about Powell and that you are Rabbit 76. It's a coincidence my ad and his article came in the same paper on the same day. But you understand the full extent of what I've just told you? Do you know what that means?"

It was the one reason why he survived the test. Question was, did Knox know about his identity back then?

"I think I do." Curtis continued to not lose momentum, "Knox has been trying to kill me since he found me after I had a DNA test. Some guy killed Gordon McNamara, and now I have Clifton Wright and Martin Green after me. They were involved in Operation Rabbit. Any of the names ring a bell?"

"I've heard of McNamara. All this must have been Knox's making years later, but this puts you in a real predicament."

Tell me about it.

Curtis ran out of questions, confused about the developments.

"What are your plans?" Buckley asked.

"I want to find the people trapped in Operation Rabbit."

"According to the message from Leon Powell, they're all dead."

"According to the message from Leon Powell, they were alive when he wrote the email."

Curtis wasn't sure if it was a snort or a laugh coming from the phone before Buckley said, "You haven't changed one bit."

"What else am I supposed to do?"

"All I can suggest for now is to stay alive. Contact me in the morning, and I'll see what I can find out in the meantime. And Shawn, promise me one thing: do *not* approach Knox or you'll never walk away again."

"Promise." He crossed his fingers not bothering to put his hands behind his back.

Buckley didn't see him anyhow, but obviously Laura did as she made her disapproval loud and clear as soon as he disconnected the call. "You heard him. Stay away from Knox!"

"He's my only lead."

"You don't know that for sure. And before we do anything we have to find a place to rest, eat, and it's getting cold. Not to mention your bandages need changing. These are the first things we need to work on."

Curtis lifted his hands, palms out. "Easily solved. We sleep in the car; I can keep you warm. The dressing we can change right here, and we have a gun. I'm sure we can find a rabbit or a deer we can shoot. I'd honestly prefer a deer. We'll manage to make a fire and cook it up. Problem solved."

Her demeanor, carrying the what-the-hell-was-that-all-about message, deflated him. In the past forty-plus hours, every expectation he had about life had turned to dust.

Robbed of everything he believed in, he swallowed once, twice, fought not to crumble, but his eyes blurred with sudden tears. "I could do with a hug."

Chapter Forty

Sutton sat on the love seat in his apartment, sipping on his second beer for the night. He'd expected Curtis to call back with the latest results, but an SMS was all he received: *Check out Hank Hiddleston former FDA Commissioner.*

It didn't take long before Sutton found Hank Hiddleston on the web and with it, what connected him to Knox. Both were born in Dallas and attended the same school but different classes. Their ways parted when adulthood asked them to take responsibility. Knox had no other option than stepping into his father's footsteps and dedicating his life to science, but he took NOKS to a higher level and to one of the leading pharmaceutical companies in the U.S.

Hiddleston had also taken on science but then had gone underground for a while until he reappeared as a professor and after many years, the Commissioner of the FDA. He resigned before the transfer from the FDA to the PRDA was complete.

Sutton sent Curtis a text asking him if he was after something specific. Curtis replied he would fill him in with details tomorrow but was wondering about Hiddleston's location. Shortly after that text, another one came in: *Please check on Wayne. Give him my number and ask him to contact me tomorrow.*

Sutton lifted his head. Wayne sat opposite, his legs sprawled over the couch, laptop on his lap. "Curtis wants to know how you are."

"I'd feel better if you'd let me contact him."

"Not yet," Sutton said and typed into the phone: *Will do. He's okay.* He lowered the phone and looked over at Wayne once more. "Were you able to find anything for me?"

"How is he?" he asked, concern furrowing his forehead.

"He's still alive." Undoubtedly Wayne wasn't happy about being kept here, sleeping in his spare bedroom until things were over, but with Clifton Wright and Martin Green still out there, Sutton deemed them a bigger threat than Knox. "Anything?"

Wayne said, "We have an amazing thirty-five-thousand clients joining up with Curtis in a span of one month before and after Knox joined."

"Wow."

"I remember Curtis said he'd hit the jackpot, but I didn't realize it was this big. I would have smelled a rat if I had more insight into his client list then. However, beyond that I only see the usual fluctuation. You can typically survive a slump here and there, but the problem was for some reason no new clients joined about two months before it all went pear-shaped. I mean literally no one. I remember Curtis called me in panic, trying to figure out what was going on. He assumed hackers were blocking his site. His research remained fruitless. In that same week, he started adding notes: 'they usually buy', next entry he wrote 'why aren't they buying?' His predictions were suddenly off, really off. Next entry he wrote 'Sayonara'."

"Any reference to who he meant by they?"

Wayne shook his head.

Sutton sighed. "I'm not very computer literate and know nothing about shares or blogs and all that stuff."

"It was an app as well."

"Whatever. What would stop people from buying?"

"I would agree with Curtis and say he was hacked by someone so good, we still haven't found the glitch."

"Is it theoretically possible people still paid into Curtis's account, or whatever you call it, and the money went somewhere else?"

"Curtis knows more about such things, but I'd say it's possible."

"Is his app or website or whatever still up and running?"

"He had to shut it all down. Legal stuff."

Sutton wondered if his legal arm was long enough to get more information. "What was his company's name again?"

He was aware this question would reap him a glower, which he promptly received, but with names and information spinning through his head, let alone worry, he put up with the glower like with a bad tempered wife.

"tri-share sc. All lower case."

"'Try' as in, attempt or test?"

"No, as in trifecta. Curtis likes word games like this. Tri means three, so it would make people believe they had more than one chance to make money. On the other hand, tri sounds the same as try, so it's a silent invite to people to try and share it. You get the drift?"

Sutton nodded. "And the S and C stands for Shawn Curtis?"

"He added it to keep him out of trouble with any other company using 'share' in their business names."

"Can you check if Hank Hiddleston was a client?"

"Hang on." Wayne typed something into the laptop, presumably Hiddleston's name. "No. Who is he?"

"Somebody Curtis mentioned." Sutton felt out of his comfort zone. He didn't know much about how such a business operated. "Did he have a main investor?"

"Share-On. Same thing here with the name. Share it on. I think it's the reason why Curtis came up with the name tri-share"

"Who are they?"

"It was his Golden Horse; that's what he called it. He said it sometimes seemed as if there was a pattern. Accordingly, he was buying and selling their shares, but he was never able to find out who's behind it, and neither could I. However, since you've given me the privilege to use data I assume I should never be able to access…"

"Well, keep that to yourself."

"Sure, and I do appreciate your trust. But since I have nothing else to do than sit here and twiddle my thumbs, I researched some companies. I mean, it would take me a year or more to go through all of them, but I randomly picked out fifty. I figured in about five of them Knox is involved. Either as chairman or investor. You work it out yourself. Five out of fifty in one million."

Sutton sipped from his beer, brooding, while doing a search on Share-On. It revealed it was nothing but a fictional company. Names led to mailboxes and addresses on the Cayman Island, which Sutton called Crook Island as it was a haven for crooks to avoid paying taxes and hide their business activities. Something Curtis wouldn't have cared about too much with his main concern being money coming in.

Sutton made a mental note to ask Curtis about the company. Maybe he knew more than he exposed. But right now, Sutton wanted to grant himself some sleep before his legs wouldn't carry him any longer. It had been a big day.

He'd shaken off the argument he had with Chief Donaghy. Who cared about him? But the squabble with Curtis this morning clung to him like bad breath. Remorse niggled at Sutton. He'd taken it too far. He'd seen it in Curtis's eyes. The hope it was a game, changing to pure begging for mercy.

But carting over six years of hope that NOKS could have lied about Emily's fate had blinded Sutton. The moment he'd captured Laura and held her in his arms, he knew she wasn't Laura. The idea Curtis knew more than the father who thought his daughter dead felt like a knife in

Sutton's heart. Now that he knew, he didn't know if it was a relief because he still didn't know how Emily became Laura. He knew so much and still knew nothing.

One day, hopefully, she'd tell him the truth. Until then it was inevitable to keep her as much as Curtis alive, though the odds were slimmer every day, every hour. Green and Clifton were out there and there was no sign of Knox. Sutton couldn't decide who was worse.

Chapter Forty-One

The full moon fought the clouds in an uncompromising battle to own the horizon, piercing the dark with laser-like beams, painting silver streaks across the black road. Curtis felt invigorated after Laura's strong but undemanding embrace, a balm to his weeping soul. He had no idea how long they stood there, but it had been long enough to wet her T-shirt with his tears.

They parted without intimacy and spoke for the first time when they were back in the car where she changed his dressing before they drove on. They stilled their hunger in a roadside cafe so empty he was confident of their anonymity. Nevertheless, he never stripped off his cap or sunglasses. If the elderly woman serving them had called the cops, they'd have taken a long time to get to this shithole—wherever it was—and he'd be long gone.

To find a bed wasn't as easy; there were mainly camping grounds, and they weren't equipped to pitch a tent. He had no issue taking a nap in the car but the little kiss and the hug they previously had didn't mean she was comfortable around his sleep-sounds which, according to Wayne, Curtis had. There'd be little choice if they didn't find accommodation.

The breeze through the half-open window chilled him despite the hoodie, but the cold kept him alert now that sleepiness began to nip at him. "I'm not sure if we're heading closer to the city which means people, which means they could recognize me. I have no idea where we are but don't want to use the GPS."

"There," she said, pointing to a barely noticeable wooden sign.

Rosa's Cottages. A gravel road led into darkness and after less than a mile, he spotted two pickup trucks parked in front of what appeared to be an office. A faint light sparkled in a small room with a sign above it. OPEN. There were cottages nestled within the trees, illuminated by moonlight. Some were A-frames, some had patios with stairs leading up to the door, others were too far away, only silhouettes recognizable.

"Should we give it a try?" he asked.

"I'll do the talking. You stay in the car."

Curtis accepted being told what to do, for as long as he agreed with her suggestions.

He parked in front of the office and watched Laura jog toward the door, his gaze on her butt. Soon after, she disappeared inside.

Minutes later she came back, a key dangling from a finger, a big grin on her face. "I don't know what it is with number 8, but that's the cottage she gave us."

"Probably cost an arm and a leg."

"Nope. She was about to close. Wanted one twenty. I said she either takes eighty or nothing. She took the eighty. Cash and no questions asked."

"I should leave the bargaining to you." He observed his surroundings. "Though, by the looks of it, this place doesn't deserve sixty."

"Apparently there's a family dispute over the land, and they aren't allowed to do renovations, etc. until they settle the case."

Amazing how much Laura could find out within a short time.

Cottage number 8 was at the bottom end of five or so buildings. Three stairs led up to the porch. Curtis opened the door. The cottage had one resemblance to the room they stayed in a few nights ago: the reek of mold hung on the walls and curtains. It had a dining area, a living section with a couch, and a TV.

In the back of the room he discovered the bathroom and the bedroom; the mattress promised comfort, and the bedding smelled fresh. "Not so bad after all. You can have the shower first. Are the painkillers in the car?"

"I'll go get them."

"I'm no invalid," he snapped, added right away, "Sorry. I'm tired, confused. Wish I could have a proper shower too. Dunk my head under the stream and wash off my anger, instead of scraping the crust from my filthy skin by hand. I feel like a pig." He lowered his head, welcomed her arms around his neck, then a kiss on his cheek.

"We can buy some waterproof bandages tomorrow. For now, what if we wash each other?"

Was it a genuine offer or a trick to find out if he was after one thing? Maybe *she* was after one thing, but he trusted his insight into human nature and put her offer down to her yearning for comfort.

"Don't take it as a rejection, but what I need is a few minutes alone. I don't feel like I'm the man I always believed I was." He pecked her cheek and whispered, "I'm sorry." He watched her disappear through the bathroom door, unsure what to do next.

~ * ~

Laura closed the door behind her.

What was I thinking? She didn't want to give him the impression that she intended to throw herself at him. She wanted to atone for what she'd screwed up, wanted to soothe him, show him he wasn't alone, that he could cry on her shoulder, that she needed a shoulder to cry on too. Gordon's death preyed on her. So did the hurt over his lying to her. How could that have happened? Why hadn't she seen her mentor for what he was?

She'd struggled when she woke with a different face six years ago, hated it at first, despite the envy she experienced every time she looked at the real Laura. Over the years, she accepted her new appearance, adapted to the smoothness of it, while she missed the face she'd grown into blinking back at her in the mirror.

What she didn't miss was her previous plump and out of shape body. After the transformation it was hot and curvy. But the intimate spots challenged her. To explore the new sensations scaring her at first, she had used some drunken idiot to learn how this new Laura felt. It had left her pleasantly surprised, wondering what pleasures she'd have missed out on if she'd remained Emily.

She could only imagine Curtis's distress. To be told he'd been created, to learn he had no blood-related parents, and no history. What did this make him?

She undressed and stepped into the shower, the man who was more than dismayed, remaining in her mind.

~ * ~

Curtis had left the cottage as soon as Laura shut the bathroom door. He didn't want to wander off too far in case somebody, like Clifton or Green, had managed to track them. Curtis didn't care about himself, didn't know who he was anymore, but there were a lot of things wrong with crying in front of a woman. It wasn't what his father had taught him. Women needed a man unshaken, unprovoked by any situation. "If you have to be a wimp, go somewhere away from the gender who needs you strong."

It sounded so wise back then. But the man Curtis looked up to as a child wasn't even his father, and he had been wrong. It had felt good when he cried in Laura's arms, but he needed her focused and not perturbed by his emotions pushing for a way out.

A stone structure resembling a decorative wishing well glittered in the moonlight and caught his eye. He sank down and backed against it. Today he'd lost his identity. His being. His existence. He shook his head, the move shaking more tears out of him.

Get your act together. He couldn't.

Who am I? What am I? He raised his tremulous hands, balled them into a fist, wanted to thrust them into his face but rammed them into the ground. He rolled to his knees, powered one fist into the well's stone wall. Again, again. *I'm nothing. I'm nothing.*

His head in his knuckle-bleeding hands, he cowered, looked up to the sky. The longer he observed the sparkling stars filtering through the unreachable treetops the more his eyes tricked him with the fantasy of the stars coming down on him, wrapping him in strength and faith. Not everything was lost.

~ * ~

Before he entered the cottage half an hour later, he stuck his head in to see where Laura was and spotted her lying on the bed, her chest moving in relaxed regularity. He sneaked to the bathroom, washed himself as best he could, bandaged his knuckles, and dressed again in the same clothes, unwilling to enter the bedroom naked. He didn't know what she expected from him, but he needed a good rest, which the couch didn't seem to promise.

She slept on the left side of the bed, her back to the middle. A bad choice. He could only sleep on his right because of his injured shoulder, therefore she would face him if she rolled over and be exposed to whatever sleeping habits he had. The bed was also narrower than a usual queen-sized, which meant he didn't know where to place his arms unless he would hug her. Couch? *Don't be a coward.*

She had covered herself with half the blanket, leaving him guessing if she was undressed. To give her the clear message he wasn't a debauchee but also wasn't rejecting her, he shoved the other half of the blanket to her side, ensuring she could use it if she wanted to.

His head pillowed on his right arm, he kept his left close to his body, watched her rhythmic breathing. It tranquilized him enough to fall asleep.

Chapter Forty-Two

Night had settled in, and the spits of rain left freckles on the road. Green had ordered Clifton to drive, his patience running thin. The failure of capturing Curtis had led to a massive fallout between the two.

When Green came to after being knocked out by Curtis, he had to deal with some moron, who tried to call the cops. Before he could do it, Green had snatched the phone from his hand and threw it wide and far. "Not needed," he'd barked at him, stomped off, and looked for Clifton.

Minutes later, in the next block, the Rover's lights had flashed. Green swung the door open, saw Clifton clutching his groin with one hand, his face blood red. No sign of Laura. It added up. She attacked the most vulnerable spot a man had. Clifton doubled over with a bent dick, and she escaped. Idiot.

The moment Green had slumped into the seat, Clifton barked, "How the fuck could you lose him?"

"At least I was outsmarted by a guy and not a chick." Green blocked Clifton's swing with a backhander straight on his cheek. Correction. Bad aiming. It ended on his eye.

Now that Green had taken over the tablet, leaving Clifton doing nothing to do but drive, moping about his shiner, he hoped he could turn the game around.

The start into their new life wasn't as easy as Green had planned. The lack of familiarity to the San Diego area worked against them, and he soon had enough of "babysitting" Clifton.

He was supposed to maintain the signal to the base, where Powell awaited results, and not lose track of Rabbit 76. Clifton hadn't been able to deliver updates to Powell either, though his message in the news could be the answer to it.

Green wondered if Powell was still alive, if anyone within O.R. was still alive, but Clifton seemed more interested in… Green still tried to figure out whether getting laid as quickly as possible took precedence or succeeding was higher on his agenda. Clifton's lack of survival-skills didn't help. Since they'd regained consciousness at a beach somewhere in San Diego, Green had to take care of essentials.

Stealing breakfast or dinner, and a car was crucial to their survival. Including a gun, which turned out to be a stupid mistake since he'd lost it to Curtis. He also admitted, though silently, that he underestimated Curtis in every way.

"Got him?" Clifton asked.

"I've got something," Green said, concentrating on the tablet's small screen delivering a weak signal dropping in and out. Technical issues, mountains. What next? "I'm not sure if it's him or some interference from another source. To be honest, I'd rather get a lock on her. We want to make sure we get to Curtis before she does because she'll sell him out like a zillion-dollar lobster frittata, and he'll be the caviar on top."

As Clifton didn't reply, Green looked over at him. The bruise was now in full swing, but it didn't stop him constantly flicking his eyes to the rearview mirror. "What's up?"

"Not sure if we got a tail," Clifton said.

Green checked behind. Headlights gained on them, a car driven faster than the legal speed on this short straight stretch of street. "Can't be him. He's about fifteen miles ahead if the signal can be trusted."

"Could be HIM HIM," Clifton said, his voice taking on a streak of panic.

"TOX-1 is dead, and HIM HIM doesn't get his hands dirty."

"From your lips to God's ears."

Green flipped down the sun visor, focused on the mirror and the reflection of two dots. "It's someone in a big rush. Just let him pass."

A few edgy seconds went by before Clifton said, "You know HE can find us."

"Our signal would have been kicking in and out the same as Curtis's."

"It's HIM." Clifton clenched his hands around the steering wheel, the car picking up speed.

"I want you to calm down. Even if it is HIM, we have what HE wants."

"No, we don't."

"We have the signal Powell's after. If HE had it too, HE would be after Curtis and not us, but you rerouted the signal so only we know where the Rabbit is. Right?" Green translated the silence as a yes, though he struggled with Clifton's erratic handling of the car, revving the engine up and down as if he'd never driven before. "I'd appreciate if you'd slow down so if it *is* HIM, I can take care of it."

"We wanted to sell Curtis to HIM."

"HE's not in the position to make deals. To be honest, since Powell spilled the beans, there has been a slight adjustment in the game. HE wants Curtis dead while we should be more interested in keeping him alive."

"So *we* can sell him off," Clifton said.

"Finally we're on the same page."

Clifton eased his foot from the gas.

Instantly, the lights swelled in the mirror. Green held on to the confidence that the car would simply overtake and mind his own business, but the minute he identified the speeding car as a white Tahoe, he regretted slowing down as much as the change from a Range Rover to a Toyota Camry.

"Floor it!" he told Clifton just as the Tahoe plowed into the Toyota's rear.

The impact and inertia forced Green's body into the seat, the rebound catapulting him forward. A blow on his head fogged his perception, but not so much he didn't recognize Clifton's yelp. Alarmed Green tried to turn but the fog won.

~ * ~

Green didn't know how long he'd been blacked out, but when he came to his world was upside down, the seatbelt cutting into his collarbone, which he guessed was broken, besides other bits hurting like hell. The worst was his right leg, caught between... he wasn't sure. He could have sworn a tree branch poked out from it. Wheezing sounds caught his attention.

Clifton hung in the seatbelt, his eyes open a slit. He wheezed again and Green acknowledged in all the years he killed people, he never watched someone die. Clifton wheezed once more... It was his last.

I'm sorry, pal. Rest in peace.

There was a crunch. In the corner of Green's eyes he perceived legs, then a head. His neck hurt too much to twist it all the way, but he knew who the legs belonged to.

"Quite a mess."

Green didn't reply, wasn't sure if he could speak; something cold and solid pressed onto his throat.

"You know what I well and truly regret? I should have denied Laura's request to lock you up in O.R. You were my best man. You were loyal, had some brains." A hand reached into the car, retrieving the tablet lying next to Green's head. "Now that I have what I need, I don't have any use for you. I don't think you would walk out of here alive anyway. You can thank me in heaven for releasing you from the pain."

A bang nearly shattered Green's eardrums. He tried to inhale. It didn't work. Tried to exhale. It didn't work. He managed to tilt his head enough to make eye contact with his killer. His pride kept him from exposing the torture he endured as he drowned in his own blood.

You'll rot in hell.

Chapter Forty-Three

Clatter woke Curtis, but his efforts to block out the noise and find more sleep were fruitless. Pillow over his head didn't help either. He lost the battle entirely when the smell of coffee wafted up to his nose. He cracked his eyes open. The sun's beam hadn't made its way through the window, but the sky was faded-denim blue.

A timid "sorry" reached his ears. Laura stood in the door, wearing only a T-shirt and underwear, her hair crunched as much as her face, though still adorable.

"What's the time?" he asked.

"Six. I couldn't sleep."

Guess my sleep has come to an end too. He flung his legs to the side of the bed.

"After I... you know—" he pointed to the bathroom— "we're going to have a chat." He said it with enough force to put across the message he wasn't happy with how things were panning out.

After he freshened up and got to the living room, she sat at the wooden table. In front of her was a cup of coffee, another one opposite. She wore jeans now and a black T-shirt.

"Thank you," he said and sat down, noticing her attention on his bandaged hands.

"What happened?"

"Doesn't matter." He ignored her grunt.

"Anyone ever told you you aren't the most pleasant man in the morning?"

"Yup. Some people compared me with that grumpy cat once gone viral on the internet."

"I can see some resemblance."

He ignored her smirk, her comment even more. He had so many things to ask her, so many things he wanted to know. Something stopped him. Was it the fear of getting hurt again, like Sarah had? Or the simple fact that he didn't know which way to go? Stuck in every way. He would have liked to share his feelings with her, but could he really? Were his feelings even real? He was manmade so who knew? Maybe his feelings were just as much created. This thought stuck to him so dominantly he struggled to find a clear mind.

She said, "I tried to get some news, but the TV is snow, and the burner doesn't have internet. We're cut off here."

He stored her information in the hindmost corner of his mind, would bring up the topic again when the time had come. Right now, one question emerged from under the mountain of thoughts. "Have you always known I'm Knox's property?"

"No."

Her quick response came across genuine enough to believe her. "Did you know I was created?"

"No."

"Where are Clifton and Green?"

"I honestly don't know."

"I need air," he said.

"I thought you wanted to talk?"

"We just did."

He had to get out. As he stepped outside, the sun had fanned over the hills. The beams streaming through the treetops calmed his inner uproar. He followed the rays as he distanced himself from the cottage that resembled a prison, a glade ahead providing him the space he needed.

He sat with his back against a tree. Sick of hiding, he had the urge to show his face, handing himself in to whomever. Knox seemed the best option. Curtis wouldn't need to bother flying to the other side of the country to confront Knox, who'd be in San Diego in a flash if he made himself available. Knox might even be in San Diego already.

The irony of the hunter turned into the hunted, hiding to escape justice for killing people or using them like guinea pigs. To Curtis it was a slam dunk that Leon Powell had referred to Sebastian Knox in his email.

The air was crisp. The day hadn't started, was neither good nor bad. Could still be created. He spotted a squirrel bouncing from one branch to another as accurately as a trapeze artist, no fear of falling. Would they ever slip, misjudge the distance, fall all the way? Fall as hard as he had?

Laura invaded his mind. She was messing with his head. During this morning's short chat, he'd caught himself studying her every move, how she held the mug or ran her fingers through her hair. Her eyes told stories without saying a word. They sparkled with enthusiasm one second, trust the next. A contradiction since she'd proven over and over he couldn't trust her. Or could he?

The smiles she sent his way continued to weaken his legs, but he feared she shared his feelings. He'd caught her out when she let her gaze linger on him longer than appropriate. The space in bed last night had narrowed as she inched closer and closer to him. Luckily, the blanket in between them kept him from spooning her right there. But something had changed. He couldn't put a finger on it, but as attracted as he was toward her, he also had to distance himself.

As a cloud covered the sun, his thoughts darkened. He didn't want to run for the rest of his life, be trapped, but he couldn't see a way out either.

He fished in his pocket for the phone he'd snatched up when leaving the cottage. Maybe it was too early to make a call, but the urge to find answers dominated him. To check for a signal, he wandered around, the phone held high until one bar showed up. Doubting he'd get more than that, he backed into another tree and dialed the number for Arthur Buckley.

This time Curtis asked him if he ever heard of Laura Webb aka Emily Sutton and informed him about her history. "I don't know if the brain transplant is true or if she's simply pulling my leg."

"There are so many things people never thought possible. We think it only happens in movies, like the ones in which faces were swapped, in others, brains. In the real world, there have been experiments in which an entire head was transplanted onto another body. That person didn't survive though. However, could it be that Laura is Emily? Absolutely. Though it would be interesting to know if she has Laura's or Emily's DNA."

"Which would decide if she's Sutton's daughter," Curtis thought out loud.

"Yes."

Curtis cleared his throat. "Sutton is under the impression he's found his dead daughter. I don't want to dampen his happiness."

"It's not up to you to tell him. But if Laura has Emily's brain, and the rest is Laura, there could be complications that haven't been explored yet. How much of Emily's brain function is in Laura and how much has been destroyed? The thing is, people from Laura's past might be able to unlock memories Emily isn't aware of. For example, if Laura had pricked her finger as a child, it's in her nerve-memory, but if Emily pricks the same finger, the body could send out a different pain signal. It would be Laura's old memory. It's difficult to explain but do you follow?"

"I think I do," Curtis said and deliberated over a comment Laura had made about her fear of the old self coming to life again.

"That's why sometimes you might deal with Laura and not Emily," Buckley said. "Considering the transfer happened six years ago, Emily probably learned how to handle surprises like this, but as far as you've told me, she's been living a secluded life, away from her past in New Jersey. But now dealing with Knox again, god knows what it will trigger. I'd be careful around her. Even if she has good intentions, there might be a few things out of her control."

"The only slight change I observed was after the encounter with Martin Green and Clifton Wright. I can't put a finger on what changed at that point, but it seems to have disappeared again. Yeah, though, something was bizarre."

"Where are they now?"

"Green and Wright? No idea. They disappeared but could reappear at any time. I assume they might be trying to find me, but I barely have a phone signal. So hopefully the one of the device in my arm is equally weak."

He went on to speculate about Gordon McNamara, and his assumption the professor also had lived two lives, though in a different way to Laura. Curtis couldn't shake the feeling Gordon may have played Laura and was working for Knox before he was killed. Nothing new came from this.

"What about my father?" For a brief second Curtis wondered why he still referred to him as his father. "Let's say he knows what's going on. Why doesn't he step in to stop it all, or at least help?"

"Maybe he doesn't know how to stop it."

Curtis picked up a rock and bounced it in his hand. "If *he* doesn't know, how am I supposed to?"

"Knox doesn't care about you as a person. It's what's inside you he wants. Use it to your advantage."

Curtis threw the rock, watched it arc through the air, then tumble as it bounced off a tree. "The web of corruption is too big to be fixed," he said. "Even if I find Knox or try to take him down, Big Brother won't let it happen."

"I can hear you fishing for excuses."

"I fear the consequences."

"What's the worst-case scenario?"

"People getting killed who shouldn't."

"You getting killed."

Buckley's words shook him up. Deep down Curtis was scared of being killed, but he didn't want to say it out loud. "I don't know what to do."

"I think you are in a situation where my words fit best: Sometimes it's wiser to accept the way things are rather than trying to change them."

"Is this why you always told me that because you expected something to go wrong one day?"

"I warned Charlie of possible consequences. Eventually it had to happen. I'm honestly amazed it's taken so long."

"It would have never happened if I hadn't done the stupid DNA test."

"If it hadn't been the test, it would have been something else. Anyway, I have to go now. Keep me up-to-date and keep your chin up."

"Thanks for listening." Curtis was about to pocket the phone when his name echoed from the speaker.

"Shawn?"

Curtis swung the phone back to his ear. "Yes."

"Please keep your promise. I know you're bursting to take Knox down, but leave it to the authorities."

"Will do." His chest was now heavier than before. He didn't like lying to Buckley, but he couldn't tell him his plans.

He'd taken but a few steps toward the cottage when his cellphone buzzed. The number showed unknown. Recent calls from unregistered numbers had turned to nightmares. He answered, heart in his throat.

"Hey, mate. Did you miss me?"

"Wayne, I'm glad to hear you. Where are you?"

"Uh, baby, that's highly confidential. Where are you?"

"Yup."

Wayne cackled. "Have you been in touch with Sutton?"

"Not since yesterday. He's cutting the cord 'cause the FBI is now on it."

"Coward."

"He's only doing it to protect himself."

"Does he know?"

"About Laura, you mean?" Curtis guessed. "Kind of, yes. No detail, though."

"What's your plan?"

"Find Knox."

"That's suicide," Wayne said.

"It's the only way."

"Powell's email was a blow. But we still have the joker. I can talk to Sutton, bring him up to speed. I'm sure he can pull some strings."

"Better not. And I'm sure he's cut you out too."

"I don't think so."

"How come?"

"I'm staying in his apartment. He thinks it's the best place for me to be."

Surprise, surprise. It was maybe not the best place for Wayne but the safest for now.

"Still, I don't want him to be part of the game, yet. No one should know. If word reaches Knox, then I'm history." After exchanging a few more theories about how best to handle the situation, Curtis added, "Call me back in about an hour. Before that, can you do me a favor?"

~ * ~

With the day still young, Curtis started creating it, forcing it into the pattern he wanted it to follow. It was time to take control of something bugging him deep down.

He entered the cottage, assumed Laura was in the bathroom as the shower's water splashed. In the kitchen he boiled water, his mind miles away as he ripped open a packet and filled the mug with instant coffee. He didn't get to pour water into the mug. Her bathing went on for too long, even for a woman.

Gripped by fear that Green and Clifton could have taken advantage of his absence and nabbed her, Curtis rapped the bathroom door. "Laura?"

The splashes stopped. "Did you call me?"

Phew. "I was wondering if… any chance you could…" How could something so easy be so tricky? "Are you up for another coffee?"

"That would be nice. I left my clothes out there. Do you mind passing them to me? I didn't expect you back so quickly."

He checked the bed, spotted her jeans, T-shirt, bra, and panties neatly folded on the bed. After gathering her clothing, he tapped at the door. "Ready?"

The doorknob twisted, her hand weaving through the gap wide enough for him to get a glimpse of pearls of water trickling down her skin toward the towel she had wrapped herself in. With his foot, he nudged the door more open.

"What were you going to say before the coffee?" she said, her mischievous smile playing with his head.

"I, um… nothing." He gave her the clothes.

"I might as well get dressed then."

What else other than getting dressed was she after? In all honesty though, he would have liked to rip that towel from her body. He cleared his throat. "I'll leave you to it."

He stopped his turn as she placed her clothes onto the counter so slowly he suspected she was replaying his words, contemplating if she wanted him to stay or not.

The towel still around her, she said, "Do you mind scratching that part, you know…" She twisted a hand up her back. "The spot where the arms are always too short to reach."

Should he reject her? Who would he reject, though? Laura or Emily? Was this woman in front of him genuinely asking for nothing other than a back scratch or did she play him if not even test him? Emily, so Curtis believed, wouldn't play or test him. That still didn't answer the question who he had in front of him. So what do to?

Then, what he would have liked to do moments ago, she did. She dropped the towel.

Now what?

Chapter Forty-Four

Curtis couldn't hide his smirk when Laura, now fully dressed, failed to gloss over her satisfied smile when she emerged from the bathroom after her second shower.

He passed her a mug of coffee.

"Do you always have sex with a woman without getting undressed?" she said.

"Technically, we didn't have sex and do you have a reason to complain?"

"God no. But I fear you've missed out."

"Not every man needs his dick to please a woman." He said it with confidence and a leer, accepting her smooch on his cheek. "I'll have a shower now."

"I can wash your back."

"Enjoy your coffee. Keep an ear open in case your dad calls."

"I thought there was no signal here."

"If you stay near the kitchen counter, there should be one."

Unable to wipe the grin from his face as he undressed in the bathroom, he wished for an ice bucket to dive into. Unwilling to go all the way to give Laura what she undoubtedly wanted, he made sure her hunger was fulfilled, for now. His own lust, which he kept at bay with utmost struggle, would get satisfied when it was time to get his share. He wanted to keep his head on straight and not let emotions shadow his common sense. And there was this wall of his own making.

To have sex it needed a man which, theoretically, he was. But it also needed a man who knew who he was, who believed in himself. But who was he really? Created! Could he even have feelings? He hoped he had and also hoped the woman who had just challenged him was the Emily in Laura and not the actual Laura.

To make sure he could trust his judgment, he'd concocted a plan.

He checked the time. There was enough for a quick shower.

Back at the basin, he washed the parts of his armpits that weren't bandaged. The reflection in the mirror told him he needed to wash his hair. The baseball cap would take care of it. The urge to shave he had to postpone. Unless he performed a wild-west stunt with soap and a knife, he had no other option than to add this utensil to his mentally formed shopping list. He added underwear to it as he reached for what he'd stripped off, tempted to not slip the already worn back on, but the idea of falling into the hands of criminals and the chance of them removing his jeans, for whatever reason, and leaving him naked left him no choice.

As he struggled with his T-shirt, he heard the buzz from the cellphone. He checked his watch, nodded, slowed his process of putting on the jeans and belting them up. Once done he brushed his teeth again.

By now he expected Laura to knock on the door to let him know about the call. She didn't. He spat out the toothpaste sharply, fighting the mistrust building in him. Was she simply waiting for him to come out of the bathroom? Could she not be trusted? Or was he paranoid? Best to find out.

He opened the door and spotted her sitting at the table, jotting down notes.

She looked up. "Wayne called, leaving a number but no name. He said he was in a rush and had no time to talk to you."

Test passed. He'd feared she would conceal the number to later pass it on to her father or Green and Clifton. She didn't. Unless she'd made the call while he was in the bathroom. She had enough time to do this. A slight pang of guilt poked him at his lack of faith in her when he saw no sign of guilt on her face. Nevertheless, he couldn't shake off the inconsistency bugging him for a while: the sniper who'd killed Gordon.

The more he pondered it, the more Curtis came to understand only Laura and Gordon knew he was in that loft. At that stage, Clifton and Green were still within O.R. Yes, Curtis always suspected Gordon played both sides, but what if it wasn't Gordon? What if Laura had a weak moment, a jumble in her brain about who she was and the bad Laura had arranged the sniper?

"Great," he said and took the note she handed to him.

"Whose number is it?"

"Just a friend. He might have some information on Gregory." An outright lie. A white lie, Curtis corrected in his mind.

She said, "I'll see if we can stay another night and where I can get food and whatever else we need like new underwear. I'm also sure you wouldn't mind a shave."

"You're good at reading minds."

"I know when I have a guy in front of me who is self-conscious."

She got off the chair. "Anything else you need?"

"Socks would be good. And a newspaper so we know what's going on since we don't have the internet or a TV. Are you going right away?"

"I was going to. I hope to be back with breakfast and other things within the hour."

"I don't think it's a good idea to head out alone."

"It's not a good idea if you join me, either."

He ripped the gun from the back of his pants, earning him a look of disgust. "Green and Clifton are still out there. I want to be ready for surprises. Take it with you, just in case." He checked the magazine, handed the Beretta to her. "You know how to—?"

"My dad's a cop."

He chuckled. *How could I forget?*

"What about you?" she asked.

"I'm sure I can find a knife somewhere." There it was again, the feeling it wasn't a good idea. "Why not check first if we can stay another night?"

"Are we dealing with trust issues here?"

Her comment came from left field. "I'm worried something will happen to you and I won't be able to help you."

"What if I come back and let you know where I'll be? Deal?"

Ten minutes later, confirming she'd booked another night, she left with the Dodge and the gun, headed to some shops less than five miles away. He hoped this wasn't a mistake when she said he had reason to worry if she didn't come back in one hour. She'd better.

~ * ~

He intended to check the cellphone to see if Laura had made any calls or sent messages while he had the shower, but it chimed in his hand before he could read the log. He cleared his throat and wiped the smirk from his face, knowing this caller wouldn't be too happy about some particular developments.

He swept his finger over the screen. "You really have a strange way of cutting the cord."

"Where are you?" Sutton snapped.

"Nice try. You know where we are."

"I don't, and don't want to know either. I just wanted to see if you'd accidentally share your location. Listen, I have some bad news, some maybe good news, and some very bad news. What do you want first?"

"The order sounds good to me."

"Somebody stole your Tahoe."

"I'd consider that as the very bad news."

"We're not sure if it was your Tahoe, but a trucker reported seeing the wreck of a Toyota rear-ended by a much bigger car, possibly a white Tahoe. The Toyota rolled down an embankment, and into trees. The driver was around thirty, curly, medium-long hair."

"Clifton Wright," Curtis said.

"The way it seems, he died on impact. The passenger was in his early forties. Light-brown hair, white shirt, jeans."

"Martin Green."

"Apparently, he was alive following the impact, but is now dead. Executed. Somebody shot him in his throat."

Curtis swallowed.

"I can only go by your description they were Martin Green and Clifton Wright as once more we can't get a proper identification. But wherever you are, Curtis, I don't want you to fall into Knox's hands. He could have shot Green in the head or the heart, made it quick. But he let him die barbarically, probably watched him drown in his own blood or bleed out, whichever came first. If this was Knox's doing, he'll maul you to death, and I don't want to be the one picking up your bits and pieces strewn all over the country. Whatever you do, I don't want you to even think about getting near Knox. Promise me this."

"Yes."

"I can't hear you."

"Yes," Curtis said louder.

"Good. Make sure Emily will do the same."

"Of course."

"And promise me you stay away from any bigger car like your Tahoe or Suburban, or a van or truck. I like my Dodge, and she won't stand a chance."

Duly noted. "Where did it happen?"

"Somewhere around the Palomar Observatory. Please don't tell me you're near there."

Close enough to consider it the really bad news.

"We're not," he said. "But it makes sense to think it was Knox. He might be unaware I signed the Tahoe over to Wayne. If anything is leading to a white Tahoe, he was hoping it would fall back onto me."

"The witness wasn't entirely certain about the make but was certain about the color, and the white scratches found on the Toyota confirmed it. Furthermore, if Wayne and I hadn't gone to his condo to get some stuff, we wouldn't know your Tahoe was stolen."

Curtis opened the door to let in some fresh air. "What's the good news?"

"Green and Clifton can't come after you any longer."

He'd hoped the good news contained more than just that. "How bad is the real bad news?"

"I suggest you sit down."

Fresh air sounded much better. "How do you know I'm not sitting?"

"Because I wouldn't be. I don't know how many Curtis-lookalikes we've sent home overnight. One is in the ICU after nearly getting beaten to death. It's a mess. Leon Powell's message has turned everyone in the city into fruit loops including the government. They set out a two-million dollar reward for your capture."

"You're kidding!"

"The good thing is the bounty is for Rabbit 76. So far nothing is linked to you."

"That is good news. Since we're already playing good news, bad news, it turns out I'm actually Knox's property or at least the government's." He closed the door, then sat at the kitchen table. "I wasn't conceived in a normal way. I was created—" the best word he could think of— "by Knox, Hiddleston, and the man who turned out not to be my father and is actually still alive. And the most likely reason I survived the hoped-for cancer vaccine was because I was... well... created." Shame he couldn't ask Laura to add whiskey to the shopping list. "Knox owns me, no matter what," he said in conclusion.

"Only if he can get you. Even then, he can't prove you're his property and creating you was illegal. Trust me, any jury will die in their chairs before they'd come to a verdict. Even so, it's important you never fall into Knox's hands."

"I'm not going to run for the rest of my life." Curtis mulled over these words. Yep, he was repeating himself. "No matter if the people in O.R. are dead or alive, Knox has to be brought to justice."

"We have nothing to prove anything besides an email with allegations against somebody called 'Seb,' coming from a man who supposedly disappeared six years ago. Therefore, Knox remains innocent until proven guilty."

The guilty one walks free while the innocent is guilty. Curtis tugged the neck of his T-shirt away from his throat. "What about Powell's list of names—the thirty-four people in O.R.?"

A heavy sigh filtered through. "Let's put it this way. At least we now know how Olivia Fitzgerald, Sophia Langdon, Samuel Dunbar, and Christian Fisher fit in."

"So there's a chance they're alive?"

"No."

"Why not?"

"Because there were crosses next to their names while Clifton and Green didn't have that. I assume they are the people who died in O.R. but again it's nothing but an assumption, and I want you to take it as that."

If Curtis had to explain how he felt right now, he would have said: slapped in the face one-hundred times.

"Anything else?" A puff coming through the line gave Curtis the impression Sutton fought with himself. He tensed. "Just say it."

"Wayne and I have been sharing a few theories."

"He would have loved that."

"I think he's right about his theory that your life has been controlled in some ways. And I don't mean only by your father. I've done a search I should have done earlier, but I think the result was blown out of the water by what you've just told me."

"Why's that?"

"I checked if anyone with the name of Curtis had died or disappeared in the past few years, and I discovered a staggering seven men, four of them killed in car accidents. They were all in the East Coast area and about your age."

Every hair on his body rose, shivering Curtis up from top to toe. He should have died the day Jessica did. Knox had been on the hunt for anyone named Curtis. Merkow's plan had backfired. Knox never believed that he'd died due to complications after his motorcycle accident.

"I'll call you back," Curtis said abruptly and disconnected, banging his fist on the table, sending the chair flying as he leaped from it.

A storm of weeping overcame him, guilt strangling him. He let the tears run until he faced the fact they wouldn't bring her back. In the bathroom, he washed his face, dried it with a towel and, now rage-ridden, contacted Sutton again. "If I ever get to Knox, I'll kill the fucking bastard!"

"I want you to calm down and not jump to conclusions. First of all, you told me Knox didn't know your father's official name but knew him as Frank Gillespie. Therefore, Knox didn't know you were his son. Not until you took the DNA test."

"Merkow told me he forged my name and death certificate, but Knox needed to find a man going by the name of Curtis."

"I studied your girlfriend's case, but I can't link the driver to Knox. It was an accident. I believe you're carrying guilt for no reason."

Curtis struggled to keep his growing agitation at bay. "The only reason she drove my car that day was because she borrowed it. Read into the case, Sutton."

"Those are serious allegations, Curtis."

"With a serious prospect for being true. Find out who the client was collecting the paintings. I bet it was a setup."

"Curtis! I'm already clutching straws trying to convince Donaghy to turn a blind eye to you in regard to the B-1 murder. You're telling me Knox conducted underground tests. The tests are confirmed in Powell's email, but that's it. Next, you're telling me Laura is Emily, and I can't get my head around that one. Now, you're telling me you're manmade. My handicap is I have nothing so far that links Knox to any of this, and I'm risking everything by helping you. So don't throw theories at me. I need facts."

Curtis balled his hands, suppressing the anger about to spill over. "Don't tell me you still think Jessica died by accident."

Sutton grunted. "Anyone ever told you you're a stubborn ass?"

"Sometimes you have to be to get somewhere in life."

"I want you to think about one thing carefully." Sutton's intonation morphed into calmness. "Is it worth it to unearth the truth, only to endure the pain you already lived though all over again? Isn't it better to let her rest?"

Curtis didn't know what to say.

Sutton said, "If anything, I believe much more that *your* accident wasn't an accident."

"Wayne would have told you that my business didn't come down by accident either."

"My thinking too."

Up to a certain degree Curtis agreed, but it still didn't make sense. He rubbed his head. On the kitchen counter, he spotted the packet of painkillers. They were just as bad as any drug: addictive. He checked the time. It had been four hours since he swallowed the last two. Was his body sending out the message he was due for the next fix? Or were the previous pills some of those bogus ones made of lemon?

"I can't just sit here and wait for a miracle to happen. If I'd put myself into the shoes of everyone else out there reading the article about Rabbit 76, I'd ask myself: why the heck don't you come forward?" He ignored the packet of pills and opened the door again.

"The people reading the article don't know the full extent. It's imperative you stay put. If you make a move I don't know about, you might work against yourself and me. Got that?"

Curtis pressed out air so hard, it hurt his chest. "Yes."

"Good. Now tell me one thing. What makes you certain Laura is who she claims she is?"

Curtis raised a brow. "Do you doubt your own daughter?"

"I still struggle to come to terms with knowing I have one again."

"If you aren't sure, how can I be?"

No answer from Sutton.

"To be honest," Curtis said, "there are still secrets surrounding her. Take Gordon's loft. Gordon knew I was coming. Laura took me to him. How did the shooter know? I had no device implanted at that stage. Laura still had her bracelet. So, what? Did she lure me into the loft to be killed by the sniper who accidentally killed Gordon? Do I trust her? No, not really. At least not fully."

"If she is Emily, and I'd like to believe that, then I'd give her the benefit of the doubt. I got to go now. Somebody I want to talk to just walked in."

"Donaghy?"

"No. I've taken your words to heart. Talk later."

As the line went dead, a part in Curtis died too: the hope to ever have a normal life.

Chapter Forty-Five

Sutton focused on Mendez, who entered the squad room, carrying a grin Sutton promised himself he'd lose soon, but he strolled leisurely as he approached his colleague, said, "Meet me in the car park," and walked on.

The wait was short. Sutton had his eyes once more on Mendez, studying his every move. He couldn't detect treachery, but Mendez was either a good actor or as clean as Sutton wished he was.

"What's up?" Mendez called out, ambling past an abutment.

Sutton hushed him between two cars to the wall behind, where he waited until Mendez was leaning against it, as he always did, either against a car or a wall or a table, never stood on his own two feet if he could avoid it, his hands always in his pockets.

Standing in front of him, hands out of the pockets, Sutton said, "Tell me more about the night you went to B-1."

Mendez frowned. "I replied to dispatch. I was near. No big deal."

"You sure you didn't intervene with dispatch and say you were taking over, despite me being the first to answer?"

Was it slight annoyance Sutton read in Mendez's face?

Mendez pushed off the wall. "What are you implying?"

"Nothing yet."

"You were finishing your shift anyway. I just started, and I was closer to the scene than you."

"Why?"

"What do you mean, why?"

"There's a difference between offering your services and insisting you must be at a crime scene. I never thought much of it until you told me you found Felicity Pike's cellphone. What's really going on?"

Mendez leaned once more against the wall. "Nothing."

The action came quicker than the thought. Sutton whacked

Mendez's head against the wall, clenched his hand around his throat, the same way he'd done with Curtis. It always worked to get a quick confession when the pressure was on the right spot. In milliseconds the brain sent the urgent call for air. A punch at the offender was near impossible as the move meant more loss of air. The instinctive reaction was more likely: get rid of the hand squeezing the pipes. But that move would come in slow motion as the seconds were already ticking.

In Mendez's case, the move hadn't even happened as he struggled getting his hands out of his pockets. Every thrust to release the grip would come limp, the brain concentrating on nothing other than air unless the guy dealing with the sudden lack of what the human body needed to live didn't fear death. Mendez wasn't such a guy. Curtis wasn't such a guy either. Neither was Sutton. It was done to him a few years ago, and he'd feared his end had come.

"You fucking better tell me what the fuck is going on or I'll twist up your dick and you'll never be able to use it again." Unmercifully, he watched Mendez's face grow red. Sutton didn't want to wait as long as he had with Curtis because Mendez wouldn't be able to handle it like Curtis had. Sutton let go.

Mendez coughed and gasped. Sutton ignored it, snatched his gun from his holster and pressed it against Mendez's temple. "I'm waiting."

"Fuck..." Coughing. "You."

"I'll fuck you right over if you don't talk."

As the redness altered to a marbled pink on Mendez's skin, his coughing relaxed to irregular breathing. Sutton didn't move the gun.

"I'm already fucked," Mendez said, his voice guttural.

Sutton waited him out.

"I... I have a..." A heavy sigh escaped Mendez. "The night Felicity was killed I lost a lot of money. Lots. I tried to win some of it back because I knew my wife would kill me. So I kept on playing. I lost more. I literally cried my eyes out..."

"Don't give me the sorry story; get to the point."

"Somebody offered to get me out of the shit."

"Keep going."

"I was given a package. In it instructions, a photo, a location, and a weird looking gun, which supposedly would not kill anyone. My job was to use the gun on the target's inner arm, insert whatever that thing fired. I was instructed to go to the airport, to domestic arrivals, and wait for the woman to come out. But she slipped through the crowd and disappeared into a cab. I shadowed her. The cab stopped less than a block short of B-1's building. I approached her, waved my badge, told her I had a few questions. But the stupid bitch knocked my balls, and in the fight, I triggered that weird gun. Whatever came out of it hit her on the lower back. She stumbled into the building. I raced back to my car, expecting dispatch to come through with a call, which it did." He stopped his story as if a train ran from its tracks. His eyes twitched. "But you weren't supposed to be there."

A cocktail of fury and disappointment heated Sutton. "I followed a dud call, you fucking piece of shit. You placed the call, wanted to keep me away." No answer was needed; now Mendez's face shot blood red. Sutton gulped his fury down. "Was she dead when you got to the scene?"

"Yes. I searched for her ID and the cellphone, which I pocketed while you spoke to Curtis, but this whole thing was getting too messy, so I made up the story that I found her phone." Mendez tried a sad-dog face. "Are you going to take that gun from my head?"

"No."

"You have no idea how much hell I've been through since then."

"I don't care about your petty sorrows. You killed Felicity."

"She wasn't supposed to die. I... *fuck*. I've been waiting every day for bullets to fucking kill me. I haven't heard another word from this guy, so I skimmed through her phone, but I couldn't find anything of importance. It had the usual I-love-you-honey messages, but they were followed by condolences from everywhere. That's when I figured her boyfriend, Gregory Whitehurst his name was, had been killed. All I could conclude was she arrived in San Diego one day after his death, but I have no idea who he was or how he fit into this whole mess."

Sutton knew. Mendez didn't need to. "Any more calls?"

"Bunches and bunches of calls to Curtis's defunct number and a few to Wayne Cantrell, starting the day her boyfriend was killed."

"I'd honestly love to smash your fucking useless head in." If only Mendez wasn't such a dickhead falling for dirty games simply out of desperation.

"Can you please take that gun from my head?"

"No. The guy who gave you the instructions—do you think he knew you're a cop?"

"I don't think he'd have approached me if he knew."

"Would you recognize him again?"

"I was pretty pissed."

Sutton dug the gun harder on his partner's skull. "You didn't appear pissed at the crime scene, and you weren't pissed enough to forget what he wanted. Who was he?"

"Knox."

Sutton couldn't explain why he was surprised. Maybe because he'd hoped it wasn't Knox. "Anything else I should know."

Mendez shook his head, but Sutton could tell there was more. "Donaghy's in his office, and nothing is holding me back from delivering you to him."

"I tried fixing the mishap. I contacted him."

"You contacted Knox?"

"I didn't know then it was Knox. I didn't even know who Knox was. It's not as if you were talking about James Bond. When I saw his photo, that's when I identified him, though he'd tried disguising his appearance with a fake moustache and longer hair. A wig I suppose. But right after leaving the crime scene, while the burner still connected me to him, I told him what happened and when I mentioned Shawn Curtis, he was hell-bent on details. He wanted me to keep him updated on his moves. So I followed him after you interviewed him and when I saw him with a woman, who I assume was Laura, going into the loft, I tipped off Knox. He must have known which loft I was talking about, so I assume he then arranged the sniper."

Sutton added up the details. *And that sniper was set to kill Curtis but instead killed Gordon McNamara.* Curtis would be overly relieved to hear it wasn't Laura who'd set him up. At least one puzzle was solved. "You still got the burner?"

"I tossed it. Things were getting too hot."

"Anything else?"

Mendez shook his head vehemently enough for Sutton to believe his last version of the story was the truth.

"Are you going to take the gun away now?" Mendez pleaded once more.

"I want you to listen carefully. I want you to head home. You'll call Donaghy and tell him you're sick. I don't want you around until this whole shit is over. If I see you here or anywhere else but home, I promise you won't see the next day."

"If I do this Donaghy might smell a rat."

"It's either that or your badge." Sutton lowered the gun and elbowed Mendez away from the wall. "Get out of my face before I have second thoughts."

Like a beaten dog, Mendez trudged to his car, turned back once more before he disappeared into his Prius and drove off. As soon as he was out of sight, Sutton took out his phone to call Curtis. No answer. He contacted Wayne.

"I was about to call you," Wayne said. "He's overdue."

Chapter Forty-Six

Curtis picked up the TV remote and hit the button. Within seconds a voice came to life, then a face. His hand tightened around the remote. Unable to strangle it, he threw it against the wall. The damn thing didn't even break.

"You fucking lying bitch!" He snorted with rage, remembering Laura told him there was only static.

He managed to focus on the woman on the screen, the same one he'd seen yesterday interviewing Donaghy. Today she wore a blue blouse which made her appear pale. Red had suited her much better.

> *"The biggest manhunt in San Diego's history, if not in the U.S., has turned people against each other. Two million dollars is a lot of money but the police are urging people to remain rational to avoid unnecessary complications, in particular if somebody was to kill Rabbit 76.*

The announcer interrupted her speech, pressed her earpiece, her eyes suddenly showing shock as much as surprise.

> *"We have breaking news about a possible suspect matching the identity of Rabbit 76. His name is Shawn Dylan Curtis. According to our source, he's linked to two recent murders. The police are working hard to locate him and are relying on the public for information. It is of utmost importance that Shawn Dylan Curtis is under no circumstances harmed as the latest developments suggest he may hold a clue to saving many people's lives."*

Curtis stretched out his legs to stop the sudden vertigo. Who was the source? Knox? Sutton? Laura? Two million could turn anyone into the snitch.

"In related news, former FDA commissioner, Hank Hiddleston, has landed this morning in San Diego, claiming he can help find Sebastian Knox, who is believed to be the man Leon Powell accuses of several felonies such as subjecting humans to unapproved medical procedures and manslaughter."

A video flashed up, showing Hiddleston leaving a limo and disappearing into a hotel. He was tall, gray-haired, wearing a suit, and he gave the impression of an educated man and in no way a criminal. The only reason Curtis hadn't planned face-to-face confrontation was he assumed Hiddleston on the other side of the country. Now, he was no more than two hours away, by car, which Curtis didn't have at the moment. He also lacked gun and money, but that didn't make reaching the city impossible.

Last night, after he smashed his knuckles against the decorative wishing well, he'd noticed the lady from the office walking to a Suburban parked out front. She searched for something, closed the door, and returned to the office. Not once did lights flash, neither when she opened nor when she closed it. There was a good chance she hadn't locked it, never thinking someone could have interest in her car.

Then, he changed his mind all over. Before adding car theft to his rap-sheet, he wanted to make sure it was worthwhile taking on the trip.

On the short footage that had appeared on the TV and as unfamiliar as he was to San Diego, he recognized the US Grant Hotel, an impressive, historical building. Five stars, he guessed and surely providing a dazzling presidential suite.

He dialed directory assistance, asked for the Grant Hotel and got connected right away.

A woman answered. "US Grant Hotel. How can I help you?"

"Could you please put me through to Mr. Hank Hiddleston?" The pause he expected. He pushed on to know for sure. "He's staying at the US Grant, isn't he? Presidential suite as far as I know."

"Sorry, I can't give you that information."

He hung up. No point wasting more time. No matter how well staff was trained in replying to calls for VIPs—Curtis was certain Hiddleston wanted to be treated as such—there was a giveaway. They first hesitated, feeling caught out as the call they were hoping would never come put them in a predicament. The woman had hesitated. Then she said she couldn't give the information. This confirmed Hiddleston was staying at the US Grant, otherwise the woman would have said, "Sorry, he's not staying with us." It was a long shot, but Curtis felt comfortable he was right.

Time to steal the car? He looked at the cellphone in his hand. Time to turn the game around. Stop running. Take action. Shake things up. He redialed.

"US Grant Hotel, how can I help you?"

To his relief, it was a different woman responding to his call. He still changed his voice's tone to more subtle. "My name is Frank Gillespie. I'm an old friend of Hank Hiddleston. Is there a chance you could put me through to him?"

"I'm not sure if I…"

"If you tell him it's Frank Gillespie, I'm sure he'll accept the call."

"I'll see if he'll accept. Please stay on the line."

He waited out those long seconds, perceived nothing but dead air besides his heartbeat. Then, a click. A voice. "You've got some nerve calling me. I thought you were dead."

"Why don't we make a deal?"

Chapter Forty-Seven

"How is this even possible?" Wayne roared into the phone, his legs moments ago comfortably sprawled out on Sutton's couch, now tensed. "You're a cop but can't trace your own car?"

"I deactivated everything for their safety. I have the FBI right up my ass and can't afford to know where Curtis is."

Sutton's apology didn't hold up with Wayne. Neither had heard from Curtis who'd promised he'd send a text every hour to let them know he was fine. Calls weren't answered and as far as Wayne could tell, Curtis and Laura had checked out of Rosa's Cottage after paying for an extra night. It made no sense, though he speculated it could have been a silent message trouble was brewing.

"Do you still think Knox got Curtis's Tahoe?" Wayne asked.

"There's a good chance. Why?"

"By the time you get back to me, I might know where he is." Wayne disconnected, dialed a number and waited, and waited. "Come on, come on, Gus."

Gustaf Rosenheim, German, freak and crazy inventor waiting for his brain to deliver the million-dollar idea, which he may have had as his latest idea had potential, now that the world had gone bananas since drones were on the market.

"Vane-Man. Vat you up to?" Gus with his usual thick German accent.

"All good here. How's your latest baby going?"

"Are you talking—?"

"Only one baby since you can't get your dick up."

"Nothing wrong with my dick. Just shooting blanks, man."

Wayne bit his tongue, doubting Gus ever had sex since he never spoke about women, or men, or sex. His inventions—they were his babies. Once they finished the development stage, he named them Adam and Eve, or Mr. Einstein. There was a Beethoven too.

Wayne asked, "Is it a he or a she?"

"Lorita."

"Nice. Exotic. Can she deliver?"

"Of course. Working on some issues as she seems colorblind, but nothing I can't solve."

"What about a black or a white car?"

"Accuracy is about eighty-seven percent. There are heaps of black cars out there, so it might be an issue. Same with white. Orange would be better."

"What if I'd give you the possible route the car is taking right now, the make, license plate? No GPS active, no cellphones to locate. That's why we need you."

"Running the license plate is still in its prototype but can help to find the car quicker. Tell me more."

"How long?"

"Depends on if I want to help."

"Let's say it's in your hands if one of my friends will end up dead or not. Best friend, if you don't mind me saying this. You in?"

"Your friends are my friends. Make sure I meet him if he doesn't end up dead."

If he doesn't end up dead, I'll personally kill him.

Chapter Forty-Eight

Curtis controlled the Dodge, controlled the situation. Sickened by learning Laura had fibbed about the TV, he clenched his fingers around the steering wheel, focused on the road, determined not to look at her.

After she returned from her shopping trip, he'd changed into new underwear and socks. The shaving cream and razor he hadn't used. At that stage, he needed strong coffee. Black, lots of sugar. He had to keep his head straight. He'd munched away a burger and changed the dressing on his shoulder by himself, which was a challenge on its own, while arguing with Laura, who didn't understand why he wanted to leave.

"First you want to stay an extra night and now you can't get out of here quick enough?"

"I don't feel safe here," he'd said, for a brief moment tempted to confront her right there.

But why bother? Anything she said was suspect. She was so damn good at it. Could smile at you and tell the biggest lie. But he was about to deliver himself to a man who could be trusted even less and she needn't know.

Now in the car, he couldn't fail but notice her sifting through the duffel, her moves jittery. He could have told her she wouldn't find what she was undoubtedly after. Again, why bother?

"Where's the cellphone?" she finally asked, eyes bulging.

"I got rid of it."

She tossed the duffel to the back seat, leaned in closer to him. "You what?"

He flicked a facetious wink. *Yeah, baby, how do you like that?*

"How are we supposed to stay in touch with my father or Wayne?"

He let her snap bounce off him. "No need to."

She snorted like a bull about to attack a red cape. "At least tell me where we're going."

"Enjoy the scenery." The road was narrow, citrus trees on one side, olive on the other; the view ahead becoming more spectacular by the mile. Sloping rugged hills, far away a lake, farther away a silvery smudge suggesting a city. How could she be complaining?

Until he got lost. The road narrowed, becoming impassible with the Dodge. He stopped, got out, sucked in the fresh air.

Laura stomped up to him. "If you'd tell me where we're going, I could tell you which road to take."

"Who said I'm lost?" He marched back to the Dodge and before slamming the door shut, yelled out, "Coming?"

She slumped into the seat, threw daggers at him. "What's changed?"

"Nothing." He started the car.

"Don't tell me 'nothing.' Since I got back, you've been acting like a sulky teenager. I have no idea what you want."

"It's all under control." He punched the gas, the tires whirling up dust.

Nothing was under control besides his plan. He'd arranged to meet with Hank Hiddleston who claimed to know Knox's location. Curtis planned to offer his blood exclusively to Hiddleston in exchange for a normal life. He would get his fame if he'd help take Knox down. Win-win both ways. All Curtis had to do was to be quicker than Knox, because now with Green and Clifton out of the picture, Knox wouldn't be far behind. She didn't know about her friends' fate. Curtis could have told her. Why bother?

He hadn't planned the trip up into the hills, which had slowed things down, though he didn't regret the mistake. Might as well enjoy the undulating scenery and the knowledge no one was following and no car could pass unnoticed. The intersection bringing him back to the highway was still a few miles away. Even though he didn't know where they were, he had a good memory once he'd driven a road. Seven miles max to get there. Seven miles of peace before he had to prepare for any type of recognition from people driving past. People looking for him. People who wanted the reward. People who wanted him dead. And Knox.

Curtis was less than a split second too late to hit the brakes and avoid what was at first a shadow in the corner of his eye, growing bigger and whiter and solid in seconds. It smashed into driver's side door. The impact knocked all his wind out, thrust him into the seatbelt. Airbags deployed, robbing him of sight and control. Laura screamed.

There was another impact. It sent the car spinning as the tires lost the battle to find grip on the loose gravel. He couldn't steer against the spin; it would send them down the hill coming dangerously close. If he hit the brakes, it would send them through the air.

He had no choice. "Hold on!"

He twitched his foot a few times, then he slammed the brakes. Laura screamed louder. He had no idea how often the car spun through the air. Once, twice, landing on the roof, the tires, roof again. Glass rained all over. The rubbing of carbon steel on gravel as the car slid on its side nearly deafened him. His head spun when the car joggled like a toy, coming to its final halt on the tires.

He took a second to compose, checked on Laura. "Are you okay?"

She had no obvious scratches or injuries besides a pale face. She nodded. "What happened?"

"My bad."

Chapter Forty-Nine

Wayne had located the Dodge with the drone, *Lorita*. It recognized the make of the car, confirmed with the license plate, but its one imperfection was the inability to follow more than one car at a time. Working under an unproven hunch that Knox had Curtis's Tahoe, Wayne had given finding the Dodge higher priority. But when he watched the Dodge being propelled through the air after the white Tahoe crashed into its side, he regretted his decision.

His mouth went dry when he studied the drone's footage. There were those seconds of hope. Were they alive? Would they come out of the car? They did, and to his surprise, both appeared more or less unhurt, though a little unsteady on their feet. A man welcomed them. *Lorita* could identify cars but not people.

Despite that, Wayne was positive it must be Knox. The car blocked the man's movements, but Curtis suddenly sagged, and then Laura. Knox then dragged two seemingly lifeless bodies to the Tahoe. Wayne shuddered. Did he just witness Curtis's and Laura's murder? Better not. He didn't spent the last few days trying to save their lives only to watch them being killed.

Gustaf's invention came with one big drawback. *Lorita's* time in the air was limited to three hours, which already exceeded the time of any other hobbyist drone, not to mention the range as he controlled the drone from up to one hundred miles using satellite signal to a certain extent.

Though the design was similar to military drones, Gustaf wasn't with the military, therefore didn't have access to drones that stayed in the air for days.

The drone had followed the Tahoe for as long as Gustaf could allow it before he had to redirect it home, inevitably taking the chance from Wayne to see where Knox went. But the short period before its recall gave Wayne information to send to Sutton. According to Google

Maps, Knox was on a dead end road. The Tahoe could handle rough terrain, but Sutton's borrowed car, Katherine's Hyundai i30, couldn't.

It had been more than twenty minutes since Wayne last heard from Sutton, who was now in a dead zone. Anxiety captured Wayne. Time was running short.

Chapter Fifty

Fed by Wayne with crucial leads of the Tahoe's direction, the very last words Sutton heard before he lost the signal was, "Watch for chimneys." When he spotted them poking out from behind treetops, Sutton surmised it was the only place Curtis and Emily aka Laura could be.

Mendez had also provided Sutton with leads. Desperate to keep his head out of the sling after his big boo-boo, he'd checked ownership of every house in the area and stumbled over a property purchased eight years ago, not by Knox but Hank Hiddleston's sister. This reeked because she'd been diagnosed with dementia years earlier.

But the most significant twist, which could explain how Curtis ended up in Knox's hands was, so Mendez told him, that Hiddleston—selflessly offering his help in finding Knox—claimed to have had a phone call from one Frank Gillespie, asking to meet but never showing up. This raised in Sutton the assumption that Curtis had purported to be Gillespie, but instead of meeting, Hiddleston sold Curtis out to Knox. Of course, there was no proof and would be difficult to find if Curtis was dead. In the meantime, no one dared to question Hiddleston's credibility.

There was one other way why Curtis ended up in trouble: Knox had tapped Hiddleston's phone. Sutton doubted it though. Knox wasn't that smart.

All this twirled through Sutton's mind until his ride in the Hyundai was abruptly halted by a gate. One of those farm gates suggesting livestock behind. The ones farmers expect you to shut so no cattle were lost. A big sign was attached to it. PRIVATE PROPERTY. TRESPASSERS WILL BE SHOT. Straightforward.

He hadn't seen the gate when he'd steered the Hyundai around the bend, expecting the road to continue in a long, wide curve. Now it resembled a trap. A camera perched on a high pole, aimed at anyone entering the property he hoped. Otherwise he would have been discovered the moment he nosed the car onto the fifty yard straight.

He reversed all the way past the curve. With any luck, and if he'd been seen, he would be considered a lost driver.

After hiding the car behind a bush, he trudged through the dense shrubs. He slipped on the black cotton jacket to camouflage better. Petrichor hung in the air from the rain that must have fallen here recently, the dust bonding and not whirling up as he slinked ahead, the chimney in his sight.

Chapter Fifty-One

The surface under Curtis felt unnervingly hard. It wasn't a bed he lay on. It was too cold, too uncomfortable. His back was slightly elevated, and it was nippy. Cold sweat pearling under his naked torso crawled down his skin. He trembled. His brain—washed out, reset, put back in. Even after he'd knocked out the rasp-tap guy, and while doing so, knocked himself out, Curtis had been in better shape.

He remembered the crash, the moment the Tahoe smashed into the Dodge still clear. The rest was a blur. The one thing he hadn't expected was for his car—how on earth did it end up here?—to come from a small side track he had seen but considered as the most unlikely place anyone could target him. All he'd been worried about at that stage was the trouble waiting for him at the highway. *I seriously have to stay on alert,* he warned himself.

A tense pull on the inside of his left elbow annoyed him. Not painful but uncomfortable. It was an automated move, his brain advising to check out the source before opening his eyes. He did it with his right arm, slowly, no jerk. A sting on his lower quadrant worsened the more he stretched his arm. He cracked his eyes open. There were wires. He studied their path. A knife attached to one end poked his naked skin. A knife!

Panic struck him. He jerked both arms, tried to reach the knife. A sharp pang jolted through him. Unmercifully, the knife broke his skin, dug into his flesh. He couldn't curl. His legs restricted. His throat constricted as if a thin snake coiled around it. On instinct he flung his hands to the snake, the knife now driving into his flesh.

"No point fighting it."

The sardonic voice jerked Curtis to a halt. In vain he fought his human reaction to reach whatever was robbing him of air, threatening to garrote him. A hand clutched around his, forced it down to his side, wires thwarting any move. There was no way to keep his other hand from the same fate.

As if the snake had lost interest, the constriction eased. The sudden intake of oxygen forced Curtis to gasp, cough, wheeze. The knife slid out of his pierced flesh, leaving a warm rivulet trickling down his skin. He quivered under the trauma, tears shooting to his eyes, his vocal cords not obeying his command to ask: Why the fuck are you doing this to me?

The tormentor appeared. Sweaty bald spots blanketed by the dark, dyed hair and a thick layer of make-up failed to hide the liver spots covering the leathery skin. His eyes were dark. Despite the common interpretation that dark eyes represented warmth, these ones reflected the opposite. So did the thin lips. His body was fleshy from indulging too many calories. And he was much shorter than Curtis expected.

Fucking Hiddleston sold me out. I should have known better.

"Nice to finally meet you."

Curtis didn't respond. Struggling to suppress a squirm, he had no intention of talking to his tormentor: Sebastian Knox.

Curtis scanned the what looked like a thirty-odd-foot square room. All he had in his view were sterile tables, racks, all glass or metal or steel or aluminum. Tubes here, vials there. The door right ahead. So close and yet so far. He couldn't see or sense walls behind him. This meant he must be smack bang in the middle of the room. What was behind him? More tools Knox planned on using on him?

A repetitive beep echoed through the room. Curtis discovered the source for the pull on the inside of his elbow. A needle was jammed into his vein. A tube ran out of it, carrying his blood into a bag on a machine rocking back and forth on a small trolley.

Knox fumbled with the bags, presumably connecting another one. Was it the first pint or the second? Maybe the third? A human male body carried around nine to eleven pints of blood. Curtis considered his height, his weight. He probably carried around ten. Two pints shouldn't be an issue, but pint three could induce the first signs of hypovolemic shock.

"Bag two," Knox hissed, repositioning the knife.

Curtis sensed the tickle on his lower abdomen.

"I wouldn't move if I were you." Knox wetted gauze with what looked like gel.

The moment Knox pressed it onto the cut, Curtis clenched his teeth, strangling a scream. He couldn't control his urge to shrink away from the unbearable heat on his skin, pinching his flesh as if someone ran it through a mincer. Desperate to prevent his body from moving, he clutched his hands around the cold steel on the side of the gurney. *The wire. Think of the wire.*

"You know," Knox said as if the torture he was giving was just day-to-day business. "Monkeys worked it out quicker than you did. You fight the fetters and the wire around your neck tightens. You stop fighting, the wire stops tightening. I readjusted the winch, so it doesn't keep tightening as otherwise your head will be snapped off just like that." He snapped his fingers as he said it. "Gone. In addition, I attached a knife. Same thing. You move and the knife will inevitably dig into you. It's how we tested intelligence on several animals. The result was astounding, rats being smarter than monkeys. I always wondered how long it would take a human to figure it out. First test failed. You're not Captain America or Superman or Einstein. Very disappointing."

Knox let go of the pressure and removed the gauze. Curtis couldn't feel his blood ooze from the wound any longer but the sting and the burn remained.

"Wow, this compound works better than I ever thought," Knox said, a flash of excitement on his face. "This will be revolutionary. I'll explain to you what just happened. I'm sure you heard of glue that's used instead of stitches?"

Curtis didn't dare to move or talk.

"The results have been amazing, but the downfall is the healing process is too slow. You need to think of soldiers here, people in combat. Certainly, there are glues capable of closing wounds within sixty seconds, but tissues and nerves still heal at normal speed. This is different. It bonds damaged nerves and tissues in seconds. It's usually used under anesthetic, but you're a tough guy, and so are soldiers. The cut wasn't as deep as I wished for, but I can confidentially say you'll give me the privilege of testing it on a good deep cut soon since I want more than just your blood."

Plagued by nausea, Curtis croaked, "Where's Laura?" If there was the slightest hint of decency in her, she was his only hope.

"She's here. She's quite a number, isn't she?" Knox's lascivious expression changed to loathing. "Fucking Gordon. If anyone knew how to play two sides, he was a real pro in it. Laura disappeared from NOKS, was never seen again. All the while he hid her from me, from anyone, right under my nose, for six fucking years."

Did this mean Knox didn't know Laura was Emily? Or was the whole Emily story bullshit and Laura was Laura? Curtis's brain ticked at overtime.

Knox said, "You see, they should have never known about you, but your DNA test got things going. Denzel should have taken care of it. Denzel was the sniper on the roof, in case you're wondering who he was.

In the system he was TOX-1. He had CIP. You know what that is?"

"No."

"Congenital insensitivity to pain. It baffles me you managed to take him down." Knox sneered when he said it. "His order was simple. He was to wait until Gordon drew your blood and then kill you. I would have taken care of Gordon. But Denzel fucked up, accidentally killed Gordon then tried to fix his mishap but ended up in the hospital because of you. He killed himself and took the truth with him, including his identity. Loyal worker he was. He was probably aware I'd kill him anyway."

So the rasp-tap guy was Denzel aka TOX-1. It sounded much better than Rabbit. No time to think about it. Curtis had a much bigger problem. The wires cutting into his wrist numbed his fingers from the lack of blood circulation. He had to gain some room to let the blood flow, fearing otherwise, and who knew how long Knox would keep him fettered like a pig on death row, he could lose his hands. Maybe it was one of Knox's sick plans.

He nudged the wire, merely an inch or two. Bad idea. The snake was back, robbing him of what he needed to survive.

"You're an idiot." Knox fiddled with the wires, eased the tension.

Curtis realized he could hardly wiggle a finger before the wires constringed. Knox mumbled something sounding like, "too tight" then the wires around his wrists eased.

Curtis pumped his fists. "How did you know I was in Gordon's loft?" The question had bugged him for so long—the one that would make or break Laura.

"A little bird told me."

"Which was?"

"The same person who killed Felicity."

A blank piece of paper revealed more. "Why was she killed?" Curtis wanted to keep Knox talking, buy time while thinking how to get out of here. Given the circumstances, he knew he was kidding himself. Clinging to hope remained his best bet. Better than nothing.

Knox said, "Gregory didn't cooperate, didn't want to reveal your location. I gave him a chance, emptied the revolver, left three shots in the chamber. Fifty-fifty chance when pulling the trigger. I thought it was fair. Honestly, I don't understand how somebody would rather die than tell me where you were. Unfortunately, I had somebody watching the mayhem. Felicity got away. And without her knowing, she led me straight to you. I was quicker than she was. The privilege of owning a private jet enabled me to have enough time and arrange for some idiot who did what I expected him to do." His laugh chilled Curtis. "That idiot is probably still thinking he accidentally killed her, but when you don't know how to inject the device, it's certain death.

"To be honest, there's hiccup. I lost track of him, but I'm sure I'll find him one day, make sure he can't talk, though doubt he will. Too scared to hand himself in for murder. I mean, what's he going to tell the authorities? 'I killed because a man offered me money?'"

Still no answer for Curtis, but he concluded it hadn't been Laura tipping off Knox. Maybe she was genuine after all.

"How are you feeling?" Knox asked. "You're turning quite green around your gills."

"You'll still lose," he managed to say. While he said it, a beep filled the room.

Curtis cursed the beep. His words were meant to distract Knox from attaching another bag, instead another pint would be gone from his body. Would he survive it? He doubted it. Fifteen to thirty percent of blood loss meant trouble. He'd lost more when he had his accident, but that blood was replaced with what put him into this situation in the first place.

Curtis held onto the hope Knox would stop once bag three was full, but it bothered him that Knox hadn't commented on his previous remark. Knox's face remained pensive, no surprise, no wrinkle of doubt. Bag three started filling.

Finally, he said, "I'll never lose."

"Even the last drop of my blood will not make it exclusive to you. My blood is already in the hands of several scientists, pharmaceutical companies, and laboratories, including the PRDA. But the PRDA won't have a chance to sweep it under the rug. Authorities are informed too. All they're waiting for is the word to go ahead."

Laura didn't know that, or Emily, or whoever she was. Only Wayne knew, and Katherine. When Curtis passed out after the meeting with Merkow, she'd drawn a blood sample at Wayne's request.

"At least you couldn't whinge about it," Wayne had told him later and added the education that whinge meant moaning. By now, Wayne would have told Sutton about it.

There was more Curtis had kept not only from Sutton, also Laura, like the phone number she received from Wayne while he was in the shower. That number was Curtis's lifeline. If she had known the importance of it, she most likely would have used it to her advantage, handed it to Knox for example. But she hadn't.

Instead she'd forwarded the number to him, therefore Curtis could send an hourly message to exactly that number, the recipient no other than Wayne, who'd be on high alert by now. No message meant trouble.

But there was one problem. Curtis was miles away from his last location: Rosa's Cottages. How could Wayne find him? There had to be a way to find some satisfaction before—and Curtis was closer than ever—he died.

"And you know what?" he said, "In some miraculous twist, Leon Powell made sure everyone knows who to look for too. So you'll lose anyway."

Chapter Fifty-Two

On closer inspection, Sutton noted the chimneys were high and colossal, the house old, the walls solid. Spooky, like in horror movies, more so in the moon's glow, pine trees casting shadows on the dark brick wall. It had three stories, porch out front with a wooden railing around it.

He approached the right of the house, the windows—four in all—unopened. Why wouldn't they be? Whoever was inside didn't want anyone joining. He checked the perimeter for other entry points.

Nothing.

Back at the front, he stepped up the porch, armed himself with his Glock, loaded a Parabellum into the chamber and rapped the door which would open outward. This suggested it was once a public building. He rapped the door again, this time harder, the vibration traveling along the walls. No reply. Somebody had to be here. The Tahoe parked only a few feet away.

Curtis would be pissed off about the dents after it got smashed into two cars. Sutton was more than pissed off when Wayne told him what had happened to his Dodge. That would cost the bastard more than just a new car.

He frowned as no one came to the door. He tried the knob. It was unlocked. Really? When he stuck his head in, a musty smell wafted up to his nose.

He wasn't exactly making a secret of his arrival. Any criminal, most of them at least, had that extra reluctance when it came to killing a cop.

Crooks killing cons wasn't that difficult. A cop meant extra years in jail, every cop out there chasing the outlaw if there was an escape. It meant a life of looking over your shoulder. It worked in theory to boost Sutton's confidence.

Ahead stretched a dim, long hallway, doors to the left and right.

Ten, eleven at least. It reminded him of a university, back in the days occupied with students running around, squealing in joy, filled with hope for a splendid future.

All he had ahead was silence. No clatter, no chatter, no breath or breeze suggesting any life other than his was near.

Until he discovered a small light emanated from under a door, the last one to the right. He inched toward it, his back to the wall, his gun chest high, his heart pounding.

Chapter Fifty-Three

It was hard to read Knox's face after the news that he wouldn't be the solitary owner of the blood he so desperately wanted. As much as there was a streak of disappointment clouding his face, anger washed it away.

"The thing is, Curtis, when you die, no one will know who you are. No matter what photos state, the authorities will have a different ID on you."

Why should that matter? "Why did Gordon implant a device?"

"How would I know?"

"Didn't he act on your behalf?"

"On my behalf?" Knox laughed sardonically. "If I'd known where he was, he'd have been dead six years ago. Besides Laura, Gordon stole crucial data and corrupted my system, which took me months to restore. I don't think he expected me to do so. But put yourself in his shoes. Your DNA set off an alarm at his end and mine. My advantage became his when you suddenly left New York and headed for San Diego. I lost you at my end, and you went straight to his."

Coincidence? Had to be.

Knox continued, "The first thing he wanted was to make sure he could find you at all times. The second thing he wanted was to make sure I couldn't find you. But he had a problem. Like me, he could only read the location the device sent out but not alter it. Nobody was supposed to do that. But Clifton was a smart boy in such matters. So, Gordon got him to do it, or Clifton altered it anyway to play me. But for Gordon to reach Clifton, he had to crack into O.R.'s system. And that opened the gate for Powell. That's how he could get that email out.

"But Gordon had to cover his own ass. He tried it by implanting the device into you. If anything unplanned happened to you, nothing would link to him when Shawn Dylan Curtis disappeared from the system. At least that's what I think he was thinking."

Curtis ran the explanation through his mind. Nothing different he could think. Besides one thing. "You're saying Gordon knew the whole time where the people from O.R. were?"

"What do you think?"

Curtis didn't like the certainty in Knox's voice. "Why didn't he get them out then?"

Knox scoffed. "Because he knew they wouldn't survive."

Like Clifton and Green. Curtis came close to asking why Powell had helped the two to escape, but the answer was given. Powell, Green, and Clifton were hoping to catch the Rabbit before Knox. Well, that didn't work.

Knox scoffed once more. "But *I am* the one who has you. I can study every bone and organ you have. I can reproduce you and don't need your permission because you're mine to start with. I still win."

Sadly, Knox was right.

Curtis asked, "Did you kill Jessica?" He had to know.

"Oh, now we're down to the nitty-gritty, but no. I'm no animal. If it is any comfort to you, her death even rattled me."

In an odd way, the words provided some solace, but it also dawned on him that Knox had showed no surprise regarding Jessica's existence.

Knox leaned over him, his face close to his. "You're under the impression it was the DNA test leading me to you, right?"

Curtis didn't dare a nod or a shake of his head.

Knox grimaced, pushed away. "And here I thought you had some brains. It was your own fault I found you. You can run a business quietly and be successful or you can be as stupid as you were. Get loud, let the people know about it. Your name alone got me going. You know why?"

Another nothing from Curtis.

"Before we get to that detail, let's start with your father. Tell me what you know about him?"

"He disappeared thirty years ago. I never saw him again."

"What was his name?"

Curtis swallowed. If he said Frank Gillespie, then Knox would want to know how he knew about the name, which would bring Buckley into the game, which Curtis wanted to avoid. If he said Charles Dylan Curtis, then Knox knew Frank Gillespie was a pseudonym.

He didn't see it coming. The first landing on his cheek traumatized his bones as much as his brain. It was the same side as the one already lacerated by the rasp-tap guy, Denzel. The same side Katherine had patched up nicely to ensure no scar was left. Interestingly, the blow didn't set off the wires to tauten but something warm crawled down his skin. So much for her efforts.

Curtis wanted to run, wanted this sick game to be over when Knox fiddled with gauze, and like before, wet it with gel. As much as Curtis choked back any groan from escaping when the gauze hit his skin, he had no chance.

Knox tossed the gauze over his shoulder, grinned, then growled as though suddenly ridden by a demon. "What was your father's name?"

"Charles." Seconds ticked by.

"Why did you hesitate?"

Think fast. "I couldn't figure out why you'd ask."

"What if I tell you I've known your father as Frank Gillespie?"

"Never heard of him."

"Haven't you?"

"No." Thin ice. Was it about to break beneath him?

"But you don't seem surprised that I knew him under a different name."

"I don't think anyone would show much emotion with a knife on their skin and a wire around their neck."

Knox rolled a swivel stool closer and sat. "Let me tell you a story. Many years ago, there was a man. He barged into the life of someone else. They became friends. Shared secrets, even women. Both were interested in science. Both wanted to change the world. Both agreed on a quest. But one became greedy. First, he stole the other's love. Next, he stole the passion of his life. What would you call this man?"

Interesting. If Curtis put this puzzle together correctly, it meant Iris, his mother, who theoretically wasn't his mother but since she gave birth to him he still considered her his mother, went out with Knox before she settled on Charles. Wow. Thank goodness she didn't stay with Knox.

But Curtis didn't think thoroughly about the answer, his cheekbone still aching from the blow. "A prick."

"A prick. What do you call the prick, running away with the woman, taking the secret which could have revolutionized the world?"

"A selfish prick."

"I'll let the mildness go on that one. What do you call the selfish prick if I told you he then sold his son's blood, but not to the one who was, supposedly, his best friend?"

Okay, that hurt. Now Curtis knew why his blood was drawn on the first day of the month for twelve years. It had nothing to do with his health. It was nothing but money. The question was where did his blood go?

Curtis composed and said, "A deceiving prick."

"A selfish, deceiving prick. But it gets better because his son wasn't his son. He was the creation for the purpose of the human study. He wasn't supposed to ever leave the lab, or have a life, or grow up. In actual fact, he was the making of three enthusiastic scientists-to-be. How do you like that one?"

Nothing new. Right now Curtis was glad it wasn't news.

"Not saying anything?" Knox's eyes flared up in anger.

"You didn't ask me what I would call him."

"You're becoming a smartass."

Curtis said nothing. Where was this heading?

"The selfish, deceiving prick ran with his wife and the... creation, until he ran out of ground. You know why that was?"

"No."

"Because I found out who he really was. And I found out who he married. Worse, he let his family sit there, all by themselves, no support, no nothing. One day, the deceived found the wife and went to see her, told her the son she was bringing up wasn't what she believed he was. It was too much for her, and she killed herself. What do you call the selfish, deceiving prick now?"

There was no knife in his heart, but there may as well be one. Curtis remembered his mother as a strong woman. She cried sometimes, he'd heard her sob, but she never showed her tears. The day she died he'd been out exploring, which hadn't been easy since the city had provided little nature, but he had his places to go to. That day some urge drew him home. He must have been minutes too late. Heart attack, the neighbor who went to see Iris to share a cup of tea with her and supposedly discovered her and called an ambulance had told him.

But the EMTs didn't come alone. Authorities weren't far behind. That's when he'd made the split-second decision—he packed his bags. The only reason for it was his mother's advice, "Whenever you see the police or anyone looking official, I want you to stay away. Should they take me, or should anything happen to me, I don't want you to come looking for me. You'll be on your own. Stay away from any doctors unless you're about to die. Watch out. At all times. Promise me this."

Instinctively, he stayed on alert all his life, used bogus addresses, changed his name around since he had three of them. Kept his promise, and never visited her grave, if there was one. He always knew something wasn't right in his life but never knew what. Now he understood his mother had prepared him for a future without her because at any day, any moment something unplanned could happen. What did this mean? She knew about his blood, knew about him, knew how he came to have a life. Knox was lying, tried to dismay him, probably even killed her. *Fucking asshole.*

"You haven't told me yet what you call this selfish, deceiving prick," Knox said.

"I'm sure you'll tell me." Curtis prepared for another blow, but it didn't come.

He wasn't sure if his heart now raced because of the horror capturing him or if the torture of looking death in the eyes caused it, or if it were the first signs of shock from blood-loss, or if it was pure rage. He couldn't control his trembling.

"You're by far the worst guinea pig I can think of, or should I say Rabbit?" Knox snorted. "Too scared to find another name for that motherfucking loser? Ah, it's the blood loss causing you to shake like a ragdoll. Tell you what. I'll give you a minute to recover while I fill you in. I guess you're burning to learn the truth. Makes dying easier. You see I'm not some cruel bastard."

Curtis didn't know what Knox was doing but assumed he stopped the blood flow because he sat back down, wiggled around on the stool, his face so close Curtis could smell his stale breath.

"As much as a, what did I just call him, motherfucking loser Frank Gillespie was, or Charles Dylan Curtis if you'd rather call him that, I have to admit he was a genius but also the biggest trouble I can think of. Not only did he steal you, he also stole every single formula revealing how we created you. He didn't care about the agreement we had. You know, we kept parts of the formula concealed; each one of us held one piece of it. But Hank was already on the edge of slipping. Frank used that weakness to his advantage, coaxed his portion of the formula out of him. In return, Hank received your blood. He wasn't much good in science, so it was wasted. However, Frank was smart and cunning and hacked into my system and stole what he needed before he destroyed it all and ran."

It answered a lot but not all. Knox was on such a roll Curtis didn't have to wait for more details.

"I knew I'd waste my time trying to find Frank. So I tried to find you. No luck. Until some years later, a small article emerged in the papers with a picture of a man named Charles Curtis and this man looked like Frank Gillespie. His biggest mistake. It led me to Iris, but you left me in a big bind, no matter how many Curtises I checked."

Sutton was right. Knox had gone on a killing spree. Target: Curtis. To keep the bubbling acids in his stomach, Curtis swallowed.

Knox said, "I had given up hope, concentrated on other matters, but luck hadn't left me. I read about a man whose predictions on the share market were beyond the norm. A photo of you. Name beneath.

Shawn Curtis. At that point it didn't mean much, but since the government pulled the rug from beneath us, I thought: What if this is my Curtis? I admit your accident didn't go as planned. It should have been a little push, a little fall, enough to hospitalize you. The loose cargo of poles… well, you survived. Unfortunately, I was fooled by a surgeon and you slipped away."

Merkow, Curtis concluded. Did Knox know he was still alive? Revealing this would shake things up, but it would come with pain. Curtis wasn't up for more as Knox hadn't filled his content of cruelty yet.

There was a sudden silence. Knox's eyes remained on his as if he studied every dimple and crease. This time Curtis saw it coming but the fist already rattled his teeth. He wanted to spit out the horrible iron taste filling his mouth, but he gulped it down, didn't cringe, didn't grimace.

A derisive laugh filled the room. "What an invention. It works a treat, holds your skin together as if it never was apart."

Vertigo bothered Curtis. He wanted it over. "What do you want?" *Besides the obvious.*

He felt Knox's spit on his cheek when he snarled, "Your father."

At that exact moment, Curtis knew he would never walk out of here again. "I don't know where he is."

"And you want me to believe this?" Knox sneered.

Curtis said nothing.

"He must have been the one behind Share-On. No man was ever so obsessed with these words. 'You have to share this.' 'Don't be greedy.' 'Share it on.'"

Words Curtis remembered. One reason why he concentrated on Share-On's moves, if not *the* reason. His father was all about sharing. Let's share food, let's share the fish he caught. Share the banana. All crap. His father never shared anything. The computer was his, the hammer was his. He never shared his feelings or shared where he'd been when he reappeared after eight weeks of absence, and he never shared where he went when he left a few days later. Despite that, and up until a few hours ago when Buckley told him that, well, that Charles wasn't his father, he'd idolized him. But Curtis realized—even though it was total irony—he wouldn't be alive if it wasn't for Charles. This apprehension catapulted strengths into him.

"Where is Frank?" Knox yelled.

Curtis wheezed. It knocked all wind out of him when Knox pounded his fist onto his belly as if he had read the thoughts twirling through his mind and wanted to kick them out of him. His gut protested from the sudden compression. The immediate reaction of convulsion activated that damn wire. Curtis had no air in him when it cut into his throat.

"Shit thing," Knox roared.

Curtis perceived some clinks. Instantly the wire fell loose on his neck. He dragged in air, Knox's words faint when he said, "Don't get too comfortable. We're not done yet."

I wish you were done. A wish Curtis knew wouldn't come true yet as Knox snatched up the stool, flung it against the wall. It crash landed, joggling to a stop on the tiled floor. Knox was far from stopping. "I'm sick of this shit!" He stormed away through the door.

Curtis concentrated on it, readying himself for Knox's next act. His heart sank, as he feared in the next minute he'd see Laura come through the door, beaten, bleeding, close to death.

It wasn't a minute and Knox returned, his hands clutched around her arms, no fetters around her. No bleeding, no beating.

The last hope vanished, replaced by a cocktail of explosive hate and disappointment. It blinded Curtis, clicked out his brain as he wiggled on the gurney. No air was taken from him. Not from the wire around his neck. The knife. It dug into his skin. It needed willpower and a hell of a lot of thinking to reverse the momentum. *Keep your hands down, don't go for the knife no matter what.* The knife pulled away from his belly. A slight relief crawled through him.

"Three attempts it needed for you to work it out," Knox mocked. "Too bad you won't last long enough to really get the hang of it."

A fact Curtis didn't doubt. His observation, clarity, thinking, blurred to a smudge of wild thoughts not making sense. The awareness Knox never stopped the blood flow was worse.

"Don't you think he's had enough?" He couldn't hear any urgency in Laura's voice. Not the slightest hint she was going to help him out of this misery.

Knox shoved her away, but not enough to be out of his reach, only far enough to backhand her in the face. She bounced backward but didn't fall. There was no blood on her face as she lifted her head, but her cheek was red. It would bruise, for sure. She didn't cry. Was she too proud to show her limitations or a tough girl? Shame she was a two-faced bitch.

"You have to make up your mind what side you're on." Knox pointed at Curtis. "You want to side with this… creation?" He shook his hand as if to shake out the pain.

Curtis shuddered. Another beep. Bag three was full.

"Change that fucking bag," Knox ordered Laura.

Don't you dare come near me.

She seemed to count the bags lined up on the trolley. "He won't survive another bag."

"I'm past the point of keeping him alive. He doesn't know where his father is. Only his father has the formula. And only he knows where the money went because he betrayed his son or whatever he is. Look at him!" Knox pointed at Curtis once more. "He's close enough to death to tell the truth. Wise enough to know he won't walk out of here. Am I right, Curtis?"

Curtis didn't nod nor blink nor move but mulled over Knox's words. What money was he talking about?

"Before he falls into somebody else's hands," Knox continued, "he's better off dead. Nobody will know who he was."

She said, "What's the point in that? You need him alive. Use him as a guinea pig if you want to but don't kill him."

Did he hear that right? Was she seriously suggesting that using him as a guinea pig was the way to go while he was on this fucking table, deathbed, whatever the heck he lay on, and about to die? This woman was unbeatable. But he needed her. She was his only ticket out. If only he knew who it was in this room. Laura or Emily. He had to think fast, find a way to the Laura he knew. But how? Something out of both their lives. Something that would take either by surprise.

He briefly held his breath before he said it. "Why did you kill Green?"

Curtis had little interest in Knox who said something about a tablet and signal and *blah blah*. He focused on Laura. It crushed him that the hoped reaction of surprise or sadness didn't come. Nothing at all. Game lost. All over. Time to come to terms with it.

One unexpected change happened within seconds. Out of nowhere, Knox had a gun in his hand and without a blink, he pressed it to her temple.

Her face drained of color.

"Go change the fucking bag or I'll blow your head off." He pushed her ahead but remained stationary a few feet away, his gun trained on her.

She inched toward the gurney. Curtis kept paying attention to Knox's movements. Remembering what had happened to Gordon, Curtis readied for her brain to rain over him.

From the corner of his eye, he watched her change the bag, but as she straightened, she dropped the full bag onto him, swapped it to one hand, while the other remained near the knife. He could feel her fumble but had no idea what she was doing.

She whispered something. Something about 'now'. He shrugged, couldn't understand what she said, his mind starting to fog.

"Pull the strings on 'now'," she mouthed. "Trust me."

Trust *her*? This had to be the joke of the year. She'd nearly killed him once before, now she wanted him to commit suicide. He pressed his lips together, grimacing his disapproval.

"Trust me," she mouthed once more.

"Fuck you," he mouthed back.

A bang echoed through the room, loud, ear battering. It shook the walls. Gun residue hung in the air. Footsteps thudded, closing in. It was Knox, tearing Laura back, one arm around her neck, gun back to her temple.

"Guessing your condition right now, Curtis, you have about five minutes left. Ten if you're lucky. Once you're unconscious or reach the state of shock, whatever comes first, nothing can help you, because there's no one to help you. But I promise you one thing: I'll let you go if you tell me where your father is."

"What about Laura?"

"You're about to die and all you're worried about is Laura?" Knox pressed her closer, one hand remaining with the gun to her temple, the other traveling over her breasts, down her belly, to her jeans. "She'll be in good hands. Don't you worry about that."

Curtis could tell she was close to revealing the truth of her identity as she blinked back tears. To stop her, he shook his head slightly. Her eyes. He tried to read them. Suddenly all his mistrust shed away. The horror in her eyes revealed a woman who had never been touched in such an invasive manner.

Knox glided his hand down her jeans, reaching where no woman ever wanted a hand without her consent. The real Laura would have known what he was like, would have experienced his touch. This Laura was petrified.

As much as Curtis wanted to intervene, he couldn't. He wanted to lift a hand, indicate that he tried to communicate. His body refused every command.

Like a piece of unwanted garbage, Knox threw her to the ground.

You fucking piece of shit, flashed through Curtis's mind, but everything around him spiraled. He closed his eyes, tried to find a focus. He opened them. Laura huddled on the ground. When Knox said once more, "Where is your father?" the words sounded as if from another room.

Curtis's eyelids didn't obey; heavily they fell close. As if a cold blanket wrapped around him, a tremble crept up. His arms light as if they were attached to a string-puppet.

Somebody screamed, "No" or was it "Now." Was it Laura? A black cloak lay over him. He couldn't shake it off.

A vibration. A bang, louder than the one before. A scream. Laura. He would have liked to look at her once more. Look her in the eye, see if she was a victim of circumstances. Hold her again. Kiss her again.

He couldn't will his eyes to open. He shivered, observed the squirrel bouncing from branch to branch, like a trapeze artist. It misjudged. It fell. There was nothing to hold onto. This awful feeling of weightlessness. No control. It was suddenly quiet. Peacefully quiet. Nothing but darkness.

Chapter Fifty-Four

This must be it. This is what it must be about. But where's the light? Curtis had experienced it once before, when his life had flashed in front of his eyes. That was what dying was about. It was warm, though. Quiet and dark. There was the light. This had to be it. No, this wasn't it. It was cold again. So cold. Too bright.

A sudden pang jolted through him. His heart jumped and ran at a million miles an hour. Heat shot through every pore. He inhaled as if it was his first breath ever. He wanted to move. Nothing moved. He tried once more. Nothing. Panic.

"Calm down."

This was neither Knox nor Laura.

"Calm down."

Curtis cracked his eyes open. The light stung. A blur manifested. Sutton. His face hung over him, his body on his chest, pressing down his shoulders and arms.

"Relax. It's over."

Curtis willed his muscles to relax, recognized Laura next to him, needle in her hand.

She sighed. "Welcome back."

Back from where? He didn't ask, too confused about Sutton strange fondness.

"Don't move."

Curtis peeked from under Sutton's armpit at Laura, who smiled at him. "You still have the wires around you."

What wires? Nothing made sense.

"I first had to make sure you wouldn't die." She lifted a syringe. "I know you don't like needles, but your heart needed a tickle. Now that you're back with us, we can take care of the wires. But before we do that, I want to make sure you know who we are and where you are."

He eyed her. "Laura." He looked at him. "Sutton."

"And Santa Claus."

Curtis turned his head to make out the source of the voice. As soon as he identified Knox, everything flooded back. Rage spilled over. He had no chance to release it as Sutton pressed him down.

"Don't move."

"You disconnect the wrong one first, he'll end up with no head." This was Knox.

Curtis focused on the hog-tied man on the floor. One leg was bleeding. Knee, by the looks of it. Curtis saved his energy. One day, he would get to him, even if he had to crawl to him. Knox was done. Dead. *I'll kill you, bastard.*

While Sutton inspected the mechanism, Curtis spotted the knife on his belly.

Laura said, "I put a coin under the knife's point. For as long as you hold still, you'll be okay."

Comforting.

"Left or right?" Sutton asked.

Curtis had no idea who the question was aimed at, but it was Knox who answered, "Eeny, meeny, miny, moe."

Sutton pointed his gun at Knox some fifteen foot away. He fired. Knox squealed.

Hand clutched to his now disfigured ear, he whimpered. "You first need to pull the pin out on the chain on the back. It will disconnect the one around his neck. Once done you start with the left hand. Remove that pin. Then the one on the right. You can detach the chain then."

"And the knife?"

No reply.

Sutton didn't have to lift the gun to make Knox talk. All it took was a smile and a wink.

"First the neck, then left hand, right hand, chest. You do one wrong, it'll tighten. You pull too hard, it'll tighten. You can do the legs at the end. They're unattached to the mechanism."

"You ready?" Sutton asked.

Curtis didn't know how to interpret his demeanor. Good luck? Goodbye? Sorry? He held his breath, prepared for a lengthy process, expected Sutton to proceed with care, but this was more like a butcher taking a bull to the slaughterhouse. *Snap*, loose, *snap*, loose, *snap*, loose. The long pause when he got to the knife nearly snapped Curtis's patience in half. The entire time, no longer than thirty seconds, he focused on Laura, holding up what he assumed was bag four, trickling blood back into his body.

He twitched as the knife, harmless now but still a threat, fell flat and cold on his stomach.

Sutton unhooked it, picked up the coin Laura had put under the blade, threw it in the air, caught it and pressed it onto Curtis's chest. "I would hang onto it. Lucky charm."

The moment the chains loosened, Curtis pumped blood into his hands. He lifted his right for the first time in a long time, releasing an army of ants to crawl through as he inched it over his body to the coin. He tried to get hold of it, but his fingers were stiff.

"Give it time," Laura said.

With a jangle, the chains and wires dropped to the floor. Sutton kicked them out of the way before he peeled his cotton jacket off and settled it around Curtis. The back of the gurney, stretcher, once deathbed, suddenly rattled.

Curtis flinched, but Laura held him back down. "I'm lowering your body so you lie flat. It'll help with the blood flow."

He tried the coin once more, wrapped his fingers around it and kept it tight in his palm.

She stymied his wiggle. "You need to remain still."

"Give him some space," Sutton said.

Silently, Curtis thanked him. This wasn't the time for cuddles and kisses. It was time to leave him to himself, let it all sink in that he still had a life ahead, although it would never be a normal life.

He clutched the jacket. The mix of shock and relief shook him up as much as the coldness altering to warmth.

"Listen to him cry like a baby," Knox mocked in the distance.

There was a thud. A howl.

"Listen to him squeal like a baby," Sutton sneered.

Curtis chuckled. Then laughed. Then whimpered as a pang traveled through him. The cut on his belly might be closed, but damn, it hurt.

Laura came back to him. "It'll take a while."

That smile, that scent. Those blue eyes. He reached for her hand, but she receded, marched to Knox and posed in front of him, proud and tall.

"Look at me," she ordered. "Remember this face. Remember this voice. Remember this name. Emily Sutton."

Knox was quiet for a long moment before he croaked, "Impossible."

"Laura died six years ago. Once more you lose." She left it at that. Nothing came from Knox. He was probably too shocked to find a word.

Back beside Curtis, the tenderness in her eyes carrying the

tenderness warming his heart, he struggled to sit, embraced her and remained like that for as long as Sutton allowed it. Fifteen seconds, twenty, thirty? Curtis didn't want to let go for a long time. He only got ten seconds out of it before Sutton cleared his throat.

"We better make a move," he said.

A move was too early. Curtis could barely feel his legs, barely keep a thought. One thought right there. Did the man who wasn't his father but whom he still considered his father because he didn't know what else to call him, really sell his blood to Hiddleston? And why did Laura say to pull on the strings on now? Was she confused about who she was? Like Buckley said: the confrontation with Knox could knock her around. Too many questions fluttered through his mind.

"He can't leave yet," Laura said to her father. "He needs more blood first."

Sutton shook his head. "We don't have the time. Who knows how many people know where we are? Take him with the blood. Get him away from here."

"Half an hour," she pleaded. "He will relapse if we get him up too early,"

"Your father's right." Curtis yanked the needle from his vein. That was the easy part. With her help, he got to his feet, lightheaded, his legs like chewed gum.

Sutton said, "I want you two to disappear before I call for backup and EMTs. It's easier for me to control this prick when the source of his anger is out of sight."

"Why don't you say you want me out of the way before I kill him?" Curtis said, trying to find footing.

"Something like that."

"You wouldn't dare, Curtis," Knox teased, his face covered in sweat and blood, one ear a bloody mess, his knee shredded. He would never walk again without a limp. "Out of all the samples your father chose the weakest, least intelligent."

Was it worth it staggering over and kicking this prick in the head? Oh yeah, but his temper would boil over if he stood any closer to this bastard.

He refused to let Knox provoke him and spoke to Sutton. "Cops will look for me all over."

"It won't take me long to break this piece of shit," Sutton said scornfully, "and you'll be cleared of murdering the woman in B-1, Felicity, before long." His forehead furrowed. "You know you'll never be a free man. There'll always be people out there hunting you, but for now, go hide somewhere. As soon as this piece of shit is in the right hands, I'll get in touch."

Curtis nodded. "Let's go," he mumbled to Laura, who packed two bags of blood into a duffel hanging over a chair and swung it onto her shoulder.

He let her lead the way through the dim hallway, glad of her supporting arm around his waist. They passed a closed door, then another. The walls were dark, no paintings or decorations brightening up the place. He wondered what was behind the doors, even more when her muscles stiffened.

"What is it?"

"I have this creepy feeling like I've been here before," she said.

Chapter Fifty-Five

He stopped. She did too as she had no choice. Without her support, he wouldn't be able to stand upright. "How familiar?"

"Too familiar."

"You game to have a closer look?"

Her face, already pale, lost its last tan. Whatever this place represented, it held a secret she seemed to believe would open old wounds.

To prevent losing her to panic, he whispered, "I don't want to leave here thinking people are hidden away, coerced or of free will, you know what I mean?"

"NOKS is in Trenton. How can O.R. be here?"

"What was the first place you remember after Gordon rescued you?"

"The beach I took you to. Everything else is a blur."

"Before that."

She scratched the back of her neck. "There's no airport here."

"Private airports aren't uncommon, and Knox told me he came in by his private jet to make sure Felicity got killed. Us not seeing an airstrip doesn't mean there is none."

"You're suggesting Gordon flew me all the way from Trenton over here?"

"And everyone used for Operation Rabbit was flown here and held here. Merkow told me everyone was brainwashed, made believe they were on a bus trip."

Her agreement to examine the place came with reluctance, but he was glad he convinced her.

Behind the first door was a copy of the room they'd just left, just smaller. The second had a bed, a desk, nothing else. So did the third and fourth. Some rooms were empty, others filled with clutter. Stairs led upstairs. Laura suggested continuing on the floor they were on. He agreed, wasn't sure if he'd make it upstairs anyway as there were at least twenty steps to climb.

The next room was bigger than the others they'd seen so far. Three-car garage size at least. It had a desk inside, antique, with bookshelves behind, also antique. Upon closer inspection, it was stacked with medical books.

Laura busied herself skimming through folders she removed from the shelving, while Curtis sat on the chair at the desk, thumbing through papers. Nothing of interest came his way, besides a contract signed by Knox for a beachside villa he apparently bought in La Jolla, worth two-point-seven-million dollars. It was clear he was planning on money coming in.

Curtis studied the switched-off computer, which was without doubt password protected. Curiosity got the better of him. "You wouldn't know his password by any chance?" he asked Laura, a field requesting those secret letters.

She didn't reply.

He swiveled the chair around, spotted her focusing on a lever poking out next to the sidewall of the shelving. Her hand was stretched out, shaking, just short of reaching it, as if she weighed up if she wanted to thrust it down, fearing what could happen. Bookshelf lever. So uninventive no one would ever look for the obvious.

"You want me to do it?" he asked.

She pushed down the lever. The bookshelf creaked as the shelving swung inward, revealing a vault. Trembling, Laura drew back. "You can't touch it. You'll get fried, you'll die."

"Knox will know, and I'll make him talk."

Weak or not, Curtis was fueled with determination to find out if anyone was behind that vault, alive hopefully. He didn't need Laura's help as he hustled to the room where Sutton had relocated Knox to the wall.

There were easy ways to get answers: ask a question and get answers. Not Knox. When Curtis asked about the vault, he denied knowing about it. Curtis exchanged a look with Sutton but didn't wait for approval.

From the trolley, Curtis snatched a scalpel before dragging Knox away from the wall, leaving him slumped to one side. Next Curtis took the nearly limp hand and pressed the blade to his thumb. "How do we get into the vault?"

Knox glared at him, shook his head.

"You really want to play tough? Fine by me, you fucking piece of shit." Curtis applied more pressure until the scalpel bit through skin.

Blood welled. Not letting go of the pressure, he sneered at Knox's grimace of pain. "Your days of holding a glass of whiskey are over if you don't talk. Last chance. How do we get past the vault?"

Sutton behind him better not interfere; Curtis was ready to slice his leg if he did.

"I know nothing about the vault," Knox said with a whimper.

"You used this building for your scummy business and not once did you discover the vault? Bullshit. How many people are in there?"

"No one's in there."

"Now you admit knowing about its existence? Say goodbye to your thumb." To get a better grip, Curtis repositioned the scalpel.

"Curtis!" Sutton cautioned in a warning tone.

Curtis shot daggers at him. "Don't give me that shit! He nearly killed me, nearly killed your daughter. Killed countless innocent people, used them as guinea pigs, took the future from them. Killed hundreds if not thousands of animals, tortured them, bled them to death like he tried with me. Even though he didn't fully testify, he killed my mother, and now you want to read me the riot act? I might end up in hell once I'm finished here, but damn, I want to make sure he doesn't walk the streets again."

"Are you done?"

"Yes."

"I don't care what you're doing to him. I'm off duty. But you don't want to add bodily harm if not murder to your list. I know you're a man with morals. All I'm asking is can you live with it?"

Deep inside, Curtis was aware that cutting off Knox's thumb meant trouble he didn't want to be in. Killing him was even worse. But there was this anger that needed to be released. What was a thumb compared to any other body part? Nothing really.

The action came before his mind had processed the swing of his hand. The scalpel slashed Knox's cheek. Blood oozed from the straight, clean cut. So clean he didn't whimper, probably oblivious to what had happened. Sutton didn't say a word when Curtis chucked the tool to the ground, marched to the trolley on which Knox had left what Curtis was after. He knelt by Knox, wet the gauze with his "revolutionary" gel.

"Next time you come up with an invention, I suggest testing it on yourself." He pressed the gauze onto his cheek, watched Knox's face contort, his screams leaving him cold. "Tell me how to get past the vault."

Knox was either unwilling or unable to talk, which infuriated Curtis. He clenched his hand around Knox's thumb, thrust it back with so much force, he felt the bones crack and tendons snap in his fingers.

Knox's shriek reminded Curtis of a puppy having its paw stood on. Some broken bones were easier explained than a slashed off thumb. The cut to his face, well, to Curtis's amazement the wound closed within seconds, leaving nothing more than a small scar. Sutton said nothing. Curtis didn't know what Laura had to say; she was out of his sight. Probably better.

"How do we get past the vault?" he asked again. The thumb now a useless limp body part, he let go of it, wrapped his hand around the other thumb and asked again, "The vault? Five seconds."

He didn't wait five seconds. As no answer came after three, he treated the thumb the same way as the other, Knox now screaming louder, his face pearling with tears.

"I can go through every single finger if you want me to."

"Rabbit 76," he sobbed.

"Why?"

"You were number seventy-six."

"And you couldn't come up with a better name than Rabbit? Tsk." Curtis shook his head. He tried to stand up but realized he needed to know more. "Where do we enter the code?"

"There's a book called *The Science of Today*. Behind it is a touchpad. You enter the code there."

As Curtis scrambled to his feet, Laura had already left the scene.

"I want you to disappear. Backup will take care of it," Sutton said.

"Sorry." Curtis pushed past him. "You might hold me back but not your daughter."

Driven by determination and hope, he gathered more strengths than he had in the past few days when he hurried to the room where she had already pressed the code into the touchpad. There was a thunderous noise, heavy bolts shifting. Was her heart pounding as much as his?

As the noises faded, she said. "I don't know if it's safe to turn the wheel."

"We'll soon find out." At the desk, he found a pair of scissors and tossed them at the vault.

No sparks, no voltage. His hands now on the wheel, he checked on Laura. Never had he seen her so overwrought before. He spun the wheel. Something moved. Another bolt, he thought. He jerked the door open. What he looked at wasn't a room. There was a staircase leading to darkness.

She pointed down the corridor. "I'd feel better if there was some light."

"A lousy attempt to keep intruders out. Let's go." He stepped ahead, Laura reluctantly following. A few steps down, there were flickers steadying, illuminating the corridor with fluorescents. "And there was light," he said.

At the bottom of the stairs, they encountered another vault. He hoped the code needed was the same. Rabbit 76. Next to the vault was the keypad. She punched in the code. Bolts shifted again.

"I want you to go first," Laura said.

"I want you to prepare for anything. An empty room or people alive." He inhaled deeply. "Or dead bodies." He pressed his shoulder to the door, Laura behind him, likely too scared to explore what was ahead.

There were no voices, clutter, anything that suggested life, only a musty smell annoying his nose. No lights filtered through. Same as before? Walk in and lights would turn on?

Curtis walked in; no lights came on. "Is there a switch on the wall?" he asked Laura, still standing outside, gaping into the room, her lips quivering. "It's not all lost," he said. "There might be another vault, another door. Don't give up yet."

Her chest expanded before she stepped inside, her hands searching for a switch, which she found as a flicker and fluorescents kicked in.

The first thing he noticed was a bed. A small cabinet. A chair. Walls, wood paneled. Hope to find life waning.

There was a small inconsistency in the wood paneling. Like a hairline cutting through. Curtis inspected it, pressed onto the board. A click. Nothing gave way. He let go. A door unlatched, revealing a wooden door. He pushed that one. It gave in instantly. In his way was a curtain which he swung back and, after he entered the room, appeared as a print of a sunset on linen to conceal the door. Smart, cheap, effective.

In front of him was a desk, a chair, a computer. A glass door. He proceeded through it and ended in a room reminding him of school, teacher's desk in the front, two lines of five desks lined up, all of them with a screen on top. Several big screens were mounted on the wall. All of them were blacked, promising no life.

Laura grew so pale, he feared she might faint as she inched into the room, her lips a thin slit, her hands clenched, her eyes widened. She fought back tears, walked up to the second desk, her hands playing over the surface.

"Clifton used to sit here. Martin Green was two rows up. Our sleeping dorms…" Remaining where she was, as though unwilling to move, she gestured to a door at the end of the room.

Curtis did what she couldn't. He opened it. A stuffy smell spilled over him. In front of him was a narrow corridor, berthing places to his left and right. Fourteen or fifteen on the bottom of each side, the same overhead. Some curtains were drawn; the beds wide enough to turn your body.

He inched forward, warily. No noise, no life, only his breathing. No clothes, no evidence anyone had ever lived here, the entire layout resembling the sleeping arrangement in submarines. It must have been a horrible life, people cramped in here like sheep. Males and females, all in the same small place. How many women had suffered assault? Or males? Did they find a way through the vault, figure out it was nothing but a hoax?

As he joined Laura again, she signaled to another door.

"That's the server room."

Upon closer inspection, Curtis found nothing in there. The servers were dead, though heat still streamed out. Laura, behind him, pointed to yet another door. It appeared heavy and thick, like a bunker door. Next to it was a red button.

He closed in on the door, his feelings mixed as he pressed the button. An alarm rang through the silence, a red light flashing above him. The heavy door required some effort so he rammed his shoulder against it. A light came on instantly. A smell he couldn't identify raised his hair, tormented his nose, invaded his throat and just sat there. Pungent, cold and heavy, and somehow nauseating sweet. The cause for the smell in front of him froze him for a few seconds. Repulsed, he swung his arm up under his nose, drew back before he dragged in air.

"What's that smell?" she called out.

Her footsteps closed in. She couldn't see it, shouldn't see it. He blocked her stride.

"What is it?" she asked.

"I'll tell you if you promise me not to check it out."

She eyed him up, held her arms out. No way was he going to move when she tried to thrust him aside. She slouched, her eyes reminding him of an innocent girl, asking for a box of chocolate.

"What's going on?" she asked.

"You don't want to…"

She propelled her foot into his shin. He howled, lost the battle to hold her back as she shoved him to the side. He gave up, unwilling to see her contorted face or hear her scream, which he heard no matter what. Not one like a woman would give when terrorized by a monstrous spider. It was a keening, guttural shriek. The tears had no chance to build; they evaporated with her anger.

"I'll kill him!" Laura roared.

"He isn't worth it." She was out of sight before he could stop her.

Once more he looked at the carnage in front of him. Bodies scrambled to a pile. Faces he didn't know. Their eyes wide open, their mouth distorted as if they'd run out of air. The first man was different. He had a wound to his thigh and another from a bullet to his head. Leon Powell. Chief execution officer. Was he the executioner or the executed?

Laura. If she was ridden by the same hate Curtis had earlier, she could make a terrible mistake.

He hauled himself up the stairs and bustled through the hallway. As he closed in on the room, he heard Sutton's voice echoing through the corridor. "What happened?"

Curtis was just in time to witness Laura kicking Knox's head as if it was a rugby ball, the force well and truly capable to cause the best player blush of jealousy. Not blushing but red was Knox's face. His jaw jutted. His nose sat crooked to the side, bleeding. She had already proven her kicking skills on the rasp-tap guy, but this was a touchdown.

Curtis looked over at Sutton who shrugged. "He fell down the stairs, hit his jaw, and broke his nose and thumbs."

"To make it more believable, he needs some broken ribs." Curtis aimed for a kick but jammed his swing. "It's the people from O.R. down there, right?"

Knox performed something like a nod.

"You killed them all?"

He shook his head.

Curtis would have liked to ask why he'd shaken his head but doubted Knox was capable of moving his lips. "How long you think he'll get?" he asked Sutton.

"A man of his caliber? He'll bribe the judge, the court, get the best lawyer he can. He'll walk free."

Beside him, Laura wound up for another kick. He swung his arms around her, spinning her around. "I have a much better idea than you landing in prison for killing him."

"Me too," Sutton said.

Chapter Fifty-Six

Thirty-six hours later, Curtis hadn't seen Laura or Sutton, who'd arranged for a motel room and asked him to remain there until further notice. Two days max, Sutton had said. Katherine had come to see Curtis and check on his health. Sleep and eat was her prescription, and she supplied him with healthy food, like fruit, nuts, steak and salad, chicken soup, which wasn't as good as Wayne's. Curtis had spoken to Wayne over the phone, told him his chicken soup was better.

"I always said I was a good cook," he said and added he had to go away for business. Life was back to normal.

Curtis had taken Katherine's advice and slept more time than being awake, watching TV to kill boredom. The latest news: Rabbit 76 aka Shawn Dylan Curtis allegedly died in a fire along with Laura Webb and Sebastian Knox, though investigators were still frantically trying to find their bodies.

Keep looking.

Curtis had way too much time at hand, awareness niggling him. Knox had said Charles had picked the weakest one out of all the *creations*. Curtis didn't see himself as weak. But he was no hero either. Over the period of the last few days, there was only one act that saved a life, or two. He'd torched a loft to get himself and Laura out. *Woohoo.* Big deal. Okay, he took down the rasp-tap guy—twice. He credited himself with a slight heroism there.

But if it hadn't been for Wayne keeping a close eye on him, he'd be dead. If it hadn't been for Sutton refraining from taking him into custody, he'd be behind bars. If it hadn't been for the same man keeping Knox at bay, he'd be dead. And there was Laura.

First, she saved Curtis when he was injured. Next, Katherine saved him because Laura wasn't so much of a doctor. Then, Laura braved Clifton, even her father. And while she battled conflicting personalities, she had the wits to place a coin under the knife's point as otherwise, he would have knifed himself—if not beheaded—the moment he… yeah, passed out. Very brave. And he missed out on all the action how Sutton took down Knox. Brilliant. Not a hero.

Curtis didn't need to be a hero, didn't need to hear people say: damn, you did great. But after everything that went down, looking back at something that would give him his own satisfaction would have been nice. He wasn't thinking of killing people, but saving lives. Sure, his blood could do that, but that wasn't the point. Knox was right. He was no Superman, Captain America, and certainly no Einstein. On the other hand, and that wasn't bad, heroes surrounded him.

Way too much time to think.

As his impatience stretched to its limits, he received a call from Sutton, ordering him to wait outside the deli two blocks down the street from the motel.

"Take everything with you, and don't kill the man picking you up. Give him a chance. And to avoid complications, wear a ball cap and sunglasses," Sutton had said.

Thirty minutes later, Curtis observed a Ford Taurus pulling over and a hand beckoning to get in the car. As he opened the door, Mendez greeted him.

"Get in."

There was a swell of hatred overwhelming Curtis. Don't kill him, Sutton had said after he told him Mendez was responsible for Felicity's death and that it was him who'd tipped off Knox when Curtis was in Gordon's loft. There must have been a good reason why Sutton sent him along, trusting enough that Curtis well and truly wouldn't kill him.

He slumped into the seat. "Where are we going?"

"Can't tell." Mendez hit the gas and after a few silent miles, he said, "I don't know how to say this. If I had known the extent… That's not the right way… not how… I didn't know she would die. I know it's no excuse to say I was drunk when Knox… I didn't know who he was. Only when I saw his photo did I know who I was dealing with. I know sorry will not cut it, and I wanted to hand myself in, but Sutton said it wouldn't bring her back and to see it as a good lesson to get my shit together, which I promised I would… I really wish you'd say something."

Curtis was more interested on the movements on the street. "We all make mistakes."

The rest of the ride remained silent and finished at the same beach where Laura had taken him a few days ago, the same beach where he learned he'd been used for experiments. If only his father had never created him.

Mendez gestured toward Sutton and Laura standing at the shore. "Good luck," he said and sped off after Curtis left the car.

As he walked up to them, his heart bounced. Laura looked good. Less stressed, and it suited her. She wore a black T-shirt and jeans, which he decided must be her favorite attire which flattered her too.

He faced Sutton and shook his hand. "I haven't had time to thank you. I couldn't have gone through all of this without you."

"If every creation was like you, then I hope the entire world will be invaded by them."

"Ha, I honestly hope there's no more of me out there." He turned to Laura, would have loved to hug her but wasn't sure of her father's approval. "Good to see you."

"How are you feeling?"

"Better." His attention back on Sutton, he said, "I don't know what your plans are, but I had plenty of time to consider options, and I guess it's best we go our separate ways." A fleeting look at Laura revealed tears building in her eyes. "I'm sorry, but it's the only way for you to start a new life, a better life, which I'll never be able to provide. Things aren't over, will never be over for me. And you know that."

Sutton pushed between the two, handed one envelope to Curtis, another to Laura.

"In some ways it was an easy decision, but it was difficult as well." Sutton ordered them to open their envelopes.

Curtis studied its contents, surprised to see a passport and a driver's license. Laura, standing to his left, held the same legal documents in her hand. "What's that about?" he asked.

"You can't run the streets as Shawn Dylan Curtis, and your name wasn't my decision."

Curtis opened the passport. The name read Jake Curtis Gillespie. He arched his brows. "Who decided on the name?"

"Not me."

"Emily Laura Gillespie?" Laura yelped.

Curtis and Laura exchanged puzzled looks. Two pairs of eyes now on Sutton.

"I had a little influence on your name, Emily. It can be a temporary thing, but for now it's the easiest. I figured it's not a good idea for you to stay here. Don't worry, we'll have time to catch up on lost days. I promise. But for now, it's better if you two stay low and disappear as far away as possible." Sutton fished out another envelope, which he handed to Curtis.

He revealed two tickets to Sydney, Australia, leaving today. He grinned, passed one ticket to Laura, or Emily. It appeared her father had decided on her name after all.

"There's your first overseas trip, Mrs. Gillespie," Curtis said, curling his lips into a smitten grin, but Laura didn't seem excited.

To Sutton, she said, "What about you? What about us?"

"Like I said, we'll catch up soon. Who knows, by then we might have an official wedding if you two haven't killed each other."

Curtis felt scrutinized as she said, "The latter is likely."

He swung his arms around her, pecked her forehead. "Time will tell." Already decided, he thought. To Sutton he said, "I'll never make it through airport security."

"It's taken care of."

Curtis ran an eye over him. "How?"

"Don't worry about it."

"Doesn't sell."

Sutton smirked conspiratorially. "Let's say somebody owes me more than just one favor and you an apology."

"Donaghy?"

"He's got his tail between his legs," Sutton said with a broad grin. "You remember the Wanted ad in the paper?"

"You telling me he put it in?"

Sutton nodded. "He wanted to speed up the process to catch you but wronged you all over."

Curtis frowned. "But that means he knows I'm alive, knows my new name."

"Does he?" Sutton clapped him on the shoulder. "Have a good trip." After a few more hugs and handshakes, he walked away.

"I have to admit, your father is quite a man."

She snorted. "Leaving his daughter behind shortly after she returned in his life?"

"He's doing it for your own good."

"What, marrying us without our consent?"

"Isn't it like in the old days, when parents decided who's marrying who?"

"Ha-ha."

He kept his attention a little longer on her, confident they were off to a good start.

"Let's go pack some things. We only have a few hours before the plane leaves." He hooked his arm into hers but didn't get to take a step as a young boy ran up to him.

"Mr. Gillespie?"

It sounded odd to be called that. "Yes."

The boy pressed an envelope into his hands. "This is for you. Goodbye." The boy hastened away.

Curtis shrugged, ripping the envelope open.

Dear Jake,

Before he read on, he skimmed the area. Nobody seemed to have an eye on him. He read on.

I named you Jake before I knew what to do with you, but as always Iris won and she decided on Shawn. I'm not saying it was a bad choice, but I hope Jake will bring you more luck in the future.

Unfortunately, quite a few things in your life didn't go according to plan, but how can the life of someone who shouldn't have had a life be planned?

The success of your company came to my surprise. Congratulations on that one. However, as you may know in the meantime, numerous clients were under Knox's flag.

Curtis had learned about it in the meantime. Wayne had told him. "I told you your life's been controlled." Wayne had been right all along but had no idea how right. And he should never know. No one should.

Curtis inched away from Laura, aware of what might be written in the letter. She should never know either that his success was actually a scam. Sure he'd created the blog and got tri-share sc up and running. It was a shaky start. In the whole process, he always thought of the movie *Field of Dreams. You build it, he'll come.* He had no idea what was supposed to come, or who. But those constant flyers and messages about the stock market; there had to be a reason for them.

As soon as Share-On joined tri-share, he'd begun receiving notes in envelopes with no return sender. At first, he had no idea what to make of the digits and numbers, though he knew the names attached were of his clients. The notes kept coming. He kept crunching them up, tossing them in the trash. Fearing somebody knew his clients, he searched for viruses in his system. No luck. One day, when he paid more attention to the notes, he understood what they were. Predictions. Bafflingly accurate. They had to come from someone who had a good knowledge about those companies' moves, Knox right within them. The business boomed. Sometimes Curtis made adjustments, thought he knew better. Win or lose. It worked fine. The messages kept coming. Day after day. Year after year. Out of the blue, they stopped.

Curtis kept on reading.

I hadn't planned on Knox joining tri-share. It should have been, let's call it our ride. But I assume he knew who you were. Why he left you alone, we'll never know. Money I imagine. But it also meant danger you weren't aware of and should have never known of.

It wasn't your fault your company went bust, but I feared Knox would pull the rug from under your feet, if not that being the reason for him to join tri-share to an extent so he had you under control. When I noticed the first signs he was exactly doing that, I took action.

My first strike was sending Sarah with the bogus story about the child. I have to admit your generosity baffled me, but I'll get to that later.

After that, I tampered with your payment system and started sending you inaccurate predictions and then stopped them.

Unfortunately, and as corny as it sounds, my health was letting me down and strike two went down the drain, but I'm trying to catch up on it. On top of it, something unplanned happened.

Even though Sarah and I had an arrangement, she returned for more money and you took the DNA test. There was nothing I could do to stop the ripple effect. Luckily, you're a clever boy, or I should say man, and you got through it with some scratches and bruises.

I'm very proud of you! I know you'd like to see me, but the two of us together is too dangerous for our futures. But I'm always somehow around you as sometimes in life things don't appear the way they are.

Charles

In seconds Curtis whipped his cell from his pocket and speed-dialed Sutton.

"Do you miss me already?"

"It's Buckley, isn't it?"

"Buckley?"

"My father. He used Buckley's name."

"The only information I have about Arthur Buckley is he's in a wheelchair, suffering MS. I doubt he's your father."

"How did he know I was meeting you here today?"

"How do I know? I haven't met your father nor have I spoken to him. Is Emily listening?"

The quick change of the topic alarmed Curtis, so he distanced himself from her. "No."

"Between you and me, I believe your father is the reason I ended up here. After Emily's death, a man came my way, shoved a note into my hand. It said: 'She's in San Diego.' I didn't know what to think of it, but it's why I moved here. I know he's been the one sending me the messages about your innocence, not Emily. He revealed that much to me in a message. In a twisted way, your father played fate or whatever you want to call it. Be thankful you have him watching over you. Have a safe trip." Sutton disconnected.

Torture. Not only not knowing where his father was, vexing Curtis was that Sarah got away with one-point-two-million dollars; money his father had literally given to her. Worse, what on earth was his father thinking, hooking him up with a woman? On top of that, his father pocketed the money he'd streamed into another account. Nice.

He flipped the letter over. There was a note. It had to be it. The one thing he wanted to know so badly.

You are predictable, though it doesn't take a mastermind to know that you would turn the letter looking for the one thing. Let's make a deal: I won't disclose how I did it. We won't disclose that we did it.

This sucked. He wanted to know how his father had predicted the stock market. Curtis folded the letter, shoved it into his back pocket under Laura's scrutiny.

"Family matters," he said. "We'd better go." It was predictable she would nag him about the letter, but he promised to keep the deal.

As they sauntered on he tried contacting Wayne on the cell, but all he got was his voice mail. He left a message, thanking him for everything and hoping to see him again, without revealing where he was traveling to. Wayne would have exploded from jealousy.

Six hours later, after packing the bare essentials, Curtis met Laura at the airport where he encountered a new problem. The seats in the plane were pre-booked. He didn't mind sitting in the middle on the short flight to LAX, allowing Laura to sit at the window since she'd never been on a plane before, but he didn't want to budge on the long flight to Sydney and insisted on an aisle seat.

"I hate being sandwiched between people. I don't have a problem with you sitting at the window. Be my guest. But I want to swap with whoever is having the aisle seat, and he can get squashed."

First, it exposed him to her complaints as she was unwilling to sit next to a stranger, then the airline refused to change the seating arrangements.

In the end, the entire huff was for nothing as nobody occupied the seat, which unnerved Curtis. "Why the hell couldn't they change the seats then?"

"You have flown before, haven't you?"

"Many times."

"Then why are you acting as if it's your first time?"

He shut her up with a kiss.

~ * ~

During the fifteen-hour flight, Laura caught up on the latest movies. Curtis closed his eyes, feigned sleep while processing the last events in the laboratory. In a mutual, silent agreement, Sutton and he thought it best to leave the dead buried. Family members had the news six years ago that their loved ones were dead or went missing and Powell's email only confirmed the worst to them.

No need to make them suffer again. No need for year-long procedures, forensics piecing together each identity which was scrambled by their device.

It wouldn't bring them back and Knox had given enough answers, which Sutton had recorded.

To finalize things, Laura, wearing gloves, typed and printed a confession on Knox's office equipment, a declaration of his guilt in gassing them all. Sutton helped Knox hold the pen to sign it.

Despite Knox's protest, she sedated him—plenty of drugs in the lab qualified for the job. Once he was out, they lugged him onto a gurney, wheeled him through the corridor, rolled him down the stairs, and dumped him in the cell with all the bodies. Of course, they removed the handcuffs and replaced them with strings. They would burn to nothing. Yes, burn.

Once more Curtis had the pleasure of setting a place on fire, this time under Sutton's watchful though blind eye of the law. To get the most effective destruction there was, they mixed whatever they found, like gasoline, chemicals, and ran a trail from the bunker up to Knox's office, from where Curtis ignited the liquids. No matter how accurately things were planned, there always had to be room for error. But they had no time to incorporate error, leaving them with a lesson learned: always check the premises before playing with fire.

Something extremely flammable and highly explosive must have been in the bunker. BOOM. A wall of heat and flames shot up the stairs and all they could do was run. Just as they jumped through the door to the open, a second boom rattled the walls, the ferocity catapulting them into grass and dirt. Luckily, they remained unscathed.

Sutton told him he wrote in his report that he observed Knox, Curtis, and Laura disappear into the building and never come out again. The good thing was the explosions knocked down surrounding trees, blocking the path, so the house's structure weakened enough to collapse and burn to the ground before the fire department found a way in.

Yes, there were the bunkers and cells, but hopefully, there had been enough heat to destroy most of it. Plus, there was so much rubble it would take a substantial amount of time before it was discovered, if anyone was ever to dig that deep.

Since it all went down differently than planned, Sutton took his time to call for backup, giving Curtis and Laura enough time to flee from the scene, though not in Curtis's Tahoe. It had to remain as evidence that Curtis was there. Good thinking from Sutton.

But there was an old battered Ford, which they assumed Powell used to run errands because this much was for sure—he would have known how to get in and out of O.R., whatever his reasons were to remain there to die.

Some people might consider it unethical to decide Knox's fate. Was it? Did a man deserve to walk free after killing thousands of animals and hundreds of people for the sake of money? The world was better off without him. Science was better off without him.

Science was now busy with Curtis's blood and studying his DNA while the government was busy replacing the PRDA's executive with new trustworthy people as one by one of the former administration confessed their knowledge about Knox's controversial methods, the allegations supported by people who worked for NOKS, its future unknown.

Coming out of retirement and offering help to clean up the mess was Hank Hiddleston. Curtis wasn't too sure what to think of it since it was he who'd sold him out to Knox and actually created him, or at least helped.

It never would be over but for now, Curtis found enough consolation in his ability to breathe deeply again, the plane's engines' hum singing him to sleep.

Chapter Fifty-Seven

The plane taxied toward the gate in Sydney. The rising sun beamed up the tarmac. Clicks from unbuckling passengers ignoring the sign urging them to remain seated left Curtis cold. He had different worries than getting out of this plane as quick as possible. He checked on Laura's moves.

She said, "We don't even know where to go from here."

"And here I thought you had it all planned out." He leaned in closer to her, pretended to kiss her but whispered, "My first worry is about making it through customs. I know your dad said he took care of it, and we made it through all the scans when we checked in. I might be dead but facial recognition doesn't change overnight."

"I'm worried about the device."

Despite all concerns, customs were no problem, and for the first time, with a name he'd received just over twenty-four hours ago, Curtis set foot in a country he'd never been to. Next to him was Laura.

"How are you feeling, Mrs. Emily Gillespie?"

"To be honest, I'm excited as much as scared."

"At least nobody wants to kill us here. I hope." His phone vibrated in his pocket. "Hmm, maybe I should have left that thing behind." He fished it out.

The message was from Wayne.

Sorry, I missed your call, mate. Get in touch once you're settled, wherever that is. I'm not going to say I'll miss you because you know I will. Just keep your ass out of trouble.

With their luggage rolling behind them, they strolled hand in hand through the doors, were welcomed by a bunch of people holding up signs with names scribbled on cardboard. Not expecting to see their names, Curtis shoved Laura ahead, but she stalled.

"Is this us?" She pointed to a sign that read Mr. and Mrs. J. & E. Gillespie.

"Your dad would have said if anyone was expecting us."

"You mean like he told us about the flights and the passports?"

It was too late to ignore a young man anyway, waving at them with a friendly grin on his face, sporting board shorts and a singlet.

"Let's hope he's got a car for us."

His hand clenched around hers, Curtis led her to the man, keeping her slightly behind, enough to avoid giving her the idea of discourtesy, but also enough to step in and protect her.

"Jake Gillespie." He stretched out his hand to greet the man and then introduced Laura as Emily.

"Peter. Hope you guys had a good flight. Please follow."

"Where are we heading?"

"There's a car waiting for you. That's all I know."

They walked outside, the heat hitting Curtis, humid and heavy wrapping him up.

Peter smiled once more. "It won't be long," he said and left.

By now, Curtis had played all sorts of scenarios through his head, but he couldn't shake off the uncanny feeling this was a set-up. Somebody was aware they were here, ready to take him to some lab, milk his blood, use him as a guinea pig, Laura's fate unknown.

"I'm not feeling too comfortable with this," he shared his concern.

"I don't know what to think of it either."

"Run?"

At that moment, a big white 4WD drove up, bull-bar at the front, four enormous tires carrying a cabin with another spare tire on the rack, which had spotlights attached. The lights flashed. The car stopped a few yards short. The lights flashed again, followed by honks.

"What do you think?" he asked Laura.

"Too late to run."

The door opened. Out jumped a man, Akubra hat kept low. His hand went up to it, ripping it off. "Mate, we don't have all fucking day. Come on."

"Wayne?"

"Couldn't let you two idiots explore the country alone. You'd get lost in bloody woop woop."

"Woop what?"

"Bush, mate."

Curtis released his relief with a tight hug.

"I missed you, buddy," he said.

"Yeah, yeah, I'll get on your nerves soon enough. Had to keep you away while I was organizing all of this. Said to Sutton if you'd get out of it alive, it's a good place to start anew. Hang on, mate." He stepped behind Curtis and stretched out his hand, kissing Laura's. "Mrs. Gillespie. Lovely to meet you... again. Hope you've had a pleasant trip so far, and I hope this dickhead is treating you nicely. If not, I'll put him straight."

"Nice to meet you... again. So far he's doing well."

"Not good enough." Wayne clapped his hands. "Anyhow, before we go anywhere, we have a certain place to go. Hop in the car."

Curtis left Laura the choice where to sit, and she decided for the back. "You sure?"

"You two have things to discuss while I'll enjoy the scenery."

Expecting Wayne to drive like a grandmother again, it surprised Curtis how confidently he maneuvered through the busy streets, particularly since the traffic rolled on the left.

"Good to be home for you?" he asked.

"Kinda. What I like is I can use my lingo and everyone understands what I'm sayin'. Y'know what I sayin'?"

Curtis laughed. "Just make sure we know what you're saying in case we are in some kind of predicament. Where are we heading?"

Wayne reached into the side compartment and tossed an envelope onto Curtis's lap.

"Found this yesty, hang on, the day before, or was it... who cares. Time difference's still doing me head in. It was in my mailbox before I flew out."

Curtis checked the contents. A key and a note.

Mr. Cantrell: Mr. Jenkins is expecting Jake Gillespie at
9 AM. Make sure he gets there. Charles.

Curtis turned the note. It read Guardian Vaults. "How did you know it was for me? I didn't even know before yesterday about my new name."

"Mate, I knew a couple of things I couldn't tell you as it would have screwed up a few things."

"You spoke to my father?"

"No, man. I used my brain. I knew your father used the name Gillespie. I had a chit-chat with Sutton about it, and it's how your passport came to live with the name Jake Curtis Gillespie."

"You named me Jake?"

"No, man, that was your dad. Look, it's too complicated. Just get used to it."

Hoodwinked by two people Curtis believed he could trust. Was there a point quarreling over it? He let it go, checked the time, checked the traffic. They only had half an hour to get to the Guardian Vaults, wherever they were, and traffic was at a crawl. "Are we going to make it on time?"

"Yeah, man. Don't worry."

Twenty-six minutes later, Wayne stopped the car, double parked, and pointed at a building. "Get out. We'll be back in half."

"You're not coming?"

"Not my business."

Curtis looked back at Laura.

"Not my business either."

He leaned back for a kiss. "See you soon."

The two lane one way street was buzzing with traffic. The glass-fronted building had, as far as he could tell, six floors. The directory guided him downstairs to another door. Also glass. He checked the time. Exactly 9 AM.

He opened the door, entered the room. The classy marble interior streamed out comfort and security, the latter the important part. He couldn't think of a reason somebody would put anything there for him, on the other side of the world.

He walked up to the counter. A blonde lady in a white shirt, black suit jacket, black skirt greeted him with a friendly smile, "Good morning. How are you today?"

Did she care how he was today? "I'm fine. I believe Mr. Jenkins is expecting me."

"Mr. Jake Gillespie?"

He nodded.

"One moment."

He readied to reveal his passport. Surely, she'd want to see identification, but the woman named Tracey, so her name-tag revealed, typed something into the computer. Then she seemed distracted by something to her side. He followed her glance and spotted a man sitting on a couch, reading a paper. His suit was impeccable, his hair peppered, neatly combed, still thick considering his age, which Curtis guessed around seventy. The angle he sat didn't give Curtis a full profile, but he observed him fold the paper and wedge it under his arm before he stood, propping a fedora onto his head. He sauntered to the exit, gave Tracey a quick nod, and disappeared through the door.

"Please follow me, Mr. Gillespie," she said.

"No ID?"

"You've been positively identified."

"By whom?"

"Mr. Jenkins."

Bamboozled, Curtis followed her. "Can you tell me more about Mr. Jenkins? Like his first name?"

"Sorry, but that's confidential. He told me you'd have questions, but my answers will be limited."

"So, he's a regular?"

"Now and then over the years."

"He'll return?"

She stopped at a door. "As of this morning, he finished his business with us. Which is a shame." She slid a key into a lock, opened a door and walked inside.

Curtis joined her in the small room. A lonely table in the middle with a cash box on top.

"Did you bring the key?" she asked.

He fished it from his pocket and passed it to her. She inserted a key into one lock, his key into the other. There was a click.

"It's not a routine procedure, but Mr. Jenkins was very specific about how to handle this. And we were specific about our safety measures. We met halfway. If you need any help, I'll be at the front desk." She left.

Curtis approached the table, his hands trembling as he opened the box. All it contained was an envelope. He ripped open one end, discovered another envelope, wrapped around it a letter. He started reading.

Dear Jake,

If you get to read this means you've made it this far. Well done. You remember I wrote about Sarah? She was supposed to get the 1.2 million you so generously paid her, but since she tried to take you for more money, we agreed you should get half of it. She didn't complain much.

When I realized Knox was involved with tri-share, I prepared for the worst, and the worst had happened.

I already mentioned that I streamed parts of your clients' money into different accounts. I did the same with the remaining profits from Share-On before it all collapsed. In all, it was a total of eight million and a bit. Out of that, all your debts will be paid. It's being taken care of while you're reading this. After I took what I think I deserve so I can finally retire, it leaves you with 2.2 million. I'm sure you'll agree.

All the paperwork is in the other envelope, including bank cards; some in Australia, some in the States, some in Europe.

There's a double bottom in the box. I want you to open it..."

Curtis had to wipe the tears from his face first. He didn't expect any of this. After a few deep breaths, he checked the box and noticed a flap enabling him to lift the bottom. As he did so, he revealed a small cylinder containing fluid and another note.

It's up to you if you want to use the contents of the cylinder. The substance will change your blood readings. However, it'll only be for a few hours. Six at the most. But it will help you out if you are in a predicament. You know it'll never be over. Use it wisely.

You'll find a card in the envelope for a doctor I fully trust. I've known him for many years. He may have made a mistake in the past, but he didn't do it by choice. He might be able to help you and Emily with the device. There's no guarantee. It's a challenge not only for him.

Good luck
Charles

PS: It was good seeing you.

In a rush, Curtis shoved the box's contents into the small bag that was added and returned to Tracey. "Anything I need to sign?"
"It's all been taken care of."
"By Mr. Jenkins?"
"Yes."
"Is he still here?"

"He left as you arrived."

"The man with the paper?"

"I can't answer more than that. Sorry."

"And he won't come back."

"No." She smiled. "It was nice doing business with you, Mr. Gillespie."

He smiled back. "Thank you." He kicked himself that he hadn't paid more attention to the face of the man with the paper. He only got a brief look, a flash of his profile. Thirty years was a long time. Torture.

He dug through the envelope to see who the person was his father trusted. He found a card. He read it and chuckled. Dr. Phil Merkow, Broken Hill, New South Wales, Australia. Wayne would know where to go.

As Curtis stepped outside to the street, he checked for Wayne's car and spotted it a few yards away but he held his stride, feeling eyes on him. Over on the other side of the street, Curtis saw a man—the man. Mr. Jenkins. The temptation was enormous. He wanted to cross the street, wanted to know for sure. The man lifted his fedora, nodded.

Curtis nodded back. Smiled. Life was good again. Great actually. There was a light at the end of the tunnel, and it occurred to him that thanks to his father—who never had been one in the first place— that man had ironically just given him a new life. If only he never had created him.

Acknowledgements

It's not supposed to become a speech at the Oscar's, but where do I start? It's certainly been a long journey, with ups and downs, frustrations as much as rewards. I shed many tears, had this little devil tapping on my shoulder saying, "Why don't you just give up?" but I hadn't spent all this time only to see dust grow on my pages.

But before I go any further, I mean, let's face it, without my parents, I wouldn't be here in the first place. Right? So, thank you for making love on that what must have been a hot August night. Or maybe it was rainy. And look what you got out of it? A little dreamer.

My apology for this slight distraction. Back to business.

A big thank you to the fabulous team of Champagne Book Group. Special thanks to Cassie Knight for believing in me, believing in my thriller, for giving me this special opportunity; my editor Judy Griffith Gill for your incredible patience and putting up with my Teutonic desires; Keith W. Willis for always freeing up time to answer my many questions while you were busy shaping your own career; and Sevannah Storm for the stunning book cover.

And in no order of importance…

My wonderful friends who haven't walked away. "OMG are you talking about books again?" Thank you for bringing me back to earth when I drifted off, distracting me when I needed a time-out, for letting me be your unlikely friend, and for always being here for me, no matter what time, no matter the problem. I can't wish for better friends, including Ray Goodworth. Ha! Maybe I should *blame* you for all of it. Thank you for disliking my very first book I wrote in English; Genia Sarafian, I'm sure you remember my very first steps in learning how to use gerunds.

Yuki Dew Miyazawa, thank you for giving me insight into San Diego; David Baker for sharing your knowledge about drones; Cherie Kean for your critical eyes on my first draft; Charlotte Erne for helping me with my tricky plot. I know you'll succeed with your children's books.

There are some people who I've never met in person but played such an important role. Victoria Gilbert, thank you for helping me with the dreaded query letter and for tirelessly being open to my questions, and for sharing your valuable knowledge into this rather confusing industry.

My lovely writer friends from different corners of the world: Wanjoo Kim, Nicholas Kotowski, Melinte Raluca. You guys kept me inspired and never shied away from giving that extra critical input to take the first pages to the next level. I have no doubt you will succeed. Never give up!

Last but not least: Google. I honestly hope my search history will never be checked.

About the Author

Born in Switzerland, T.C. Correy always felt *strangely* drawn to Australia. From a young age she wrote short stories, but inspired by a TV series, her first novel based Down Under gave T.C. the perfect excuse to head for the land of Kangaroos and Koalas, which she now calls home.

With barely enough English to get by—let alone Aussie slang—she gathered enough material during her adventurous solo trip traveling the Outback to write an entire book, but it was thrillers she grew an undying passion for.

Tackling the new country, T.C. didn't shy away from teaching herself proper English, and since then, under the watchful eye of her beloved Mini Foxy, she's completed four thrillers, though oddly enough, they're based in San Diego.

During the day working in hospitality in one of Australia's top destinations, at night she's like a sponge and researches facts for her thrillers—no matter the topic—though leaves enough conspiracy for everyone's mind. Her science thriller, *If Only He Never*, is the first (but not the last) of her books to be published.

T.C. loves to hear from her readers. You can find and connect with her at the links below.

Facebook: https://www.facebook.com/authortccorrey
Twitter: https://twitter.com/tccorrey

~ * ~

Thank you for taking the time to read *If Only He Never* and hope you enjoyed reading it as much as we loved bringing it to you. If you enjoyed the story, please tell your friends and leave a review. Reviews support authors and ensure they continue to bring readers books to love and enjoy.

A cure, a cover-up and a reporter willing to give his life for the ultimate story.

Money makes the world go around. People will lie, steal, and kill for the number on a bill. As a reporter, Jack lived a life of exposing such things, uncovering the cold truth for the readers of *The Chicago Tribune*. That is until he uncovers a truth that the FDA can not let out.

Jack takes on a renegade force but soon finds that it is a battle he need not wage himself. A hidden sect, a group of insiders wants the company taken down and Jack may be their key to finally completing their goal.

Chapter One
Kill the Story

Tribune Company, Chicago, IL, August 19th

The windy city provided no breeze to stave off the dog days of summer. Heat brought common courtesy to the brink of extinction; a prolonged wave engulfed the Second City. Jack Randolph, an eager thirty-one-year-old reporter, had a Nobel Prize mentality that often led him to stories too magnificent for a mainstream newspaper such as the *Tribune*. An investigator first and a writer second, his potential was untapped.

He entered his editor's office, the daily paper in his hand. He tossed the paper onto Mike's desk, scattering the work his chief tooled away on. Mike sat back in his chair; this wasn't the first time Jack had come in with the idea of creating a scene.

"Why did you pull my story? You told me front page—it's not even in here."

"Wasn't my call."

"You're the editor. You have final say, Mike. Don't try and put this on someone else."

Mike shook his head at the eager reporter. He put both hands on his desk and calmly rose. He replied, "Jack, you need to shut my door and sit down."

"I'm not taking this. I busted my ass on this story. I'd be pissed if you buried it in the middle, but not to run it at all is just chicken shit. You know I have something here."

"Shut the door, and we can talk."

Calming himself, Jack closed his editor's door, walked to his Mike's desk, then plopped petulantly into his chair. Expecting the usual spiel on how his work was seen as too edgy and poked at the wrong people, Jack sat back to listen.

Armed with his customary retorts on the matter, he readied himself. "So give it to me."

"You really burned some people here. I know we've done this before, but trust me, it's not me you're dealing with anymore. I got the call from the big guys this morning. They told me to pull the story… and they told me to fire you. I'm sorry, Jack, I tried everything, but I have to let you go. You have talent, but you just lack the focus. It wasn't my call."

Jaw opened wide, Jack turned to his boss with both arms in the air. "What? You're serious? I write the piece of the year, of the decade, and instead of the front page, I am canned. What is this, the Soviet Union? Call the wrong people out and your story gets killed."

"If there was anything I could do, I would have. You've just rubbed them the wrong way too many times. You had to know this was gonna happen sooner or later."

"So, freedom of speech means nothing to you or this paper. Mike, I have sources who can confirm everything I wrote. This isn't some quack trying to sell a story."

"It doesn't matter. They killed the story—it's over."

"Then you need to ask yourself why they would do it. Why would they pull a story that would expose corruption if they weren't getting something out of it? I'll tell ya why—because the *Tribune's* in bed with these people."

"Jack, everything isn't some conspiracy. That's your biggest problem. Everything is us versus them with you. It wore thin, I got sick of it, they got sick of it, and it finally caught up to you. You only look for the big story. I've sent you out for hard news, but you saw it as trivial. Clean out your desk."

"You can't report the news if you're part of it, Mike. Remember those words." Jack sought conspiracy theories over hard print news and pursued only those angles that produced such a story.

He had spent more time in his editor's office than his articles spent on the front page, but there had always been something that kept him on the payroll. Until now.

"Goodbye, Jack."

"I'll break this story, Mike."

"For once, just let things go. It wasn't your story. It was your career. Your constant paranoia about the government, city, state, or local. Hell, Jack, you went after a school board claiming they passed kids just to ensure funding. You're getting a nice severance package in this. Take it and try to relax for a while. If anything changes here, I'll let you know. But don't count on it."

"You can tell them to take their severance package and shove it up their asses. Someone is going to want this story. You can tell them I'll get it out there one way or another. I don't need you, and I sure as hell don't need them."

"Jack…"

Not allowing his boss to finish his statement, Jack picked up his paper and threw it. The pages separated and slowly floated to the floor. He slammed the office door then hurried to his desk. He rummaged through his drawers and picked up only one item—the pen he used to take most of his notes. Not wanting to make any more of a scene, he left the building without another word spoken.

The loss of his job and his already proven track record for finding conspiracies where there weren't any revved him up with the story brewing inside of him. They'd fired him for the wrong reasons; it motivated him more than ever to get his story out.

Upset, he turned to the one person he always counted on—his girlfriend, Kate. Just a phone call away, the voice that comforted him through his problems and listen to his gripes awaited him. His cellphone might as well have had therapist written all over it.

Jack called and connected with her.

"Hey, hun, I'm kinda in the middle of something." Kate sounded like she was trying to get through a tough workday of her own.

"I was fired," he said, deciding not to coat the blow.

"Why? What happened?"

"I went in this morning, and Mike told me the board decided I was too controversial for the paper. They think I'm on the wrong track for their liberal bullshit. But I know what it was."

"And what's that?"

"You know what I think. I think the FDA has pockets that reach a lot further than I dug. I think they didn't want that article to reach the eyes of people paying for all their treatments. I think—"

Kate cut to the point. "Jack, even if that is true, what does the FDA and the paper have to do with one another?"

"Money, everything has to do with money. The rich watch out for one another. Think about it. How else can you run this government?

If one limb falls, there's a chance another might, and they won't let that happen. There's a connection here, and they think I'm getting to close to it."

"Do you want me to come home?"

"No. I want to go talk with Martini."

"Martini is the last guy you need to be talking with right now. I'm sure my boss will let me leave. Why don't you just meet me at home? We can go out and do something, get your mind off the whole thing for a little while."

He sighed. "I just want to run this by him. Besides, yours is the only income we might have for a while."

Her turn to sigh. "Every time you go and see that guy you come back with all these weird ideas. You know he's probably the reason you lost your job in the first place."

"You don't know that."

"Did you get your last story idea from him?"

Jack paused. He had thought he had something he could really sink his teeth into. "He helped me on it, and it hit a nerve, Kate. It wasn't my editor who fired me, it was the board. The board barely gets involved even when a story's faked, so why now? I'm telling you, they didn't want this story out."

"Okay, let's just say they didn't want this out. You aren't in a position to get it out there anymore. Maybe you should just let this one go."

"I'll see you when you get home. I love you."

"Please don't do anything to get in trouble."

After hanging up, Jack turned to hail a cab; one met him immediately. Martini influenced Jack's conception of the government. Martini, really named Josh Gibson, took the nickname for his constant drinking habit and fascination with James Bond.

A hard-hitting conspiracy theory buff, Martini saw agents for big brother in every face he did not recognize, found a plot behind every news story and new piece of legislation. It made his life more difficult than it had to be.

When Jack had done a story some years ago on rebels from the '70s, he'd focused on Martini for the article, and they became friends. Martini was a hippie with anti-establishment mentality, a holdover a bit too young for the experimentation period of the '60s and too cynical for the mellowed lifestyles of the '70s, he became an icon of revolution.

Somewhat frail, getting up in age, he had a long, scruffy beard and unkempt clothing that completed the typical image of diluted renegade, an image that set him apart from the norm. Theirs became a protégé-mentor relationship. Martini took young Jack under his wing. Years had gone by with Jack going to Martini to find out the story behind the story.

Jack's cab pulled up to Martini's dilapidated apartment building. A curtain drew in and fell back into place at the window where the always suspicious introvert surveyed his surroundings. Jack knew his friend watched from inside and smiled at the notion that Martini had always been on guard.

Jack went up the stairs and knocked. The door opened. Within the apartment lay a pack rat's heaven, with no wall visible throughout the home; every inch covered with newspaper articles with segments circled and margins scribbled in. All counter space and tables littered with stacks of papers and notebooks that gave the impression of paranoia.

At a glance, the sanity of the hermit came into question. Nonetheless, Jack had confidence in this man and believed the scripture he spouted.

Jack walked into the apartment and sat down. His fists balled, his stomach tightened, and his mind swirled as anger dominated his emotions. "Martini, you won't believe what happened."

"What's wrong?"

"I got canned."

"That article, 'Cures outside the United States'?"

"Exactly."

"I thought there might be some backlash from that. What the fuck happened to free speech in this country? What reason did they give you?"

"They just told me that I was rubbing people the wrong way." Jack reached into his backpack and pulled out his notes, four separate folders, all of them titled "Cures." He placed them on Martini's table and opened each, showing his friend all the time that went into the research.

Martini smiled. "I'd bet. Telling the world that there's cures for disease out there that the FDA covers up for profit might get some people pissed."

"Well, I'm gonna get this story out there one way or another."

"Jack, I don't know if this is one you should tackle."

"That doesn't sound like you. They're sticking it to us. There are millions of people suffering out there with diseases we can cure, and the FDA and pharmaceutical companies are hiding them so they can keep selling drugs that only push the symptoms to the side for a while. If we don't bring it out, we're just as bad as they are. We'd be letting all those people suffer for no reason. I'm not gonna do that."

"You know I'm the first one in line for taking these guys on, but this is like taking on an elephant with a toothpick."

"So you're out?"

"No. We just have to figure out how to use that toothpick."

"We can bring this to the national news," Jack said, excited about the prospect of uncovering something big.

"Then we need solid evidence. What do you have?"

"I have a list of remedies used by other nations. Things the US government won't okay or are denying altogether. My source told me some less respectable members of the medical community are paying researchers to shut up too."

"They'll just dispute it. They have the media, and the backing of the entire medical association. If those two tell the public that all those cures are unproven, the people will believe 'em. They'll just say it's unsafe or not okayed for use in the U.S. *yet.* They can mask it with studies for years until it blows over."

"Long enough for the pharmaceutical companies to make their profit."

"Exactly."

"So what's the next step?"

"You have to go to the source."

"What do you mean?"

"Somebody found these cures. Some individual scientist figured it out, and I'm sure they went to the FDA with it. You need to find one of them. If there's one thing that I know about our government, follow the money and you'll find what you're looking for. You said the government had to pay them to shut up about the cure so the drug companies can make billions fighting the symptoms right?"

"Right."

"Did your source give you a name or anything?"

"I didn't get any specific names."

Martini nodded as if he wanted Jack to follow through on his thoughts. "Then what proof do you have?"

"I have dozens of people who were cured. Patients that the medical world said were terminal that were treated by these quote questionable methods and walked away without a sign of anything ever being wrong."

"That's a good start, but things go into remission, people self-heal, hell, some people will just tell you it was a miracle. Without hard proof that you can take to a lab, you have nothing. So what do you really have?"

"I know this is gonna sound unbelievable, but one source

claimed that a research company in Canada found a cure for cancer. He didn't know where the treatment came from, but when he opened his wallet wide enough he was given an off-the-market treatment, and in a matter of weeks, the cancer was gone. The only thing he was told was that it wasn't given the go-ahead in the U.S., and he wasn't to tell anyone about it. After he started feeling better, his conscience got the best of him, and he knew he had to share it. He wants this exposed more than I do, but he's too scared to come out."

"It doesn't sound strange at all. The money that goes into all the research and failed treatments makes it a great candidate for a cover-up. You should start there. Follow that survivor to the doctor that helped him; he either came up with the cure or knows the lab that discovered it."

"Can I use your computer?" Jack asked, hoping to start his research immediately.

"Hell no. I don't know how far you want to go with this, but I can't get involved. I know what these people are willing to do, and I can't take that chance. I suggest you go to a library and don't sign in under your name. The more paths you allow them to follow, the more roadblocks they'll put in your way. Be careful with that article you wrote, they already know that you're on to them. You're a blip on the radar screen now, kid."

Without hesitation, Jack gathered the notes he had strewn about the table and left to uncover his latest mystery. With the knowledge of just a few cures, he went to the city library, hoping to track down a name.

Taking Martini's advice, Jack signed in under the alias Ryan Bennett, a name he used on the many occasions he felt the reporter angle might not get him the story. Bennett had many background stories of his own. Some people might know him as a roving businessman, others might remember a land surveyor, and some might even recall Ryan Bennett as a homeless drifter. Jack wore many hats with his alter ego.

At the computer, he decided to conduct a broad search for various research companies. He typed in "cancer" and saw the numerous foundations looking for the cure and the money involved in such an undertaking.

For page after page, he scrolled the endless studies assigned to the topic. He compared the grants given to each foundation by the federal government and the dates they gave them, trying to find some favorites that suddenly disappeared after a large payoff. He clicked his mouse on each questionable entry to save it onto his disk. The hours passed.

He performed more click and drags at a monotonous pace. He moved onto the individual pharmaceutical companies and the business they gave to research scientists.

More hours passed as the FDAs turn came and Jack traced the money flowing freely and extensively to these corporate giants. The day turned to night, and he felt he had played this idea out to the fullest. He printed out all he'd found and decided to take them back to Martini's to go over the data.

Feeling a little of the paranoia that Martini planted, Jack covered his work and walked out of the library. His eyes surveyed everyone's movement with obsessed worry. The short walk was filled every emotion he had. He quivered, shook, and intermingled hot and cold sensations.

In his car, he looked around again and chuckled at the idea that he had fallen for all the "men in black" talk his friend had given him over the past couple years. During routine investigations Jack had dealt with dangerous matters but never truly saw anything that brought him to alert like the subject at hand.

He drove to Martini's apartment. Streetlights switched on, and few people walked the streets as it approached 10:30 on Tuesday; Jack felt the lack of excitement in the area would help to him discover a tail if he in fact had one. His confidence grew—no one followed him. He pulled into Martini's parking lot. He walked slowly up the stairs to the third-floor apartment.

He knocked on the door, and several bolt locks clicked open. His friend greeted him.

"Did you find anything?" Martini asked.

Jack lifted the stack of papers he acquired from the library. "I don't know. There was too much for me to go through. I thought I might call on you for some help."

"Come in. Let's see what we can find."

Inside the apartment, Jack put a sports bag on the table and opened it to show hundreds of documents on the appropriations of funds to go along with the papers he carried. The vast lists covered the table and flowed to the floor: lists, names, columns, chaos. It was not a task for one.

Martini gazed upon the papers and introduced his theory. "The root of all evil lays right here in front of us."

"Do you really think our answers will be in here?"

"I don't know, but at least we know who the people are that are in the game. You take half, and I'll take half."

The two sat, each at their own end of the table and sorted through the documents. The work went by with nary a word. Hour after hour drained the mind and the determination. Each man held a notepad and took notes during the search, each filling a page or two of his own. They poured coffee often; before long the moon yielded to the morning sun and both men started to fade. They compared notes upon notes looking for a common string.

Jack perked up. "Here's one that received three payments in two years."

Martini frowned and shook his head. "Na, not enough. I've seen dozens of these companies already that received more than that."

They continued through the paperwork.

Jack frowned, staring. Not sure of what he looked at, he turned to Martini. "Have you ever heard of Starfish Laboratories?"

"No. Why?"

"I just can't figure out why they're getting grants from companies that are getting grants. And they're out of Canada, not even a U.S. company."

"Show me."

"Look at this. It says that April 18th 2004, the federal government gave Wheaton Labs a ten-million dollar grant for a breast cancer study, and Wheaton turned around and gave Starfish Labs two million for the same study on the same day. And Bind Labs got a three-million dollar grant and subbed five hundred thousand to Starfish. There are about five more here. Kossier Labs, granted two million after getting three just the day before."

"It looks more like money laundering than research. What did you say the name of that lab was?" Martini asked.

"Starfish Labs."

"Well, they seem to be one of the biggest money-makers here. It might be the best place to start. Why don't you look 'em up?"

"Should I go to the library?"

"No. Fuck 'em. If they get nervous, we'll know we're on the right track. Use my computer."

Jack typed STARFISH LABS into the search engine, and the two sat back and hoped for something to send up a red flag. Before long, they got some information but nothing that excited them immediately. Starfish Labs did have a website, professional looking but dull and outdated.

"Okay, kinda a small lab, only five researchers in Canada," Jack stated.

"Yeah but being out of the States gives them a lot more cover than you'd think. And I don't think it's all that common for the U.S. to fund research outside the U.S., do you? If the taxpayers got a hold of this, votes might be swayed."

"But that's all speculation. It's doesn't really tell us anything. So what, they applied for a U.S. grant."

"Then how about that?" Martini asked, pointing at the screen.

"What?"

"Look at that date. It says Starfish closed its research department two months ago. Tell me, why would they get a grant a month before they close their doors?"

"I don't know... maybe they didn't expect to close."

"Do you know how hard it is to get one of these grants? They'd have to show research from years of study. These guys have more grants than most of these companies combined. Something's up with them. Something's dirty."

"Who's the head researcher? Maybe finding out more about him will tell us more about the research they did."

"Dr. William Lamb."

"So what's next?"

"It's your call but I think you need to introduce yourself to the good doctor. He might have something to say."

Jack researched Dr. Lamb to the full capacity the internet allowed. He had the location of Starfish labs, the last known address of Lamb, and directions to each. Jack and Martini decided that furthering their case hinged on finding this man. A shot in the dark at best but the evidence drove them to him.

Chapter Two
Finding the Source

During the next two days, Jack took his theory and produced a scenario in his mind that he must play out. He felt the reporter searching for a story would not do much to help his cause, so Ryan Bennett became a father, a father who was losing his daughter to cancer. If the government paid off Dr. Lamb, he was not going to come right out and say it.

Jack planned to play on the emotions and the idea that Dr. Lamb got into this field to truly help. He thought any man, father or not, would crumble at the notion of a grief-stricken family. He put his creative side to the test in an attempt to paint the picture of a desperate man who would do anything to find a way for his child to live. He needed to awaken the empathy in Dr. Lamb that he'd replaced with cold hard cash.

Jack flew to the nearest airport he could find to the small, secluded area in southeastern Canada, the home of Dr. Lamb. He rented a car at the airport using his real credentials as Jack Randolph but knew from here on out, he needed to become Mr. Bennett.

Within an hour of his arrival, he had pinpointed the doctor's home and decided to make the initial contact. He approached the house, his hopes heightened by the researcher's luxurious-looking home. Three stories high, the brick structure outlined in beautiful shrubbery. An oak door invited guests, and a windowpane that stretched from the first floor to the third gave a grand impression. A half-circle driveway, complete with two automobiles, let Jack know that someone was home. He could only think that this was where the grant money was. The root of all evil lay in front of him.

He knocked on the door, his heart beating with hopes of uncovering the ultimate conspiracy. A man answered.

"Dr. Lamb?" Jack asked.

"Yes. How can I help you?"

"Are you the Dr. Lamb who founded Starfish Labs?"

"Yes, I am but I'm afraid the lab has been closed."

"Sir, I need your help."

"What can I do for you?"

"My daughter has cancer," Jack explained, going with the story he had made up for himself, already knowing a lie would help a bit more than the truth on this occasion.

"Like I said, the lab has been closed," Dr. Lamb replied.

Lamb started to shut his door, obviously more than a little uneasy with this conversation.

"Dr. Lamb, David Green told me you could help."

He laid it out on the table, the name of his source, hoping it would find its target. The doctor looked up at Jack without a word. Jack understood the silent reflection. Whether he intended to or not, the doctor had quietly admitted that he knew David Green.

Shock overcame Jack as he pondered the notion that he might have actually found who he was looking for. He gathered himself and pushed forward. "You are the Doctor Lamb I'm looking for, aren't you?"

"I don't know what Mr. Green said, but I can't help you."

"But you do know David Green."

"No. I'm sorry, I can't help you."

"Doctor, please."

"I'm sorry."

The door closed, and Jack had his answer. Dr. Lamb knew his source, whether he admitted it or not.

~ * ~

In his motel room in town, Jack perfected the story he wanted to tell Dr. Lamb to try to get into his confidence. He wanted to find out if Martini had any thoughts or any insight on a predicament he felt lost in. Jack called. Just a few rings away, Martini answered.

"Martini, it's Jack. I found Dr. Lamb."

The always skeptic Martini replied, "And let me guess, he had nothing to say."

"He wouldn't say a word, but I know it's him. When I gave up my source's name, I might as well have dropped a hammer on his foot."

"You're sure?"

"One hundred percent, there's no doubt. I just don't know if I can get him to talk to me."

"Well he has been paid well, or he could be terrified. The people that dish out that kind of money expect to get what they paid for. Lamb knows they'll do anything to keep this under wraps. There's not a question in his mind that they won't get rid of him if he slips. It's gonna be hard to convince him to talk to you, but you can do it."

"I know. I'll tug on the strings as long as it takes. You think he'll crack or go to the people that paid him off?" Jack asked.

"I don't know. It's a story he wants to tell. He became a researcher to help —he just got lost along the way. It has to be eating him alive to see all those people out there suffering when he has the means to stop it. Play on that, and he'll break. He might have sold his soul, but he's still human."

"Oh I'm gonna play, but who knows how much of a soul this man has left. By the look of his house, he might have traded it in for a twenty-four karat life."

"You need to be careful, Jack. Too many people don't want this out there. If things get hairy, you're an awful long way from home. You should study the area. Get yourself all the maps you can and look at the layout before you go too far. You need at least four ways to get out of each hideout you find and enough places to duck if you're on the run."

"There's the Martini I know."

"Hey, I've been called a kook for longer than you've been alive. If you pay attention you might make it to my age."

Jack looked around the room and saw a port. "Don't worry, I'll look around town, but hey, this room has an internet jack. Do you think they'd be safe?"

"The internet's never safe, but it's probably as safe as it gets out there. Did you or Ryan Bennett sign in?"

"I'll be playing the role of Mr. Bennett this go around."

"Good. I was hoping you didn't get caught up in all this and forget. But you know the people that are watching you probably know about Bennett by now. I mean, you have used him quite a bit. I think you need to come up with something else soon."

"I will. I just don't have identification for anyone else up here."

"Just keep it in mind. I'll start making up some fakes."

"All right, I have to get some sleep. I'll scout the area tomorrow before I go see Dr. Lamb. I'll call you when I know something."

Not too big for some friendly advice and always having trusted Martini, Jack looked up some maps of the area on the internet and searched for places to run and, if worse came to worst, hide.

He took out several scraps of paper and doodled rough sketches of the town and routes to travel in case the worst happened. In the end, Jack had mapped no less than eight different routes from the doctor's home to his motel and from his motel out of town. He felt prepared, but the night went by with paranoid thoughts intermingling with hope. If he got Dr. Lamb to talk, everything in his life, all his theories, all the case scenarios, would come to fruition; if he could not, he lost his job, credibility, and more importantly, his belief that there was something bigger out there to find.

Jack stood at his pinnacle; on one side laid the gradual slide of victory; the other, the abrupt plummet of defeat.

Out Now!

What's next on your reading list?

Champagne Book Group promises to bring to readers fiction at its finest.

Discover your next
fine read!
http://www.champagnebooks.com/

We are delighted to invite you to receive exclusive rewards. Join our Facebook group for VIP savings, bonus content, early access to new ideas we've cooked up, learn about special events for our readers, and sneak peeks at our fabulous titles.

Join now.
https://www.facebook.com/groups/ChampagneBookClub/

Printed in Great Britain
by Amazon

28337484R00171